Lost Lenore: The Adventures of a Rolling Stone

by Mayne Reid

Copyright © 7/21/2015
Jefferson Publication

ISBN-13: 978-1515165064

Contents

Volume One—Chapter One.

Family Affairs.

The first important event of my life transpired on the 22nd May, 1831. On that day I was born.

Six weeks after, another event occurred which no doubt exerted an influence over my destiny: I was christened Rowland Stone.

From what I have read of ancient history—principally as given by the Jews—I have reason to think, that I am descended from an old and illustrious family. No one can refute the evidence I have for believing that some of my ancestors were in existence many hundred years ago.

The simple fact that I am in existence now is sufficient proof that my family is of a descent, ancient and noble, as that of any other on earth.

Perhaps there is no family, in its wanderings and struggles towards remotest posterity, that has not experienced every vicissitude of fortune; sometimes standing in the ranks of the great; and in the lapse of ages descending to the lower strata of the social scale, and there becoming historically lost.

I have not yet found it recorded, that any individual of the family to which I belong ever held a very high position—not, in fact, since one of them named Noah constructed a peculiar kind of sailing craft, of which he was full owner, and captain.

It was my misfortune to be brought into existence at a period of the world's history, when my father would be thought by many to be a man in "humble circumstances of life." He used to earn an honest living by hard work.

He was a saddle and harness-maker in an obscure street in the city of Dublin, and his name was William Stone.

When memory dwells on my father, pride swells up in my soul: for he was an honest, temperate, and industrious man, and was very kind to my mother and his children. I should be an unworthy son, not to feel pride at the remembrance of such a father!

There was nothing very remarkable in the character of my mother. I used to think different once, but that was before I had arrived at the age of reason. I used to think that she delighted to thwart my childish inclinations—more than was necessary for her own happiness or mine. But this was probably a fault of my wayward fancy. I am willing to think so now.

I was a little wilful, and no doubt caused her much trouble. I am inclined to believe, now that she treated me kindly enough—perhaps better than I deserved.

I remember, that, up to the time I was eight years of age, it was the work of two women to put a clean shirt on my back, and the operation was never performed by them without a long and violent struggle. This remembrance, along with several others of a like nature, produces upon me the impression, that my parents must have humoured my whims—too much, either for my good or their own.

When I was yet very young, they thought that I was distinguished from other children by a *penchant* for suddenly and secretly absenting myself from those, whose duty it was to be acquainted with my whereabouts. I often ran away from home to find playmates; and ran away from school to avoid the trouble of learning my lessons. At this time of life, so strong was my propensity for escaping from any scene I did not like, and betaking myself to such as I deemed more congenial to my tastes, that I obtained the soubriquet of *The Rolling Stone.*

Whenever I would be missing from home, the inquiry would be made, "Where is that Rolling Stone?" and this inquiry being often put in the school I attended, the phrase was also applied to me there. In short it became my "nickname."

Perhaps I was a little vain of the appellation: for I certainly did not try to win another, but, on the contrary, did much to convince everybody, that the title thus extended to me was perfectly appropriate.

My father's family consisted of my parents, a brother, one year and a half younger than myself, and a sister, about two years younger still.

We were not an unhappy family. The little domestic cares, such as all must share, only strengthened the desire for existence—in order that they might be overcome.

My father was a man without many friends, and with fewer enemies, for he was a person who attended to his own business, and said but little to any one. He had a talent for silence; and had the good sense not to neglect the exercise of it—as many do the best gifts Nature has bestowed upon them.

He died when I was about thirteen years old; and, as soon as he was gone from us, sorrow and misfortune began for the first time to show themselves in our house.

There are many families to whom the loss of a parent may be no great calamity; but ours was not one of them; and, young as I was at the time, I had the sense to know that thenceforward I should have to war with the world alone. I had no confidence in my mother's ability to provide for her children, and saw that, by the death of my father, I was at once elevated from the condition of a child to that of a man.

After his decease, the work in the shop was carried on by a young man named Leary—a journeyman saddler, who had worked with my father for more than a year previous to his death.

I was taken from school, and put to work with Mr Leary who undertook to instruct me in the trade of a harness-maker. I may say that the man displayed considerable patience in trying to teach me.

He also assisted my mother with his counsel—which seemed guided by a genuine regard for our interests. He managed the business in the shop, in what appeared to be the best manner possible; and the profits of his labour were punctually handed over to my mother.

For several weeks after my father's death, everything was conducted in a manner much more pleasant than we had any reason to expect; and the loss we had sustained seemed not so serious to our future existence, as I had at first anticipated.

All of our acquaintances thought we were exceedingly fortunate in having such a person as Mr Leary, to assist us in carrying on the business. Most of the neighbours used to speak of him in the highest terms of praise; and many times have I heard my mother affirm that she knew not what would become of us, if deprived of his assistance.

Up to this time Mr Leary had uniformly treated me with kindness. I knew of no cause for disliking him; and yet I did!

My conscience often rebuked me with this unexplained antipathy, for I believed it to be wrong; but for all that, I could not help it. I did not even like his appearance; but, on the contrary, thought him the most hideous person I had ever beheld. Other people had a different opinion; and I tried to believe that I was guided by prejudice in forming my judgment of him. I knew he was not to blame for his personal appearance, nor for any other of my fancies; but none of these considerations could prevent me from hating Matthew Leary, and in truth I *did* hate him.

I could not conceal my dislike—even from him; and I will do him the justice to state that he appeared to strive hard to overcome it with kindness. All his efforts to accomplish this were in vain; and only resulted in increasing my antipathy.

Time passed. Mr Leary daily acquired a greater control of the affairs of our family; and in proportion as his influence over my mother increased, so did my hostility towards him.

My mother strove to conquer it, by reminding me of his kindness to all the family—the interest he took in our common welfare—the trouble he underwent in teaching me the business my father had followed—and his undoubted morality and good habits.

I could not deny that there was reason in her arguments; but my dislike to Mr Leary was independent of reason: it had sprung from instinct.

It soon became evident to me that Mr Leary would, at no distant period, become one of the family. In the belief of my mother, younger brother, and sister, he seemed necessary to our existence.

My mother was about thirty-three years of age; and did not appear old for her years. She was not a bad looking woman—besides, she was mistress of a house and a business. Mr Leary possessed neither. He was but a journeyman saddler; but it was soon very evident that he intended to avail himself of the opportunity of marrying my mother and her business, and becoming the master of both.

It was equally evident that no efforts of mine could prevent him from doing so, for, in the opinion of my mother, he was every thing required for supplying the loss of her first husband.

I tried to reason with her, but must admit, that the only arguments I could adduce were my prejudices, and I was too young to use even them to the best advantage. But had they been ever so just, they would have been thrown away on my father's widow.

The many seeming good traits in the character of Mr Leary, and his ability for carrying on the work in the shop, were stronger arguments than any I could urge in answer to them.

My opposition to their marriage—now openly talked about—only engendered ill-will in the mind of my mother; and created a coldness, on her part, towards myself. When finally convinced of her intention to become Mrs Leary, I strove hard to overcome my prejudices against the man: for I was fully aware of the influence he would have over me as a step-father.

It was all to no purpose. I hated Mr Leary, and could not help it.

As soon as my mother had definitively made known to me her intention of marrying him, I felt a strong inclination to strengthen my reputation as a runaway, by running away from home. But such an exploit was then a little too grand for a boy of my age to undertake—with much hope of succeeding in its accomplishment. I did not like to leave home, and afterwards be compelled to return to it—when I might be worse off than ever.

I formed the resolution, therefore, to abide in my mother's—soon to be Mr Leary's—house, until circumstances should force me to leave it; and that such circumstances would ere long arise, I had a painful presentiment. As will be found in the sequel, my presentiment was too faithfully fulfilled.

Volume One—Chapter Two.

A Sudden Change of Character.

Never have I witnessed a change so great and sudden as came over Mr Leary, after his marriage with my mother.

He was no longer the humble journeyman—with the deportment of a respectable young fellow striving to retain a situation, and gain friends by good conduct. The very day after the wedding, his behaviour was that of a vain selfish overbearing plebeian, suddenly raised from poverty to wealth. He no longer spoke to me in his former feigned tone of kindness, but with threats, in a commanding voice, and in accents far more authoritative, than my father had ever used to me.

Mr Leary had been hitherto industrious, but was so no longer. He commenced, by employing another man to work in the shop with me, and plainly expressed by his actions that his share in the business was to be the spending of the money we might earn.

Up to that time, he had passed among his acquaintances as a temperate man; but in less than three weeks after his marriage, he came home drunk on as many occasions; and each time spoke to my mother in an insulting and cruel manner.

I took no trouble to conceal from Mr Leary my opinion of him and his conduct; and it soon became evident to all, that he and I could not remain long as members of the same family.

Our difficulties and misunderstandings increased, until Mr Leary declared that I was an ungrateful wretch—unworthy of his care; that he could do nothing with me; and that I should remain no longer in his house!

He held a long consultation with my mother, about what was to be done with me—the result of which was, that I was to be sent to sea. I know not what arguments he used; but they were effectual with my mother, for she gave consent to his plans, and I was shortly after bound apprentice to Captain John Brannon, of the ship "Hope," trading between Dublin and New Orleans.

"The sea is the place for you, my lad," said Mr Leary, after the indenture had been signed, binding me to Captain Brannon. "Aboard of a ship, you will learn to conduct yourself in a proper manner, and treat your superiors with respect. You are going to a school, where you will be taught something—whether you are willing to learn it, or not."

Mr Leary thought, by sending me to sea, he was obtaining some revenge for my ill-will towards him; but he was mistaken. Had he known what pleasure the arrangement gave me, he would, perhaps, have tried to retain me a little longer working in the shop. As I had already resolved to leave home, I was only too glad at being thus sent away—instead of having the responsibility of an indiscretion resting on myself. I had but one cause for regret, and that was leaving my mother, brother, and sister, to the tender mercies of a man like Mr Leary.

But what was I to do? I was not yet fourteen years of age, and could not have protected them from him by staying at home. The hatred between us was mutual; and, perhaps, when his spite was no longer provoked by my presence, he might treat the rest of the family better. This was the only thought that consoled me on parting with my relatives.

I could do nothing but yield to circumstances, leave them to their destiny, whatever that was to be, and go forth upon the world in search of my own.

My brother bore our father's name, William Stone. He was a fair-haired, blue-eyed boy, with a mild, gentle disposition, and was liked by everyone who knew him. He never did an action contrary to the expressed wishes of those who had any authority over him; and, unlike myself, he was always to be found when wanted. He never tried to shirk his work, or absent himself from school.

My little sister, Martha, was a beautiful child, with curly flaxen hair, and I never gazed on anything more beautiful than her large deep blue eyes, which seemed to express all the mental attributes of an angel.

It pained me much to leave little Martha—more than parting either with my mother or brother.

My mother wished to furnish me with a good outfit, but was prevented from doing so by Mr Leary—who said that he could not afford the expense. He declared, moreover, that I did not deserve it.

After my box was sent aboard the ship, and I was ready to follow it, little Willie and Martha were loud in their grief, and I had to tear myself away from their presence.

When it came to parting with my mother, she threw her arms around me, and exclaimed, "My poor boy, you *shall* not leave me!"

Mr Leary gave her a glance out of his sinister eyes, which had the effect of suddenly subduing this expression of grief, and "we parted in silence and tears."

Often, and for hours, have I thought of that parting scene, and wondered why and how Mr Leary had obtained so great an influence over the mind of my poor mother.

I once believed that she had a will of her own, with the courage to show it—an opinion that had been formed from observations made during the life of my father, but since her marriage with Mr Leary, she seemed afraid of giving utterance to a word, that might express independence, and allowed him, not only to speak but think for her.

I knew that she had much affection for all of us, her children—and her regret at thus sending me, at so early an age to encounter the hardships of a long voyage must have been deep and sincere.

I know that her heart was nearly breaking at that moment. The expression of her features, and the manner in which she wrung my hand, told me so; and yet the passion of my grief was not equal in power to that of her fear for the frowns of Mr Leary.

My amiable step-father accompanied me to the ship, which was lying in Dublin Bay; and on our way thither, he became much excited with drink. He was so elated with whiskey, and with the idea that I was going away, that he did not speak to me in his usual unpleasant tone. On the contrary, he seemed all kindness, until we had got aboard the ship.

"Now my little 'Rolling Stone,'" said he, when about to take leave of me, "you are going to have plenty of rolling now, and may you roll so far away, as never to roll across my path again."

He appeared to think this was very witty, for he was much amused at what he had said, and laughed long and loudly.

I made no reply, until he was in the boat, which was about to shove off from the ship, when, looking over the bulwarks, I called after him.

"Mr Leary! if you ill-use my mother, brother, or sister, in my absence, *I will certainly kill you when I come back.*"

Mr Leary made no reply, further than to answer me with a smile, that a hyena might have envied.

Volume One—Chapter Three.

Stormy Jack.

There have been so many stories told of the sufferings of boys, when first sent to sea, that I shall not dwell long on those that befell myself.

What a world to me was that ship! I little knew, before it became my home, how many great men there were in the world. By great men, I mean those high in authority over their fellows.

I went aboard of the ship, with the idea that my position in it would be one which ordinary people might envy. I was guided to this opinion by something said by the captain, at the time the indentures of my apprenticeship were being signed. No sooner were we out to sea, than I learnt that there were at least a dozen individuals on board, who claimed the right of commanding my services, and that my situation on board was so humble, as to place me far beneath the notice of the captain in command. I had been told that we were to be *friends*, but before we were a week out, I saw that should it be my lot to be lost overboard, the captain might only accidentally learn that I was gone. The knowledge of this indifference to my fate was not pleasant to me. On the contrary, I felt disappointed and unhappy.

Aboard of the ship were four mates, two boatswains, a carpenter and *his* mate, and a steward, besides some others who took a little trouble to teach me my duty, by giving me orders which were frequently only given, to save themselves the trouble of doing what they commanded me to do.

Only one of these many masters ever spoke to me in a pleasant manner. This was the boatswain of the watch, in which I was placed, who was called by his companions, "Stormy Jack," probably for the reason that there was generally a tempest in his mind, too often expressed in a storm of words.

For all this, Stormy Jack was every inch a sailor, a true British tar, and all know what that means.

Perhaps I should have said, that all know what it might have meant in times past, for Stormy Jack was not a fair specimen of English sailors of the present day. The majority of the men aboard of British ships are not now as they were thirty years ago. English sailors, in general, seem to have lost many of the peculiarities that once distinguished them from other people, and a foreign language is too often spoken in the forecastle of English ships.

To return to Stormy Jack.

One day the carpenter had ordered me to bring him a pannikin of water. Leaving a job on which I had been set to work by Stormy Jack, I started to obey. In doing so, I caught the eye of the latter, who was standing a little to one side, and had not been seen by the carpenter as he gave me the order.

Stormy shook his head at me, and pointed to the work he had himself ordered me to perform, in a manner that plainly said, "go at it again."

I obeyed this interpretation of his signal, and resumed my task.

"Did you hear what I said?" angrily shouted the carpenter.

"Yes, sir," I answered.

"Then why do you not start, and do what I told you?"

I stole a sly glance at Stormy Jack, and seeing upon his face a smile, approving of what I did, I made bold to answer, in a somewhat brusque manner, that I had other work on hand, and, moreover, it was not my business to wait upon him.

The carpenter dropped his adze, caught up his measuring rule, and advanced towards me.

He was suddenly stopped by the strong hand of Stormy placed firmly on his shoulder.

"Avast!" said the sailor, "don't you molest that boy at his work. If you do, I am the one to teach you manners."

The carpenter was a man who knew "how to choose an enemy," and with such wisdom to guide him, he returned to his own work, without resenting in any way the check he had thus met with.

The fact that I had refused to obey the carpenter, and that Stormy Jack had interceded in my behalf, became known amongst the others who had been hitherto bullying me, and I was afterwards permitted to go about the ship, without being the slave of so many masters.

Some time after the incident above related, Stormy Jack chanced to be standing near me, and commenced a conversation which was as follows:

"You are a boy of the right sort," said he, "and I'll not see you mistreated. I heard what you said to the lubber as brought you aboard, and I always respects a boy as respects his mother. I hope that man in the boat was not your father."

"No," I answered, "he is my step-father."

"I thought as much," said Stormy, "by his appearing so pleased to get rid of you. It's my opinion no one ought to have more than one father; but you must brace up your spirits, my lad. Two or three voyages will make a man of you, and you will then be able to go back home, and teach the lubber manners, should he forget 'em. Do the best you can aboard here to larn your duty, and I'll keep an eye on you. If any one goes to boxing your compass, when you don't deserve it, I'll teach him manners."

I thanked Stormy for his kind advice, and promised to do all I could to merit his protection.

After having made a friend of Stormy, and an enemy of the carpenter, I began to be more at home on the ship, and took a stronger interest in its mysteries and miseries. Familiarity does not with all things breed contempt. That it should not is a wise provision of Nature, for the accommodation of the majority of mankind—whose necessity it is to become familiar with many cares, annoyances, and disagreeable circumstances.

Second nature, or habit, is only acquired by familiarity, and seamen become so familiar with all that is disagreeable in a life on the sea, that they are never satisfied long with any home, but a floating one. The mind of youth soon becomes reconciled to circumstances, however unpleasant, much sooner than that of an older person, and this was probably the reason why, although greatly dissatisfied at the beginning of the voyage, I soon became so contented with a life on the sea, that I preferred it to one on land—at least in a home with Mr Leary as my master.

Upon occasions, Stormy Jack permitted the storm in his soul to rage a little too wildly. One of these occasions occurred about two weeks, before we reached New Orleans. He had got into a dispute with the second mate about the setting of a sail, and both becoming intemperate in the use of the Queen's English, words were used which had to be resented with violence.

The first assault was made by the mate, who soon found that he was but a child in the hands of Stormy Jack.

The first mate happened to be on deck smoking his pipe, as also the carpenter, and, as in duty bound, both ran to the relief of their brother officer. Poor Stormy was knocked down with the carpenter's mallet, his hands were tied behind him, and he was dragged below.

The next day I was allowed to take him his dinner, and found him well pleased with his situation. I was expecting to see him in great grief over his misfortune—which to me appeared very serious—and was agreeably surprised to find him in better spirits than I had ever seen him before.

"It's all right, Rowley, my boy," said he. "If they can afford to keep me in idleness, and pay me wages for doing nothing, I'm not the one to complain. I'm glad this has happened, for I never liked the first breezer, nor yet Chips, and now I've got an opportunity for letting them know it. I'm going to leave the ship, and when I've done so, I'll teach them manners."

I expressed the opinion, that it could not be very pleasant to be kept so long in a dark place and alone.

"That's no punishment," said Stormy. "Can't I sleep? I've been served worse than this. On a voyage to India I refused duty on the second week out. I was put in a pen along with some turkeys and geese, and was told whenever I would go to my duty, I should be taken out. I never gave in, and finished the voyage in the turkey coop. That was far worse than this, for the noise on deck, with the conversation between my companions, the turkeys and geese, often used to keep me from sleep. That was a queer plan for teaching a fellow manners, but I did not let it succeed.

"I was going to say one place was as good as another, but it a'nt. This ship is no place for me. After we reach New Orleans I shall leave it, and if ever I come across eyther the first breezer, or carpenter, ashore, they'll both larn what they never knew afore, and that's manners. When two men are fighting, another has no right to interrupt either of 'em with a blow of a mallet, and the man who does so has no manners, and wants teachin'."

I was pleased to hear Stormy say that he intended to leave the ship, for the idea of doing so myself had often entered my thoughts, and had been favourably entertained.

I had no great hopes of finding a better home than I had on board the ship, but I had been placed there by Leary, and that was sufficient reason for my wishing to leave her. He had driven me from my own home, and I would not live in one of his choosing.

I resolved, therefore, to take leave of the ship if Stormy would allow me to become his companion, and even if he should not, I had more than half determined upon running away.

Volume One—Chapter Four.

A Change of Calling.

Two days before we reached New Orleans, Stormy Jack expressed some sham contrition for what he had done, with an inclination to return to his duty. He was liberated, and once more the deck was enlivened by the sound of his rough manly voice giving the necessary orders for working the ship.

I found a favourable opportunity of telling him, that I should like to go along with him. At first he objected to aid me, and urged me to remain, as a reason for my doing so, urging the argument: that a boy serving his apprenticeship was much better off than one wandering about without a home.

To me this argument was worth nothing. The idea of remaining for seven years in a situation chosen for me by Mr Leary, was too absurd to be seriously entertained for a moment. I told Stormy so; and he finally consented that I should go with him.

"My reason for objecting at first," said he, "was because I did not like to be troubled with you; but that's not exactly the right sort o' feeling for a Christian to steer by. One should expect to have some trouble with those as need a helping hand, and I don't know why I should try to shirk from my share of it."

I promised Stormy that I would try not to cause him any trouble, or as little as possible.

"Of course you will try," said he, "or if you don't, I'll teach you manners."

Stormy's threat did not alarm me; and our conversation at the time ended—leaving me well pleased with the prospect of getting clear of the ship, by his assistance.

Stormy's return to duty was only a pretence. It was done to deceive the officers—so that he might the more easily find an opportunity of escaping from the ship.

Two days after our arrival in the port of New Orleans, he was allowed liberty to go ashore; and I was permitted to accompany him. The Captain probably supposed that the wages due to Stormy would bring him back; and the suspicion, that a boy like myself should wish to leave the ship, had never entered into his mind.

Several of our shipmates went ashore along with us; and the first thing we all thought of was, what the reader will readily imagine, to find a place where strong drink was sold. This is usually a sailor's first thought on going ashore after a voyage.

After having taken two or three glasses with our shipmates, Stormy gave me a wink, and sidled towards the door. I followed him; and slipping unperceived into the street, we turned a corner, and kept on through several streets—until we had arrived at another part of the city. The little that Stormy had drunk had by this time only sharpened his appetite for more.

"Here I am," said he, "with clear twelve shillings in my pocket. What a spell of fun I could have, if 'twas not for you! Seven weeks without a spree, and now can't have it because I've you to take care of. Thought 'twould be so. Rowley, my boy! see what I'm suffering for you. You are teaching me manners, whether I'm willing to larn 'em or not."

I allowed the sailor to go on uninterrupted with his storm of complaints, although there was a reflection in my mind, that if I was keeping him from getting drunk, the obligation was not all on my side.

Stormy had but twelve shillings, and I half-a-crown, which the Captain had given to me before coming ashore.

It was necessary that something should be done, before this money should be all spent.

Under ordinary circumstances, the sailor need not have felt any apprehension, about being out of money. He could easily get employment in another vessel; but as matters stood, Stormy was afraid of being caught, should he attempt to join another ship—before that from which he had deserted had taken her departure from the port. If caught, Stormy knew he would be punished; and this rendered him a trifle serious.

The next day we passed in wandering about the city—taking care to avoid all places where we would be likely to meet with any of the officers, or men of the ship "Hope."

Stormy's thoughts were all day in a fearful storm, commingled with anxiety as to what we should do to make a living.

"On your account, Rowley," said he, "I'm not misinclined for a spell on shore, if I could find anything to do, but that's the trouble. There's not much work ashore, that be proper for an honest man to bear a hand in. What little of such work there is here, is done by darkies, while white men do all the cheating and scheming. Howsomever, lad, we must try to get at something."

The next day Stormy did try; and obtained work at rigging a new ship, that had just been launched. The job would last for a month. The wages were good; and the storm in Stormy's mind had now subsided into an agreeable calm.

We sought a cheap lodging-house, not far from where his work was to be performed; and that evening the sailor indulged in a pipe and a glass, from which he had prudently refrained during all the day.

I was unwilling that the burden of supporting me should be borne by my generous protector; and being anxious to do something for myself, I asked him what I should go about.

"I've just been thinking of that," said he, "and I believe I've hit upon an idea. Suppose you sell newspapers? I see many lads about your age in that business here; and they must make something at it. It's not hard work, besides it appears to be very respectable. It is a lit'rary business, as no boy should be 'shamed of."

I approved of the plan, and joyfully agreed to give it a trial.

It was arranged that the next morning I should go to the office of a daily paper—buy a bundle of copies; and try to dispose of them at a profit.

Early the next morning, Stormy started off to his work on the ship, and I to a newspaper office.

I reached the place too early to get out the papers; but found several boys waiting like myself. I joined their company, listened to them, and was much interested in their conversation, without very clearly comprehending what they were talking about.

I could distinctly hear every word they said; but the meaning of the words I knew not, for the most of them were slang phrases—such as I had never heard before.

I could see that they were very fast boys—much faster than I was—although the "Rolling Stone" had not been for several years rolling through the streets of Dublin, without learning some city sharpness.

I entered into conversation with two of the boys, in order to find out something of the business of news-vending; and could see from their manner that they regarded me, as they would have said, "not all thar."

They pretended to give me such information as I required; but I afterwards learnt that they had not told me one word of truth.

When the papers were published, I went in with the others, put down a half dollar, and received in exchange the correct number of copies. I hurried out, walked some distance from the office, and commenced offering my wares for sale.

On turning down a wide street, I met three gentlemen, each of whom took a copy out of my hands and gave me a picayune in return.

I was doing business for myself—buying and selling; and in my soul arose a feeling of independence and pride that has never been so thoroughly awakened since.

I passed along the street, till I came to a large hotel, where I saw two other gentlemen under the verandah.

I went up to them, offered my goods as before, and each took a newspaper. As one of them offered me payment for his copy, I had hardly the strength to hand him the paper and take his money. I nearly dropped to the pavement. The man was Captain Brannon, of the ship "Hope," to whom I had been apprenticed!

I moved away from him as fast as my trembling limbs would carry me; and the glance which I could not help throwing over my shoulder, told me that I had not been recognised.

This was the man, who had promised to treat me as he would his own son; and yet during a long voyage had taken so little notice of me, that I could thus transact business with him, without being recognised!

By twelve o'clock my work for the day was finished; and I returned to the lodging-house with a dollar in picayune pieces—having made a hundred per cent on my capital.

I was at that hour the happiest boy in New Orleans.

I was happy, yet full of impatience, as I waited through the long afternoon for the return of Stormy Jack.

There was pride and pleasure in the anticipation of his approval of my exertions, when I should show him the money I had made. It was the first money I had ever earned—my only transactions with the circulating medium before that time, having been to spend it, as fast as it could be obtained from a fond father.

I entered into an elaborate calculation by an arithmetical rule I had learned under the name of "reduction," and found that I had made in one day, by my own exertions, over two shillings of English money.

I had pride—pride in my ability to make money at all, and pride in my scholastic acquirements, which enabled one so young to tell how much had been gained, for I was not able to comprehend fully the amount, until I had brought it into shillings and pence.

With burning impatience I waited for the return of Stormy. Being fatigued, however, I fell asleep, and dreamt of having made a fortune, and of having had a fight with Mr Leary, in which that gentleman—to make use of Stormy's favourite expression—had been "taught some manners."

When I awoke, I looked eagerly at a clock. It was past seven in the evening, and Stormy Jack had not returned!

He had been due more than an hour. The happiness I had been all day indulging in, suddenly forsook me; and a sickening sensation of loneliness came over my soul.

I sat up waiting and watching for him until a very late hour—in fact until I was driven to bed by the landlady; but Stormy did not return.

Volume One—Chapter Five.

God Help Us!

No week of my life ever seemed so long, as that night spent in waiting for the return of Stormy Jack. It was not until the sun beams were gushing through my window in the morning, that I was able to fall asleep.

By nine o'clock I was up, and out upon the streets in search of my companion and protector. My search was continued all day without success.

I did not know the name of the ship on which he had gone to work; and therefore I had no clue to his whereabouts. In fact I had such a slight clue to guide me, that my search was but little less than the pursuit of folly.

I did not like to believe that Stormy had wilfully deserted me.

In my lone and friendless condition, with the memory of the way in which I had left my mother, to have thought so, would have made me desirous of dying. I had rather think that some serious accident had happened him, than that he had abandoned me to my fate, to avoid any further trouble I might give him.

Another idea occurred to me. He might have been found by some of the officers of the "Hope," and either taken aboard, or imprisoned for deserting. This was so probable, that for awhile I was tempted to go back to the ship and resume my duties.

Reflection told me, that if he had fallen into the hands of the captain, he would not leave me alone in a city like New Orleans. He would tell the captain where I was staying, and have me sent for and brought aboard.

The only, or what seemed the best thing I could do, was to return to the lodging-house, and there await the event.

After a long weary day spent in vain search for my lost companion, I carried this idea into effect, and went back to the lodging-house. As I anticipated, Stormy had not returned to it.

The landlady was a woman of business; and fancied, or rather believed, that my responsible protector had deserted me, leaving her with a boy to keep, and a bill unpaid.

She asked me if I had any money. In reply, I produced all I had. All but one "picayune" of it was required, for the payment of the score we had already run up.

"Now, my lad," said she, "you had better try to find some employment, where you will earn a living. You are welcome to stay here to-night, and have your breakfast in the morning. You will then have all day to-morrow to find another home."

The next morning, after I had swallowed my breakfast, she came to me and bid me an affectionate "good bye." It was a broad hint that she neither expected, nor wished me to stay in her house any longer.

I took the hint, walked out into the street, and found myself in a crowd, but alone, with the great new world before me.

"What shall I do?" was the question set before a full committee of my mental faculties, assembled, or awakened, to deliberate on the emergency of the moment.

I could be a newsvendor no longer: for the want of capital to invest in the business.

I could return to the ship, and perhaps get flogged for having run away; but I was so disappointed in the treatment I had received at the hands of the captain, that nothing but extreme suffering could have induced me to seek protection from him.

The restraint to which I had been subjected on board the ship, seemed partly to have emanated from Mr Leary, and for that reason was to me all the more disagreeable.

I wandered about the streets, reflecting on what I should do until both my brain and legs became weary.

I sat down on some steps leading to the door of a restaurant. My young heart was still strong, but beating wildly.

Over the door of a grocer's shop in front of me, and on the opposite side of the street, I read the name "John Sullivan." At sight of this familiar name, a glimmering of hope entered into my despairing mind.

Four years previous to that time, the grocer with whom my parents used to deal had emigrated to America. His name was John Sullivan. Was it possible that the shop and the name before me belonged to this man?

I arose, and crossed the street. I entered the shop, and inquired of a young man behind the counter, if Mr Sullivan was at home.

"He's up stairs," said the youth. "Do you wish to see him in particular?"

I answered in the affirmative; and Mr Sullivan was called down.

The man I hoped to meet was, when I saw him last, a little man with red hair; but the individual who answered the summons of the shop boy, was a man about six feet in his stockings, with dark hair and a long black beard.

I saw at a glance, that the grocer who had emigrated from Dublin and the man before me were not identical, but entirely different individuals.

"Well, my lad, what do you want?" asked the tall proprietor of the shop, looking down on me with a glance of curious inquiry.

"Nothing," I stammered out, perhaps more confused than I had ever been before.

"Then what have you had me called for?" he asked, in a tone that did little to aid me in overcoming my embarrassment.

After much hesitation and stammering, I explained to him that from seeing his name over the door, I had hoped to find a man of the same name, with whom I had been acquainted in Ireland, and who had emigrated to America.

"Ah!" said he, smiling ironically. "My father's great-grandfather came over to America about two hundred and fifty years ago. His name was John Sullivan. Perhaps you mean him?"

I had nothing to say in answer to this last interrogation, and was turning to leave the shop.

"Stop my lad!" cried the grocer. "I don't want to be at the trouble of having come downstairs for nothing. Supposing I was the John Sullivan you knew—what then?"

"Then you would tell me what I should do," I answered, "for I have neither home, friends, nor money."

In reply to this, the tall shopkeeper commenced submitting me to a sharp examination—putting his queries in a tone that seemed to infer the right to know all I had to communicate.

After obtaining from me the particulars relative to my arrival in the country, he gave me his advice in exchange. It was, to return instanter to the ship from which I had deserted.

I told him that this advice could not be favourably received, until I had been about three days without food.

My rejoinder appeared to cause a change in his disposition towards me.

"William!" said he, calling out to his shop-assistant, "can't you find something for this lad to do for a few days?"

William "reckoned" that he could.

Mr Sullivan then returned upstairs; and I, taking it for granted that the thing was settled, hung up my hat.

The grocer had a family, living in rooms adjoining the shop. It consisted of his wife and two children—the eldest a girl about four years of age.

I was allowed to eat at the same table with themselves; and soon became well acquainted with, and I believe well liked by, them all. The little girl was an eccentric being, even for a child; and seldom said a word to anyone. Whenever she did speak, she was sure to make use of the phrase, "God help us!"

This expression she had learnt from an Irish servant wench, who was in the habit of making frequent use of it; and it was so often echoed by the little girl, in a parrot-like manner, that Mr Sullivan and his wife—at the time I joined the family were striving to break her from the habit of using it.

The servant girl, when forbidden by her mistress ever to use the expression in the child's presence, would cry out: "God help us, Mem! I can't help it."

Whenever the words were spoken by little Sarah—this was the child's name—Mrs Sullivan would say, "Sarah, don't you ever say that again. If you do, you shall be locked up in the cellar."

"God help us!" little Sarah would exclaim, in real alarm at the threat.

"There you go again. Take that, and that," Mrs Sullivan would cry, giving the child two or three slaps on the side of the head.

"Oh mother! mother! God help us!" little Sarah would cry out, altogether unconscious of the crime she was committing.

Every effort made, for inducing the child to refrain from the use of this expression, only caused its more frequent repetition; and often in a manner so ludicrous, as to conquer the anger of her parents, and turn it into laughter.

When I had been about five weeks with Mr Sullivan, I was engaged one morning in washing the shop windows, and accidentally broke a large and costly pane of plate glass. A sudden shock came over my spirits—one more painful than I had ever experienced. Mr Sullivan had been so kind to me, that to do him an injury, accidentally or otherwise, seemed the greatest misfortune that could happen to me.

He was upstairs at the time; and I had not the moral courage to face him. Had I waited for him to come down, and see what had been done, he might have said something that would have pained me to hear; but certainly nothing more serious would have happened, and all would have been well again.

I must have a disposition constitutionally inclined to absconding. To run away, as my mother had often told me, must be my *nature*. I would rather believe this than otherwise, since I do not wish to be charged with the voluntary indiscretion of deserting a good home. It was only an overwhelming sense of the kindness with which I had been treated, and the injury I had inflicted on my benefactor, that caused me to dread an encounter with Mr Sullivan.

Perhaps a boy with a smaller sense of gratitude and less sensitiveness of soul, would have acted differently; and yet would have acted right: for it is always better to meet a difficulty boldly, than to flee in a cowardly manner from the responsibilities attending it.

Little Sarah Sullivan happened to be in the shop at the time I broke the window. I heard her exclaim, "God help us!"

I did not stay to hear any more: for in six seconds after, I had turned the nearest corner; and was once more homeless in the streets of New Orleans.

Volume One—Chapter Six.

Once More upon the Ocean!

I did not dislike a sea life; and would not have been dissatisfied with any situation on a ship, providing it had not been procured for me by Mr Leary.

On running away from Mr Sullivan's shop, my inclination was to leave New Orleans in some ship; but, unfortunately, I knew not the proper manner of going to work to accomplish my desires.

I walked along the levee, till I reached a ship, that was just being hauled from the wharf—evidently for the purpose of standing down the river and out to sea.

I stepped aboard intending to apply for work; and after looking around for a while, I observed a man who, to all appearance, was the captain.

When asked to give me some situation in the ship, he appeared too busy to pay any attention to my request.

I was on a vessel proceeding to sea; and, knowing my ability to make myself useful, I determined not to go ashore without a hearing.

I walked forward; and amidst the confusion of getting the ship under way—where there was so much to be done—I found work enough to do; and took much care, while doing it, to keep out of the way of others—which, to a boy aboard of a ship, is a task of some difficulty.

No one seemed to take any notice of me that afternoon or evening; and about nine o'clock at night I laid down under the long boat, fell asleep, and slept till morning.

I turned out at the earliest hour, and lent a hand at washing the decks; but still no one seemed to know, that I was not one of the ship's company!

At eight o'clock the crew were mustered, and divided into watches. My name was not called: and the captain observing the circumstance, requested me to walk aft.

"Who are you?" asked he, as I drew near.

Something whispered me not to undervalue myself, but to speak up with confidence; and in answer to his demand, I told him that I was a *Rolling Stone*.

"A Rolling Stone, are you?" said the captain. "Well, what have you rolled here for?"

"Because I wanted to go somewhere," I answered.

He then asked me if I had ever been at sea; and, on learning the name of the ship I had deserted, he said that she had sailed the week before, or he would have sent me back to her.

He concluded his examination, by giving the steward orders to look after me—telling him that I could assist in the slop work to be done in the cabin.

To this arrangement I decidedly objected, declaring that I was a *sailor*, and would not be made a *cuddy servant*!

I have every reason to believe, that this declaration on my part elevated me several degrees in the captain's good opinion.

He replied by expressing a hope, that I would not aspire to the command of the ship; and if not, he would see what could be done for me.

The vessel was bound for Liverpool with cotton; and was owned by the captain himself, whose name was Hyland.

I was never better treated in my life, than on board that ship.

I was not assigned to any particular occupation, or watch; but no advantage was taken of this circumstance, on the captain's part, to make me do too much, or by me to do too little.

I was generally on deck all the day; and whenever I saw anything useful that I could do, it was done.

In this way, both watches had the aid of my valuable services—which, however, were not always sufficiently appreciated to prevent a few sharp words being applied to me. But a boy aboard of a ship soon learns to take no notice of such trifles.

I was ordered to mess with the sailmaker, who—as I afterwards learnt—was directed by the captain to look well after me.

On our arrival in Liverpool, the ship was docked, and the crew went ashore, with the exception of two men—both strangers to me—who with myself were left on board.

One of the men had something to do with the Custom House; and tried hard to induce me to go ashore, along with the rest of the crew. But the ship being my only home, I was not willing to leave her; and I resisted all the inducements held out by the Custom House officer to that effect. The captain had gone away from the ship, after seeing her safe into port; but I would not leave the vessel lest I should never meet him again: for something told me he was my truest friend.

The next day he came on board again; and seemed rather surprised at finding me there.

"Ah! little Rolling Stone," said he, "I've been inquiring for you; and am pleased to see you have not gone ashore. What do you intend to do with yourself?"

"Stay here," I answered, "until the ship sails again."

"No, you can't stop here," said the captain. "You must come ashore, and live somewhere—until the ship is made ready for sea."

He continued to talk with me for half-an-hour; and obtained from me a full account of the circumstances under which I had left my home.

"If I thought that you would stay with me, and do something for yourself," said Captain Hyland, after hearing my story, "I would endeavour to make a man of you."

My reply to this was, that I preferred a life on the sea to any other, and that I left Captain Brannon, for the simple reason that I did not like either him, or the man who had placed me under his control.

"Very well," said the captain, "I'll keep you awhile on trial; and if you prove ungrateful for what I shall do for you, you will injure yourself, more than you can me."

After this conversation, he took me ashore, bought me a suit of clothes; and then told me to accompany him to his own home.

I found that Captain Hyland had a wife and one child—a girl about ten years of age.

I thought there could be nothing in the universe more beautiful than that girl. Perhaps there was not. Why should not my opinion on such subjects be as correct as that of others? But no man living could have looked upon Lenore Hyland, without being convinced that she was very beautiful.

Six weeks passed before the ship was again ready for sea; and during that time I resided at the captain's house, and was the constant companion of his little daughter, Lenore.

In the interval, my kind protector asked me—whether I would not like to go to Dublin for a few days, and see my mother.

I told him that the "Hope" would then be in Dublin; and that I would certainly be handed over to Captain Brannon.

He reflected for a moment; and then allowed the subject to drop.

I did feel some anxiety concerning my relatives; but was too happy in Liverpool, to change my condition by going to visit them.

In order to satisfy my conscience, I thought of several reasons why I should not go home. They were easily found: for very idiotic, indeed, is that mind that cannot find arguments, in support of desires emanating from itself—whether they be right or wrong.

I knew that in whatever state I might find my relatives—or whatever might have been the conduct of Mr Leary towards them—I would be powerless either to aid them or punish him.

I strove my best to make as little trouble as possible in my new home, and to gain the good will of Mrs Hyland. I had every reason to believe that my efforts were successful.

In justice to her, I should state that my task was not so difficult, as it would have been with most women: for she was a kind-hearted lady, who had the discernment to perceive that I was anxious to deserve, as well as obtain her esteem.

Before the ship was ready to sail, Lenore had learnt to call me *brother*; and when parting with her to go on board, her sorrow was expressed in a manner that gave me much gratification.

Perhaps it is wrong for any one to feel pleasure at the demonstrations of another's grief; but there are circumstances when such will be the case, whether wrong or not. Unfortunate, indeed, is that lonely being, who has not in the wide world one acquaintance from whom he can part, with eyes dimmed by the bright drops of sorrow.

There are thousands of seamen, who have wandered long and far from every early tie of kindred and friendship. They form no others; but wander over the earth unloving, unloved and unknown—as wretched, reckless and lone, as the "last man," spoken of by the poet Campbell.

There is ever a bright spot in the soul of that man, who has reason to believe that there is some one, who thinks of him with kindness when far away; and that one bright spot will often point out the path of virtue—which otherwise might have been passed, undiscovered, or unheeded.

Volume One—Chapter Seven.

Choosing a Horse.

The reader may justly say that I have dwelt too long on the incidents of my early years. As my excuse for having done so, I can only urge, that the first parts we play on the stage of life appear of more importance to us than what they really are; and are consequently remembered more distinctly and with greater interest than those of later occurrence.

I will try not to offend in the same way again; and, as some compensation for having been too tedious, I shall pass over nearly three years of my existence—without occupying much space in describing the incidents that transpired during this period. Circumstances aid me in doing so, for these three years were spent in a tranquil, happy manner. They produced no change in my situation: for I remained in the same employment—in the service of Captain Hyland.

The ship "Lenore," owned and commanded by him, was a regular trader between Liverpool and New Orleans.

In our voyages, the captain took as much trouble in trying to teach me navigation—and all other things connected with the profession of the sea—as he could have done had I been his own son.

I appreciated his kindness; and had the gratification to know that my efforts to deserve it met with his warmest approbation.

At every return to Liverpool, and during our sojourn there, his house was my home. At each visit, my friendship for Mrs Hyland, and her beautiful daughter Lenore, became stronger. It was mutual too; and I came to be regarded almost as one of the family.

When in Liverpool, I had frequent opportunities of going to Dublin to see my mother, and with shame I confess that I did not make use of them. The attractions of my home in Liverpool proved too great for me to leave it—even for a short interval.

I often thought of going to Dublin; and reflected with pride on the fact that I was getting to be a man, and would be able to protect my relatives from any ill-treatment they might have received at the hands of Mr Leary. With all this, I did not go.

Aboard of the ship, I had one enemy, who, for some reason not fully understood, seemed to hate me as heartily, as one man could hate another. This was the first mate, who had been with Captain Hyland for several years.

He had witnessed with much disfavour the interest the captain took in my welfare, from the time of my first joining the ship; and jealousy of my influence over the latter might have had much to do in causing the mate's antipathy towards myself.

The steward, sailmaker, and one or two others, who were permanently attached to the vessel, were all friends to the "Rolling Stone," the name by which I was generally known; but the hostility of the first mate could not be removed by any efforts I made towards that end.

After a time, I gradually lost the nickname of the "Rolling Stone," and was called by my proper name, Rowland. I suppose the reason was, that my actions having proved me willing and able to remain for some time in one situation, it was thought that I deserved to be called a "Rolling Stone" no longer.

I had been nearly three years with Captain Hyland, and we were in New Orleans—where the ship, lying at the wharf, was left under my charge. The captain himself had gone to stay at a hotel in the city; and I had not seen him for several days.

The first mate was at this time neglecting his duty, and frequently remained over twenty-four hours absent from the ship. On one occasion, just as the latter came aboard to resume his duties, I received intelligence, that the captain was very ill, and wished to see me ashore.

Notwithstanding this message from the captain himself—the mate, whose name was Edward Adkins—refused to allow me to leave the ship.

The season was summer; and I knew that many people were dying in the city—which was scourged at the time with yellow fever.

The captain had undoubtedly been taken ill of that disease; and, disregarding the commands of the mate, I went ashore with all haste to see him.

I found him, as I had anticipated, suffering from yellow fever. He had just sufficient consciousness to recognise, and bid me an eternal farewell, with a slight pressure of his hand.

He died a few minutes after; and a sensation came over me similar to that I had experienced a few years before—when bending over the cold inanimate form of my father.

Mr Adkins became the captain of the "Lenore," and at once gave me a discharge. My box was sent ashore; and I was not afterwards allowed to set foot on board of the ship!

I appealed to the English Consul; but could obtain no satisfaction from him. I could not blame the official: for the mate was entitled to the command, and consequently had the right of choosing his crew.

My wages were paid me—besides some trifling compensation, for being discharged in a foreign port.

Again the new world was before me; and the question once more came up: "What am I to do?"

I wished to return to Liverpool to see Mrs Hyland and Lenore. They were to me as a mother and sister. Who should carry to them the sad news of their great misfortune? Who but myself?

The beautiful Lenore, I must see her again. I had been fancying myself in love with her for some time; but, now that her father was dead I reflected more sensibly on the subject, and arrived at the conclusion that I was a fool. I was but seventeen, and she only thirteen years of age! Why should I return to Liverpool? I had a fortune to make; and why should I return to Liverpool?

I thought of my mother, brother, and sister. They were under the ill-treatment of a man I had every reason to hate. They might need my protection. It was my duty to return to them. Should I go?

This question troubled me for some time; but in the end it was settled. I did not go.

Many will say that I neglected a sacred duty; but perhaps they have never been placed in circumstances similar to mine. They have never been in a foreign country, at the age of seventeen, in a city like New Orleans.

There was at this time a great commotion in the place. The fife and drum were continually heard in the streets; and flags were flying from houses in different parts of the city—indicating the localities of "recruiting stations."

The United States had declared war against Mexico; and volunteers were invited to join the army.

Among other idlers, I enrolled myself.

It was probably a very unwise act; but many thousands have done the same thing; and I claim an equal right with others to act foolishly, if so inclined. We are all guilty of wise and foolish actions, or more properly speaking, of good and bad ones; and often, when desirous of doing the one, it ends by our committing the other.

After being "mustered into the service," we were sent into the country to a rendezvous, where the corps to which I belonged, which was to form part of a cavalry regiment, received its allotted number of horses.

To have pointed out a particular horse to a particular man, and have said "that is yours," would have given occasion for many to declare that partiality had been shown. For this reason, an arrangement was made by which each man was allowed to choose his own horse.

The animals were ranged in a line, by being tied to a rail fence; and then we were all mustered in rank, about two hundred and fifty yards to the rear. It was then made known, that on a signal being given, each one of us might take the horse that suited him best.

The word of command was at length given; and a more interesting foot race was perhaps never witnessed, than came off on that occasion.

I was good at running; but unfortunately but a poor judge of horse flesh.

Only three or four of the company reached the fence before me; and I had nearly all the horses from which to make my choice.

I selected one, with a short neck and long flowing tail. He was of coal-black colour; and, in my opinion, the best looking horse of the lot. It was an intellectual animal—a horse of character—if ever a horse had any mental peculiarities entitling him to such distinction.

It was the first steed I ever had the chance of bestriding; and the movement by which I established myself on his back must have been either very cleverly, or very awkwardly executed: since it greatly excited the mirth of my companions.

The horse had a knack of dispensing with any disagreeable encumbrance; and having been so long a "Rolling Stone," I had not yet acquired the skill of staying where I was not wanted.

15

When I placed the steed between my legs, he immediately gave me a hint to leave. I know not whether the hint was a strong one or not; but I do know that it produced the result the horse desired: since he and I instantly parted company.

I was informed that the animal came from Kentucky; and I have not the least doubt about this having been the case, for after dealing me a sommersault, it started off in the direction of the "dark and bloody ground," and was only stopped on its journey by a six foot fence.

Those who were dissatisfied with the result of their choice, had permission to exchange horses with any other with whom they could make an arrangement.

In the corps to which I belonged was a young man from the State of Ohio, named Dayton. When the scamper towards the horses took place, instead of running with the rest, Dayton walked leisurely along; and arrived where the horses were tied, after every other individual in the company had appropriated a steed. The only horse left for Dayton had also a character—one that can only be described by calling him a sedate and serious animal.

This horse had a sublime contempt for either whip or spurs; and generally exercised his own judgment, as to the pace at which he should move. That judgment equally forbade him to indulge in eccentric actions.

Dayton proposed that we should exchange steeds—an offer that I gladly accepted. When my absconding horse was brought back to the camp, I made him over to Dayton, by whom he was at once mounted.

The animal tried the same movements with Dayton that had proved so successful with me; but they failed. He was a good rider, and stuck to his horse, as one of the men declared, "like death to a dead nigger."

The creature was conquered, and afterwards turned out one of the best horses in the troop.

Volume One—Chapter Eight.

An Episode of Soldier-Life.

American authors have written so much about the Mexican war, that I shall state nothing concerning it, except what is absolutely necessary in giving a brief account of my own adventures—which, considering the time and the place, were neither numerous nor in any way remarkable.

While in the service of the United States during that campaign, I was the constant companion of Dayton. On the march and in the field of strife, we rode side by side with each other.

We shared many hardships and dangers, and such circumstances usually produce firm friendships. It was so in our case.

Dayton was a young man who won many friends, and made almost as many enemies, for he took but little care to conceal his opinions of others, whether they were favourable or not. Although but a private, he had more influence among his comrades than any other man in the company. The respect of some, and the fear of others, gave him a power that no officer could command.

I did not see much of the war: as I was only in two actions—those of Buena Vista and Cerro Gordo.

I know that some of the people of Europe have but a very poor opinion of the fighting qualities of the Mexicans, and may not dignify the actions of Buena Vista and Cerro Gordo by the name of battles. These people are mistaken. The Mexicans fought well at Buena Vista, notwithstanding that they were defeated by men, said to be undisciplined.

It has been stated in a London paper that the Mexicans are more contemptible, as an enemy, than the same number of Chinamen. The author of that statement probably knew nothing of either of the people he wrote about; and he was thus undervaluing the Mexicans for no other reason, than that of disparaging the small but brave army to which I belonged.

The Mexicans are not cowards. An individual Mexican has as much moral and physical courage as a man of any other country. As a general thing they have as little fear of losing life or limb as any other people. "Why then," some may ask, "were they beaten by a few thousand American volunteers?"

Without attempting to answer this question, I still claim that the Mexicans are not cowards.

In the battle of Buena Vista I lost the horse obtained by exchange from Dayton. The animal had been my constant care and companion, ever since I became possessed of him; and had exhibited so much character and intellect, that I thought almost as much of him, as I did of Dayton, my dearest friend.

In my opinion, it is not right to take horses on to the field of battle. I never thought this, until I had my steed shot under me—when the sight of the noble animal struggling in the agonies of death, caused me to make a mental vow never again to go on horseback into a battle.

This resolve, however, I was soon compelled to break. Another horse was furnished me the next day—on which I had to take my place in the ranks of my corps.

One day the company to which I belonged had a skirmish with a party of guerilleros.

We were charging them—our animals urged to their greatest speed—when Dayton's horse received a shot, and fell. I could not stop to learn the fate of the rider, as I was obliged to keep on with the others.

We pursued the Mexicans for about five miles; and killed over half of their number.

On returning to camp, I traced back the trail over which we had pursued the enemy—in order to find Dayton. After much trouble I succeeded; and I believe no person ever saw me with more pleasure than did Dayton on that occasion.

The dead horse was lying on one of his legs, which had been broken. He had been in this situation for nearly three hours; and with all his exertions had been unable to extricate himself.

After getting him from under the terrible incubus, and making him as comfortable as possible, I sought the assistance of some of my companions. These I fortunately found without much trouble, and we conveyed our wounded comrade to the camp. Dayton was afterwards removed to a hospital; and this was the last I saw of him during the Mexican war.

I had but very little active service after this: for my company was left behind the main army; and formed a part of the force required for keeping open a communication between Vera Cruz, and the capital of Mexico.

The rest of the time I remained in the army, was only remarkable for its want of excitement and tediousness; and all in the company were much dissatisfied at not being allowed to go on to the Halls of Montezuma. The duty at which we were kept, was only exciting for its hardships; and American soldiers very soon become weary of excitement of this kind. We were only too delighted, on receiving orders to embark for New Orleans.

On the Sunday before sailing out of the port of Vera Cruz, I went in search of some amusement; and commenced strolling through town in hopes of finding it. In my walk, I came across a man seated under an awning, which he had erected in the street, where he was dealing "Faro." A number of people were betting against his "bank," and I lingered awhile to watch the game.

Amongst others who were betting, was a drunken mule-driver, who had been so far unfortunate as to lose all his money—amounting to about one hundred dollars.

The "MD"—as the mule-drivers were sometimes styled—either justly, or not, accused the gambler of having cheated him. He made so much disturbance, that he was at length forced away from the table by others standing around it—who, no doubt, were interested in the game.

The "MD" went into a public-house near by; and soon after came out again, carrying a loaded rifle.

Advancing within about twenty paces of the table where the gambler was engaged, he called out to the crowd to stand aside, and let him have a shot at the "skunk," who had cheated him.

"Yes," said the gambler, placing his hand on a revolver, "stand aside, gentlemen, if you please, and let him have a chance!"

Those between them, obeyed the injunction in double quick time; and, as soon as the space was clear enough to give a line for his bullet, the gambler fired—before the "MD" had raised the rifle to his shoulder.

The mule-driver was shot through the heart; and the game went on!

We had an interesting voyage from Vera Cruz to New Orleans. The hardships of the march and camp were over. Some were returning to home and friends; and all were noisy—some with high animal spirits, and some with strong ardent spirits, known under the name of *rum*.

There was much gambling on the ship, and many rows to enliven the passage; but I must not tarry to describe all the scenes I have met, or the narrative of the Life of a Rolling Stone will be drawn out too long for the patience of my readers.

We landed in New Orleans, were paid what money was due to us, and disbanded—each receiving a bounty warrant for one hundred and sixty acres of land.

In the company to which I belonged, were some of my countrymen, who had been in the English army; and I often conversed with them, as to the comparative treatment of the soldiers of the English and American armies. I shall give the conclusion we came to upon this subject.

A majority of English soldiers have relatives whom they visit and with whom they correspond. The reader will easily understand that when such is the case, thousands of families in the United Kingdom have more than a national interest in the welfare of the army, and the manner its soldiers are treated. The sympathies of the people are with them; and a soldier, who may be ill-used, has the whole nation to advocate his cause.

The majority of American regular soldiers are isolated beings—so far as home and friends are concerned—and about the only interest the nation at large takes in their welfare is, that they do their duty, and earn their pay.

This difference is understood by the soldiers of both armies; and it has its effect on their character.

In England, the army is regarded as an important part of the nation.

In the United States, it is not; but only as a certain assemblage of men, employed by the people to do a certain work—for which they receive good wages, and plenty of food: for in these respects, the American soldier has an advantage over the English, almost in the ratio of two to one!

Volume One—Chapter Nine.

A Fruitless Search.

There were speculators in New Orleans, engaged in buying land warrants from the returning volunteers. I sold mine to one of them, for one hundred and ten dollars. Besides this amount, I had about fifty dollars saved from my pay.

I shall now have the pleasure of recording the fact that I made one move in the right direction. I set sail for my childhood's home.

Conscience had long troubled me, for having neglected to look after the welfare of my relatives; and I embarked for Dublin with a mind gratified by the reflection that I was once more on the path of duty.

So much pleasure did this give me, that I resolved ever after to follow the guiding of reason, as to my future course in life. The right course is seldom more difficult to pursue than the wrong one, while the wear and tear of spirit in pursuing it is much easier.

How many strange thoughts rushed into my brain—how many interrogations offered themselves to my mind, as we dropped anchor in Dublin Bay. Should I find my mother living? Should I know my brother William and my sister Martha? What had become of Mr Leary? Should I have to kill him?

Such questions, with many others of a similar nature, coursed through my soul while proceeding towards the city.

I hurried through the streets, without allowing anything to distract my thoughts from these themes. I reached the house that had been the home of my childhood.

At the door, I paused to recover from an unusual amount of excitement; but did not succeed in quelling the tumultuous emotions that thrilled my spirit with an intensity I had never experienced before.

I looked cautiously into the shop. It was no longer a saddle and harness-maker's, but a dingy depot for vending potatoes, cabbages, and coals!

I thought a great change must suddenly have taken place in the whole city of Dublin.

It did not occur to me, that six years was a sufficient period of time for turning a saddler's shop into a greengrocer's—without any reason for being surprised at the transformation.

I stepped inside; and inquired of a stout, red-haired woman the whereabouts of a Mrs Stone, who formerly occupied the premises. The woman had never heard of such a person!

It suddenly occurred to me—and I heaved a sigh at the recollection—that my mother's name was not *Stone*, but that she was *Mrs Leary*.

I renewed my inquiry, substituting the latter name.

"Mistress Leary?" said the vulgar-looking hag before me, "lift here five year ago."

The vendor of cabbages did not know where Mrs Leary had gone. Neither did I; and this knowledge, or rather absence of knowledge, produced within me a train of reflections that were new and peculiar.

I turned out of the house, and walked mechanically up the street. A familiar name met my half-vacant gaze. It was painted on a sign, over the door of a cheese-monger's shop—Michael Brady.

I remembered that Mrs Brady, the wife of the man whose name I saw, was the intimate acquaintance and friend of my mother. Perhaps, I might learn something from her; but what, I almost feared to ascertain.

I went into the shop, and found Mrs Brady seated among her cheeses. She did not look a day older than when I last saw her. When asked, if she remembered ever having seen me before, she gazed at me for some time, and made answer in the negative.

I was not astonished at her reply. I could easily understand her stupidity; my appearance must have greatly altered since she had seen me last.

"Do you remember the name of Rowland Stone?" I asked.

"What! the little Rolling Stone?" she exclaimed, gazing at me again. "I do believe you are," said she, "Now when I look at you, I can see it is. How you have changed!"

"What has become of my mother?" I cried out, too impatient to listen longer to her exclamatory reflections.

"Poor woman!" answered Mrs Brady, "that's what I have wished to know for many years."

I was called upon to exercise the virtue of patience—while trying to obtain from Mrs Brady what information she could give concerning my family. With much time spent and many questions put, I obtained from her the following particulars:

After my departure, Mr Leary became very dissipated, and used to get drunk every day. Whenever he sold anything out of the shop, he would go to a public-house, and stay there until the money obtained for the article was spent. He would then return, abuse my mother, beat the children, take something else out of the shop; and pawn it for more money to spend in drink or dissipation. This game he had continued, until there was nothing left in the establishment that Mr Leary could sell for a shilling.

The neighbours remonstrated with my mother for allowing him to proceed in this manner; but the deluded woman seemed to think that everything done by her husband was right; and was even offended with her friends for interfering. No arguments could persuade her that Mr Leary was conducting himself in an improper manner. She appeared to think that the drunken blackguard was one of the best men that ever lived; and that she had been exceedingly fortunate in obtaining him for a husband!

When Mr Leary had disposed of everything in the shop, and had spent the proceeds in drink, he absconded—leaving my mother, brother and sister to suffer for the necessaries of life.

Instead of being gratified at getting clear of the scoundrel, my mother was nearly heart-broken to think he had deserted her!

Her first thought was to find out where he had gone. He had served his apprenticeship in Liverpool; and my mother had reasons to believe that he had betaken himself thither. The house in which she resided, had been leased by my father for a long term. At the time Mr Leary deserted her, the lease had several years to run. Since the time when it had been taken, rents in the neighbourhood had greatly risen in value; and my mother was able to sell the lease for ninety pounds. Obtaining this sum in cash, she left Dublin with her children; and proceeded to Liverpool to find Mr Leary, as Mrs Brady said, that she might give him the money to spend in drink!

My mother's friends had advised her to remain in Dublin; and told her that she should be thankful her husband had deserted her; but their advice was either unheeded, or scornfully rejected. In spite of all remonstrance, she took her departure for Liverpool; and Mrs Brady had never heard of her again.

I was intensely interested in what was told me by Mrs Brady. For awhile, I believed that my poor beguiled parent deserved her fate, however bad it may have been; and I was half inclined to search for her no more. But when I came to reflect that nearly five years had elapsed since she left Dublin, I fancied that, if unfortunately successful in finding Mr Leary, she might by this time have recovered from her strange infatuation concerning him. Though for her folly, she deserved almost any fate Mr Leary might bring upon her, I believed it to be my duty to see her once more. Besides, I had a strong desire to renew the rudely broken links of affection, that had existed between myself and my sister and brother.

When a boy, I was very proud of having a sister like little Martha, she was so kind, affectionate, and beautiful. And William, too, I remembered him with a brother's fondness. Although my mother had acted ever so foolishly, it was not the less my duty to look after her. Perhaps, for her unaccountable delusion, she had been by this time sufficiently punished. It was my desire to find her, if possible, and learn if such was the case. She was my mother, and I had no other wish than to act towards her as a son. I determined, therefore, to proceed to Liverpool.

I may confess that something more than duty summoned me thither—something even stronger than filial affection. It was the design of visiting Mrs Hyland—or, rather her daughter. I knew there would be danger to my happiness in again seeing Lenore; and I strove to strengthen my resolution by the belief that I was acting under a call of duty.

I had been with Captain Hyland when he died. I alone saw his eyes closed in death, and alone followed him to the grave. Why should I not visit his wife and child?

I could fancy that that pressure of the hand given me by the Captain in his dying struggle, was a silent command to me—to carry to them his last blessing.

Besides, Mrs Hyland had been very kind to myself; and during my sojourn in Liverpool, had made her home to me both welcome and pleasant. Why should I refrain from seeing her again—simply because her daughter was beautiful? I could think of no sufficient reason for denying myself the pleasure. The dread of its leading to pain was not enough to deter me; and I resolved to renew my acquaintance with Lenore.

Before leaving Dublin, I tried to get some information that would aid me in my search after Mr Leary and my relatives; but was unsuccessful. None of Mr Leary's former acquaintances could give me any intelligence as to what part of the city of Liverpool he might be found in. I could only learn that my mother, before leaving, had some knowledge to guide her, which had probably been obtained, sometime or other, from Mr Leary himself.

In my search, therefore, I should have no other traces than such as chance might throw in my way.

Volume One—Chapter Ten.

A Chilling Reception.

I do not like Liverpool as a city; and less do I admire a majority of its citizens. Too many of them are striving to live on what they can obtain from transient sojourners. Being the greatest shipping port in the United Kingdom—and that from which most emigrants take their departure—it affords its inhabitants too easy opportunities for exercising their skill—in obtaining the greatest amount of money for the least amount of service—opportunities of which many of them are not slow to avail themselves.

My dislike to the people of Liverpool may perhaps, arise from the fact that I claim to be a sailor; and that thousands of people in that great seaport—from beggars, thieves, and the like who crowd its crooked, narrow, dirty streets in search of a living, up to merchants, agents, and ship-owners—imagine that there is no harm in taking advantage of a sailor, and, under this belief, seldom lose an opportunity of doing so.

The first thing I did after arriving in this precious seaport, was to possess myself of a city directory, and make a list of all the saddle and harness-makers in the place—putting down the address of each opposite his name.

I then wrote a note to each of them—requesting, that if they knew anything of a journeyman saddler named Matthew Leary, they would have the goodness to communicate with me; if not, no answer to my note would be required.

Having completed this interesting correspondence—which occupied me the whole of a day—I repaired to the residence of Mrs Hyland. There had been no change there. I found her still living in the same house, where years before, I had parted with her and her daughter.

I was conducted into the drawing-room; and the next instant one of the most beautiful creatures man ever beheld, stood before me.

Lenore was beautiful when a child; and time had only developed her young charms into the perfection of feminine loveliness. To me, her beauty transcended everything I had ever seen; although I had been in Dublin, New Orleans, and Mexico—three places which are not the least favoured with the light of woman's loveliness.

Lenore was now sixteen years of age, and looked neither more nor less. The only description I can give of her is that there was nothing remarkable about her, but her beauty. I can give no particulars of how she appeared. If asked the colour of her hair and eyes, I should have been unable to tell; I only knew that she was beautiful.

I was painfully disappointed at the reception she gave me. She did not meet me with those manifestations of friendship I had anticipated. It was true that I had been a long time away; and her friendship towards me might have become cooled by my protracted absence. But this was a painful consideration. I endeavoured to dismiss it—at the same time I strove to awaken within her the memories of our old companionship.

To my chagrin, I saw that I was unsuccessful. She seemed to labour under some exciting emotion; and I could not help fancying that it was of a painful character.

Her whole behaviour was a mystery to me, because so different from what it had formerly been, or what I had hoped to find it.

I had left Lenore when she was but little more than a child, and she was now a young lady.

In the three years that had intervened, there was reason for me to expect some change in her character. With her mother, no change I presumed could have taken place. I left Mrs Hyland a woman; and such I should find her, only three years older. In her I expected to meet a friend, as I had left her. She entered the room. I was again doomed to disappointment!

She received me with even more coldness than had been exhibited by Lenore. She did not even offer me her hand; but took a seat, and with a more unpleasant expression than I had ever before observed on her face, she waited apparently with impatience for what I might have to say.

The sensitive feelings of my soul had never been so cruelly wounded. I was in an agony of anger and disappointment; and unable any longer to endure the painful excitement of my emotions, I uttered a few common-place speeches, and hastily withdrew from their presence.

What could their conduct mean? In the excited state of my thoughts, I was unable to form even a conjecture, that seemed in any way consistent with my knowledge of their previous character.

It might be that when Lenore was a child, and I was a boy, they had seen no harm in befriending and being kind to me; but now that Lenore was a young lady, and I a man—a sailor, too—they might have reasons for not having any further acquaintance with me.

Could it be that they were endued with that selfishness—in this world possessed by so many? That they had been my friends only because Captain Hyland was my protector—to fall away from me now, that his protection could be no longer extended to me?

I could hardly think this possible: for it would be so much out of keeping with all that I had ever known of the character either of Mrs Hyland or her daughter.

I had long anticipated great pleasure in revisiting them; and had thought when again in their presence I should be with friends. Never had I been so cruelly disappointed; and for awhile I fancied that I should never care to meet with old acquaintances again.

I am capable of forming strong attachments. I had done so for Mrs Hyland and her daughter, and their chill reception had the effect of causing me to pass a sleepless night.

In the morning, I was able to reflect with a little more coolness, as well as clearness. A cause, perhaps *the* cause, of their strange conduct suddenly suggested itself to my mind.

Adkins, the first mate of the ship Lenore, had been, and, no doubt, still was—my enemy. He had turned me out of the ship in New Orleans; and had, in all likelihood, on his arrival in Liverpool, poisoned the mind of Mrs Hyland, by some falsehood, of which I was the victim. I knew the scoundrel to be capable of doing this, or any other base action.

There was a consolation in the thought that this explanation might be the real one, and for a while it restored the tranquillity of my spirit.

I would see them again, demand an explanation; and if my suspicions proved true, I could refute any change made against me—so as once more to make them my friends.

I did not desire their friendship from any personal motives. It might not now be worth the trouble of having it restored; but in memory of their past kindness, and out of regard for my own character, I could not leave them labouring under the impression that I had been ungrateful.

Alas! there was a deeper motive for my desiring an explanation. Their friendship was worth restoring. It was of no use my endeavouring to think otherwise. The friendship of a beautiful creature like Lenore was worth every thing. The world to me would be worthless without it. I was already wretched at the thought of having lost her good opinion. I must again establish myself in it, or failing, become more wretched still.

The next day, I returned to the residence of Mrs Hyland. I saw her seated near the window, as I approached the house. I saw her arise, and retire out of sight—evidently after recognising me!

I rang the bell. The door was opened by a servant—who, without waiting to be interrogated, informed me that neither Mrs nor Miss Hyland were at home!

I pushed the door open, passed the astonished domestic, entered the hall; and stepped unceremoniously into the apartment—in the window of which I had seen Mrs Hyland.

No one was inside—excepting the servant, who had officially followed me. I turned to her, and said in a tone savouring of command:

"Tell Mrs Hyland that Mr Rowland Stone is here, and will not leave until he has seen her."

The girl retired, and soon after Mrs Hyland entered the room. She did not speak; but waited to hear what I had to say.

"Mrs Hyland," I began, "I am too well acquainted with you, and respect you too much, to believe that I am treated in the manner I have been, without a good cause. Conscious of having done nothing intentionally to injure you, or yours, I have returned to demand the reason why your conduct towards me has undergone such a change. You once used to receive me here as though I was your own son. What have I done to forfeit your friendship?"

"If your own conscience does not accuse you," she answered, "it is not necessary for me to give you any explanation, for you might not understand it. But there is one thing that I hope you *will* understand: and that is, that your visits here are no longer either welcome or desirable."

"I learnt that much yesterday," said I, imitating in a slight degree the air of sneering indifference, in which Mrs Hyland addressed me. "To-day I have called for an explanation. Your own words imply that I was once welcome; and I wish to know why such is no longer the case."

"The explanation is then, that you have proved unworthy of our friendship. There is no explanation that *you* can give, that will remove the impression from my mind that you have been guilty of ingratitude and dishonesty towards those who were your best friends; and I do not wish to be pained by listening to any attempt you may make at an apology."

I became excited. Had the speaker been a man, my excitement would have assumed the shape of anger.

"I only ask," I replied, endeavouring, as much as possible, to control my feelings, "I only ask, what justice to you, as well as myself, demands you to give. All I require is an explanation; and I will not leave the house, until I have had it. I insist upon knowing of what I am accused."

Mrs Hyland, apparently in high displeasure at the tone I had assumed, turned suddenly away from me, and glided out of the room.

To calm my excitement, I took up a paper, and read, or attempted to read.

For nearly half an hour I continued this half involuntary occupation. At the end of that time, I stepped up to the fire-place, caught hold of the bell pull, and rang the bell.

"Tell Miss Lenore," said I, when the servant made her appearance, "that I wish to see her; and that all the policemen in Liverpool cannot put me out of this house, until I have done so."

The girl flounced back through the door; and shortly after Lenore, with half of a smile on her beautiful face, entered the room.

She appeared less reserved than on the interview of the day before; and, if possible, more lovely. I was too happy to interpret from her deportment, that she had not yet entirely forgotten the past; and that what I now wished to know, she would not hesitate to reveal.

"Lenore," said I, as she entered, "in you I hope still to find a friend—notwithstanding the coldness with which you have treated me; and from you I demand an explanation."

"The only explanation I can give," said she, "is, that mamma and I have probably been deceived. There is one who has accused you of ingratitude, and other crimes as bad—perhaps worse."

"Adkins!" I exclaimed. "It is Adkins, the first mate of the 'Lenore!'"

"Yes, it is he who has brought the accusation; and, unfortunately, whether false or no, your conduct has been some evidence of the truth of the story he has told us. Oh! Rowland, it was hard to believe you guilty of ingratitude and crime; but your long absence, unexplained as it was, gave colour to what has been alleged against you. You have never written to us: and it will be nearly impossible for you to be again reinstated in the good opinion of my mother."

"In yours, Lenore?"

She blushingly held down her head, without making reply.

"Will you tell me of what I am accused?" I asked.

"I will," she answered. "And, Rowland, before I hear one word of explanation from you learn this; I cannot believe you guilty of any wrong. I have been too well acquainted with you to believe that you could possibly act, under any circumstances, as you have been accused of doing. It is not in your nature."

"Thank you, Lenore!" said I, with a fervour I could not restrain myself from showing. "You are now as you have ever been, more beautiful than anything in the world, and wise as you are beautiful."

"Do not talk thus, Rowland! Nothing but your own words can ever change the opinion I had formed of your character—long ago, when we were both children. I will tell you why my mother is displeased with you. There are more reasons than one. First, when my father died in New Orleans, Mr Adkins brought back the ship; and you did not return in it. We were surprised at this; and called Mr Adkins to account for not bringing you home. He did not appear willing to give us any satisfaction concerning you; but we would insist on having it; and then, with apparent reluctance, he stated that he had not wished to say anything against you—fearing that from our known friendship for you, it might be unpleasant for us to hear it. He then told us, that you had not only neglected, and proved cruel to my father—when on his death-bed—but, that, as soon as it became certain there was no hope of his recovery, you behaved as though you thought it no longer worth while to trouble yourself with a man, who could not live to repay you. He said that you had previously deserted from the ship, and left my father—notwithstanding his earnest entreaties that you should remain with him. It cannot be true. I know it cannot be true; but so long as my mother thinks there is a particle of truth in Mr Adkins' statement, she will never forgive you. Your accuser has also stated that when you left the ship, you took with you what was not your own; but this he did not tell us until several months had elapsed, and there appeared no probability of your returning."

"What has become of Mr Adkins now?" I asked.

"He is on a voyage to New Orleans in the 'Lenore.' He obtained my mother's confidence, and is now in command of the ship. Lately he has been trying to make himself more disagreeable to myself—by professing for me—what he, perhaps, believes to be an affection. Oh! it is too unpleasant to dwell upon. My mother listens, I fear, too consentingly, to all he has to say: for she is grateful to him for his kindness to my father before he died—and for the interest he appears ever since to have taken in our welfare. His manner towards us has greatly changed of late. Indeed, he acts as if he were the head of our family, and the owner of the vessel. I believe he is expected to return to Liverpool at any time: as the time for the voyage has expired, and the ship has been due for some days."

"I wish he were in Liverpool *now*" said I. "When he does arrive, I will make him prove himself a liar. Lenore! I have ever been treated with the greatest kindness by your father and mother. It is not in my nature to be either ungrateful or dishonest. Your father's ship was my home, I did not leave that home without good reason. I was turned out of it by the very villain who has accused me. I shall stay in Liverpool until he returns; and when I have exposed him, and proved myself still worthy of your friendship, I shall again go forth upon the world with a light heart, as I can with a clear conscience."

Requesting Lenore to tell her mother that she had been deceived—and that I should stay in Liverpool till I proved that such was the case—I arose to take my departure. I lingered only to add: that I would not again annoy them with my presence until the return of the ship—when I should challenge Adkins to appear before them, and prove him guilty of the very crimes he had charged against myself—ingratitude and dishonesty.

With this promise did I close my interview with Lenore.

Volume One—Chapter Eleven.

On the Track of Mr Leary.

After leaving Mrs Hyland's house, I had much to occupy my thoughts. The principal subject that engaged their attention was the wonderful beauty of Lenore.

She was beautiful; and she professed to be my friend. But while I felt a consoling pride in possessing the friendship of one so lovely, there was much that was unpleasant in the thought that her mother could, even for an instant, have believed me guilty of the grave charges brought against me by Adkins.

To be thought ungrateful by one who had treated me with so much kindness, and more especially one who was the mother of Lenore, was a reflection full of bitterness.

Adkins had now done enough to make me his deadly enemy. He had never used me well aboard ship; and would have caused me still more trouble there had he not been restrained by his fear of Captain Hyland. He had turned me out of the ship in New Orleans. He had returned to Liverpool, and accused me of the basest of crimes.

But what was still more unpleasant to dwell upon; he was endeavouring to deprive me of what was of almost equal consequence with my character—of her whom I had hoped might one day become my wife. Yes, there could be no doubt of the fact. He was trying to win Lenore.

This last I could scarce look upon as a crime on his part. To aspire to win one so lovely was no crime; and one who should do so would only be acting as Nature commanded.

But at that time, I did not view it in this light; and the idea of Edward Adkins aspiring to the hand of Lenore Hyland was proof to me that he was the vilest wretch that ever encumbered the earth.

For a while, I forgot my hatred for Mr Leary in my dislike to Mr Adkins.

Hatred with me had never before reached a thirst for revenge; but to this degree of hostility had it attained, within an hour after leaving Lenore.

But what could I do? When my enemy returned, I could confront him in presence of Lenore and her mother. I could make one statement, which he would certainly contradict by making another. I was in a country where the laws do not allow a man any chance of obtaining redress for the cruellest wrong, or insult, he may suffer.

I passed that night, as the preceding one, without sleep.

The day after that on which I had addressed my letters to the saddle and harness-makers of Liverpool, I received answers from two of them—both men who had been acquainted with Mr Leary.

I lost no time in calling upon these correspondents.

One of them frankly informed me that Mr Leary's time, as an apprentice, had been served in his shop, that he did not think him exactly honest; and had been only too glad to get rid of him. He had not seen or heard anything of Mr Leary for seven years; and hoped never to behold that individual again. He had taken Leary, when a boy, from the work-house; and believed he had no relatives, who would know where he was to be found.

I called on the other saddler, and learnt from him that Mr Leary, after having served his time, had worked in his establishment as a journeyman, though only for a very short while. Leary had left him to go to Dublin; but had returned three or four years afterwards, and had again been employed by him for a few days. On leaving the second time, Mr Leary had engaged to go out to New South Wales, with a saddle and harness-maker from that colony, who, as the Liverpool tradesman laughingly stated, had been so foolish as to pay for Leary's passage, in the hope of being repaid by his services after he got there.

With painful interest, I inquired, whether Mr Leary had taken along with him to Australia a wife and family.

"No," said the saddler, "nothing of the kind. He was not able to do that: since he had to tell a thousand lies to induce the saddler to take himself. But I remember, there was a woman from Dublin inquiring for him after he had sailed; and she, poor creature, appeared well nigh heart-broken, when she learnt that he had gone without her. I suppose she must have been his wife."

The saddler had heard nothing since from either Leary or the woman.

A part of this intelligence was very satisfactory. My mother had *not* found Mr Leary in Liverpool, and that wretch was now far away.

But where was my mother? Where had she and her youngest children been for the last five years? How should I learn their fate?

Surely I had plenty of work before me. My relatives were to be found; and this would be no easy task: since I had not the slightest clue to guide me in the search. I had to convince Mrs Hyland that I was still worthy of her friendship. I had to obtain revenge on my enemy Adkins; and a greater task than all would still remain. I had to win, or forget Lenore.

My last interview with her, had revived within my mind the sweet remembrances of the past, along with thoughts of the present, and dreams of the future—thoughts and dreams that would not again sleep. A mental vision of her loveliness was constantly before me.

What was I to do first? I had but little money in my pockets; and could not leave Liverpool at present to obtain more. I must stay until the return of Adkins; and it would not do to spend my last shilling in idly waiting.

Without friends I could only get such occupation, as required the severest labour to perform; but, fortunately for that, I had the will, health, and strength I feel a pride in stating, that I acted, as a man should under the circumstances. Instead of strolling about in hopeless idleness, I went to the docks, and obtained labourer's work.

For two weeks I worked at handling cotton bales, and bags of sugar. The toil was humble, and the pay for it was proportionately small; but duty commanded me, and I worked on, cheered by hope, and without repining at my fate.

Sometimes in the evening, I would walk up and down the street in front of the residence of Mrs Hyland—with the hope of seeing Lenore, or with the knowledge of being near her, whether she might be seen or not. I found pleasure even in this.

I did not like to call on her again—until I had given her mother some proof of my innocence.

Sometimes it occurred to me to ask myself the question, why should I see her more, even after I had cleared myself? She was beautiful, dangerously beautiful; and I was friendless, homeless, and without fortune. Why should I endanger my future peace of mind, by becoming more and more infatuated with one whose heart I could scarce hope ever to possess?

Duty as well as reason told me to pursue the search for my relatives, and see Lenore Hyland no more. But where is the heart love-stricken that will listen to the call, either of reason, or duty?

Mine did not, and could not. It was deaf to such an appeal. I could think only of Lenore, yearn to see her again—to speak with her—to listen to her—to love her!

Volume One—Chapter Twelve.

An Encounter with a Coward.

About a week after my interview with Mrs Hyland and her daughter, I saw what I had been daily looking for—a notice in one of the Liverpool papers, under the head of "Shipping Intelligence," announcing the arrival of the ship "Lenore," Captain Adkins, from New Orleans.

After reading the notice, I hastily flung aside the paper; and proceeded direct to the docks—where I found the vessel had already arrived.

As I might have expected, Adkins was not aboard. He had landed several hours before, while the ship was still in the river. Having ascertained the name of the hotel where he was in the habit of staying, while in Liverpool, I lost no time loitering on board the ship, but went in search of him. On reaching the hotel, I found that he had slept there the night before, but had gone out after breakfast in the morning.

My conjecture was, that he would be found at the house of Mrs Hyland; and it now occurred to me that I had been wonderfully stupid in not looking for him there in the first instance.

From the hotel, I proceeded direct to Mrs Hyland's residence, as I walked along, anticipating much pleasure in the task of compelling Adkins to refute his own falsehoods. I feared, however, that shame would hinder him telling the truth; and that even in my presence he would stick to his infamous story. I feared it, because I did not wish to kill him.

As I had conjectured, he was visiting at Mrs Hyland's. Just as I reached the door, Adkins was coming out.

I controlled my temper as well as I could. I did not wish to defeat my purpose by an exhibition of idle anger.

"Good morning Mr Adkins!" said I. "We meet again; and I assure you, on my part, with profound pleasure."

He would have passed without speaking, had I not placed my body so as to block the way.

"Who the devil are you; and what do you want?" he asked, with a bullying tone and air that I had often known him assume before.

"I am Rowland Stone," I answered, "and I wish to see you on a matter of considerable importance."

"You see me then! what the important business?"

"It can only be made known in the presence of Mrs Hyland and her daughter."

"Mrs Hyland does not wish to see you," said Adkins, "and much less her daughter, I should think. As for myself, I want nothing to do with you."

"I can believe the latter part of your assertions," I answered, "but it is necessary that we should sometimes do what may not be exactly agreeable to us. If there is a spark of manhood in you, walk back into the house, and repeat to Mrs Hyland in my presence, what you have said behind my back."

"I shall not take the trouble to do any thing of the kind. I tell you again, I want nothing to say to you. Give me the way!"

As Adkins said this, he made a gesture as if he intended to pass me.

"I'll give you the way to hell," said I, "unless you do as I bid you," and I caught him by the collar to drag him into the house.

He resisted this attempt by aiming a blow at me, which I returned with such interest, that while I still kept my legs, the captain of the "Lenore" missed his; and, staggering backward, he fell heavily on the door-step.

I had now lost all command of myself; and, after ringing the bell, to have the door re-opened, I seized him by the hair of the head—for the purpose of hauling him inside.

My purpose would have been accomplished. I would have broken down the door, dragged him into the house, confronted him with Mrs Hyland, and made him swallow his false words, but for the arrival of a trio of policemen.

I was not overcome until after a long struggle, in which the exertions of the three policemen, Adkins himself, and another man, who was passing at the time, were united against me. It ended in their putting me in irons.

As I was led away from the house, I noticed that Mrs Hyland and Lenore were both at the window—where, I had no doubt, they had been witnesses of the affray.

I was at once taken to a police station, and locked up in one of its cells.

Next morning I was brought before a magistrate. Adkins was there to prosecute. The three policemen were present as witnesses, as also the Liverpool citizen, who had aided in putting me in irons.

After evidence was heard against me, I was called upon for my defence. I had nothing to say to the charge.

The magistrate emphatically declared that a case of a more unprovoked assault had never been brought before him; and that he did not think the ends of justice would be met by the infliction of a fine. He therefore sentenced me to fourteen days' imprisonment.

I thought none the less of myself for that; and, under other circumstances, two weeks in a prison might not have been passed unpleasantly. But it was bitterness to reflect, that while I was passing my time in the companionship of petty thieves, Edward Adkins was daily visiting Lenore.

Fourteen days must I pass as a prisoner, while my vile enemy would be enjoying the society of Mrs Hyland and her daughter—no doubt doing all he could to blacken my character, and lower me still further in their estimation!

The reflection was anything but pleasant, though I might have partly consoled myself by another: that I was much better off inside the gaol, than millions of my fellow countrymen outside of it. Had I committed some crime, that really deserved this confinement, then would I, indeed, have felt really wretched; but conscience accused me of no wrong; and I was not without those tranquillising emotions ever springing from a sense of rectitude and innocence.

I was not afraid that Adkins would gain any great advantage over me in winning the affections of Lenore—even though aided by the influence of her mother. It was not that which troubled me during my sojourn within the walls of a prison. If Lenore should prove capable of choosing such a man for her husband, I need not regret her loss. My spirit was more harassed by the thought: that wrong should have thus triumphed—that Adkins should be in the society of Lenore, when he should have been in my place in the prison, and I in his.

After I had passed eight days of my confinement, I was surprised one morning by the announcement that I was to receive visitors.

Two persons had called, and inquired for Rowland Stone. They were outside—waiting to be admitted to my cell.

Both proved to be old acquaintances. One was a man named Wilton, who had been the second mate of the ship "Lenore," under Captain Hyland. The other was Mason, the steward of the same ship.

As both these men had been very kind to me when I was in the ship, I was pleased to see them; but much more so, when I learnt to whom I was indebted for their visit. Mason told me that he was still steward of the "Lenore," and that Miss Hyland had come to him on board: for the purpose of obtaining a true account of the circumstances that stood between me and Adkins.

"I was glad to learn, Rowley, that you had turned up again," said Mason, "but at the same time, sorry to hear of your present trouble. I at once resolved to try and get you out of at least a part of it, although I may lose my situation by doing so. I told Miss Hyland, plainly enough, that Adkins was a villain, and that I could prove it. I promised her that I would come and see you. Wilton here, is now the skipper of a tug-boat on the river, and I brought him along—knowing that he can lend a hand to help us."

"Nothing can please me more than to see Adkins lose the command of the 'Lenore,'" interposed Wilton, "for I know that he is not an honest man; and that he has been all along robbing the widow. We must decide on some plan to convince Mrs Hyland, that she is placing confidence in a scoundrel."

Wilton and Mason remained with me nearly an hour; and it was decided that nothing should be done openly, until my term of imprisonment should expire. We were then to ascertain when Adkins would be on a visit to Mrs Hyland's house, when we should all three go together, meet him there, and tell Mrs Hyland the whole story of his falsehood and dishonesty.

"Should she not believe us, and still continue to trust him," said Wilton, "then she deserves to be robbed, that's my way of thinking."

I thought the same, so far as robbing her of her worldly wealth; but it was bitter to believe that the rascal might also rob her of a jewel more priceless than all else—of Lenore. But I could not believe that the most insane folly on her part would deserve so extreme a punishment, as that of having Adkins for a son-in-law!

Mason gave me his address, so did Wilton, and I promised to call on them, as soon as I should be set at liberty.

They left me happy, and hopeful. I was happy, not because I was young, and in good health—not because I had found friends who would aid me in subduing an enemy; but because the beautiful Lenore had interested herself in my misfortunes, and was trying to remove them.

That was a theme for many long and pleasant reveries, which while they rendered me impatient to be free, at the same time enabled me to pass the remainder of my term of imprisonment, with but slight regard for the many petty annoyances and discomforts of the situation.

I accepted my liberty when it was at length given me; and on the same day went to visit Mason and Wilton.

What had been done already by Lenore, left me under the impression that she would still further aid me in establishing the truth. I felt confident, that she would not object to letting us know on what day and hour we might meet Adkins at her mother's house; and with this confidence, I wrote a note to her, containing the request that she would do so. Then, in pleasant expectation of soon having an opportunity of clearing my character, I awaited the answer.

Volume One—Chapter Thirteen.

A Reckoning Up.

Lenore did not disappoint me. Two days after getting out of the prison, I received her reply—informing me that Adkins would be at her mother's house the next day, and advising me to call with my friends, about half-past ten. I had made known to her the object of my desire to meet him.

After receiving her note, I went immediately to Mason and Wilton; and we appointed a place of rendezvous for the next morning.

That evening, I was as uneasy as the commander-in-chief of an army on the eve of a great battle. I had an enemy to confront and conquer—a reputation already sullied to restore to its former brightness.

I could not help some anxiety as to the result.

In the morning, I met my friends at the appointed place; and as the clock struck ten, we started for the residence of Mrs Hyland.

As we came within sight of the house, I perceived Lenore at the window. She recognised us, rose from her seat, and disappeared towards the back of the room. When I rang the bell, the door was opened by herself.

Without hesitating, she conducted us all three into the parlour, where we found Adkins and Mrs Hyland.

The latter appeared to be no little astonished by our unexpected entrance; but as for Adkins himself, he looked more like a frightened maniac than a man.

"What does this mean?" exclaimed Mrs Hyland, in a voice that expressed more alarm than indignation.

"These gentlemen have called to see you on business, mother," said her daughter. "There is nothing to fear from them. They are our friends."

Having said this, Lenore requested us to be seated; and we complied.

Adkins did not speak; but I could read from the play of his features, that he knew the game was up, and that he had lost.

"Mrs Hyland," said Wilton, after a short interval of silence, "I have called here to do what I believe to be a duty, and which I ought to have done long ago. If I am doing any wrong, it is only through my ignorance of what's right. I was your husband's friend, and we sailed together, for nine years or thereabouts. I was on the ship 'Lenore' when Captain Hyland died, in New Orleans; and I have heard the stories that Mr Adkins here has told about this young man. Those stories are false. When in New Orleans, at the time of your husband's death, Adkins was most of the time drunk, and neglecting his duty. Rowley did not desert from the ship, neither did he neglect the captain, but was the only one of the ship's company with him, or taking care of him, when he died. Mr Adkins never liked Rowley; and the only reason I can think of for his not doing so, is just because it is natural for a bad man to dislike a good one. When Mr Adkins obtained the command of the ship, he would not let Rowley come aboard again—much less return in her to Liverpool. I made one voyage with Adkins as first mate after Captain Hyland's death, and learnt, while making it, that I could not continue with him any longer—unless I should become nearly as bad as himself. For that reason I left the ship.

"Mrs Hyland!" continued Wilton, fixing his eye upon Adkins, and speaking with determined emphasis, "I have no hesitation in pronouncing Mr Adkins to be a wicked, deceitful man, who has been robbing you under the cloak of friendship; and still continues to rob you."

"These men have formed a conspiracy to ruin me!" cried Adkins, springing to his feet. "I suppose they will succeed in doing it. Three men and one woman are more than I can contend against!"

Mrs Hyland paid no attention to this remark; but, turning to Mason, said, "I believe that you are Mr Mason, the steward of the 'Lenore.' What have you to say?"

"I have to state that all Mr Wilton has told you, is true," said Mason. "Rowley, to my knowledge, has never done anything to forfeit your friendship. I have long known that Captain Adkins was a scoundrel; and my desire to expose him—overcome by the fact that I have a large family to support, and was afraid of losing my situation—has caused me to pass many a sleepless hour. I had made up my mind not to go another voyage along with him—before learning that my testimony was wanted in aid of Rowley here. On hearing that he had robbed the young man—not only of his old friends, but of his liberty—I no longer hesitated about exposing him. He is a dishonest villain; and I can prove it by having the ship's accounts overhauled."

"Go on! go on!" cried Adkins. "You have it all your own way now. Of course, my word is nothing."

"He is telling the truth for once in his life," said Mason to Mrs Hyland. "For his word *is* just worth nothing, to any one who knows him."

"Now, Rowland," said Mrs Hyland, "what have you to say?"

"Very little," I answered. "I did not wish you to think ill of me. There is nothing that can wound the feelings more than ingratitude; and the kindness with which you once treated me, was the reason why I have been so desirous of proving to you that I have not been ungrateful. You have now evidence that will enable you to judge between Adkins and myself; and after this interview, I will trouble you no more, for I do not desire to insist upon a renewal of the friendship you have suspected. I only wished you to know that I had given you no cause for discontinuing it."

"Now, gentlemen!" said Adkins, "having been amused by all each of you has to say, I suppose I may be allowed to take my leave of you; and," said he, turning to Mrs Hyland, "I'll see you again, madam, when you have not quite so much interesting company to engage your attention."

He arose, and was moving towards the door.

"Stop!" shouted Mason, stepping before him. "Mrs Hyland," continued the steward, "I know enough about this man, and his management of your business, to justify you in giving him in charge to a policeman. Shall I call one?"

For a minute Mrs Hyland was silent.

I looked at Adkins, and saw that my triumph over him was complete. His own appearance condemned him; and anyone to have seen him at that moment—humiliated, cowed, and guilty—would ever after have dreaded doing wrong; through very fear of looking as he did.

In truth, he presented a melancholy spectacle: for he had not the courage to assume even a show of manliness.

To complete my triumph, and his discomposure, Lenore, who had been all the while listening with eager interest, and apparent pleasure to what had been said, cried out, "Let him go, mother, if he will promise never to come near us again!"

"Yes, let him go!" repeated Mrs Hyland. "I must think before I can act."

Mason opened the door; and Adkins sneaked out in a fashion that was painful, even for me—his enemy—to behold. After his departure, each waited for the other to speak.

The silence was broken by Mrs Hyland, who said:

"Of you, Mr Wilton, and you, Mr Mason, I have often heard my late husband speak in the highest terms; and I know of no reason, why I should not believe what you have told me."

25

"With you, Rowland," she continued, turning her eyes upon me, with something of the old friendly look, "with you, I have been acquainted many years; and the principal reason I had for doubting your integrity and truthfulness, was because I thought that, had you possessed the regard for us, you should have had, you would certainly have come back after the death of my husband.

"You did not; and the circumstance, as you will admit, was strong against you. I have now much reason to believe that I have been deceived in Adkins; and I do not know whom to trust. I must suppose that all of you have come here without any ill feeling towards me: for I know not why you should wish to do me an injury.

"I have a respect for those in whom Mr Hyland placed confidence. I have heard him speak well of all of you; and I do not remember now of anything he ever said that should give me a favourable opinion of Adkins. Indeed, I never heard Mr Hyland speak much concerning him. It is my duty to think of the past as well as the present, before I can say anything more."

Wilton and Mason both assured Mrs Hyland that they had only acted under the influence of a sense of duty—inspired by the respect they had for the memory of her husband.

We left the house; but not till Mrs Hyland had shaken hands with me, and at the same time extended to me an invitation to call the next day; and not till Mrs Hyland's daughter had given me reason to believe that my visit would be welcome.

Volume One—Chapter Fourteen.

Once More Friends.

I did call the next day, and had no particular reason to be dissatisfied with my reception.

Mrs Hyland did not meet me in the same motherly manner, she once used to exhibit; but I did not expect it; and I could not feel displeased at being admitted on any terms, into the presence of a being so beautiful as Lenore.

Neither did *she* receive me in the same manner she used to do in the past; but neither was I annoyed by that circumstance. It was necessary that the child-like innocence and familiarity, once existing between us, should cease; and it was no chagrin to me to perceive that it had done so.

I confessed to Mrs Hyland, that I had acted wrong in not returning to Liverpool after her husband's death; but I also explained to her how, on being discharged from the ship, I had felt myself sorely aggrieved; and, having no longer a home, I had to wander about as circumstances dictated. I added, of course, that could I have had the least suspicion that my absence would have been construed into any evidence of crime or ingratitude, I would have returned long before to refute the calumny.

Lenore did not try to conceal her pleasure, at seeing her mother and myself conversing once more as friends.

"You must not leave us again, Rowland," said she, "for we have not many friends, and can ill-afford to lose one. See how near we have been to losing you—all through your being absent."

"Yes, Rowland," said Mrs Hyland. "My house was once your home; and you are welcome to make it so again. I shall only be fulfilling the wishes of my husband, by renewing the intimate friendship that once existed between us."

Her invitation to make her house once more my home, I reluctantly declined. Lenore seemed no longer my sister; and with some sorrow the conviction forced itself on my mind—that my fate was to love—to love, yet wander far from the one I loved.

Lenore was now a young lady. I thought myself a man. As children, we could no longer live together—no longer dwell under the same roof. Lenore was too beautiful; and I was too much afflicted with poverty. Any further acquaintance between us might not contribute to my future happiness but the contrary.

I left the house with mingled feelings of pleasure and despair, pleased to find myself once more restored to the good opinion of Mrs Hyland—despairing of being able to resist the fascinations of her daughter's beauty.

Every time I gazed upon her fair face, could only add to my misery. I was young; and as I had been told, good-looking. Lenore and I had been old friends and playmates. It was possible for me to win her love; but would it be honourable?

Would it be a proper return for the kindness of Captain Hyland and his widow, for me, a penniless "rolling stone," to try to win the affections of their only child, and subject her to the misery of my own unfortunate lot? No! I could love Lenore; but I could not act in such an unworthy manner.

Then followed the reflection, that Mrs Hyland had some property. Her home would be mine. She needed a son-in-law to look after the ship; and I was a seaman.

These thoughts only stirred within me a feeling of pride, that would not allow me to receive any advantage of fortune from one I could choose for a wife. I knew that with all the exertions a man may make—and however correct his habits may be—he cannot live happily with a wife who brings into the firm of husband and wife more money than himself.

Another unpleasant consideration came before me. Why should I be seeking for reasons against marrying Lenore, when perhaps she might not consent to marry *me*? Because we were old friends, was no reason why she should ever think of me as a husband. By trying to make her love me, I might, as she had said of Mr Adkins, cause her only to hate me.

The day after my visit to Mrs Hyland and Lenore, I went to see Mason, the steward, in order that I might thank him for the good word he had spoken for me—as well as for much kindness he had shown towards me, when we were shipmates in the 'Lenore.' He received me in a cordial manner, that caused me to think better of mankind, than I had lately done. In a long conversation I held with him, he told me of many acts of dishonesty, in the committal of which he had detected Adkins, who, he said, had been robbing Mrs Hyland in every way he could.

"Captain Hyland took much trouble in giving you some education," said he; "why don't you marry the daughter, and take command of the ship?"

"I am a poor penniless adventurer," I replied, "and dare not aspire to so much happiness as would be mine, were I to become the husband, as well as captain, of 'Lenore.' I am neither so vain nor ambitious."

"That's a fact," said Mason. "You have not enough of either. No man ever did any thing for himself, or any one else, without thinking something of himself, and making such a trial as you decline to undertake. He is a lucky man who wins without trying."

There was truth in what the steward said; but the Hylands had been my friends, and were so again; and I could not bring myself to abuse the confidence they had placed in me. I could not speak of love to Lenore, and so I told the steward.

In this interview with Mason, I learnt from him that Adkins had disappeared, and could no more be found!

"His flight," said Mason, "will be positive proof to Mrs Hyland that he was unworthy of the confidence she had placed in him. She cannot be too thankful, that your return has been the means of her discovering his true character. I would have exposed him long ago, but I did not think that I could succeed; and that I would only be doing myself an injury—in short, ruining my poor family, without the consolation of knowing that I had also ruined a scoundrel. Thank the Lord for all his mercies! The villain has been uncloaked at last."

With this pious thanksgiving ended the interview, between the honest steward and myself.

Volume One—Chapter Fifteen.

Love and Poverty.

From that time I called every day to see Lenore and her mother; and each time came away more hopelessly infatuated.

My money was gradually growing easier to count—until I found that I had but a few shillings left, and necessity must soon force me to seek employment. Of course I contemplated going to sea, and making my living on board some ship; but I found it impossible to come to a determination.

How was I to leave Liverpool, where I could gaze each day on the beauty that adorned Lenore?

I could not take my departure until circumstances should compel me. In order to protract my stay as long as possible, I lived on but one meal per diem; and as I had also to keep a little money for my lodgings, I made that meal upon a penny roll.

Mrs Hyland had determined on giving up the ship—a resolution no doubt due to the mismanagement, or rather dishonesty, of him who had lately commanded her. I assisted her in finding a purchaser; and she was very fortunate in disposing of the vessel at a good price.

She had plenty of money, and was willing to aid me. But pride prevented me from accepting of anything but her friendship; and ofttimes did I appear in the presence of Lenore while suffering the pangs of hunger! Was that love?

I thought it was; and on this fancy, and a single roll of bread, I lived from day to day. Never had I been so happy, and, at the same time, so wretched. I could look upon her I loved, and converse with her for hours at a time. That was happiness. But I loved Lenore, and must leave her. That was misery.

Lenore seemed to meet me with so much cheerfulness, that my resolution to leave her—without being absolutely compelled to it—was often nearly broken; and I believe there are but few who would have resisted the temptation to stay. But pride, a sense of justice, and a love of independence, prompted me to go forth again upon the world, and seek fortune afresh. Perhaps, too, the fact that I was naturally a "rolling stone," might have had much to do in my determination, at length arrived at, of bidding adieu to Lenore. There was yet another motive urging my departure—one which had been too long allowed to lie dormant within my bosom; my relatives were lost, and I knew not where to find them. This thought often arose, causing me much regret. I had as yet no reason to believe that they had left Liverpool; but if such should prove to be the case, the sooner I started in search of them, the sooner would my conscience be satisfied.

I waited till my last shilling was spent; and then sold a signet ring—which I had taken from the finger of a dead Mexican, on the field of battle—obtaining thirty shillings for it. With this trifling sum I had a great deal to accomplish. It constituted the sole fund with which my relatives were to be sought and found. It was the capital I had to invest, in the business of making a fortune worthy of Lenore!

I advertised for my mother in some of the Liverpool papers; but the only result was the loss of the greater part of my cash. She had probably gone after Mr Leary to Australia. Having followed him from Dublin to Liverpool, was proof that she was foolish enough to follow him to the Antipodes; and the money she had received for the lease of her house, would enable her to go there.

Had I been certain that she had sailed to Australia, I should have gone after her; but I could scarce believe that she had been guilty of an act of folly; which even the absence of common sense would neither excuse nor explain. Because she had once acted foolishly, was not positive proof that she still continued the victim of her unfortunate infatuation.

The mere conjecture that my mother had emigrated to Australia, would not have been a sufficient reason for my going so far in search of her—so far away from Lenore. Still it was certain I must go somewhere. I had a fortune to make; and, in my belief, Liverpool was the last place where an *honest* man would have stood any chance in making it.

My clothing had become threadbare, and my hat and boots were worn to such a dilapidated condition, that I became every day more ashamed to pay my visits to Lenore. I at length resolved upon discontinuing them.

I arose one morning, with the determination of making a move of some kind during the day: for the life that I had been leading for the past six weeks could be endured no longer.

I made an excursion to the docks, where I soon succeeded in finding a berth; and shipped for the "run" in a large vessel—a "liner"—bound to New York. This business being settled, I proceeded to the house of Mrs Hyland—to bid her and her daughter "good-bye."

They showed every evidence of regret at my departure; and yet they did not urge me very strenuously to remain: for they knew something of my disposition.

I had a long conversation with Lenore alone.

"Miss Hyland," said I, "I am going in search of a fortune—a fortune that must be obtained by hard toil; but that toil shall be sweetened by hope—the hope of seeing *you* again. We are both young; and the knowledge of that gives me encouragement to hope. I shall not now speak to you of love; but I shall do so on my return. I believe that we are friends; but I wish to make myself worthy of something more than your friendship."

I fancied that Lenore understood me. I cannot describe the exquisite pleasure that thrilled me, as I noted the expression of her features while she stood listening. It did not forbid me to hope.

"I will not try to detain you, Rowland," she answered, "but if you are unsuccessful abroad, do not remain long away. Return to us; and you will find those who can sympathise with your disappointments. I shall pray that no harm may befall you; and that we may soon meet again."

I could perceive her bosom trembling with some strong emotion, as she uttered these parting words.

As I took her hand to bid the final "good bye," we were both unable to speak; and we parted in silence.

The memory of that parting cheered me through many a dark and stormy hour of my after life.

Volume One—Chapter Sixteen.

Atlantic Liners.

Perhaps the most worthless characters, who follow the sea as a profession, are to be found among the crews of Atlantic liners—especially those trafficking between Liverpool and New York.

These men seldom make voyages to any other ports, than the two above mentioned; and their custom is to "ship for the run" in one vessel, and return in another. They do not affect long voyages; and prefer that between Liverpool and New York to any other.

There are several reasons for this preference on their part.

One is the facility with which—on an Atlantic liner—they can rob each other, and steal from the passengers.

Another is, that being, even for seamen, a profligate, dissipated set, these short voyages give them more frequent opportunities of being in port—where they can indulge in the vices and habits so congenial to their vulgar tastes.

A third reason is, the great number of emigrant-passengers carried between those ports, along with the loose observance of the Passenger Act—the rules of which are less strictly enforced upon Atlantic liners, than aboard ships going on longer voyages.

It may be inferred from this, that the ruffians comprising the crews of the Atlantic liners, have a better opportunity of plundering the passengers than in any other ships.

When embarking on one of these vessels to recommence my duties as a seaman, I was not encumbered with much luggage; and I was not very long in her forecastle, before discovering that this was rather an advantage than a misfortune!

I had spent so much of my money, that I should have been absolutely unable to buy an outfit for any other "trip" than that between Liverpool and New York.

The less a sailor takes aboard with him on such a voyage, the less will he lose before it is terminated.

One of the crew of the ship in which I sailed, was a young seaman, who had never made the voyage from Liverpool to New York; and therefore lacked experience of the evil doings incidental to such a trip. He had been foolish enough to bring on board a large "kit" of good clothing. The first night out of port, when this young man was keeping his watch on deck, one of his comrades below took notice of his chest.

"It's locked," said the man, stretching out his hand to try the lid.

"Blast him!" cried another, "I suppose he thinks we are all thieves here!"

"Sarve him right if he were to lose every-things that's in it," significantly remarked a third.

"So say I," chimed in a fourth speaker, drawing nearer to the kit, in order to be at hand in case of a scramble—which the moment after was commenced.

The chest was turned over, all hands taking share in the act; and without further ado, its bottom was knocked in. Most of the sailor's effects were pulled out, and scattered about—each of the ruffians appropriating to himself some article which he fancied.

Amongst other things, was a new pair of heavy horseskin boots, which were obtained by a fellow, who chanced to stand in need of them; and who pulled them on upon the spot.

The next day, the young sailor having missed his property, of course created a disturbance about it. For this, he was only laughed at by the rest of the crew.

He complained to the officers.

"Had your clothes stole, have you?" carelessly inquired the first mate. "Well, that's what you might have expected. Some of the boys are queer fellows, I dare say. You should have taken better care of your togs—if you cared anything about them."

The next day, the young sailor saw one of the men with the stolen boots upon his feet, and at once accused the wearer of the theft. But the only satisfaction he obtained, was that of getting kicked with his own boots!

We had on board between three and four hundred passengers—most of them Irish and German emigrants.

Several deaths occurred amongst these poor people. Whenever one of them died, the fact would be reported to the officers; and then the first mate would order the sailmaker to enclose the body in a sack—for the purpose of its being thrown overboard. This command to the sailmaker was generally given as follows:

"Sails! there's a dead 'un below. Go down, and sack 'im."

As these words were heard by the passengers—alas! too often repeated—the sailmaker was known during the remainder of the voyage by the name of Mr Sackem; and this unfortunate functionary became an object of mysterious dread to many of the passengers—especially the women and children.

Women generally have a great horror of seeing the dead body of any of their relatives thrown into the sea; and Mr Sackem incurred the ill-will of many of the female emigrants, who were simple enough to think that he was someway or other to blame for the bodies being disposed of in this off-hand, and apparently unfeeling fashion!

A young child—one of a large family of Irish people—had died one night; and the next morning the sailmaker went into the steerage where the body lay—to prepare it for interment in the usual way.

The first attempt made by Mr Sackem, towards the performance of his duty, brought upon him an assault from the relatives of the deceased child, backed by several others who had been similarly bereaved!

Poor Sails was fortunate in getting back upon deck with his life; and he came up from the hatchway below with his clothing torn to rags! He had lost the greater part of a thick head of hair, while his countenance looked like a map of North America, with the lakes and rivers indicated in red ink.

It was not until the captain had gone down—and given the passengers a fine specimen of the language and manners of the skipper of an Atlantic liner in a rage—that the body was allowed to be brought up, and consigned to its last resting place in the sea.

I landed in New York, with the determination of trying to do something on shore, for I was by this time convinced, that a fortune was not to be made by following the occupation of a common sailor.

I did not remain long in New York. Too many emigrants from Europe were constantly arriving there; and continuing that same struggle for existence, which had forced them into exile.

I had every reason to believe, that a young man like myself was not likely to command his full value, where there were so many competitors; and I determined to go on to visit the West.

Is it true, a life on the sea might have been preferable to the hardships, that were likely to be encountered beyond the borders of civilisation; but Lenore was not to be won by my remaining a common sailor, nor would such a profession be likely to afford me either time or opportunity for prosecuting the search after my lost relations. I knew not whether I was acting prudently or not; but I directed my course westward; and did not bring to, until I had reached Saint Louis, in the State of Missouri. There I stopped for a time to look about me.

On acquaintance with it I did not discover much in this western city to admire. A person of sanguine hopes, and anxious to accomplish great things in a very little time, is, perhaps, not in a fit frame of mind to form correct conclusions; and this may account for my being discontented with Saint Louis.

I could not obtain a situation in a city where there was but little to be done, and no great wages for doing it. I was told that I might find employment in the country—at splitting rails, cutting wood, and other such laborious work; but in truth, I was not in the vein to submit myself to this kind of toil. I was disappointed at finding, that in the great West I should have much more work to do than I had previously imagined.

It chanced that at this time there was a grand commotion in Saint Louis. Gold had been discovered in California—lying in great quantities in "placers," or gold washings; and hundreds were departing—or preparing to depart—for the land where fortunes were to be made in a single day.

This was precisely the sort of place I was looking for; but to reach it required a sum of money, which I had not got. I had only the poor satisfaction of knowing that there were many others in a similar situation—thousands of them, who wished to go to California, but were prevented by the same unfortunate circumstances that obstructed me.

Many were going overland—across the prairies and mountains; but even this manner of reaching the golden land required more cash than I could command. A horse, and an outfit were necessary, as well as provisions for the journey, which had to be taken along, or purchased by the way.

I regretted that I had not shipped in New York, and worked my passage to California round the Horn. It was too late now. To get back to any seaport on the Atlantic, would have required fifteen or twenty dollars; and I had only five left, of all that I had earned upon the liner. I spent these five dollars, before I had succeeded in discovering any plan by which I might reach California. I felt convinced that my only chance of finding my relatives, and making myself worthy of Lenore, lay in my getting across, to the Pacific side of America.

While thus cogitating, I was further tantalised by reading in a newspaper some later accounts from the diggings. These imparted the information that each of the diggers was making a fortune in a week, and spending it in a day. One week in California, was worth ten years in any other part of the world. Any one could get an ounce of gold per diem—merely for helping the giver to spend the money he had made!

Should I—the Rolling Stone—stay where I could find employment at nothing better than splitting rails, while Earth contained a country like California?

There was but one answer to the interrogation: No.

I resolved to reach this land of gold, or perish in the attempt.

Volume One—Chapter Seventeen.

On Horseback Once More.

The same newspaper that had imparted the pleasing intelligence, supplied me with information of another kind—which also produced a cheering effect upon my spirits.

The emigrants proceeding overland to California, required protection from the Indians—many hostile tribes of whom lived along the route. Military stations, or "forts" as they were called, had to be established at different points upon the great prairie wilderness; and, just then, the United States' Government was enlisting men to be forwarded to these stations.

Most of the men enrolled for this service, were for its cavalry arm; and after my last quarter of a dollar had been spent, I became one of their number. My former experience in a dragoon saddle—of which I could give the proofs—made it no very difficult matter for me to get mounted once more.

Enlisting in the army, was rather a strange proceeding for a man who was anxious to make a fortune in the shortest possible time; but I saw that something must be done, to enable me to live; and I could neither hold a plough, nor wield an axe.

At first, I was not altogether satisfied with what I had done, for I knew that my mother was not to be found in the wilds of America; and that, after remaining five years in the ranks of the American army, I would be as far as ever from Lenore.

There was one thought, however, that did much to reconcile me to my new situation; and that was, that our line of march would be *towards California*!

Three weeks after joining the cavalry corps, we started for a station lying beyond Fort Leavenworth.

Our march was not an uninteresting one: for most of my comrades were young men of a cheerful disposition; and around our camp-fires at night, the statesman, philosopher, or divine, who could not have found either amusement or instruction, would have been a wonderful man.

Our company was composed of men of several nations. All, or nearly all, of them were intelligent; and all unfortunate: as, of course, every man must be, who enters the ranks as a common soldier.

Man is the creature of circumstances, over which he has no control. The circumstances that had brought together the regiment to which I belonged, would probably make a volume much more instructive and interesting than any "lady novel," and this, judging from the taste displayed by the majority of readers of the present day, is saying more than could be easily proved.

Many European officers would have thought there was but slight discipline in the corps to which I was attached; but in this opinion, they would be greatly in error.

The efficiency of our discipline consisted in the absence of that pretty order, which some French and English martinets would have striven to establish; and which would have been ill-suited for a march over the sterile plains, and through the dense forests encountered in the line of our route. This absence of strict discipline did not prevent us from doing a good day's march; and yet enabled us to have plenty of game to cook over our camp-fires by night.

We had no duty to trouble ourselves with, but what the common sense of each taught him to be necessary to our safety and welfare; and we were more like a hunting party seeking amusement, than like soldiers on a toilsome march.

For all this, we were proceeding towards our destination, with as much speed as could reasonably be required.

We had one man in the company, known by the name of "Runaway Dick"—a name given to him after he had one evening, by the camp-fire, entertained us with a narration of some of the experiences of his life.

He had run away from home, and gone to sea. He had run away from every ship in which he had sailed. He had started in business several times, and had run away each time in debt. He had married two wives, and had run away from both; and, before joining our corps, he had run away from the landlord of a tavern—leaving Boniface an empty trunk as payment for a large bill.

"Runaway Dick" was one of the best marksman with a rifle we had in the company; and it was the knowledge of this, that on one occasion caused me perhaps the greatest fright I ever experienced.

I had risen at an early hour one morning, which being very cold, I had lighted a fire. I was squatted, and shivering over the half kindled faggots, with a buffalo robe wrapped around my shoulders, when I saw "Runaway Dick" steal out from his sleeping place under a waggon. On seeing me, he turned suddenly round, and laid hold of his rifle.

I had just time to throw off the hairy covering, and spring to my feet, as the rifle was brought to his shoulder. Three seconds more, and I should have had a bullet through my body!

"Darn it! I thought you was a bar," said Dick coolly, putting down his rifle, as I fancied, with a show of some chagrin at having been undeceived, and "choused" out of his shot.

I afterwards heard that he was only trying to frighten me. If so, the experiment proved entirely successful.

After reaching the post we were to occupy, I was not so well satisfied with my situation, as when on the march.

The discipline became more strict, and we had a good deal of fatigue-work to do—in building huts, stables, and fortifications.

Besides this unsoldierly duty by day, we had at night to take our turn as sentinels around the station.

Emigrants on the way to California passed us daily. How I envied them their freedom of action, and the bright hopes that were luring them on!

One morning, "Runaway Dick" was not to be found. He had run away once more. It was not difficult to divine whither—to California.

In this, his latest flight, he appeared to give some proof that he had still a little honesty left: for he did not take along with him either his horse, or his rifle.

I overheard some of the officers speaking of him after he was gone, one of them pronounced him "a damned fool" for not taking the horse—so necessary to him upon the long journey he would have to perform, before reaching his destination.

On hearing this remark, I registered a resolve, that, when my turn came to desert, they should not have occasion to apply the epithet to me, at all events, not for the same reason that Runaway Dick had deserved it.

Whether Dick's example had any influence on me, I do not now remember. I only know that I soon after determined to desert, and take my horse with me.

I had served the Government of the United States once before; and did not think myself any too well rewarded for my services. I might probably have believed that "Uncle Sam" was indebted to me; and that by dismissing myself from his employ, and taking with me some of his property, it would be only squaring accounts with him; but I did not then take the trouble to trifle with my conscience—as I do not now—to justify my conduct by any such excuse. To carry off the horse would be stealing; but I required the animal for the journey; and I did not like to leave my officers under the impression that I was a "damned fool."

"Every one who robs a government is not called a thief," thought I, "and why should I win that appellation when only trying to win Lenore?"

I could not afford to squander the best part of my life in a wilderness—standing sentry all the night, and working on fortifications all the day.

It was absurd for any one to have enlisted an intelligent-looking young fellow like myself, for any such occupation. Was I not expected to take French leave on the first favourable opportunity? And would I not be thought a "fool" for not doing so?

These considerations did not influence me much, I admit, for the true cause of my desertion, was the knowledge that neither my relatives nor Lenore would ever be encountered in the middle of the great American prairie, and that to find either I must "move on."

One night I was dispatched on patrol duty, to a place some two miles distant from the fort. The sky was dark at the time; but I knew the moon would be shining brightly in an hour.

A better opportunity would perhaps never occur again; and I resolved to take advantage of it and desert.

By going through the wilderness alone, I knew that I should have many dangers and hardships to encounter; but the curiosity, of learning how these were to be overcome, only added to my desire for entering upon them.

My patrol duty led me along the trail of the emigrants proceeding westward; and even in the darkness, I was able to follow it without difficulty, riding most of the way at a trot. When the moon rose, I increased my pace to a gallop, and scarce halted until daybreak, when, perceiving a small stream that ran through the bottom of a narrow valley, I rode toward it. There dismounting, I gave my horse to the grass—which was growing so luxuriantly as to reach up to his knees.

The horse was more fortunate than I: for the long night's ride had given me an appetite, which I had no means of satisfying. I was hungry and happy—happy, because I was free; and hungry for the same reason! A paradox, though a truth.

There were birds warbling among the trees by the side of the stream. I could have shot some of them with my rifle, or revolver, and cooked them over a fire—for I had the means of making one. But I was not hungry enough to risk the report of a shot being heard; and after tethering my horse, to make secure against *his deserting me*, I lay down upon the long grass and fell fast asleep.

I dreamt no end of dreams, though they might all have been reduced to one; and that was: that the world was my inheritance, and I was on my way to take possession of it.

When I awoke, the sun was in the centre of the sky. My horse had satisfied his hunger; and, following the example of his master, had laid down to sleep.

I did not hesitate to disturb his repose; and, having saddled and remounted him, I once more took to the emigrant trail, and continued on towards fortune and Lenore!

Volume One—Chapter Eighteen.

Old Johnson.

I travelled along the trail all that afternoon and evening, until, just as twilight was darkening into night, I came in sight of some camp-fires. On seeing them, I paused to consider what was best to be done.

To halt at the camp—if, as I supposed, it was a party of emigrants—might lead to my being taken, in case of being pursued from the fort, for my dress, the U.S. brand on the horse, and the military saddle, all proved them the property of "Uncle Sam."

This determined me to avoid showing myself—until I should have put a greater distance between myself and the fort.

I dismounted on the spot where I had halted, tethered my horse, and tried to take some rest. I soon found that I could not sleep: hunger would not admit of it.

Within sight of me were the camp-fires, surrounded by people, who would probably have relieved my wants; and yet I feared to go near them.

Conscience, or common sense, told me, that emigrants in a wilderness might not look very favourably upon one, employed to protect them, deserting from his duty, and taking property along with him—of which every citizen of the United States believes himself to be the owner of a share. They might not actually repel me. In all probability they would give me something to eat; but they might also give information concerning me—should I be pursued—that would enable my pursuers to make a prisoner of me.

Before daybreak I awoke, having enjoyed a brief slumber; and, silently mounting my horse, I rode beyond the emigrants' camp—deviating widely from the trail to get around them.

I soon recovered the track; and pursued it as fast as my steed was willing to carry me. When, looking out for a place where water could be obtained—with the intention of stopping awhile and killing some bird or animal for food—I came in sight of another party of emigrants, who were just taking their departure from the spot where they had encamped for the night.

I had put one train of these travellers between me and the fort; and now fancied myself tolerably safe from pursuit. Riding boldly up to the waggons, I told the first man I encountered, and in very plain terms that I must have something to eat.

"Now, I like that way of talking," said he. "Had you asked for something in the humble manner many would have done, perhaps you would not have got it. People don't like to carry victuals five hundred miles, to give away for nothing; but when you say you *must* have something to eat, then, of course, I can do nothing but give it to you. Sally!" he continued, calling out to a young woman who stood by one of the waggons, "get this stranger something to eat."

Looking around me, I saw a number of people—men, women, and children of every age. There appeared to be three families forming the "caravan" no doubt emigrating together, for the purpose of mutual protection and assistance. There were five or six young men—who appeared to be the sons of the elder ones—and a like number of young women, who were evidently the daughters of three others of middle age, while a large flock of miscellaneous children, a small flock of sheep, a smaller number of cattle, several horses, and half-a-dozen half-famished dogs completed the live-stock of the train.

"I guess you're a deserter?" said the man, to whom I had first addressed myself, after he had finished his survey of myself and horse.

"No," I answered. "I'm on my route to Fort Wool. I have lost my way, and gone without eating for two days."

"Now, I like that way of talking," responded the emigrant, who appeared to be the head man of the party. "When a man tells me a story, I like it to be a good one, and well told—whether I believe it, or not."

"What reason have you to disbelieve me?" I asked, pretending to be offended at having my word doubted.

"Because I think, from your looks, that you are not a damned fool," answered the man, "and no other but a fool would think of staying in a military fort, in this part of the world, any longer than he had a chance to get away from it."

I immediately formed the opinion, that the person speaking to me was the most sensible man I had ever met—myself not excepted: for it was not necessary for him to have seen Lenore, to know that I had done well in deserting.

After my hunger had been appeased, I moved on with the emigrant train, which I found to consist of three Missouri farmers and their families, on their way to the "Land of Promise." The man with whom I had conversed, was named Johnson, or "old Johnson," as some of his juniors called him. He was a sharp, brisk sort of an old fellow; and I could perceive, at a glance there was no chance of his being humbugged by any made-up story. I, therefore, changed my tactics; and frankly acknowledged myself to be a deserter from the United States' troops, occupying the last fort he had passed. It was scarce necessary to add, that my destination was California. I finished by proposing: that he would have my services in whatever capacity he might require them, in consideration of furnishing me with food upon the journey.

"Now, I like that way of talking," said old Johnson, when I had concluded, "we just chance to need your help, and that of your horse, too; and we'll try to do the best we can for you. You must expect to see some hard times, before we get through—plenty of work and no great feeding—but do your share of the work, and you shall fare like the rest of us."

I could ask nothing fairer than this; and the next day, found me dressed in a suit of "linsey wolsey," working my passage to California, by taking my share with the others, in clearing the track of obstructions, driving the cattle, and such other duties as fall to the lot of the overland emigrant.

The journey proved long, fatiguing, and irksome—much more so than I had expected; and many times a day did I swear, that, if I ever worked a passage to California again, it should be by water. I was impatient to get on; and chafed at the slow pace at which we crawled forward. Horses and cattle would stray, or make a stampede; and then much time would be lost in recovering them.

Sometimes we would reach a stream, where a bridge had to be built or repaired; and two or three days would be spent at the work. The draught horses and oxen would die, or, becoming unable to proceed farther, would have to be left behind. The strength of our teams was being constantly weakened—until they were unable to draw the heavily loaded waggons; and it became necessary to abandon a portion of their contents—which were thrown away upon the prairies. The first articles thus abandoned, were carpets and other useless things, not required on the journey, but which to please the women, or at their instigation, had been put into the waggons at starting, and dragged for six or seven hundred miles!

The dogs, that, at the commencement of the journey, had for each mile of the road, travelled about three times that distance, having worn the skin from the soles of their feet, now crawled along after the waggons without taking one unnecessary step. They seemed at length to have reached the comprehension: that the journey was to be a protracted one; and that while undertaking it, the idle amusement of chasing birds was not true canine wisdom.

I shall not startle my leaders with a recital of any remarkable adventures we had with the hostile Indians: for the simple reason that we had none. They gave us much trouble for all that: since our fear of encountering them, kept us constantly on the alert—one of our party, and some times more, standing sentry over the camp throughout the whole of every night.

If my readers reason aright, they will give me credit for not drawing on my imagination for any part of this narrative. They may easily perceive that, by thus eschewing the subject of an encounter with Indians, I lose an excellent opportunity for embellishing my true tale with an introduction of fiction.

As we approached the termination of our journey, the teams became weaker—until it took all of them united in one yoke to draw a single waggon, containing only the youngest of the children, and a few pounds of necessary provisions!

The old ladies, along with their daughters, performed the last hundred miles of the journey on foot; and when we at length reached the first settlement—on the other side of the mountains—a band of more wretched looking individuals could scarce have been seen elsewhere. My own appearance was no exception to that of my companions. My hat was a dirty rag wrapped around my head like a turbann while my boots were nothing more than pieces of buffalo hide, tied around my feet with strings. For all this, I was as well dressed as any of the party.

My agreement with old Johnson was now fulfilled; and I was at liberty to leave him. I was anxious to be off to the diggings, where his eldest son, James, a young man about twenty years old, proposed accompanying me. Old Johnson declined going to the diggings himself—his object in coming to California being to "locate" a farm, while the country was still "young."

He furnished us with money to buy clothing and tools, as well as to keep us in food for awhile—until we should get fairly under weigh in the profession we were about to adopt.

I promised to repay my share of this money to his son—as soon as I should earn its equivalent out of the auriferous earth of California.

"Now, I like that way of talking," said old Johnson, "for I'm a poor man; and as I have just come here to make a fortune, I can't afford to lose a cent."

I parted with Mr Johnson and his party of emigrants with some regret, for they all had been more kind to me than I had any reason to expect.

I have never found the people of this world quite so bad as they are often represented; and it is my opinion, that any man who endeavours to deserve true friendship, will always succeed in obtaining it.

I have never met a man whose habit was to rail against mankind in general, and his own acquaintances in particular, whose friendship was worth cultivating. Such a man has either proved unworthy of friendship, and has never obtained it; or he has obtained, and therefore possesses that, for which he is ungrateful.

Volume One—Chapter Nineteen.

A "Prospecting Expedition."

On parting with the Californian colonists, young Johnson and I proceeded direct to the diggings on the Yuba, where, after looking about for a day or so, we joined partnership with two others, and set to work on a "claim" close by the banks of the river.

We had arrived at an opportune season—the summer of 1849—when every miner was doing well. There was a good deal of generosity among the miners at this time; and those who could not discover a good claim by their own exertions, would have one pointed out with directions how to work it!

Our party toiled four weeks at the claim we had chosen, and was very successful in obtaining gold. Never did my hopes of the future appear so bright. Never did Lenore seem so near.

No gold washing could be done on the Yuba during the winter—the water in the river being then too high—and, as we had not much longer to work, it was proposed by three men, who held the claim adjoining ours, that we should join them in prospecting for some new diggings—where we might be able to continue at work all the winter, unembarrassed by too much water and too many miners.

One of our neighbours who made this proposal, had visited a place about forty miles farther up the country—where he believed we might find a "placer" such as we required. He had been upon a hunting expedition to the place spoken of; and while there did not look for gold—having no mining tools along with him; but from the general appearance of the country, and the nature of the soil, he was convinced we might find in it some rich dry diggings, that would be suitable for working in the winter.

It was proposed that one of us should accompany the man on a prospecting expedition, that we should take plenty of provisions with us, and search until we should discover such diggings as we desired.

To this proposal, both parties agreed; and I was the one chosen, by Johnson and my other two companions, to represent them in the expedition—the expenses of which were to be equally shared by all.

Before starting, I left with young James Johnson my share of the gold we had already obtained—which amounted to about sixty ounces.

The hunter and I started—taking with us three mules. Each of us rode one—having our roll of blankets lashed to the croup of the saddle. A sixty pound bag of flour, some other articles of food, a tent, and the necessary "prospecting" tools formed "the cargo" of the third mule, which, in the language of California, was what is called a "pack-mule."

My fellow prospector was only known to me by the name of Hiram. I soon discovered that he was not an agreeable companion—at least, on such an expedition as that we had undertaken. He was not sociable; but, on the contrary, would remain for hours without speaking a word; and then, when called upon to say something, he would do so in a voice, the tones of which were anything but musical.

The animal I bestrode had been christened "Monte," that of Hiram was called "Poker," and the mule carrying "the cargo" was "Uker." With such a nomenclature for our beasts, we might easily have been mistaken for a pair of card-sharpers.

Our progress over the hills was not very rapid. We were unable to go in a direct line; and were continually wandering around steep ridges, or forced out of our way by tributaries of the main river—which last we were frequently compelled to ascend for miles before we could find a crossing place.

Although fortunate in having good mules, I do not think that our travel averaged more than fifteen miles a day, in a direct line from where we started, though the actual distance travelled would be over thirty!

Late in the evening of our third day out, our pack-mule, in fording a stream, got entangled among the branches of a fallen tree; and, while trying to extricate the animal out of its dilemma, Hiram was pulled into the water, and jammed against a limb—so as to suffer a serious injury.

That night we encamped by the stream—near the place where the accident had happened; and, about midnight, when I was changing my mule—Monte—to a fresh feeding place, the animal became suddenly alarmed at something, and broke away from me—pulling the lazo through my hands, till not only was the skin peeled clean off my fingers, but one or two of them were cut clean to the bone. I reproached myself for not sooner having had the sense to let go; but, as usual, the reproach came after the damage had been done.

The mule, on getting free, started over the ridge as though she had been fired from a cannon—while Poker and Uker, taking the hint from their companion, broke their tethers at the same instant, and followed at a like rate of speed.

I returned to Hiram, and communicated the unpleasant intelligence: that the mules had stampeded.

"That's a very foolish remark," said he, "for you know I'm not deaf."

This answer did not fall very graciously on my ear; but having made up my mind, to remain in good humour with my companion as long as possible, I pretended not to notice it. I simply said in reply, that I thought there must either be a grizzly bear, or Indians, near us—to have stampeded the mules.

"Of course thar is," said Hiram, in a tone more harsh than I had ever before heard him use.

I fancied that he was foolish enough to blame me for the loss of the mules; and was a little vexed with him, for the way in which he had answered me.

I said nothing more; but, stepping aside I bandaged up my fingers, and tried to obtain a little sleep. At sunrise I got up; and, having first dressed my wounded fingers, I kindled a fire, and made some coffee.

"Come, Hiram!" said I, in an encouraging tone, "turn out, mate! We may have a hard day's work in looking for the mules; but no doubt we'll find them all right."

"Find them yourself," he answered. "I shan't look for them."

I had much difficulty in controlling my temper, and restraining myself from giving Hiram an uncourteous reply.

To avoid subjecting myself to any more of his ill-natured speeches, I returned to the fire, and ate my breakfast alone.

While engaged in this operation, I pondered in my own mind what was best to be done. It ended by my coming to the determination to go in search of my mule Monte; and, having found her, to return to my partners on the Yuba. I felt certain, that should I attempt farther to prosecute the expedition along with Hiram, and he continue to make the disagreeable observations of which he had already given me a sample, there would certainly be a row between us. In some parts of the world, where people think themselves highly enlightened, two men getting angry with one another, and using strong language, is not an unusual occurrence; and very seldom results in anything, more than both proving themselves snarling curs. But it is not so in California, where men become seriously in earnest—often over trifling affairs; and had a row taken place between my comrade and myself, I knew that only one story would have been told concerning it.

I finished my breakfast; and, leaving Hiram in his blankets, I started off over the ridge to find Monte. I searched for the mules about six hours; and having been unsuccessful in my search, I returned to the camp without them.

Hiram was still wrapped up in his blanket, just as I had left him; and then the truth suddenly flashed into my dark mind, like lightning over a starless sky.

Hiram was ill, and I had neglected him!

The bruise on his side, received against the fallen tree, was more serious than I had supposed; and this had misled me. He had made no complaint.

The moment I became aware of my mistake, I hastened to his side.

"Hiram," said I, "you are ill? Forgive me, if you can. I fear that my thoughtlessness, and passionate temper, have caused you much suffering."

He made no reply to my conciliatory speech. He was in a very high fever; and asked faintly for water.

I took the tin vessel, in which I had made the coffee; and having filled it at the stream, gave him a pint cup full.

He drank the water eagerly; and then found voice to talk to me. He said that he was glad that I had returned, for he wished to tell me where he had buried some gold, and where his wife and child were living, and could be written to.

He spoke with great difficulty; and soon called for more water.

I again filled the cup nearly full, and handed it to him. After drinking every drop that was in it, he requested me to give him the coffee-can; but, thinking that he had drunk enough water, I declined acceding to his request; and tried to persuade him, that too much water would do him a serious injury. He only answered me by clamouring for more water.

"Wait but a little while," said I. "In a few minutes you shall have some more."

"Give it me now! Give it me now! Will you not give me some now?"

Knowing that the quantity he had already drunk, could not fail to be injurious to him, I refused to let him have any more.

"Give me some water!" he exclaimed, with more energy of voice and manner, than I had ever known him to exhibit.

I replied by a negative shake of the head.

"Inhuman wretch!" he angrily cried out. "Do you refuse? Refuse to give a dying man a drop of water!"

I once more endeavoured to convince him, that there would be danger in his drinking any more water—that there was yet a chance for him to live; but, while talking to him, I perceived a change suddenly stealing over his features. He partly raised himself into a sitting position; and then commenced cursing me, in the most horrible language I had ever heard from the lips of a dying man!

After continuing at this for several minutes he sank back upon the grass, and lay silent and motionless.

Allowing a short interval to elapse, I approached the prostrate form, and gently laid my hand upon his forehead. I shall never forget the sensation that thrilled through me, as I touched his skin. It was already cold and clammy—convincing me that my prospecting companion had ceased to live!

I passed the whole of the following day in trying to recover the mules. Had I succeeded, I would have taken the body to some camp of diggers, and buried it in a Christian manner.

As this was not possible, with my lame hands, I scooped out a shallow grave; and buried the body as I best could.

Having completed my melancholy task, I started afoot to rejoin my partners on the Yuba—where I arrived—after several days spent in toilsome wandering—footsore and dispirited.

The adventure had taught me two lessons. Never to refuse any one a drink of water when I could give it; and to be ever after careful in interpreting the language of others—lest some wrong might be fancied, where none was intended.

Volume One—Chapter Twenty.

Richard Guinane.

On my return to the Yuba, with the sad tale of my comrade's death—and the consequent unfortunate termination of our prospecting scheme—Hiram's partners made search for his gold, in every place where it was likely to have been buried.

Their search proved fruitless. The precious treasure could not be found. Unfortunately, none of us knew where his family resided. He had been incidentally heard to say, that he came from the state of Delaware; but this was not sufficient clue, to enable any of us to communicate with his relatives.

His wife has probably watched long for his return; and may yet believe him guilty of that faithlessness—too common to men who have left their homes on a similar errand.

As our claim on the Yuba was well nigh exhausted, we dissolved partnership—each intending to proceed somewhere else on his own account. Young Johnson—who had been my companion across the plains—never before having been so long away from his parents, determined upon going home to them, and there remaining all the winter.

I had heard good accounts of the southern "placers," which, being of the sort known as "dry diggings," were best worked during the rainy season. Three or four men, from the same "bar" where we had been engaged, were about starting for the Mocolumne; and, after bidding James Johnson and my other mates a friendly farewell, I set out along with this party.

After reaching our destination, I joined partnership with two of my travelling companions; and, during the greater part of the winter, we worked upon Red Gulch—all three of us doing well.

Having exhausted our claim, my two partners left me both to return home to New York. Being thus left once more alone, I determined upon proceeding still farther south—to the Tuolumne river, there to try my fortune during the summer.

On my way to the Tuolumne, I fell in with a man named Richard Guinane, who had just come up from San Francisco City. He was also *en route* for the diggings at Tuolumne; and we arranged to travel together.

He was going to try his luck in gold seeking for the second time; and, finding him an agreeable companion, I proposed that we should become partners. My proposal was accepted—on the condition that we should stop awhile on the Stanislaus—a river of whose auriferous deposits my new partner had formed a very high opinion.

To this I made no objection; and, on reaching the Stanislaus, we pitched our tents upon its northern bank.

When I became a little acquainted with the past history of my companion, I might reasonably have been expected to object to the partnership. From his own account, he was born to ill-luck: and, such being the case, I could scarce hope that fortune would favour me—so long as I was in his company. Assuredly was Richard Guinane the victim of unfortunate circumstances. There are many such in the world, though few whom Fortune will not sometimes favour with her smiles—when they are deserved; and, ofttimes, when they are not.

Richard Guinane, according to his own account of himself, was one of these few. Circumstances seemed to have been always against him. Each benevolent, or praiseworthy action he might perform, appeared to the world as dictated by some base and selfish feeling! Whenever he attempted to confer a favour, the effort resulted in an injury, to those whom he meant to benefit. Whenever he tried to win a friend, it ended by his making an enemy!

His hopes of happiness had ever proved delusive—his anticipations of misery were always realised!

Pride, honour, in short, every noble feeling that man should possess, appeared to be his; and yet fate so controlled those sentiments, that each manifestation of them seemed, to the world, the reverse of the true motive that inspired it. Such was Guinane's character—partly drawn from statements furnished by himself, and partly from facts that came under my own observation.

Certain circumstances of his life, which he made known to me, had produced an impression on my memory; but more especially those of which I was myself a spectator, and which brought his unhappy existence to an abrupt and tragical termination. The history of his life is too strange to be left unrecorded.

Richard Guinane was a native of New York State, where his father died before he was quite five years of age—leaving a wife and three children, of whom Dick was the eldest.

So early had Dick's ill-fortune made its appearance, that before he had reached his fourteenth year, he had established the reputation of being the greatest thief and liar in his native village!

When once this character became attached to him, no church window could be broken, nor any other mischief occur, that was not attributed to Dick Guinane, although, according to his own account, he was really the best behaved boy in the place!

Near the residence of his mother, lived the widow of a merchant, who had left a small fortune to his only child, a daughter—the widow having the sole charge both of the fortune and the heiress—already a half grown girl.

With a charming voice, this young lady would answer to the name of Amanda Milne. She had seen Dick every day, since her earliest childhood; and she had formed a better opinion of him than of any other lad in the village. She was the only one in the place, except his own mother, who felt any regard for Dick Guinane. All his other neighbours looked upon him, as a living evidence of God's amazing mercy!

Like most young ladies, Amanda was learning some accomplishments—to enable her to kill time in a genteel, and useless manner.

The first great work achieved by her fingers, and to her own entire satisfaction, was a silk purse—which it had not taken her quite two months to knit. This purse, on a favourable opportunity having offered itself, was presented to Dick.

Not long after, her mother wished to exhibit her needle-work to some friends—as a proof of the skill and industry of her daughter, who was requested to produce the purse.

Amanda knew that Dick was not liked by the inhabitants of the village; and that her own mother had an especially bad opinion of him. Moreover, the Guinane family was not so wealthy as the widow Milne; and in the opinion of many, there was no equality whatever between the young people representing each.

Though Amanda was well aware of all this, had she been alone with her mother, in all likelihood she would have told the truth; but, in the presence of strangers, she acted as most other girls would have done under similar circumstances. She said she had lost the purse; and had searched for it everywhere without finding it. About that time, Dick was seen in possession of a purse; and would give no account, of how he came by it. The two facts that Amanda Milne had lost a purse, and that Dick Guinane had one in his possession, soon became the subject of a comparison; and the acquaintances of both arrived at the conclusion: that Amanda, as she had stated, must have lost her purse, and that Dick must have stolen it!

Time passed on—each month producing some additional evidence to condemn poor Dick in the estimation of his acquaintances.

Mrs Guinane was a member of the Methodist Church, over which presided the Reverend Joseph Grievous. This gentleman was in the habit of holding frequent conversations with Mrs Guinane, on the growing sinfulness of her son. Notwithstanding her great reverence for her spiritual instructor, she could not perceive Dick's terrible faults. Withal, the complaints made to her—of his killing cats, dogs, and geese, stealing fruit, and breaking windows—were so frequent, and apparently so true, that she used to take Dick to task, and in a kindly way read long maternal lectures to him.

Dick always avowed his innocence—even in the presence of Mr Grievous—and would use the best of arguments to prove himself as "not guilty." This pretence of innocence, in the opinion of the Reverend Grievous, was a wickedness exceeding all his other misdeeds; and the sanctimonious gentleman suggested the remedy, of having Dick beaten into confession and repentance! To this course of treatment, however, Mrs Guinane firmly refused to give her consent.

One day, Dick had been to a neighbouring town; and when returning, had passed a house—to the gate of which the old and well known horse of the Reverend Grievous stood tied. Simply noticing the horse, and reflecting that his reverend owner must be inside the house, Dick continued on.

When near his mother's house, he was overtaken by the horse, that had come trotting along the road after him. The horse was without a rider, which proved that not being properly secured, he had got loose.

Dick caught the horse, mounted him, and commenced riding back—for the purpose of delivering him to the minister, for he could not permit, that so pious a person should have to walk home through the mud.

The road was bad—like most of the country roads in the United States—and Dick was already fatigued with a long walk. To take the horse to the house where his owner was visiting, would give him more than a mile to walk back; but no personal consideration could deter the lad from doing what he thought to be his duty.

On coming out of the house—where he had been visiting one of the members of his church—Mr Grievous was surprised not to find his horse; but the mystery was fully explained when, after proceeding a short distance, he saw Dick Guinane on the horse's back.

Here was evidence welcome to Mr Grievous. Dick was at one of his old games—caught in the very act—riding another man's horse—and that horse the property of his own minister!

The Reverend Joseph was rejoiced, as he had long been looking for an opportunity like this. He attributed all Dick's misdeeds to the want of proper chastisement; and here was a good reason for administering it to him. Dick had no father to correct his faults; and, in the opinion of Mr Grievous, his mother was too lenient with the lad.

He had long promised, that if ever he caught Dick in any misdemeanour, he would himself administer a lesson that would not only benefit the boy, but the community in which he dwelt. He would be only fulfilling a duty, which his sacred office imposed upon him; and the present opportunity was too good a one to be lost.

Dick rode up to the minister, dismounted, and accosted him in a manner that should have been proof of innocence. Perhaps it would have been, by any other person; but to the Reverend Grievous, Dick's confident deportment—inspired by the consciousness of having acted rightly—only aggravated the offence of which he was supposed to be guilty. His bold effrontery was but the bearing of a person long accustomed to crime. So reasoned Mr Grievous!

Without giving Dick time to finish his explanation, the minister seized him by the collar; and, with his riding whip, commenced administering to him a vigorous chastisement.

Dick was at the time over sixteen years of age; and was, moreover, a strong, active youth for his years.

So great was his respect, for all persons, whom he thought superior to himself, that for some time he bore the chastisement—unresistingly permitting the minister to proceed in the execution of his fancied duty.

36

Human nature could not stand such treatment long; and Dick's temper at length giving way, he picked up a stone, hurled it at the head of the reverend horsewhipper—who, on receiving the blow, fell heavily to the earth.

He rose again; and in all probability would have returned to a more vigorous use of his horsewhip, had his victim been still within reach; but Dick had secured himself against farther punishment, by taking to his heels, and placing a wide distance between himself and his irate pastor.

Next day, Dick was brought before a magistrate, the Reverend Grievous, upon oath, being compelled to make a somewhat true statement of the affair. The justice had no other course than to discharge the prisoner, which he did with reluctance—expressing regret that the strict letter of the law did not allow him to deal with the offence in the manner it so justly merited!

His native village no longer afforded a peaceful home for Dick Guinane.

He was pointed at in the streets. Other boys of his age were forbidden by their parents to play with him; and the little school girls crossed the road in terror, as they saw him approach. In the opinion of the villagers, he had reached the climax of earthly iniquity.

He was sent to reside with an uncle—his mother's brother—who lived in the city of New York. Before leaving his native place, he attempted to make a call on Amanda Milne; but was met at the door by her mother, who refused either to admit him within the house, or allow her daughter to see him.

Shortly after reaching his new home in the great city, he received a letter from his mother—enclosing a note from Amanda, the contents of which partly repaid him for all the injuries he had suffered.

During a residence of five years in New York, he was unsuccessful in everything he undertook; and, unfortunately, though from no fault of his own, lost the confidence of his uncle, as also his protection.

He returned to his native village, where he found that he was still remembered with disfavour.

He talked of love to Amanda Milne; but his suit was rejected. She admitted being much prepossessed in his favour, and that he had no rival in her affections; but what woman can brave the ridicule of all her acquaintances, and the anger of an only parent, by accepting a lover universally shunned and condemned?

Dick once more bade adieu to his native village; and after various vicissitudes in different cities of the United States, at length found his way to California. He had been one of the most fortunate miners on the Feather river; and had invested the money made there in a dry goods store in San Francisco.

Just one week after entering upon his new business, the city of San Francisco was burnt to the ground; and Dick's dry goods store, including the contents, along with it.

With only one hundred dollars in his purse, he again started for the diggings; and it was while journeying thither that he and I came together, and entered into partnership as above related.

Volume One—Chapter Twenty One.

After breaking ground upon the Stanislaus, we toiled for three weeks without any success. Every one around us seemed to be doing well; but the several mining claims worked by Guinane and myself seemed to be the only places in the valley of the Stanislaus where no gold existed. Not a grain rewarded our labours.

"For your sake we had better part company," said Guinane to me one evening, after we had toiled hard all day, and obtained nothing. "You will never have any luck, so long as you are my partner."

I was inclined to think there was some truth in what my comrade said; but I did not like the idea of leaving a man, merely because he had been unfortunate.

"Your fate cannot long contend with mine," I answered. "I am one of the most fortunate fellows in the world. If we continue to act in partnership, my good fortune will, in time, overcome the ill-luck that attends upon you. Let us keep together awhile longer."

"Very well," assented Guinane, "but I warn you that some one above—or below, may be—has a 'down' on me; and the good genius attending you will need to be very powerful to make things square. However, you lead the way, and I will follow."

I did lead the way; and we went to Sonora, further south, where we entered upon a claim at a place called Dry Creek. Here we met with success, of which we could not reasonably complain.

We often used to walk into Sonora in the evening; and amuse ourselves, by witnessing the scenes occurring in the gambling houses, or having a dance with the bright-eyed Mexican señoritas.

One evening, while loitering about in one of the gambling houses, we saw a digger who was intoxicated, almost to the degree of drunkenness. He was moving about in half circles over the floor, keeping his feet under him with much difficulty, unknown to himself. Every now and then, he loudly declared his intention of going home, as if he thought such a proceeding on his part, was one in which all around him must be highly interested. Each time, before going, he would insist upon having another drink; and this continued, until he had swallowed several glasses of brandy, on the top of those that had already produced his intoxication. In paying for these drinks, he pulled out a bag of gold dust, which carried, judging from its size, about one hundred ounces; and a man behind the bar, weighed from it the few specks required in payment for the liquor.

There was something in the appearance of this miner that strangely interested me. I fancied that I had seen him before; but could not tell where. While I was endeavouring to identify him, he staggered out of the house into the street—leaving me in doubt, as to whether we had met before or not.

The thoughts of my companion Guinane, were not absorbed by wanderings like mine; and he had been more observant of what was transpiring around him. After the miner had gone out, he came close up to me, and whispered:—

"That man will be robbed. When he pulled out his bag of gold to pay for the drink, I saw two men exchange glances, and walk out before him. They will waylay, and rob him. Shall we let them do it?"

"Certainly not," I answered, "I like the look of the man; and do not think that he deserves to lose his money."

"Come on then!" said Guinane; and we both stepped out into the street.

The first direction in which we turned was the wrong one: for, after proceeding about a hundred yards, nothing of the drunken man was to be seen; and we knew that he was too drunk to have got any farther away.

We turned back; and walked at a quick pace—indeed, ran—in the opposite direction. This time our pursuit was more successful. We saw the drunken miner lying on the pavement, with two men standing over him, who pretended, as we came up, that they were his friends; and that they were endeavouring to get him home.

Had the drunken man been willing to accept of their assistance, we might have found no excuse for interfering; but as we drew near, we could hear him exclaiming, "Avast there, mates! I can navigate for myself. Be off, or, dammee! I'll teach you manners."

"Stormy Jack!" I exclaimed, rushing forward, followed by Guinane. "'Tis you Stormy? What's wrong? Do you want any help?"

"Yes," replied Jack, "teach these fellows some manners for me. My legs are too drunk; and I can't do so myself."

The two men moved silently, but rapidly away.

"Have you got your gold?" I asked, ready for pursuit in case the fellows had robbed him.

"Yes, that's all right. One of them tried to take it; but I wouldn't let him. I'm sober enough for that. It's only my legs that be drunk. My hands are all right."

Stormy's legs were indeed drunk, so much so, that Guinane and I had much difficulty in getting him along. We were obliged to place him between us, each supporting one of his sides. After considerable labour, we succeeded in taking him to a house where I was acquainted. Here we put him to bed; and, after leaving instructions with the landlord, not to let him depart until one of us should return, we went home to our own lodgings.

Next morning, at an early hour, I called to see Stormy; and found him awake and waiting for me.

"You done me a good turn last night," said he, "and I shall not forget it, as I have you."

"Why do you think you have forgotten me?" I asked.

"Because last night you called me Stormy Jack; and from that, I know you must have seen me before. I've not been hailed by that name for several years. Now, don't tell me who you are: for I want to find out for myself."

"You could not have been very drunk last night," said I, "or you would not remember what you were called?"

"Yes, would I," answered Stormy, "according as the land lay, or what sort of drunk it was. Sometimes my mind gets drunk, and sometimes my legs. It's not often they both get drunk together. Last night it was the legs. Had you been a man six or seven years ago, when I was called Stormy Jack, I should remember you: for I've got a good memory of things that don't change much. But when I used to be called Stormy Jack, you must have been a bit o' a tiny boy. Now, who can you be? What a stupid memory I've got!" continued he, scratching his head. "There's no way of teaching it manners, as I knows of. But what boy used to call me Stormy Jack—that looked as you ought to have looked a few years ago? Ah! now I have it. Bless my eyes, if you arn't the Rollin' Stone!"

Stormy then rushed forward, grasped my hand, and nearly crushed it between his strong, sinewy fingers.

"Rowley, my boy!" said he, "I knew we should meet again. I've thought of you, as I would of my own son, if I'd had one. I've looked the world over, trying to find you. How come you to hail me by name last night? You are an astonishing chap. I knew you would be; and some one has larnt you manners. Ah! I suppose 'twas Nature as did it?"

I need not say, that Stormy and I, after this singular renewal of companionship, were not likely to part in a hurry. We passed that day together, talking over old times—Stormy giving me a history of some events of his life, which had transpired since our parting in New Orleans.

"On the morning I last saw you," said he, "I went to work on the ship, as I intended; and did a hard day's work—for which I've never yet been paid.

"When I was going home to you, I met an old shipmate; and, in course, we went into a grog-shop to have something to drink.

"After having a glass with my friend at his expense, of course, it was but right for him to have one at mine. We then parted company; and I made tracks for the lodging-house, where I had left you.

"Them two glasses of brandy, after working hard all the afternoon in the hot sun, did more for me, than ever the same quantity had done before. I was drunk somewhere, though I was not exactly certain where.

"Just before reaching the house where we were staying, I met the first breezer, who, you remember, had knocked me down with the carpenter's mallet. Well! without more ado, I went to work to teach him manners.

"While giving him the lesson, I larnt that it was my head that was drunk: for my legs and arms did their duty. I beat and kicked him in a way, that would have rejoiced the heart of any honest man. Just as I was polishing him off, two constables came up, and collared me away to gaol.

"The next morning, I was sentenced to one month's imprisonment. Captain Brannon did not like that: for he wanted me back aboard of his ship. But the magistrate, mayor, or whatever he was, that sentenced me, had too much respect for me to allow the captain to have his own way; and I was lodged and fed, free of all expense, until the 'Hope' had sailed.

"After coming out of the gaol, I went straight to the boarding-house, in hopes of finding you still there; but I larnt that you had gone away, the next day after I was jugged; and the old woman could not give any account of where you had drifted to. I thought that you had joined the 'Hope' again, and gone home. I've been everywhere over the world since then; and I don't know how I could have missed seeing you before now!

"I came to San Francisco Bay in an English ship—the captain of which tried to hinder the crew from deserting, by anchoring some distance from the city, and keeping an armed watch over them. He thought we were such fools as to leave San Francisco in his ship for two pounds a month, when, by taking another vessel, we could get twenty! He soon found his mistake. We larnt him manners, by tying and gagging him, as well as his first officer, and steward. Then we all went ashore in the ships' boats—leaving the ship where I suppose she is now—to rot in the bay of San Francisco.

"After coming up to the diggings, I had no luck for a long time; but I'm now working one of the richest claims as ever was opened."

During the day, I told Stormy the particulars of my visit to Dublin; and the trouble I was in concerning the loss of my relatives.

"Never mind 'em!" said he, "make a fortune here—and then make a family of your own. I've been told that that's the best way to forget old friends, though, for myself, I never tried it."

Stormy's advice seemed wisdom: as it led me to think of Lenore. Before parting with my old messmate, I learnt from him where he was living. We arranged to see each other often; and as soon as we should have an opportunity of dissolving the respective partnerships in which each was engaged, we should unite and work together.

Stormy was the first friend who took me by the hand—after I had been turned out upon the cold world; and time had not changed the warm attachment I had long ago conceived for the brave sailor.

Volume One—Chapter Twenty Two.

On leaving San Francisco, Guinane had declared his intention of going to the Stanislaus river; and his acquaintances, left behind in that city, had been directed to write to him at the latter place.

One Saturday morning, he borrowed a mule from one of the neighbouring miners, to ride over to the post-office for his letters.

The miner owning the mule, was just going to his work; and pointed out the animal to Guinane. It was grazing on the hill-side, about half a mile distant from our tents. In addition to pointing it out, the owner described it to be a brown mule, with rat tail, and hog mane.

He then brought the saddle and bridle out of his tent; and, placing them at Dick's disposal, went off to his work.

Dick proceeded towards the hill, caught and saddled the mule, and, bidding me good-day, rode off on his journey.

I was expecting him back that evening; but he did not return. I felt no concern on account of his remaining absent all that night. The next day was Sunday; and knowing that he would not be wanted to do any work on the claim, he might, for some purpose that did not concern me, have chosen to stay all night in the town.

Sunday evening came, without Guinane; and, fearing that some accident might have befallen him, I resolved to start next morning for the post-office, should he not return before that time.

The next morning came, without bringing back the absentee; and I set out in search of him.

After going about five miles, I met him returning; and, to my surprise, saw that he was afoot! I was still more surprised as he drew near, and I obtained a close view of his face and features. Never in my life had I seen such a change in the person of any individual, in so short a time. He seemed at least ten years older, than when he left me at the diggings two days before.

His face was pale and haggard; and there was a wild fiendish expression in his eyes, that was fearful to behold. I could not have believed the eyes of Richard Guinane capable of such an expression. His clothing was torn to rags, bedaubed with dirt, and spotted with dry blood. In short, his whole appearance was that of a man who had been badly abused.

"What has happened?" I asked, mechanically—as soon as my surprise at his appearance permitted me to speak.

"I can't tell now," said he, speaking with much difficulty. "I must have water."

I turned back; and we walked on towards our tents, in which direction we had not far to go, before arriving at a coffee-shop. There he drank some water, with a glass of brandy; and then, ordering a breakfast, he went out to have a wash in the river—an operation of which I had never seen a human being in greater need.

He ate his breakfast in haste—scarce speaking a word until he had finished. Then, starting suddenly from his seat, he hurried out of the house; and moved on along the road towards the place where our tents were pitched.

"Come on!" cried he. "I cannot stop to talk. I've work to do. I want revenge. Look here!"

He stopped till I came up—when, lifting the long dark hair from the sides of his head, he permitted me to see that he had *no ears*!

"Will you aid me in obtaining revenge?" he asked.

"Yes," I answered, "with my body and soul!"

"I knew you would!" he exclaimed. "Come on! we have no time to lose."

As we walked homeward, I learnt from him the particulars of the terrible misfortune that had befallen him.

On the Saturday morning, after starting off for the town, he had got about a mile beyond the place where I had met him, when he was overtaken by a party of four Mexicans.

Before he was well aware that they had any intention to molest him, a lazo was thrown over his shoulders; and he was dragged to the ground—where his arms were instantly pinioned.

39

By signs, he was made to understand: that his captors claimed the mule, upon which he had been riding.

Guinane could speak but few words of Spanish; and therefore could not make the Mexicans understand, how the mule came into his possession.

After holding a consultation amongst themselves, they took his revolver from him; and, whilst three of them held him, the fourth cut off both of his ears! They then mounted their horses, and rode away—taking with them the mule Guinane had borrowed from the miner.

After going about three hundred yards, they halted, took off the saddle and bridle—which they did not claim to own—threw them on the ground, as also Guinane's revolver; and then continued their course.

Nothing can be said to justify these men for what they had done; but probably they could have alleged some excuse for their conduct.

They undoubtedly believed that Guinane had stolen the mule; and they knew that if one of their own countrymen had been caught in a similar act, he would have been fortunate to have escaped with his life. They saw no reason why an American should not be punished for a misdeed—as well as a Mexican.

Guinane pursued them at the top of his speed, insane with grief, and burning with indignation.

They soon rode out of his sight; but he continued on after them—until he fell exhausted to the earth. He must have lain for some hours in a state of insensibility, partly caused by loss of blood—partly by the fatigue that had followed the wild raging of his passions.

It was night when he recovered his senses; and in his endeavours to reach home, he had wandered among the hills, in every direction but the right one.

I have said that he recovered his senses. The expression is hardly correct. He only awoke to a consciousness that he still existed—a horrible consciousness of the inhuman treatment he had been submitted to. His most sane thought was that of a burning thirst for vengeance; but so intense had been this desire, that it defeated its own object, rendering him unconscious of everything else, and to such a degree, that he had only discovered the right road to our camp a few minutes before I had met with him.

"The truth is," said he, as he finished telling me his story, "I returned to the place where I lost my ears, with the insane hope that I might meet the Mexicans. After having a look at the place, I recovered my senses once more, enough to direct me towards the only object for which I now care to live and that is, revenge. I'm not in so much haste for it now, as I was an hour ago. There's plenty of time. I'm young, and will find them sometime. Come on! Come on! How slow you walk!"

We were then going at a pace that might be called running.

On reaching our tents, we learnt that Guinane had actually taken *the wrong mule*! The miner from whom he had borrowed it, had not thought it necessary to describe its brands. Not supposing there was another mule in the neighbourhood, in any way resembling his own, he had not imagined there could be any mistake.

From some diggers, we learnt that the Mexicans we wished to find, had encamped for the night—near the place where Guinane had caught the mule; and it was not strange they had accused him of having stolen it. On recovering the animal, in the manner described, they had returned to their camp, and shortly afterwards had resumed their journey. By making some inquiries, we found that they had gone southward.

As they had no mining tools along with them, we came to the conclusion, that they were on their way home—into some of the northern provinces of Mexico. If so, we might easily overtake them, before they could pass out of California.

We lost no time in making preparations for the pursuit—the most important part of which was the providing ourselves with good horses. In due time, this difficulty was got over, although my bag of gold dust was much lighter, after the purchase of the horses had been completed.

By daybreak of the next morning, we were ready for the road. Guinane kept urging me to expedition—in pursuit of those who had awakened within his soul a thirst for vengeance, that blood alone could assuage!

Volume One—Chapter Twenty Three.

A Curious Case of Self-Murder.

The pursuit conducted us southward; and, at almost every place where we made inquiry, we heard of four mounted Mexicans—who could be no other than the men we were desirous of overtaking.

For the first two days, we were told, in answer to our inquiries, that they were about forty-eight hours in advance of us.

On the third morning, we again got word of them at a rancho, where they had stopped to bait their horses. The owner of the rancho gave a description of a mule which they were leading along with them—a brown mule, with rat tail and hog mane. It could be no other than the one, which had cost Dick so dearly.

After feeding their animals, the Mexicans had made no further halt; but had taken the road again—as if pressed for time. So fancied the ranchero.

They must have been under some apprehension of being pursued—else they would not have travelled in such hot haste. It was about forty hours—the man said—since they had taken their departure from the rancho. We were gaining upon them; but so slowly, that Guinane was all the while chafing with impatience.

He seldom spoke. When he did, it was to urge me to greater speed. I had much trouble in holding him sufficiently in check to prevent our horses from being killed with over riding.

From information obtained at the rancho, we could now tell that the Mexicans were making for the sea coast, instead of directing their march towards the interior. If they intended going overland to the city of Mexico, they were taking a very indirect road towards their destination.

At each place where we got word of them—on the fourth day of our pursuit—we learnt that the distance between us was rapidly lessening.

Near the evening of this day, we stopped at another rancho, to refresh our horses—now nearly done up. The Mexicans had stopped at the same place, six hours before. On leaving it, they had taken the road to San Luis Obispo. We should arrive there about noon on the following day.

"To-morrow," said Guinane, as he lay down to snatch a short repose, while our horses were feeding, "to-morrow I shall have revenge or death! My prayer is, *God let me live until to-morrow*!"

Again we were in the saddle—urging our horses along the road to San Luis Obispo.

We reached that place at the hour of noon. Another disappointment for my companion!

San Louis is a seaport. A small vessel had departed that morning for Mazatlan, and the Mexicans were aboard of her!

On arriving at the port, they had hastily disposed of their animals; and taken passage on the vessel—which chanced to be on the eve of sailing. We were just one hour too late!

To think of following them further would have been worse than madness—which is folly. By the time we could reach Mazatlan, they might be hundreds of miles off—in the interior of Mexico.

Never have I witnessed such despondency, as was exhibited by Guinane at that moment.

So long as there had appeared a chance of overtaking the men, who had injured him, he had been sustained by the hope of revenge; but on our relinquishing the pursuit, the recollection of the many misfortunes that had darkened his life, added to this new chagrin, came palpably before his mind, suggesting thoughts of suicide!

"'Twas folly to pursue them at all," said he. "I should have known that the chance of overtaking them would have been a stroke of fortune too good to be mine. Fate has never yet been so kind to me, as to grant a favour I so much desired; and I was a fool to expect it. Shall I die?"

I used every means in my power to direct his thoughts to some other subject; but he seemed not to heed, either what I said or did.

Suddenly arousing himself from a long reverie, he emphatically exclaimed:

"No! I will war with fate, till God calls me hence! All the curses of fortune shall not make me surrender. All the powers of Hell shall not subdue me. I will live, and conquer them all!"

His spirit, after a terrible struggle, had triumphed; and now rose in opposition to fate itself.

We rode back to the Stanislaus. It was a dreary journey; and I was glad when it was over. There had been an excitement in the chase, but none in returning from it. Even the horses seemed to participate in the cloudy change that had come over our thoughts.

After arriving at the Stanislaus, I went to see Stormy Jack. I found him hard at work, and doing well in his claim—which was likely to afford him employment for several weeks longer. I was pleased to hear of his success; and strongly urged him to abstain from drink.

"I don't intend to drink any more," said he, "leastwise, as long as I'm on the diggings; and sartinly not when I have any gold about me. That last spree, when I came so near losin' it, has larnt me manners."

Guinane accompanied me on this visit to Stormy; and on our return, we passed through the town. My partner had left his name at the office of "Reynold's Express," for the purpose of having his letters forwarded from the General Post-office in San Francisco. As we passed the Express Office, he called in, to see if any had arrived for him.

A letter was handed to him—for which he paid in postage and express charges, one dollar and fifty cents!

After getting the letter, we stepped into a tavern, where he commenced reading it.

While thus occupied, I noticed that he seemed strangely agitated.

"We are friends," said he, turning short towards me. "I have told you some of my troubles of the past. Read this letter, and make yourself acquainted with some more. It is from Amanda Milne."

He held the letter before my eyes, and I read:—

"I know your upright and manly spirit will see no impropriety in my writing to you. I have done you injustice; and in doing so, have wronged myself, as much as you. I have just learnt that your character has been injured by a fault of mine—by my not having acknowledged giving you the purse. Forgive me, Richard! for I *love* you, and *have loved* you, ever since I was a child."—Guinane crumpled the letter between his fingers, and I was able to read no more. I saw him suddenly raise his hands towards the place where once were his ears—at the same time that I heard him muttering the words, "Too late! too late!" Another movement followed this—quick and suspicious. I looked to ascertain its meaning. A revolver was in his hand—its muzzle touching his temples!

I rushed forward; but to use his own last words, I was "too late."

There were three distinct sounds; a snap, the report of a pistol, and the concussion of a body falling upon the floor.

I stooped to raise him up. It was too late. He was dead!

Can the reader comprehend the thought that dictated this act of self-destruction? If not, I must leave him in ignorance.

In preparing the remains of my comrade for the grave, a silk purse, containing a piece of paper, was found concealed beneath his clothing. There was writing upon the paper, in a female hand. It was as follows:—

"Dick,

41

"I do not believe the stories people tell of you; and think you are too good to do anything wrong I am sorry you have gone away. Good bye.

"Amanda."

It was, no doubt, the note he had received from Amanda, after his first parting with her—enclosed in the letter of his mother, sent after him to New York. It was replaced in the purse, and both were buried along with his body.

Poor Amanda! She may never learn his sad fate—unless chance may direct her to the reading of this narrative.

Volume One—Chapter Twenty Four.

An Impatient Man.

I have not much fault to find with this world—although the people in it do some strange things, and often act in a manner that puzzles me to comprehend. The man of whom Guinane had borrowed the mule, was himself an original character. After my comrade's death, I became slightly acquainted with this individual; and was much amused, though also a little pained, at what I thought to be his eccentric behaviour.

Original types of mankind are, perhaps, more frequently met with on gold fields than elsewhere. Men without a certain spirit and character of their own, are less likely to adopt a life of so many perils and hardships, as gold diggers must needs encounter.

But there are also men who can *appear* eccentric—even amongst gold diggers; and the individual to whom I have alluded was one of these. His name was Foster.

The mail from the Atlantic States was due in San Francisco every fortnight; and, of course, at about the same interval of time, in the different diggings to which the letters were forwarded—the Stanislaus among the rest. Three days, before its arrival, at the last mentioned place, Foster used to leave his work, and go to the post-office—which stood at a considerable distance from his claim—for letters. He would return to his tent, as a matter of course, disappointed; but this did not prevent him from going again to the post-office, about six hours after.

"Has the mail arrived yet?" he would inquire of the post-master.

"No. I told you a few hours ago, that I did not expect it in less than three days."

"Yes, I know; but the mail is uncertain. It is possible for it to arrive two or three days earlier than usual; and I want my letters as soon as they get in."

"No doubt," the post-master would say, "no doubt you do; and I advise you to call again in about three days."

"Thank you; I will do so," Foster would answer; and six hours after he would call again!

"As soon as the mail arrives," the post-master would then tell him, "I will *send* your letters to you. It will be less trouble for me to do that, than to be so often unnecessarily annoyed."

"No, no!" Foster would earnestly exclaim, "pray don't trust them into the hands of any one. They might be lost. It is no trouble for me to call."

"I can easily believe that," the post-master would rejoin. "If it was any trouble, you would not come so often. I must, therefore, adopt some plan to save me from this annoyance. As soon as the mail arrives I will put up a notice outside the window here, and that will save you the trouble of coming in, and me of being bothered with your questions. Whenever you come in front of the house, and do not see that notice, you may be sure that the mail has not arrived. You understand?"

"Yes, thank you; but I don't wish to give any unnecessary trouble. I dare say the mail will be here by the time I come again. Good-day!"

Six hours after, Foster would be at the post-office again!

"Any news of the mail?" he would ask.

"Are you working a good claim?" inquired the post-master once—in answer to this perpetual dunning.

"Yes," replied Foster. "Tolerably good."

"I am sorry to hear it."

"Why?"

"Because if you were not doing well, you might be willing to go into some other business—the post-office for instance—and buy me out. If you were here yourself, you would have your letters as soon as they arrived. Since getting *them* seems to be your principal business, you should be on the spot to attend to it. Such an arrangement would relieve me, from a world of annoyance. You worry me, more than all the rest of the several hundred people who come here for letters. I can't stand it much longer. You will drive me mad. I shall commit suicide. I don't wish to be uncivil in a public capacity; but I can't help expressing a wish that you would go to Hell, and never let me see your face again."

Foster's chagrin, at not getting his letters, would be so great, that the post-master's peculiar wish would pass unheeded; and the letter-seeker would only go away to return again, a few hours after.

Usually about the tenth time he called, the mail would be in; and in the general scramble of the delivery, Foster would get *two letters*—never more, and never less.

One evening, near mail time, he was, as usual on a visit to the post-office after his letters; and his mate—whose name was Farrell—having got weary of sitting alone in his tent, came over to mine—to pass an hour or two in miner's gossip. He told me, that Foster had been for his letters seven times during the two days that had passed!

"He will have to go about three times more," said Farrell, "and then he will probably get them. The mail should be in this evening."

"Forster appears to think very much of his family?" I remarked to his partner. "I never saw a person so impatient for news from home."

"He is certainly very anxious to hear from home," said Farrell, "but not exactly for the reasons you may be supposing. Foster and I are from the same neighbourhood, and have known each other for many years. We came to California together; and I am well acquainted with all the circumstances under which he is acting. Now, if you hailed from anywhere near that part of the world to which we belong, I should say nothing about him; but as you don't, and it's not likely you'll ever drift in that direction, there can be no more harm in my telling you what I know, than there would be in talking about some one of whom we have read, and who has been dead a thousand years ago."

"Foster married when he was very young—his wife being a woman about ten years older than himself. She was worse than old—she was plain; and besides had but very little sense. Add to this, that she was always ill; and ill-tempered, and you have a woman, whom you will admit could not be very agreeable for a wife.

"He had not been married over a week, before he discovered that he had been making a fool of himself.

"You have noticed his anxiety about the letters. Well—I shall explain it. By every mail, he expects news of the death of his wife; and it is his impatience to hear *that* which makes him so uneasy about the arrival of the post. If he should get a letter to-night containing the news of her death, he would be the happiest man in California; and I dare say would start for home, within an hour after receiving it."

I expressed some surprise, that one man should intrust another with such a disgraceful secret; and plainly proclaimed my disapprobation of Foster's conduct.

"You are wrong, my friend," rejoined his partner. "For my part, I admire his frank and manly spirit. What is the use of one's pretending that he wishes his wife to live, if he really desires her to die? I hate a hypocrite, or a person who will, in any way, deceive another. I don't suppose that Foster can help disliking his wife—any more than he can keep from sleeping. The feeling may be resisted for a while; but it will conquer in the end. Foster is a man, in whom I cannot be deceived; and I respect him for the plain straightforward manner, in which he avows his sentiments."

"This indecent impatience to hear of the death of his wife," said I, "cannot wholly arise from hatred. There is probably some other woman with whom he is anxious to be united?"

"That is very, very likely," answered Farrell, "and the second letter he always receives along with the one from his wife may serve as an affirmative answer to your conjecture. Well! he is one of the most open-hearted honourable fellows I ever met; and I don't care how soon his hopes are realised. Because a man has been foolish a little in his youth, is no reason why he should always be punished for it."

Our conversation was interrupted by the arrival of Foster himself—who appeared in a high state of pleasant excitement.

"Come on, Farrell!" cried he, "let us go to the tent, and settle up. It is all over with the old lady; and I start for home by daybreak to-morrow morning."

Farrell bade me good-night and Foster, who did not expect to see me again, shook hands at parting—bidding me a final goodbye.

There was much in the expression of Foster's countenance that I did not admire; and, notwithstanding, the apparent openness of his speech, I could not help thinking him a fellow not only without good feeling, but hypocritical, and treacherous.

Farrell purchased his mule, and also his share of the mining tools; and by break of day the next morning, Foster was on his way to San Francisco.

The post-master of Sonora was annoyed by him no more; and Farrell was left to regret the loss of his plain-speaking partner.

Volume One—Chapter Twenty Five.

A Bull and Bear Fight.

One Sunday afternoon, seeking for amusement, I walked into Sonora; and, following a crowd, I reached the "Plaza de Toros."

The proprietor of this place had gone to a great expense, to get up a grand entertainment for that day.

A large grizzly bear had been caught alive in the mountains—about twenty miles from the town—and, at great trouble and expense, had been transported in a strong cage to Sonora—to afford amusement to the citizens of that lively little city.

To bring the bear from his native wilds, had required the labour of a large party of men; and several days had been spent in the transport. A road had to be made most part the way—of sufficient width to permit the passage of the waggon that carried the cage. Bridges had also to be thrown over streams and deep ravines; and the bear was not securely landed in Sonora, until after he had cost the proprietor of the Bull-ring about eleven hundred dollars.

Several savage bulls had also been provided for the day's sport; and the inhabitants of the town, and its vicinity, were promised one of the most splendid, as well as exciting, entertainments ever got up in California.

I had before that time witnessed two or three Spanish bull fights; and had formed a resolution never to see another. But the temptation in this case—being a bull and bear fight—was too strong to be resisted: and I paid two dollars—like many others as foolish as myself—for a ticket; and, armed with this, entered the amphitheatre.

The *Plaza de Toros* was a circular enclosure with benches—on which about two thousand people could be comfortably seated; but, before the performance had commenced, the place contained three thousand or more. The first performance was an ordinary Spanish bull fight; and excited but little interest. The bull was soon killed, and dragged out of the arena.

After a short interval, a second bull made his bow to the spectators. The instant this one showed himself, everybody predicted an exciting scene: for the animal leaped into the arena, with a wild bellowing, and an expression of rage, that portended a very different spectacle, from that exhibited by his predecessor.

The *toreros* appeared surprised—some of them even confounded—by the fierce, sudden and energetic spring with which the bull charged into their midst.

A matador standing alone, in the arena, is in but little danger—even when pursued by the fiercest bull. It is when three or four of the toreros are in the ring together—getting in one another's way while turning to avoid his horns—that the bull has the advantage over his adversaries. At such times, the bull-fighter runs a great risk of getting badly gored, or even killed outright.

The latter misfortune happened to one of the men, on the occasion in question. The second bull that had promised such a savage exhibition of his fierce strength, did not disappoint the spectators. In the third or fourth charge which he made among the matadors, he succeeded in impaling one of their number upon his horns. The body of the unfortunate man was lifted clear up from the ground, and carried twice round the ring—before the bull thus bearing him could be despatched!

Of course, the man was dead; and had been so, long before being taken off the animal's horns. His heart's blood could be seen running in a thick stream down the shaggy forehead of the bull, and dripping from his nose, as he carried the inanimate form around the arena!

The dead bodies of both man and animal were taken out of the place together, and on the same cart, the only interval allowed to elapse between the sports, was the short half hour necessary to making preparation for the grand spectacle of the day—the fight between the bear and a bull!

The cage containing the grizzly was drawn into the ring by a span of horses—which were at once taken away; and then a small, and not a very formidable "toro," was led into the arena by several men, who guided him with their long lazos.

The appearance of this bull was disappointing to the spectators, who fancied that a much larger animal should have been chosen to encounter the savage monster of the mountains. The explanation was conjectured by all. The bear was worth over one thousand dollars, while the bull cost only twenty-five; and from this disparity in price, it was evident that the owner of both wished to give grizzly the advantage in the fight. This was made certain, by the proprietor himself coming forward with the unexpected proposal: that before commencing the fight, the bull should have the tips shaved off from his horns! "This," he said, "would hinder the bear from receiving any serious injury; and it could be exhibited in a fight on some other Sunday!"

But the spectators wished to see a good fight on this Sunday, and a fair fight as well. They did not wish to see the poor bull deprived of his natural means of protecting himself; and then torn to pieces by the claws of the favoured bear.

The master of the amphitheatre was about to carry out his economic project—when a scene ensued that beggars all description. It ended in the bull being allowed to retain the tips of his horns.

The action now commenced. The hind leg of the bear was pulled out of the cage door—which was partially opened for the purpose. The leg was made fast, by a strong log chain, to a stake that had been driven deep into the ground near the centre of the arena. The door was then thrown wide open; but, notwithstanding this apparent chance of recovering his liberty, the bear refused to take advantage of it.

A rope was then made fast to the back of the cage, and attached to a horse standing outside the enclosure. By this means, the cage was dragged away from the bear, instead of the bear being abstracted from the cage—leaving the animal uncovered in the centre of the arena. The lazos were next loosed off from the horns of the bull; and the two combatants were left in possession of the ground—at liberty to exercise their savage prowess upon each other.

The bull on regaining his feet, rolled its eyes about, in search of something on which he might take revenge, for the unseemly way in which he had just been treated. The only thing he could conveniently encounter was the bear; and, lowering his muzzle to the ground, he charged straight towards the latter.

Bruin met the attack by clewing himself into a round ball. In this peculiar shape he was tossed about by the bull, without sustaining any great injury. After he had been rolled over two or three times, he suddenly unclewed himself; and, springing upward, seized the bull's head between his fore paws.

So firm was his grip, that the poor bull could neither advance nor retreat—nor even make movement in any direction. It appeared as if it could only stand still, and bellow.

To make the grizzly let go his hold—in order that the fight might proceed with more spirit—a man, in the employ of the proprietor, entered the arena with a bucket of water—which he threw over the bear. The latter instantly relinquished his hold of the bull; and, rapidly extending one of his huge paws, seized hold of the servant who had douched him; and, with a jerk, drew the man under his body.

Having accomplished this feat, he was proceeding to tear the unfortunate man to pieces; and had squatted over him with this intention, when a perfect volley of revolvers—in all about two hundred shots—were fired at his body. The bear was killed instantly, though strange to say, his death was caused by a single bullet, out of all the shots that had hit him; and there were more than a hundred that had been truly aimed! The only wound, that could have proved fatal to such a monster, was a shot that had entered one of his ears, and penetrated to the brain. Many balls were afterwards found flattened against the animal's skull, and his skin was literally peppered; but, though the man, at the time the shots were fired, was clutching the bear's throat with both hands, he was not touched by a single bullet!

There were two circumstances connected with this affair, that, happening in any other land but California, would have been very extraordinary. One was, the simultaneous discharge of so many shots, at the moment when the bear was seen to have the man in his power. It might have been supposed, that the spectators had been anticipating such an event, and were ready with their revolvers: for the bear's seizing the man, seemed a preconcerted signal for them to fire.

Another remarkable circumstance was, that, although the discharge of so many pistols was sudden and unexpected, and proceeded from every point round the circle of the amphitheatre—where thousands of people were crowded together—no one but the bear was injured by the shots!

It was a striking illustration of some peculiarities in the character of the energetic self-relying men of the world, that then peopled California.

In the "Plaza de Toros"—witnesses of the scenes I have attempted to describe—were many young girls belonging to the place, as well as others, from Mexico, Chili, and Peru. During the continuance of that series of exciting scenes—which included the killing of one person by empalement upon a bull, the mutilation of another by the claws of a grizzly bear, and the destruction of the bear itself, by a volley of revolvers—these interesting damsels never allowed the lights of their cigarritos to become extinguished; but calmly smoked on, as tranquil and unconcerned, as if they had been simply assisting at the ceremony of a "fandango!"

Volume One—Chapter Twenty Six.

Stormy's Autobiography.

In my rambles about Sonora and its vicinity, when seeking amusement, on what is called the "first day of the week." I was generally accompanied by Stormy Jack.

During my early acquaintance with the old sailor, I was too young to have formed a correct opinion of his character; and my respect for him, was based entirely upon instinct.

Now that I was older, and possessed of a more mature judgment, that respect—instead of having diminished—had increased to such a degree, as to deserve the name of admiration. I could not help admiring his many good qualities. He loved truth; and spoke it whenever he said anything. He was frank, honest, sociable, and generous. He had an abhorrence of all that was mean—combined with a genuine love for fair play and even-handed justice of every kind. He was in the habit of expressing his opinions so frankly, that, on the slightest acquaintance, every honest man became his friend, and every dishonest one his enemy.

Stormy was, in truth, one of nature's noblemen—such a one as is seldom met with, and never forgotten. He was instinctively a gentleman; and the many long years in which he had been associated, with those who are thought to be lowest in the scale of civilisation, had not overcome his natural inclination.

Stormy was strong on all points but one; and that was, in the resisting his appetite for strong drink. To this he too often yielded.

"Do not think, Rowley," said he one evening, when I chanced to allude to this subject, "that I can't keep from thinking, if I tried. I never drank when I was young: for I had some hope and ambition then; and I could see the silliness of giving way to such a habit. It is only since I have become old Stormy Jack, and too old for my bad habits to be of any consequence to myself, or any one else. No, Rowley, it don't signify much now, how often I get drunk—either in my mind or legs. When I was young, like you, I had no one to teach me manners—except the world; and it did larn me some. Wherever I went, every one appeared to think it was their business to teach me manners; and the way they went about it, was not always very gentle. I've seen hard times in this world, Rowley, my lad."

"I have no doubt of it, Stormy," said I, "for you have that appearance. You look as though, man, fate, and time had all used you roughly."

"And so they have. I've nobody to thank for anything, unless it is the Almighty, for having given me health and strength to out-live what I have passed through; and I'm not sartin that I should be thankful for that. If you like, Rowley, I'll tell you something of my history; and it'll give you an idea of the way the world has used me."

"I should like it much."

"Here goes then! The first thing I can remember, is a father who used to get drunk in the legs; and the second, a mother who would as often get drunk in the head.

"As my father, when intoxicated, could not stand on his feet, nor move from the place in which he chanced to be, my mother would take advantage of his helplessness; and used to teach him manners, in a way that always kept his countenance covered with scratches, cuts, and bruises. I may add, that she served myself in a very similar manner. If ever either my father, or I, were seen in the streets without a fresh wound on our faces, the neighbours knew that there was no money in the house, or anything that would be received at a pawn shop for so much as sixpence. The soundness of our skins would prove the scarcity of cash in my father's establishment; or as they say here in Californy, that we were 'hard up.'

"About the time I was thirteen years of age, my parents discovered that they could no longer maintain themselves, much less me; and they sought, and found, a home in the work-house—whither I was taken along with them.

"Both died in the work-house the year after entering it; and I was apprenticed, or I might say hired out, to a baker.

"In this situation, I had a world of work to do. I had to sit up all night, helping the journeymen to make the bread; and then I had to go out for two or three hours every morning—with a heavy basket of loaves on my head, to be delivered to the customers living here and there. In addition to this hard work, I was nearly starved. The only time I could get enough to eat, was when I was out on my rounds with the bread, when I could steal a little scrap from each loaf—in such a way that the morsel wouldn't be missed.

"I've not yet told you, that my native place is London; and if you know anything of that city, you may have some idea of the life I lived when a child, with two miserable, poor, and drunken parents.

"Well, I staid with the baker above two years; and though I was nearly killed with hard work and want of food—as well as sleep—that, perhaps, wasn't the most unhappy part of my life. There was a worse time in store for me.

"The baker and his wife, who owned and ill-treated me, had a little girl in the house—a slavey they had taken from the same work-house from which they had fetched me. This girl wasn't treated any better than I was; and the only happy moments either of us ever had, were when we could be together, and freely express our opinions of our master and mistress—both of whom behaved equally bad to us—if anything, the woman the worst. The girl and I used to encourage each other with hopes of better times.

"I had seen many little girls in the streets, dressed very fine, and looking clean, well-fed, and happy; and some of them I thought very beautiful. But none of them appeared so beautiful, as the one who was being worked and starved to death in the same house with myself—though her dress was nothing but a lot of dirty rags.

"By the time I had got to be sixteen years of age, I was too much of a man to stand the ill-usage of the baker and his wife any longer; and I determined to run away.

"I did not like to leave behind me my companion in misery; but as I thought, that, in a few weeks I should make a little fortune, and be able to find her a better home, we became reconciled to the idea of parting with one another.

"One morning I bade her good-bye; and started off with the basket of bread on my head to go my rounds.

"When I had nearly completed the delivery, and had left with different customers all but the last loaf, I set down the basket, took this loaf under my arm, and was free.

"I went straight to the docks to look out for something; and, before the day was over, I found a situation aboard a schooner in the coal trade—that was about to sail for Newcastle.

"The skipper of this vessel was also its owner; and himself and his family used it as their regular home.

"I was determined to please this man—not only by doing my duty, but as much more as I could. I succeeded in gaining his good will.

"We went to Newcastle, took in a cargo; and by the time we reached London again, the skipper would not have been willing to part with me, had I desired to leave him. When we got back to London, he gave me liberty to come ashore; and made me a present of half-a-crown, to spend as I liked.

"It was the largest sum of money I had ever owned; and, with it in my possession, I thought that the time when I might take my little fellow servant away from the hard life she was leading, could not be far away. I determined not to spend one penny of the money upon myself; but to go ashore at once, and make a bold push towards getting the girl away from the place where she was staying.

"I told the skipper all about her—what sort of a home I had left her in—and the cruelties she was still likely to be enduring.

"He talked to his wife; and after they had asked me a good many questions: as to whether the girl was well-behaved, and used no bad language—they told me that I might bring her aboard the vessel then lying in the river; and that she might look after the three children, and do anything else to make herself useful.

"I started off on my errand, in better spirits than I had ever been in before. I was afraid to go near the baker's house, for fear I should be seen from the shop and might have trouble in getting away again: for I had been regularly bound as his apprentice. So I watched the public-house—where I knew the girl would be sure to come for the supper beer in the evening.

"After I had been looking out for about half an hour, she came, looking more beautiful, more ragged and dirty, than when I had last seen her, four weeks before.

"'Come on, Ann!' I cried. (Ann was her name.) 'Come on! Fling away your jug, and follow me!'

"I ran up to her, while I was speaking.

"She dropped the jug—not because I had told her to do so—but from the excitement of her surprise at seeing me. It fell out of her hands on the pavement; and was broken to pieces.

"'Follow me,' said I, 'I've another home for you.'

"She gave one glance at the broken jug; and probably thought of her mistress, and the beating she would be sure to get, should she go home without the jug and the supper beer. That thought decided her. She then took my hand; and we started off towards the river.

"I am going to cut my story short," said Stormy, after a pause—during which he seemed to suffer from some painful reflection. "For nine years I worked for that girl. Part of the time I was getting good wages—as the second mate of a large ship, running to Charleston, in the United States; and all of my money was spent in keeping Ann in a good home, and in having her taught to read and write, and behave herself like a lady.

"To deny myself every comfort, for the sake of saving money for her, was my greatest pleasure. I have often crossed the Atlantic without proper clothing; so that Ann might be placed beyond the danger of want, while I was gone.

"During these nine years, I drank no grog, nor liquor of any kind. I would not even take a glass at the expense of any of my messmates, because I would be expected to stand a glass in return; and there was more pleasure in saving the money for Ann, than in spending it on what could only injure me. I have often walked the cold wet decks with my feet freezing for the want of a pair of socks and good boots— because these things would cost money: and all that I could make I wished to spend only for the benefit of Ann, who was always in my thoughts—the idol of my soul.

"While making my voyages across the Atlantic, I got some of my companions to learn me to read and write a little. I worked very hard at this, when I could find time. There were two reasons for my wishing to be able to write: the first, because I had some desire to learn on my own account; and the other reason was, that when I should marry Ann, I did not wish her to have a husband who could not write his own name.

"When I had got to be about twenty-three years of age, I began to think of getting married. I was earning good wages; and had saved enough money to furnish a little house for Ann. Just about that time, however, I noticed she had begun to treat me with a little coldness. I had been so very saving of my money, that I always went rather shabbily dressed; and I at first thought that she might be a little ashamed of my appearance. I knew that this would not be right on her part; but I also knew that women have got vanity; and that they cannot help a feeling of that kind. I could not think that it was possible for Ann not to love me—after the many sacrifices I had made for her—for I deserved her love, and had fairly earned it. I thought that if there was a man worthy of being loved by her, and having her for his wife, I was that man, for I had done all that I was able to gain her good will; and no one can do more. I was under the belief, too, that she loved me: for she had many a time told me so. You may imagine, then, how I was taken aback, when one time that I returned from a voyage to give her all the money I had earned, I found that she treated me very coldly; and that every day she grew colder and colder, and seemed as if she only wanted to get clear of my company."

At this interesting crisis of his story, Stormy was interrupted by the entrance of two of our mining neighbours, who came into our tent to have a quiet game of "uker" along with us.

Volume One—Chapter Twenty Seven.

Ann.

I had been much interested in Stormy's story of his early life; and the next evening, I went over to his tent, and taking a seat upon the ground, requested him to continue it.

"All right, Rowley, my boy," said he, in answer to my appeal. "I believe that I left off last night, where the girl, after my having worked nine years for her, had begun to treat me with coldness.

"Well, on becoming sure of this, I determined to find out the reason. I knew there must be something wrong; and I made up my mind to find out what it was—though it might lead to the breaking up of all my fine prospects. One day, when my ship was about to start on a new trip to Charleston, I settled scores with the captain, and left her. Ann was under the belief, that I had gone off in the vessel; but she was mistaken. I had stopped behind, to keep an eye on herself. A few months before, I had given her some money—to enable her to go into partnership with a widow, in keeping a little stationery and toy shop—and she was now in that business. My scheme was to keep an eye on the shop; and see what was going on. I had not been very long playing spy, before I found out the lay of the land. A young fellow of a swellish appearance, used to pay visits to the shop, nearly every day of the week. He came in the evening; and Ann would go out with him to theatres and dancing places.

"I watched the fellow to his home, or to his lodgings—for he lived in a two-pair back; and from there I tracked him to his place of business. I found that he was what in London is called a 'clerk.' He was a thing unworthy of Ann; but, of course, that being the case, he did not know it; and I could see from his vain looks that he thought sufficiently of himself—too much to marry Ann. From what I saw, I had no doubt that he was deceiving her.

"I scarce knew what to do: for there was no use in telling the girl that she was being deceived. She would not have believed me.

"If she had believed me, and given the puppy up, it would not have made much difference to me. My confidence in her was gone. I could have had it no more. She had acted ungrateful to me—by giving her preference to a conceited swell—who took her about to places of amusement, where men do not take young girls, whom they intend afterwards to marry. Ann had proved herself unworthy of a love like mine. I had toiled for her, and loved her, for nine long years; and this was the return.

"My good resolutions all forsook me—by the shock which her ingratitude gave me; and ever since that time, I've been only Stormy Jack, and nothing more. You know what he is." Stormy once more relapsed into silence, as if his story had been concluded. More deeply interested than ever, I desired to know more. In answer, to my request, he resumed his narrative.

"Well," continued he. "My next voyage was a long one. I made the trip to India, and was gone fourteen months; but on my return, at the end of that time, I had not forgotten Ann. I still loved her—although I knew that she could never be my wife. Even had she consented, my pride would not allow of my marrying her now.

"When I got back from India, I went to the little shop to enquire for her. She was no longer there. I found her in the work-house—the same from which she had been taken when a child. She was the mother of a child, seven months old; and had never been married. I determined to teach her manners. You may think it strange, Rowley, but I was now, more than ever, resolved she should love me. It would be some satisfaction for what I had suffered on her account. I knew my motive wasn't altogether as it ought to have been, but I could not help doing as I did.

"When paid the wages, owing me by the East Indiaman, I had about twenty-five pounds to the good; and, with this money, I took Ann out of the work-house, and placed her in a comfortable home. I acted, to all appearance, as kindly to her, and seemed as affectionate as I had ever been; and I even gave her more of my company than I had ever done before. When she came to contrast my conduct with that of the heartless villain who had ruined and deserted her, she could not help loving me. On her knees, and with tears in her eyes, she confessed her folly, and sorrow for the past; and prayed for me to forgive her.

"'Of course, I forgive you, Ann,' said I, 'or I would not have returned to you.'

"'And will you love me as much as you once did?' she then asked.

"'Certainly I will.'

"'John,' she said, 'you are the most noble-minded man in the world; and I only begin to know your real worth. Oh! what a fool I have been, not to have known it before! You are better than all other men on the earth!'

"Ann had got over the folly of her girlhood. The sorrows which she had suffered during the last few months, had taught her wisdom, and brought repentance; and she now believed, that such love as I had offered her was of some value.

"I visited her every day; and appeared to take such an interest in the welfare, both of herself and her child, that I, at length, became certain that she loved me. She could not have helped it, had she tried. Poor girl! she fancied she was going to be happy again; but she was mistaken.

"When my money was all spent, I prepared to take leave of her. Before going, I told her the truth, that I had loved her, ever since she was a child; and that I ever would; but that I could never make her my wife. After what had transpired, I could never be happy as her husband.

"'I shall never forget you, Ann,' said I. 'Whenever I have a pound in my pocket, you are welcome to fifteen shillings of it; but *my* happiness, for this world, you have entirely destroyed; and I can never marry you, as I once intended to do. You know the many years that I toiled for you; and was that not proof that I loved you dearly? All that I have done, I am willing to do again; but what I had hoped to do, is no longer possible. You have not proved worthy of my love, and can never be my wife.'

"As I said this, she was nearly distracted; and declared that she would never accept another shilling from me. She promised to do for me all that I had done for her: to work for me, and let me live in idleness. I had at last succeeded in winning her love.

"Perhaps I was wrong in having done so; but the manner in which I had been myself wronged, rendered me incapable of acting honest. I could not help taking this way to larn her a little manners. There was another I intended larning a lesson to, before I left London; but I determined to teach him in a very different way. It was the swell that had ruined Ann.

"I looked out for him; and found him in the street, on the way to his place of business. I laid one o' my flippers on his shoulder, to keep him from escaping, while I gave him his lesson with the other. I flattened his nose, nearly tore off one of his ears; and did him some other damage besides. The police pulled me off o' him; and I was taken away to the station, and next day brought before a magistrate.

"I only got two months for giving the conceited snob his lesson, which I didn't much regret, for I was just as well off in the gaol as anywhere else. My time or my liberty was worth nothing more to me. When again set free, I made another voyage to India, and got back in fourteen months.

"When I returned, Ann was dead. She had died in the same work-house, in which she was born.

"Since then, there has been no particular reason why I should behave myself; and I have been, as you see me, old Stormy Jack. I never again thought of getting married. I could only love but one; and that one it was not my fate to be spliced to. I suppose it was never intended I should get married. At all events, I don't mean to try. I made one girl miserable by not marrying her; and I might make another miserable if I did."

With this hypothetical reflection, Stormy concluded his sad story.

End of Volume One.

Volume Two—Chapter One.

A Strange Summons from Stormy.

As already stated, I had left the northern diggings with the design of going to the Tuolumne river; and that on my way to the latter place I had met Guinane—who had induced me to relinquish my design, and stop awhile on the Stanislaus.

Now that Guinane was gone, and the claim in which we had been partners worked out, there was nothing to hinder me from carrying out my original intention; and I resolved, to leave the Stanislaus' diggings, and proceed onward to the Tuolumne.

Stormy Jack, who stayed behind, promised to join me, as soon as he should have worked out his claim on the Stanislaus—which he expected to do in about three weeks.

On reaching the Tuolumne, I proceeded to Jacksonville—a little mining village, where, after looking about a couple of days, I purchased two shares in a claim that lay upon the bank of the river.

Not liking the sort of work required to be done on this claim—which was wet—I employed men to work it for me. I could afford to do this: for, having toiled hard ever since my arrival in the diggings, and not having been either unsuccessful or extravagant, I had begun to believe that Lenore might yet be mine. The brighter this hope became, the more value did I set on my life; and was therefore careful not to endanger my health by working in a "wet claim."

Another change had taken place in my domestic arrangements. I no longer lived in a miner's tent, nor did I continue to act as my own cook and washer-woman. I was worth several hundred pounds; and began to have a better opinion of myself than ever before. So proud was I of possessing such a sum of money, that had I been in Liverpool at that time, I should not have hesitated to talk of love to Lenore.

The life of most gold-diggers is wretched beyond belief. The inconveniences and hardships they endure are but poorly repaid, by their freedom from the irksome regulations and restraints of more civilised life. I have seen miners eating bread that had been kneaded *in a hat*, and baked in the hot ashes of their camp fire! I have seen them suffering many hardships—even hunger itself—at the very time they were encumbered with ponderous bags of gold!

In the days when gold-digging was romantic and fashionable, I have seen learned lawyers, skilled physicians, and eloquent divines—who had been seduced by the charms of a miner's life—passing the Sabbath day at the washtub, or seated outside their tents, needle in hand, stitching the torn seams of their ragged and scanty clothing. I had myself been following this rude manner of life, ever since my arrival at the diggings; but it had now lost its charms, and after reaching the Tuolumne, I took up my residence in a French boarding-house.

My two shares in the claim I had purchased soon began to yield a rich return, so that I was able to purchase several more, and also employ more men in working them.

One day I received a visit from Stormy Jack, who had come over from the Stanislaus, as he said, "to take bearings before sailing out from Sonora."

He saw how comfortably I was living in Jacksonville; and that I was making money without much hard work.

"I'll come and live like you," said he, "for I am getting too rich myself to go on as I've been doing. I won't stand hard work any longer."

After spending the day with me, he returned to Sonora—with the intention of selling out his claims on the Stanislaus, and coming to reside at Jacksonville.

The day after he had gone away—which chanced to be Saturday—at a late hour of the evening, I received a letter from him. He had written it that morning, and sent it to me by a shopkeeper who chanced to be returning to Jacksonville. So badly was the letter written, that I was occupied all the rest of the evening deciphering it; but after spending much time, patience, and ingenuity upon the epistle, I arrived at a tolerable understanding of the intelligence it was intended to convey.

Stormy commenced by stating, that I must excuse all faults: for it was the first letter he had written for a period of more than thirty years. In fact, all correspondence of an epistolary kind on Stormy's part had been discontinued on the death of Ann!

I was then informed, in the old sailor's characteristic fashion, that a murder had just been committed on the Stani. A woman had been killed by her husband; and the husband had been summarily tried, and found guilty of the crime.

The next day, at noon, the miners were going to teach the murderer "manners," by hanging him to a tree. I was advised to come over, and be a spectator of the lesson—for the reason that Stormy believed we had both seen the guilty man before. Stormy was not sure about this. The murderer bore a name, that he had never heard me make use of; but a name was nothing. "I've a bit of a fancy in my head," wrote Stormy, "that I have seen the man many years ago; and that *you* will know who he is—though I can't be sartain. So come and see for yourself. I'll expect you to be at my tent, by eleven o'clock in the mornin'."

Who could the murderer be, that *I* should know him? Could Stormy be mistaken? Had he been drinking; and this time become affected in the brain, instead of the legs?

I could hardly think it was drink. He would not have taken the trouble to write, his first epistle in thirty years, without some weighty reason.

I went to see the store-keeper who had brought the letter. From him I learnt that a murder *had* been committed by a man from Sydney, and that the murderer was to be hung on the following day.

As I continued to reflect on the information I thus received, a horrid thought came into my mind. Could the murderer be Mr Leary? Could his victim have been my mother?

There was a time when this thought would have produced on me a different effect from what it did then, a time when, dark as might have been the night, such a suspicion would have caused me to spring to my feet and instantaneously take the road to Sonora.

It did not then. I now felt less interest in the mystery I had so long been endeavouring to solve. Time, with the experience it brought, had rendered me less impulsive, if not less firm in purpose. I could not, however, sleep upon the suspicion; and after passing a wretched night, I was up before the sun.

Sonora was about thirteen miles distant from the Tuolumne diggings. It would be a pleasant morning walk; and I determined to go afoot. The exercise would only give me an appetite—so that I should enjoy my breakfast after reaching the Stanislaus. I could take plenty of time on the way, and still be there by nine o'clock—two hours sooner Stormy expected me.

I started along the road—meditating as I walked onward, what course I should pursue, supposing the murderer should turn out to be Leary, and supposing the murdered woman to be my mother!

Mr Leary was the husband of my mother. He was my stepfather. Should I allow him to be hung?

Such thoughts coursed rapidly through my mind, as I proceeded along the solitary path. I could not check them, by the reflection that, after all, the man might *not* be Mr Leary. Why I had thought of him at all, was because I could think of no other man that Stormy and I had both known before—at least, none who was likely to have committed a murder. But my correspondent might still be mistaken; and the condemned criminal be a stranger to both of us?

When I had walked about a mile along the main road to Sonora I left it—knowing that I could make a shorter cut by a path, leading over the ridge that separates the valleys of the Stanislaus and Tuolumne.

I had got, as I supposed, about half-way to Sonora; and was passing near a chapperal thicket, when a large grizzly bear rushed out of the bushes, and advanced straight towards me.

Fortunately a large live oak tree was growing near, with limbs that extended horizontally. I had just time to climb up among the branches. A second more, and I should have been grasped by the claws of the grizzly. Unlike his congener the brown bear, the *grizzly* cannot climb a tree, and knowing this I fancied myself safe.

Taking a seat on one of the limbs of the live oak, I proceeded to contemplate the interesting position in which I was placed. The bear had a brace of cubs playing in the chapperal near by. I could hear them sniffing and growling; and soon after got sight of them, engaged in their uncouth, bearish frolics. It would have been pleasant enough to watch these creatures; but the prospect of how I was to regain my liberty soon became the sole subject of my thoughts—by no means a pleasant one.

I saw that, the bear was not inclined to leave the tree, while her interesting family was so near. That seemed certain. The chance of any person passing, near that lonely place, was one against a hundred. The path was very little used, and only by an occasional pedestrian like myself.

To ensure the safety of her offspring, the bear might keep me up that tree until her cubs had arrived at the age of discretion, and be able to take care of themselves. Under the circumstances, I could not subsist so long.

Always having allowed myself to believe, that a civil tongue, a good bowie-knife, and the sense to mind my own business, were a much better protection than fire-arms, I seldom carried a revolver—as most people in California, at that time, were in the habit of doing. I now found need of the weapon, when I had it not.

I was not, however, wholly unprovided with what might console me in my dilemma: for I had some good cigars and a flask of brandy,—that happened to have been put into my pocket the night before. To aid me in calculating the chances of regaining my liberty, I took a pull at the flask, and then lighted a cigar.

Volume Two—Chapter Two.

A Grizzly on Fire.

During all this time, the bear had been energetically trying to pull down, or eat up, the tree; and I only felt secure, when I saw that she had not the ability to do either.

But the business upon which I was bound to Sonora now came before my mind. It seemed to have become greatly magnified in importance, so much so, that I began to fancy, that all my hopes for the future depended on my finding Stormy Jack before twelve o'clock. Time was rapidly passing, without my making any progress towards the place of appointment.

"What shall I do?" was the thought that seemed to run like hot lead through my skull.

The excited state I was in hindered the enjoyment I usually have in smoking a good cigar; and the fire of the one I had lit soon became extinguished.

Imbued with the belief that smoking tranquillises an agitated mind, and brings it to a fitter state for contemplation, I relighted the cigar.

I knew from the implacable disposition of the grizzly bear, that the old she that besieged me was not likely to leave the tree so long as I was in it; and the length of my captivity would probably depend on which of us could longest resist the demands of hunger.

My cigars—unlike some that I have often been compelled to smoke—could not be used as *substitute for food*: since they were composed neither of turnip tops nor cabbage leaves.

The day was intensely hot; and I had grown thirsty—a sensation that brandy would not remove. The longer I kept my perch, the more my impatience pained me, indeed, life seemed not worth possessing, unless I met Stormy at the time he had appointed. I felt the terrible exigency; but could not think of a way to respond to it. There was every probability of the next day finding me no nearer Sonora, but much nearer death, than I was then. The agony of thirst—which the feverish anxiety caused by my forlorn condition each moment increased—would of itself make an end of me.

The idea of descending from the tree, and fighting the bear with my bowie-knife, was too absurd to be entertained for a moment. To do so would be to court instant death.

I have already stated that at the time of which I write, California was disgraced by such spectacles as combats between a grizzly bear and a bull.

I had witnessed three such exhibitions; and the manner in which I had seen one of the former knock down and lacerate a bull with a single blow of its paw, was enough to make me cautious about giving the old she an opportunity of exhibiting her prowess upon myself.

The remembrance of such scenes was enough to have made me surrender myself to positive despair. I had not, however, quite come to that.

A scheme for regaining my liberty at length suggested itself; and I believe it was through smoking the cigar that the happy idea occurred to me.

To the branch on which I was sitting was attached a tuft of a singular parasitive plant. It was a species of "Spanish moss," or "old man's beard," so called, from the resemblance of its long white filamentary leaves to the hairs of a venerable pair of whiskers.

The plant itself had long since perished, as I could tell from its withered appearance. Its long filaments hung from the limb, crisp and dry as curled horse-hair.

Reaching towards it, I collected a quantity of the thread-like leaves, and placed them, so that I could conveniently lay hands upon them when wanted.

My next move was to take out the stopper of my brandy flask—which done, I turned the flask upside down, and spilled nearly the whole of its contents upon the back of the bear. What was left I employed to give a slight moistening to the bunch of Spanish moss.

I now drew forth my lucifers—when, to my chagrin, I saw that there was but one match left in the box!

What if it should miss fire, or even if igniting, I should fail with it to light the dry leaves?

I trembled as I dwelt upon the possibility of a failure. Perhaps my life depended upon the striking of that one match? I felt the necessity of being careful. A slight shaking of the hand would frustrate my well-contrived scheme.

Cautiously did I draw the match over the steel filings on the box, too cautiously, for no crackling accompanied the friction.

I tried again; but this time, to my horror, I saw the little dump of phosphorus that should have blazed up, break from the end of the stick, and fall to the bottom of the tree!

I came very near falling myself, for the bright hope that had illumed my mind was now extinguished; and the darkness of despondency once more set over my soul.

Soon, however, a new idea came into my mind—restoring my hopes as suddenly as they had departed. There was fire in the stump of the cigar still sticking between my lips.

The match was yet in my hand; and I saw that there remained upon it a portion of the phosphoric compound.

I applied its point to the coal of the cigar; and had the gratification of beholding it blaze upwards.

I now kindled the Spanish moss, which, saturated with the brandy, soon became a blaze; and this strange torch I at once dropped on the back of the bear.

Just as I had expected, the brandy, with which I had wetted the shaggy coat of the bear, became instantly ignited into a whishing, spluttering flame, which seemed to envelope the whole body of the animal!

But I was not allowed to have a long look at the conflagration I had created: for the moment the bear felt the singeing effects of the blaze, she broke away from the bottom of the tree, and retreated over the nearest ridge, roaring as she went like a tropical hurricane!

Never before had I beheld a living creature under such an elevated inspiration of fear.

Her cries were soon answered by another grizzly, not far away; and I knew that no time was to be squandered in making my escape from the place.

I quickly descended from the tree; and the distance I got over, in the succeeding ten minutes, was probably greater than I had ever done before in twice the time.

Volume Two—Chapter Three.

Lynch versus Leary.

I reached Stormy's tent about ten o'clock; and found him waiting for me. I proposed proceeding at once towards the gaol where the condemned man was kept. I was more impatient than my companion—impatient to see whether I might identify the criminal.

"Come on!" said I, "we can talk and walk at the same time."

The old sailor followed me out of his tent, and then led the way without speaking.

"Storm along, Stormy," cried I, "Let me hear what you have to say."

"It's not much," replied he; "I'm afraid I've been making a fool of myself, and you too. I saw the man yesterday, who's going to be hung to-day. I fancied that he was the same as brought you aboard the 'Hope' in Dublin Bay, when you first went to sea—he that you told me was your stepfather—and who you promised to larn manners if ever you should come back, and find he had been misbehaving himself. Now it may be all my own fancy. That was so many years ago that I mightn't remember; but I couldn't rest satisfied, without having you see him, for yourself."

I told Stormy that he had acted right; and that I hoped, and should be pleased, to find that he was mistaken.

Stormy's doubts had the effect of tranquillising me a little. I was now very hungry too; and at the first restaurant in our way, I went in, and ordered some breakfast, which was eaten with an appetite I hoped never to have again—a hope that was no doubt shared by the proprietor of the restaurant.

We then pursued our journey to the place where the prisoner was under guard.

The prison was merely a public-house—around which a crowd of people were beginning to assemble.

I wished to see the prisoner; but he was in an inside room, with the men who guarded him; and these were a little particular as to who was admitted into his presence. I had to wait, therefore, until he should be led out to execution.

On finding that I could not be allowed to see the murderer—and as I was anxious to learn something immediately—I determined on taking a look at his victim. It would be easy to do this: as the house where the dead woman was lying was not far distant, from that which contained her murderer.

Accompanied by Stormy, I walked over to the house; and we were admitted into the room where the corpse was lying. The face of the murdered woman was concealed under a white cloth; and while standing over the body, I was more strangely agitated than I had ever been before. Should I, on removing that slight shrouding of cotton, behold the inanimate features of my mother?

The suspense was agonisingly interesting. The covering was at length removed; and I breathed again. The body was not that of my mother; but of a young woman apparently about nineteen or twenty years of age. She had been a beautiful woman, and was still so—even in death!

Less tortured by my thoughts, I followed Stormy back to the public-house—around which the crowd had greatly increased: for it was now twelve o'clock, the hour appointed for the execution.

My heart beat audibly, as the criminal was led forth, surrounded by his guards and attendants.

Stormy was right. The murderer was Matthew Leary!

"What shall I do?" I inquired of Stormy, as we followed the criminal to the place of execution.

"You can do nothing," answered Stormy. "Let *them* teach him manners. If you interfere, you'll be larnt some yourself."

There was truth in this. From the temper of the men, who had judged and condemned the murderer, it was evident I could do nothing to save him. Perhaps I did not contemplate trying.

The prisoner was led from the public-house he had been kept in since his condemnation, to a live oak tree, growing on the top of a high hill, about half a mile from the town. Under this tree was a grave, that had been freshly dug. The murderer, as he was conducted forward, must have seen the grave, and know it to be his final resting-place. For all that, he approached the tree without any apparent emotion!

"He is either a very good man, or a very bad one," said one by my side, "he is going to die game!"

A cart was drawn up under the live oak; and into it climbed four or five respectable-looking men—who appeared to be taking a prominent part in the proceedings.

One of them requested silence—a request which was immediately complied with—and the man who made it, then addressed the assembly, in, as near as I can remember, the following words:—

"Gentlemen! Before commencing to execute the painful duty, we have met to perform, I deem it necessary to give you a brief description of the circumstances, under which we are called upon to act. The prisoner before you—*John Mathews*,—has been tried by a jury of twelve men; and found guilty of the murder of his wife—or a woman living with him as such. He has been defended by able counsel; and the trial has been conducted with all the decorum and ceremony required by an occasion so solemn and important. It has appeared in evidence against the prisoner, that he was an habitual drunkard; and that his principal means for indulging, in his unfortunate habits of dissipation, were derived from his wife—who supported herself, the prisoner, and their child, by working as a washer-woman. There has been full evidence brought before the jury, that, on the day the murder was committed, the prisoner came home drunk, and asked the woman for money. She told him that she had but three dollars in the house; and that she wanted that to procure necessaries for her child—in fine, she refused to let him have it. The prisoner demanded the three dollars, and the woman still refused to give them up. After he had made a vain attempt to extort the money by threats, he went across the room, and procured a pistol, with which he unsuccessfully made an attempt to shoot her. Finding that the weapon was unloaded, he turned it in his hand, and struck the woman two heavy blows on the head with its butt. These blows were the cause of her death—which occurred two hours afterwards. The man who committed this crime is now before you. As I do not wish to prejudice the mind of any one, I have simply stated what was proved on the trial; and the question I now put is—what shall we do with him?"

The speaker finished by putting on his hat, which was as much as to say, that his part in the solemn ceremony was performed.

The firm, earnest voice, in which the address had been delivered, convinced me that the speaker, who had thus distinguished himself, was actuated neither by prejudice nor passion.

From the tenor of the speech he had delivered, I could tell that the criminal's fate, to a certain extent, still depended on a vote of the crowd; and in their decision I felt more interested, than even Mr Leary himself appeared to be!

Another of the men in the cart now took off his hat; and the murmuring noise once more subsided.

"Fellow citizens!" said this second speaker, "I am not here either to apologise for, or sanction the crime this man has committed. I know, as well as any man present, the necessity that exists in a land like this, or, rather, in the state of society in which we live, for the severe punishment of crime. All I ask of you is, to let this man be punished by the laws of the country. A system of government—of which you all approve—has lately been established among us; and arrangements have been made for the trial and punishment of criminals. Do not take the law into your own hands. People living in the civilised communities of Europe and our own country are crying 'Shame! shame!' at many transactions, similar to this, which have occurred in California; and the same words will be uttered against the proceedings that are taking place here to-day. I am a magistrate; and have with me a constable. I will pledge my life that if you will allow us to remove the prisoner, he shall be brought before a jury and tried by the laws of our country. I trust that no good citizen will make any objection to our taking that course with him."

The magistrate then put on his hat—as a signal that *he* had nothing more to say.

The murmur of the crowd rose higher; and there were heard many cries of dissent from what had been last said.

"He's had a fair trial—hang him!" exclaimed one.

"Hang him now, or he'll escape!" vociferated another.

There were also a few voices raised on the other side. "Give him up! Let the magistrate have him!" shouted these last.

A man now stood up in the cart; and called for a show of hands.

All in favour of delivering the prisoner into the custody of the law officers were requested to hold up their right hands.

About twenty arms were extended into the air!

A number of these belonged to men who had the appearance of being what in California were called "Sydney Ducks"—old convicts from New South Wales; but most of the hands raised were those of well-known gamblers—all of whom have an instinctive horror of Justice Lynch.

Those who were in favour of the prisoner being hung, *then and there*, were next invited to hold up their right hands.

In an instant about three hundred arms were held aloft. All of them that I saw were terminated with strong, sinewy fists, stained only with toil, and belonging to miners—the most respectable portion of the population.

This silent, but emphatic, declaration was considered final. After it had been delivered, there commenced a scene of wild excitement.

I rushed through the crowd, towards the tree under which the criminal stood. As I came up to him, I saw that a rope had been, already noosed around his neck.

A man was climbing into the live oak—for the purpose of passing the rope over one of its branches.

"Stop!" I cried, "stop for one minute! Let me ask this man a question, before he dies."

Mr Leary turned towards me with a stare of surprise; and for the first time, since being brought upon the ground, did he appear to take any interest in what was passing!

"I am the Rolling Stone," I shouted to him, "Tell me, where is my mother?"

The murderer smiled, and such a smile! It was the same fiendish expression he had thrown at me, when I last saw him in the boat in Dublin Bay.

"Tell me where I can find my mother!" I again asked, nearly frantic with rage.

At this moment the slack end of the lazo, that had been passed over the branch and then slung back among the crowd, was instantly seized by a hundred hands. The condemned man seemed not to notice the movement, while, in answer to my question, the malignant expression upon his features became stronger and deeper.

"Away!" I cried, scarcely conscious of what I said or did, "Away with him!"

Those holding the rope sprang outward from the tree, and up rose Mr Leary.

A few faint kicks, and his body hung motionless from the limb of the live oak.

An empty sardine box was nailed to the tree, on which the murderer was hanging. Above it was pinned a piece of paper—on which were written the words, "For the orphan."

Many miners stepped up to the spot, opened their purses; and slipped a few dollars' worth of gold dust into the box.

Their example was followed by Stormy Jack; and from the quantity of yellow dust I saw him drop into the common receptacle, I could tell that his purse must have been three or four ounces lighter, when he came away from the tree!

Volume Two—Chapter Four.

The Orphan.

Shortly after the termination of the melancholy drama, in which I had taken so prominent a part, Stormy Jack and I went to see the child—now left without either father or mother.

We found it in the keeping of a young married couple—who had lately arrived from Australia; and who had there been acquainted with its unfortunate mother.

They told us, that the murdered woman was the daughter of a respectable shopkeeper in Sydney, that she had run away with Mr Mathews—the name under which Leary had passed in Australia—and that her parents had been very unwilling she should have anything to do with him.

She was an only daughter; and had left behind a father and mother sorely grieved at her misconduct. Everybody that knew her had thought her behaviour most singular. They could not comprehend her infatuation in forsaking a good home and kind parents for such a man as Mathews—who, to say nothing of his dissipated habits, was at least twenty years older than herself.

Perhaps it was strange, though I had learnt enough to think otherwise. Experience had told me, that such occurrences are far from being uncommon, and that one might almost fancy, that scoundrels like Leary possess some peculiar charm for fascinating women—at least, those of the weaker kind.

The orphan was shown to us—a beautiful bright-eyed boy, about a year old; and bearing a marked resemblance to its mother.

"I shall take this child to its grandfather and grandmother in Sydney," said the young woman who had charge of it; "they will think all the world of it: for it is so like their lost daughter. May be it will do something to supply her place?"

From the manner in which the young couple were behaving towards the child, I saw that it would be safe in their keeping; and added my mite, to the fund already contributed for its support.

In hopes of learning whether my mother had ever reached Sydney, I asked them if they had been acquainted with Mathews there; or knew anything of his previous history. On this point they could give me no information. They had had no personal acquaintance with Mathews in Australia; and all that they knew or had ever heard of him was unfavourable to his character. In Sydney, as elsewhere, he had been known as a dissolute, intemperate man.

Before we left the house, three men came in—bringing with them the gold that had been for the orphan.

It was weighed in the presence of the young man and his wife, and the amount was fifty ounces—in value near two hundred pounds of English money. My own contribution increased it to a still greater sum. The married couple had some scruples about taking charge of the gold, although they had none in regard to encumbering themselves with the child!

"I will go with you to an Express Office," said the man to the deputation who brought the money, "and we will send it to Mr D—, in San Francisco. He is a wholesale merchant there, and came from Sydney. He is acquainted with the child's grandparents; and will forward the money to them. As for the child, I expect soon to return to Sydney myself—when I can take it along with me, and give it up to those who have the right to it."

This arrangement proving agreeable to all parties concerned, the gold was at once carried to the Express Office, and deposited there—with directions to forward it to Mr D—, the merchant.

Having passed the remainder of the day in the company of Stormy Jack, I returned to my home on the Tuolumne, but little better informed about what I desired to know, than when I left it. I had seen Mr Leary for the last time; but I was as ignorant as ever of the fate of my relatives.

Leary was now gone out of the world, and could trouble my mother no more—wherever she might be. It was some satisfaction to be certain of that.

As I walked homeward my reflections were sufficiently unpleasant: I reproached myself with having too long neglected the duty on which I had started out—the search after my relations.

Nor was I without some regret, as I suffered my mind to dwell on the spectacle just past. The criminal was my stepfather. I had, though half unconsciously, given the word, that had launched his body from the scaffold, and his soul into eternity!

My regrets could not have been very deeply felt. They were checked by the reflection, that he could have given me some information concerning my mother, and that he had died apparently happy with the thought, that he had disappointed me by withholding it!

Mr Leary had been my mother's husband—my own stepfather—yet without shame I have recorded the fact, that he died an ignominious death. I am not responsible for his actions. I stand alone; and the man who may think any the less of me, for my unfortunate relationship with a murderer, is one whose good will I do not think worth having.

Volume Two—Chapter Five.

Stormy's Last Spree.

Shortly after my return to the Tuolumne, I was joined by Stormy Jack, who came to Jacksonville, as he had promised he would, with the determination to take the world a little easier.

Since his childhood Stormy had never spent a whole week in idleness—at least not at a single spell—and such a life he soon found, did not help him to that supreme happiness he had been anticipating from it.

In the little town of Jacksonville an idle man could only find amusement, in some place where strong drink was sold; and to be, day after day, continually called upon to resist the temptation to drink, was a trial too severe for Stormy's mental and physical constitution. Both had to yield. He got drunk frequently; and on several occasions so very drunk, as to be affected both in his head and legs at the same time!

He was himself somewhat surprised at finding himself so often in this condition of "double drunkenness,"—as he termed it. It was not often in his life he had been so. It was a serious affair; and he made some sort of a resolution that it should not occur again.

To avoid its recurrence, he saw that he must employ himself in some way; and he purchased a rifle, with the design of transforming himself into a hunter.

By following this profession he could combine business with amusement, as there were other hunters making a very good thing of it, by supplying the citizens of Jacksonville with venison and bear meat.

Stormy prosecuted his new calling for about three days. At the end of that time he had been taught three things. One was, that hunting was hard work—harder, if possible, than mining. Secondly, he discovered that the amusement of the chase was, after all, not so grand—especially when followed as a profession, or by a man of peculiar inclinations, altogether different to his own. Finally, Stormy arrived at the conclusion, that the business didn't pay.

The truth is, Stormy was no marksman; and could only hit a barn, by going inside, and closing the door before firing off his piece.

The calling of a hunter was not suited to the old "salt," nor was it of the kind he required, to keep him from backsliding into his bad habit. He therefore determined to give it up, and take to some other.

While deliberating on what was to be done, he again yielded to the old temptation; and got gloriously drunk.

Alas, for poor Stormy! It proved the last intoxication of his life!

The story of his death is too sad to be dismissed in a few words; and when heard, will doubtless be thought deserving of the "full and particular" account here given of it. I record the facts, in all the exactitude and minuteness, with which memory has supplied them to myself.

At that time there was staying in Jacksonville a man known by the name, or soubriquet, of "Red Ned." I had casually heard of the man, though I had not seen him, as he had only arrived in the place a few days before; and was stopping at one of the gambling taverns, with which that mining village was abundantly provided.

I had heard that Red Ned was a "dangerous man,"—a title of which he was no little vain; and, probably, ever since his arrival in the place, he had been looking for an opportunity of distinguishing himself by some deed of violence.

In my wanderings over the world I have encountered many of those men known as "bullies." Notwithstanding the infamy attached to the appellation, I have found some of them—perhaps unfortunately for themselves—endowed with genuine courage, while others were mere cowardly wretches—ever seeking to keep up their spurious reputation, by such opportunities as are offered in quarrelling with half-grown lads, and men under the influence of drink.

Such swaggerers may be met with in all parts of the world; but nowhere in such numbers, as in California—which for a country so thinly peopled, appears to be more than ordinarily afflicted with the propensity for "bullyism." At least, it was so, at the period of which I am writing.

At that time, a man, who was known to have killed three or four of his fellow-creatures, was looked upon with admiration by many, with fear by as many more, and with abhorrence by a very few indeed.

Quarrels in California, three times out of every four, terminated fatally for one or other of the combatants; and the survivor of several such sanguinary affairs was certain to obtain among his fellows a reputation of some kind—whether of good or evil—and for this, unhappily, the majority of mankind are but too eager to strive.

Where society exists in a state of half civilisation—such as was that of California fifteen years ago—it is not so strange that many should be met, who prefer having the reputation of a bully to having no reputation at all.

It was the unfortunate fate of my old comrade, to encounter one of these contemptible creatures—who combine the bully with the coward—in the person of Red Ned.

Stormy, after giving up the calling of the chase, had found himself once more afloat, and in search of some business that would be more suited to his tastes and abilities. While beating about, as already stated, he had once more given way to his unfortunate propensity for strong drink; and had got intoxicated both in his mind and his limbs.

While in this state, he had involved himself in a coffee-house quarrel with the man above mentioned; and who, no doubt, well understood the helpless condition of his adversary: for it was Red Ned himself who provoked the quarrel.

When unmolested by others, I never knew a man of a more harmless, inoffensive disposition than was the old sailor.

Even when under the influence of liquor, he never, to my knowledge, commenced a dispute; but when in that state, he was inclined to "teach manners" to any one who might interfere with him.

Red Ned had met Stormy in one of the gambling taverns, where the latter was carrying on his carouse; and perceiving that the old sailor was helplessly intoxicated, and moreover, that he was only a sailor—whom he could affront, without offending any of the company present—his bullying propensity would not permit him to let pass such a fine opportunity of gaining the distinction he coveted.

In Stormy's state of inebriety there was but little danger to be dreaded from any personal conflict with him, for although he was still able to keep his feet, his legs had reached a degree of drunkenness, that caused him occasionally to reel and stagger over the floor of the bar-room.

The ruffian, perfectly conscious of all this, made some slurring remark—intended to reflect upon Stormy's condition, and loud enough for the latter to hear it.

As might have been expected, the old sailor did not take the slur in good part; but in return poured forth his displeasure in his usual frank and energetic manner.

Stormy, when excited by drink, was somewhat extravagant in the use of vituperative language; and there can be no doubt that the bully was compelled to listen to some plain-speaking that he did not much relish.

He submitted to the storm for a while; and then rushing upon Stormy, he struck the old sailor a slap with his open hand.

Stormy, of course, returned the blow with closed fists, and then proceeded to defend himself, by throwing his body, as well as its intoxicated legs would allow, into a boxing attitude.

But the bully had no intention to continue the fight in that cowardly fashion—as he would have called it; and drawing his bowie-knife out of his boot, he closed suddenly upon Stormy, and buried its blade in the old sailors side.

Of course this terminated the strife; and the wounded man was conveyed to his lodgings.

Volume Two—Chapter Six.

Red Ned.

At the time that Stormy was teaching, or rather receiving, that terrible lesson of manners, I was not in the village. I had gone some two or three miles up the river, to look after my miners at their work.

A messenger brought me the news; and, in breathless haste, I hurried homewards.

On arriving at the house where Stormy lived, I found him stretched upon his bed—with a doctor bending over him.

"Rowley, my boy, it's all over with me," said he. "The doctor says so; and for the first time in my life I believe one."

"Stormy! Stormy! my friend, what has happened?" I asked, as across my soul swept a wave of anguish more painful than words can describe.

"Never mind any explanation now," interrupted the doctor, turning to me, and speaking in a low voice. "Do not excite your friend, by making him converse. You can learn the particulars of his misfortune from some one else."

The doctor was in the act of leaving; and, interpreting a sign he gave me, I followed him out. I was told by him, that Stormy had been stabbed, and that his wound would prove mortal. The man of medicine imparted some other details of the affair, which he had collected from the spectators who had witnessed it.

On parting from me, the surgeon gave me warning, that the wounded man might live two days—certainly not longer.

"He has received an injury," said he, "that must cause his death within that time. You can do nothing, beyond keeping him as quiet as possible."

After pronouncing this melancholy prognosis, the surgeon took his departure, with a promise to call again in the morning.

I returned to the bedside of my doomed comrade.

He would talk, in spite of all I could do, or say, to prevent him.

"I *will* talk," said he, "and there's no use in your trying to stop me. I've not much longer to live; and why should I pretend to be dead, before I really am?"

I saw it was no use to attempt keeping him either quiet or silent. It only excited him all the more; and would, perhaps, do more harm to him than letting him have his way—which I at length did. He proceeded to inform me of all the particulars of the affair. His account slightly differed from that given me by the doctor, who had doubtless heard a one-sided statement, from the friends of the bully.

"I don't know whether I've been sarved right or not," said Stormy, after concluding his account. "I sartinly called the man some ugly names; and every one about here is likely to say that it was right for him to teach me manners. But why did he stab me with a knife? My legs were staggering drunk; and he might have thrashed me without that!"

On hearing Stormy's statement, I became inspired with a feeling of fell indignation against the scoundrel, who had acted in such a cowardly manner: a determination, that my old comrade should be avenged.

I knew it would be idle to go before a magistrate, for the purpose of getting the bully punished, for the two men had come to blows, *before* the knife had been used.

The affair would be looked upon as an affray—in which either, or both, had the right to use whatever weapons they pleased—and Stormy would be thought deserving of his fate, for not protecting himself in a more efficient manner!

I knew that he was drunk; and that even if sober he would not have used a deadly weapon in a bar-room row; but although I knew this, others would tell me, that my friend's being drunk was not the fault of the man who had stabbed him; and that if he had not chosen to defend himself according to custom, he must bear the consequences.

Impelled by my excited feelings, I left Stormy in the care of a miner who had come in to see him; and stepped over to the tavern, where the horrible deed had taken place.

About forty people were in the bar-room when I entered. Some were seated around a table where "Monte" was being dealt, while others were standing at the bar, noisily swilling their drinks.

Without making remark to any one, I listened for a few minutes to the conversation. As the affair had occurred only that afternoon, I knew that they would be talking about it in the bar-room—as in reality they were. Several men were speaking on the subject, though not disputing. There was not much difference of opinion among them. They all seemed to regard the occurrence, as I expected they would, in the same light.

Two men had got into a quarrel, and then come to blows. One had stabbed the other—in California an everyday occurrence of trifling interest. That was all the bar-room loungers were disposed to make of it.

I differed in opinion with them; and told them, in plain terms, that the fight they were talking about had not been a fair one, that the man who had stabbed the other had committed a crime but little less than murder.

A dozen were anxious to argue with me. How could I expect a man to be called hard names in a public room without his resenting it?

"But why did the man use a knife?" I asked. "Could the insult not have been resented without that?"

I was told that men had no business to fight at all, if they could avoid it; but when they did, each had a right to be in earnest, and do all the harm he could to the other.

I was also admonished that I had better not let "Red Ned" hear me talk as I was doing, or I might probably get served as bad as the sailor, who had offended him that same day.

I thus learnt, for the first time, that the man who had wounded Stormy was "Red Ned," and from what I had heard of this ruffian already, I was not the less determined that Stormy should be avenged.

I knew, moreover, that if "Red Ned" was to receive punishment, it would have to be inflicted by myself.

He was not in the tavern at the time; or, perhaps, he might have received it on the instant.

I returned to Stormy; and passed that night by his side.

He was in great pain most part of the night. The distress of my mind at the poor fellow's sufferings, determined me to seek "Red Ned" the next morning; and, as Stormy would have said, "teach him manners."

When the day broke, the wounded man was in less pain, and able to converse—though not without some difficulty.

"Rowley," said he, "we must attend to business, before it be too late. I know I shan't live through another night, and must make up my reckoning to-day. I've got about one hundred and eighty ounces; and it's all yours, my boy. I don't know that I have a relation in the world; and there is no one to whom I care to leave anything but yourself. I can die happy now, because I know that the little I leave will belong to you. Had this happened before our meeting in Sonora, my greatest sorrow at going aloft would have been, to think some stranger would spend what I have worked hard to make, while my little Rowley might be rolling hungry round the world."

At Stormy's request, the landlord of the lodging was called in; and commanded to produce the bag of gold which the sailor had placed in his keeping.

At this the man, apparently an honest fellow, went out of the room; and soon returned with the treasure, which, in the presence of the landlord and a miner who had come in, its owner formally presented to me. It was a bequest rather than a present—the act of a dying man.

"Take it, Rowley," said he, "and put it with your own. It was got in an honest manner, and let it be spent in a sensible one. Go to Liverpool, marry the girl you told me of; and have a home and family in your old age. I fancy, after all, that must be the way to be happy: for being without home and friends I know isn't. Ah! it was that as made me live the wretched roaming life, I've done."

The exertion of talking had made Stormy worse. I saw that he began to breathe with difficulty; and seemed to suffer a great deal of pain. So great was his agony, that it was almost equal agony for me to stand by his side; and I stole out, leaving him with the surgeon—who had meanwhile arrived—and the miner before mentioned.

I stole out *upon an errand.*

Volume Two—Chapter Seven.

My Comrade Avenged.

Perhaps ere this my errand may have been conjectured. If not I shall disclose it. I left the bedside of Stormy to seek Red Ned.

I went direct to the tavern—knowing that the bully frequented the place, and that if not there, some one could probably tell me where he might be found.

As I entered the bar-room, a tall, slender man, with red hair, was talking, in a loud voice, to a knot of others collected in front of the bar.

"Let him dare tell me that it was murder," said the red-haired man, "and I'll serve him in the same way I did the other. Murder indeed! Why, there was a dozen men by, who can prove that I listened for ten minutes to the man insulting and abusing me in the most beastly manner. Could flesh and blood stand it any longer? What is a man worth who'll not protect his character? Whoever says I acted unfair is a liar; and had better keep his cheek to himself."

As soon as I heard the speaker's voice, and had a fair look at him, I recognised him as an old acquaintance.

It was Edward Adkins, first mate and afterwards captain of the ship "Lenore"—the man who had discharged me in New Orleans after the death of Captain Hyland—the man who had accused me of ingratitude and theft! Yes, it was Adkins, my old enemy.

I knew that *he* was a coward of the most contemptible kind, and a bully as well.

What I had witnessed of his conduct on the Lenore, during many years' service with him, had fully convinced me of this. A thorough tyrant over the crew, while cringing in the presence of Captain Hyland—who was often compelled to restrain him, from practising his petty spite upon those under his command. It did not need that last interview I had had with him in Liverpool—in the house of Mrs Hyland—to strengthen my belief that Edward Adkins was a despicable poltroon.

In answer to the question he had put: "What's a man worth who'll not protect his character?" I walked up to him and said:—"You have no character to protect, and none to lose. You are a cowardly ruffian. You purposely started a quarrel with an inoffensive man; and drew your knife upon him when you knew he was helpless with drink."

"Hell and damnation! Are you talking to me?" inquired Adkins, turning sharply round, his face red with rage.

But his features suddenly changed to an expression that told me he wished himself anywhere else, than in the presence of the man to whom he had addressed the profane speech.

"Yes! I'm talking to you," said I, "and I wish all present to listen to what I say. You are a cowardly wretch, **and worse**. You have taken the life of a harmless, innocent man, unable to protect himself. You, to talk of resenting an insult, and protecting your character—your character indeed!"

Had we two been alone, it is possible that Adkins would not have thought himself called upon to reply to what I had said; but we were in the presence of two score of men, in whose hearing he had just boasted—how he would serve the man who had been slandering him. That man was myself.

"Now!" I cried impatient for action, "you hear what I've said! You hear it, all of you?"

The bully had been brought to bay.

"Gentlemen!" said he, addressing the crowd who had gathered around, "what am I to do? I was driven yesterday to an act I now regret; and here is another man forcing me into a quarrel in the same way. Take my advice," said he, turning to me, "and leave the house, before my blood gets up."

"There is not the least danger of your blood getting up," said I; "your heart's gone down into your heels. If I was so drunk, as to be just able to keep my legs, no doubt you would have the courage to attack me. You haven't got it now."

The greatest coward in the world can be driven to an exhibition of courage—whether sham or real; and Adkins, seeing that he could no longer in California lay claim to the title of a *dangerous man*, without doing something to deserve it, cried out—

"Damnation! if you want it, you shall have it!"

As the words passed from his lips, I saw him stoop suddenly—at the same time jerking his foot upward from the floor. I divined his intention, which was to draw his bowie out of his boot; and while his leg was still raised, and before he could fairly lay hold of the knife, I dealt him a blow that sent him sprawling upon the floor. The knife flew out of his hand; and, before he could regain his feet, I stepped between him and the place where it was lying.

I have neglected to tell the reader, that I could no longer with propriety be called "The *little* Rolling Stone," though Stormy still continued to address me occasionally by that appellation. At the time of this—my last encounter with Adkins—I was six feet *without* my boots; and was strong and active in proportion. I have called it my *last* encounter with this ruffian—it was so. Before he was in a position to attack me a second time, I drew my own knife from its sheath; and threw it on the floor alongside his. I did this, to show that I scorned to take any advantage of an unarmed man—as my cowardly opponent had done with poor Stormy Jack. I did not at the moment think of the wrongs Adkins had done to myself—of my imprisonment in a common gaol—of the falsehoods he had told to Mrs Hyland—of his attempt to win Lenore. I thought only of poor Stormy.

Adkins again rushed on me; and was again knocked down. This time he showed a disposition for remaining on the floor—in the hopes that some of his friends might come between us, and declare the fight to be over; but I kicked him, until he again got up, and once more closed with me.

I met the third attack, by picking him up in my arms—until his heels were high in the air, and then I allowed him to fall down again on the crown of his head. He never rose after that fall—his neck was broken.

Before I left the room, every man in it came up and shook hands with me—as they did so, telling me that I had done a good thing.

Volume Two—Chapter Eight.

Stormy Tranquil at Last.

When I returned to Stormy he was worse; and I saw that he had not much longer to live. He was not in so much pain as when I left him; but it was evident he was sinking rapidly.

"Stormy," said I, "what would you wish me to do to the man, who has brought you to this?"

"Nothing," he answered; "he's a bad man—but let him go. Promise me that you will not try to teach him manners—let the Lord do it for us."

"All right, comrade," said I, "your wishes shall be obeyed: for I cannot harm him now. He has gone."

"I'm glad of that," said the dying man, "for it shows that he knew himself to be in the wrong. By his running away, others will know it too; and will not say that I desarved what I've got."

"But he has *not* run away," said I, "he is dead. I went to the house, where you met him yesterday. I found him there. Before I came out, he died."

Stormy's expressive features were lit up with a peculiar smile.

It was evident that he comprehended the full import of my ambiguous speech, though he made no comment, further than what gave me to understand, that his object, in making me promise not to harm Red Ned, was only from fear that I might get the worst of it. I could tell, however, by the expression upon his features, that he was rather pleased I had not left to the Lord the work of teaching manners to his murderer.

I remained by the bedside of my dying comrade—painfully awaiting the departure of his spirit. My vigil was not a protracted one. He died early in the afternoon of that same day, on which his murder had been avenged.

There was no inquest held, either upon his body, or that of his assassin. Perhaps the latter might have been brought to trial, but for the judgment that had already fallen upon him. This being deemed just by all the respectable people in the place, there were no farther steps taken in the matter, than that of burying the bodies of the two men—who had thus fallen a sacrifice to the play of unfortunate passions.

I have seen many gold-diggers undergo interment, by being simply rolled up in their blankets, and thrust under ground without any ceremony whatever, all this, too, only an hour or two after the breath had departed from their bodies. Such, no doubt, would have been the manner in which the body of Stormy Jack would have been disposed of, had there not been by him in his last hour a friend, who had been acquainted with him long, and respected him much.

I could not permit his remains to be thus rudely interred. I had a good coffin made to contain them; and gave the old sailor the most respectable burial I had ever seen among the miners of California.

Poor Stormy! Often, when thinking of him, I am reminded of how much the destiny of an individual may be influenced by circumstances.

Stormy Jack was naturally a man of powerful intellect. He possessed generosity, courage, a love of justice, and truth—in short, all the requisites that constitute a noble character. But his intellect had remained wholly uncultivated; and circumstances had conducted him to a calling, where his good qualities were but little required, and less appreciated. Had he been brought up and educated to fill some higher station in society, history might have carried his name—which to me was unknown—far down into posterity. In the proportion that Nature had been liberal to him, Fortune had been unkind; and he died, as he had lived, only Stormy Jack—unknown to, and uncared for, by the world he might have adorned.

After having performed the last sad obsequies over his body, I recalled the advice he had given me, along with his gold, to return to Lenore.

I resolved to follow a counsel so consonant with my own desires. I found no difficulty in disposing of my mining shares; and this done, I made arrangements for travelling by the stage conveyance then running between Sonora and Stockton.

Before leaving the Stanislaus, I paid a visit to the young couple, who had been entrusted with the care of Leary's child.

My object in going to see them was to learn, if possible, something more of that gentleman's doings in Australia.

It was true, they had said, that they were unacquainted with him there; but there were several questions I wished to ask them—by which I hoped to learn something concerning my mother, and whether she had followed Leary to the colonies.

I found the guardians of the child still living where I had seen them, on the day the murderer was executed. The orphan was no longer in their keeping. They had sent it to its grandparents in Sydney, in charge of a merchant—who had left California for the Australian colonies some weeks before.

Though I obtained from the man and his wife all the information they were capable of giving, I learnt but little of what I desired to know. They thought it likely, that in San Francisco, I might hear more about the subject of my enquiries. They knew a man named Wilson—who had come from Sydney in the same ship with them; and who was now keeping a public-house in San Francisco. Wilson, they believed, had been well acquainted with Mathews—for this was the name which Leary had assumed in the colonies.

Such was the scant information I succeeded in obtaining from the friends of the late Mrs Leary; and with only this to guide me, I commenced my journey for the capital of California.

Volume Two—Chapter Nine.

A Rough Ride.

The stage, by which I travelled from Sonora to Stockton, was nothing more than a large open waggon, drawn by four Mexican horses.

We started at six o'clock in the morning, on a journey of eighty-four miles. This we should have to perform before four o'clock in the afternoon of the same day—in order to catch the steamer, which, at that hour, was to start from Stockton for San Francisco.

Notwithstanding that the road over most of the route was in reality no road at all, but an execrable path, we made the eighty-four miles within the time prescribed: for the stage arrived at Stockton more than twenty minutes before the time appointed for the sailing of the steamer!

In spite of this rapidity of transit, I did not at all enjoy the journey between Sonora and Stockton. I was all the time under an impression that my life was in imminent danger; and, as I was at last on my way to Lenore, I did not wish to be killed by the overturning of a Californian stage coach—behind four half-wild horses, going at the top of their speed.

Sometimes we would be rushing down a steep hill, when, to keep the horses out of the way of the waggon they were drawing, the driver would stand up on his box, and fling the "silk" at them with all the energy he could command. On such occasions there would be moments when not a wheel could be seen touching the ground; and not unfrequently the vehicle would bound through the air, to a distance equalling its own length!

We were fortunate enough to reach Stockton, without breaking either the wheels of the waggon, or the bones of any of the passengers, which to me at the time seemed something miraculous.

I do not relish describing scenes of a sanguinary character; but, to give the reader some idea of the state of society in California, at the time I write of, I shall mention a circumstance that transpired during my twenty minutes' sojourn in Stockton—while waiting for the starting of the steamer.

Just as we were getting out of the stage waggon, several pistol-shots were heard, close to the spot where we had stopped. They had been fired inside the gambling room of a public-house, on the opposite side of the street; and several men were seen rushing out of the house, apparently to escape the chances of being hit by a stray bullet.

As soon as the firing had ceased, the retreating tide turned back again; and re-entered the house—along with a crowd of others, who had been idling outside.

I walked over; and went in with the rest. On entering the large saloon, in which the shots had been fired, I saw two men lying stretched upon separate tables—each attended by a surgeon, who was examining his wounds.

I could see that both were badly—in fact mortally—wounded; and yet each was cursing the other with the most horrible imprecations I had ever heard!

One of the surgeons, addressing himself to the man upon whom he was attending, said:—

"Do not talk in that profane manner. You had better turn your thoughts to something else: you have not many hours to live."

Neither this rebuke, nor the unpleasant information conveyed by it, seemed to produce the slightest effect on the wretch to whom it was addressed. Instead of becoming silent, he poured forth a fresh storm of blasphemy; and continued cursing all the time I remained within hearing.

I was told that the two men had quarrelled about a horse, that one of them first fired at the other, who fell instantly to the shot; and that the latter, while lying on the floor, had returned the fire of the assailant, sending three bullets into his body.

I heard afterwards that the shots had proved fatal to both. The man who had fired the first shot died that same night—the other surviving the sanguinary encounter only a few hours longer.

I had no desire to linger among the spectators of that tragical tableau; and I was but too glad to find a cue for escaping from it: in the tolling of the steam-boat bell, as it summoned the passengers aboard.

A few minutes after, and we were gliding down the San Joaquin—*en route* for the Golden City.

The San Joaquin is emphatically a crooked river. It appeared to me that in going down it, we passed Mount Diablo at least seven times. Vessels, that we had already met, could be soon after seen directly ahead of us, while those appearing astern would in a few minutes after, encounter us in the channel of the stream!

A "Down-easter," who chanced to be aboard, made the characteristic observation:—that "the river was so crooked, a bird could not fly across it: as it would be certain to alight on the side from which it had started!"

Crooked as was the San Joaquin it conducted us to the capital of California—which we reached at a late hour of the night.

So impatient was I to obtain the information, which had brought me to San Francisco, that on the instant of my arrival I went in search of the tavern, kept by Mr Wilson.

I succeeded in finding it, though not without some difficulty. It was a dirty house in a dirty street—the resort of all the worthless characters that could have been collected from the low neighbourhood around it, chiefly runaway convicts, and gay women, from Sydney. It was just such a hostelrie, as I might have expected to be managed by a quondam companion of Mr Leary.

Mr Wilson was at "home," I was at once ushered into his presence; and, after a very informal introduction, I commenced making him acquainted with my business.

I asked him, if, while at Sydney, he had the pleasure of being acquainted with a man named Mathews.

"Mathews! Let me see!" said he, scratching his head, and pretending to be buried in a profound reflection; "I've certainly heard that name, somewhere," he continued, "and, perhaps, if you were to tell me what you want, I might be able to remember all about it."

I could perceive that my only chance of learning anything from Mr Wilson was to accede to his proposal, which I did. I told him, that a man named Mathews had been hung a few weeks before on the Stanislaus, that it was for the murder of a young girl, with whom he had eloped from Australia; and that I had reason to believe, that the man had left a wife behind him in Sydney. I had heard that he, Mr Wilson, had known Mathews; and could perhaps tell me, if such had been the case.

"If it was the Mathews I once knew something about," said the tavern-keeper, after listening to my explanation, "he could not have left any money, or property, behind him: he hadn't a red cent to leave."

"I didn't say that he had," I answered. "It is not for that I make the inquiry."

"No!" said the tavern-keeper, feigning surprise. "Then what can be your object, in wanting to know whether he left a wife in Sydney?"

"Because that wife, if there be one, is my mother."

This answer was satisfactory; and Mr Wilson, after healing it, became communicative.

He had no objections to acknowledge acquaintance with a man who had been hung—after my having admitted that man's wife to be my mother; and, freely confessed, without any further circumlocution, that he had been intimate with a man named Mathews, who had eloped from Sydney with a shopkeeper's daughter. He supposed it must be the same, that I claimed as my stepfather.

Wilson's Mathews had arrived in Sydney several years before. About a year after his arrival he was followed by his wife from Dublin—with whom he had lived for a few weeks, and then deserted her.

Wilson had seen this woman; and from the description he gave me of her, I had no doubt that she was my mother.

The tavern-keeper had never heard of her, after she had been deserted by Mathews, nor could he answer any question: as to whether she had brought my children to the colony. He had never heard of her children.

This was the sum and substance of the information I obtained from Mr Wilson.

My mother, then, had actually emigrated to Australia; and there, to her misfortune, no doubt, had once more discovered the ruffian who had ruined her.

Where was she now? Where were her children? My brother William, and my little sister Martha, of whom I was once so fond and proud?

"I must visit Australia," thought I, "before going back to England. Until I have recovered my relatives I am not worthy to stand in the presence of Lenore!"

Volume Two—Chapter Ten.

The Partner of the Impatient Man.

As my return to Liverpool and Lenore was now indefinitely postponed, I was in less haste to leave San Francisco. I wished to see something of this singular city, which had grown up, as it were, in a single day.

The citizens of the Californian capital—composed of the young and enterprising of all nations—were at that time, perhaps, the fastest people on record; and more of real and active life was to be seen in the streets of San Francisco in a single week, than in any other city in a month—or, perhaps, in a year.

The quick transformation of the place—from a quiet little seaport to a large commercial city—astonished, even those who had witnessed its growth, and played a part in the history of its development.

Half of the present city is built upon ground, which was once a portion of the bay, and under the water of the sea. Boats used to ply where splendid buildings now stand—in the very centre of the town!

On my visit to San Francisco on this occasion, I saw fine substantial houses, where, only one year before, wild bushes were growing—on the branches of which the bachelors of the place used to dry their shirts! Mountains had been removed—carried clear into the bay—and hundreds of acres had been reclaimed from the encroachments of the sea.

Twice, too—within a period of only two years—the city had been burned down, and rebuilt; and for all this work that had been done, prices had been paid, that would seem extravagant beyond belief—at least, when compared with the small wages of labour, in any other country than California.

The amusements, manners, and customs, of almost every nation upon earth, could, at this time, have been witnessed in San Francisco. There was a Spanish theatre patronised by Chilians, Peruvians, and Mexicans. For the amusement of these people there was also a "Plaza de Toros," or amphitheatre for their favourite pastime—the bull fight.

In visiting these places of amusement—or the French and Italian opera houses—or some of the saloons where Germans met to continue the customs of their "Faderland"—one could scarce have supposed himself within the limits of a country, whose citizens were expected to speak English.

I paid a visit to all the afore-mentioned spectacles, and many others—not wholly for the sake of amusement; but to learn something of the varied phases of life there presented to observation. I could have fancied, that, in one evening, I had been in Spain, France, Italy, Germany, China, and over all parts of both North and South America!

For several days I wandered about the streets of San Francisco, without meeting a single individual I had ever seen before.

I was beginning to feel as if I knew no one in the world, when one afternoon I was accosted by a person bearing a familiar face.

It was Farrell, whom I had known at the diggings of the Stanislaus—the partner of the impatient man, who used to worry the postmaster of Sonora; and who had gone home in such haste, after learning of the death of his wife.

"Come along with me," cried Farrell, "I have got a queer story to tell you."

I accompanied him to the "Barnum House," where he was staying; and we sat down to have a talk and a drink.

"You were quite right about that fellow Foster," said he, as soon as we had got settled in our chairs; "a more treacherous deceitful villain never trod Californian turf—nor any other, for that matter."

"You are a little mistaken." I replied, "I never accused him of being either treacherous, or deceitful."

"Do you not remember our having a talk about him, the evening before he started home; and my telling you, that he was an honest, plain-speaking fellow?"

"Yes; and I remember telling you, that if your statement, of the reason of his anxiety to get his letters, was true, he could not be so very deceitful, or he would have had the decency to have concealed the cause of that anxiety even from you."

"I have never been more deceived in my life, than I was in that man," continued Farrell. "Do you know why he was so desirous to hear of his wife's death?"

"You said something about another woman."

"I did. Who do you suppose that other woman was?"

"I haven't the slightest idea."

"I'll tell you then. *It was my wife!* He wanted his own wife to die, so that he could go home and elope with mine. It's a fact—*and he's done it too.* That's who the second epistle he used to get, was from. I have just got a letter from my brother, giving me the whole news. It's interesting, isn't it?"

"Yes; what are you going to do?"

"Find them, and kill them both!" said Farrell, hissing the words through his teeth.

"I should not do that. A man is fortunate in getting rid of a wife, who would treat him after that fashion. Your thanks are rather due to your fair-dealing friend, for relieving you of any further trouble with such a woman."

"There's some truth in what you say," rejoined Farrell. "But I don't like being humbugged. He was such a plain-speaking fellow, I wonder why he didn't tell me what he was intending to do, and who was writing to him all the time. In that case, perhaps, I should have made no objection to his running away with her. But there *is* one thing, I should have decidedly objected to."

"What is that?"

"Furnishing the money to pay their travelling expenses—as well as to keep them comfortably wherever they have gone."

"Did you do that?"

"I did. When Foster left the Stanislaus to go home, I entrusted all my gold to him—to take home to my precious wife. For all his frank open ways, and plain-speaking, he did not tell me that he intended to assist my wife in spending it; and that's what gives me the greatest chagrin. I've been regularly sold. Over every dollar of that money—as they are eating or drinking it—will they be laughing at the fool who worked so damned hard to make it. Now I don't like that; and I should like to know who would. Would you?"

"Not exactly. But where do you expect to find them?"

"In this city—San Francisco."

"What! They surely would not be such simpletons as to come out to California, and you here?"

"That's just what they'll do," replied Farrell. "They'll think their best plan to keep clear of me, will be to leave the States, and get out here, by the time I would be likely to reach home. They will expect me to start from this place, the moment I hear the news of their elopement; and that by coming here, they will be safe not to see me again—thinking I would never return to California. For that reason I don't intend going home at all; but shall stay here till they arrive."

After spending the evening in his company, I admonished the injured husband—in the event of his meeting with his false partner and friend—to do nothing he might afterwards regret.

Farrell and I then parted; and I saw no more of him before leaving San Francisco.

I sojourned another week in the capital of California; and, having learned enough of its mysteries and miseries, I began to make preparation for my voyage across the Pacific.

An eminent banking firm in London had established an agency in San Francisco; and by it I forwarded to England all the gold I had collected—excepting a few ounces retained for my travelling expenses to Australia.

I found no difficulty in obtaining a passage from San Francisco to the latter place. Gold-diggings had been recently discovered in New South Wales—in Port Philip, as Victoria was then called; and as many people from the colonies wished to return, for their accommodation, numbers of large ships were being "laid on" for Sydney and Melbourne.

There is no class of passenger so profitable as the gold-digger *going away from a diggings*; and this being a fact, well-known among the captains and owners of ships, there was no scarcity in the supply of vessels then fitting out in the harbours of California.

Volume Two—Chapter Eleven.

A Difference among Diggers.

I engaged passage in the Dutch brig "Ceres," bound for Sydney; and sailed in the early part of June out of San Francisco Bay.

When I again embark as a passenger in a Dutch vessel, it will be after I have learnt to speak that detestable lingo. Of all the crew of the "Ceres," only the first officer could speak a word of English; and, during the time I was aboard the brig, I discovered more than one good reason for my resolve never again to embark in a ship, where I could not understand the language by which she was worked.

A majority of the passengers had originally come from the Australian Colonies to California; and were now returning to their homes—dissatisfied with a country, where they were not regarded as good citizens.

The worst characters amongst them had conceived a strong antipathy for everything American.

This will be easily understood, by taking into consideration the fact, that many of the people from the Australian Colonies who went to California, were men of infamous character. Indeed it is rather to the credit of the Californians: that they had treated with some severity these English convicts, who had made their appearance amongst them, for the express purpose of thieving and robbing.

I do not wish to be understood as saying, that all the gold seekers from Australia were of this character. I formed the acquaintance of many Anglo-Australian diggers, who had won the respect of all who knew them.

Too many of the class, however, were undoubtedly bad men. They had been bad men in their mother country, were bad men in the colonies, bad in California; and will continue to be bad wherever they go. They justly merited the contempt, which the Americans had bestowed upon them.

I have more respect for the great nation to which I belong than to defend the conduct of its convicts, against the opinions formed of them by the people of California.

There were three or four Californians amongst the passengers of the "Ceres," who appeared to be respectable, as they were well conducted young men, yet they were intensely hated by a majority of the passengers—merely because they were Americans, and not English convicts from the colonies.

The Australians, while in California, when not drunk, generally behaved themselves like other people. This, however, arose from the absolute compulsion of circumstances, and the dread of being punished for their misdeeds; but no sooner had we got clear of the Golden Gate, than they resumed their former vulgar habits of acting and speaking; and not a sentence could be uttered by one of them, without reference to the circulating fluid of the body.

Early in the month of August, we came in sight of one of the numerous groups of islands with which the Pacific ocean is enamelled.

About twelve o'clock at night—while going at a speed of not more than five knots an hour—we ran straight upon a reef of rocks.

A scene of wild confusion then ensued—every one expecting the brig to go immediately to the bottom—but it was soon ascertained, that she was hanging or resting on a point of the rocks, which had penetrated her timbers; and that she was in no immediate danger of sinking. Fortunately the weather was calm at the time, and the sea perfectly tranquil, else the brig would certainly have been knocked to pieces.

As usual, the long boat was found to be *not* sea-worthy; and there was but one other, a small pinnace, that would hold about twelve of the seventy-six passengers comprising the cargo of the "Ceres"—to say nothing of her crew!

We could see land, about a mile from our position; and it was evident, that no watch could have been kept aboard; else the brig could not have been lost.

As soon as order had been somewhat restored, and our exact situation ascertained, the crew, assisted by the passengers, commenced building a raft, upon which, when finished, we were to attempt making a passage to the shore.

At daybreak we obtained a better view of the land—indistinctly seen during the darkness. It was a small island—apparently about three miles in circumference—with groves of palm trees standing thickly over it.

The raft having been at length got ready, the work of landing commenced.

By nine o'clock all hands were ashore; and then some efforts were made towards transporting to the beach such provisions as could be saved from the wreck of the brig.

The men, who first volunteered their services for this duty, were some of the most disreputable of the passengers.

Their object in returning to the brig was simply to plunder. The boxes belonging to their fellow-passengers were broken open by these scoundrels, who appropriated to themselves every article of value they could conceal about their persons.

When the work of saving the provisions really commenced, it was found that there was but little to be saved. All the bread, and most of the other stores, had got soaked in the sea-water, and consequently spoilt. A barrel of beef, and another of pork, were all the stores that could be procured in a fit condition for food.

Before we had been ashore over an hour, we became acquainted with the unpleasant circumstance that no fresh water was to be found upon the island.

This intelligence produced great consternation; and the wreck was revisited—for the purpose of ascertaining if any could be procured there. But very little water fit for drinking could be had on board the brig—most of her supply being down in the hold, and of course submerged entirely out of reach.

Some mining tools and American axes had constituted a portion of the cargo. Some of these were now brought ashore, and put into requisition in the search for water.

With the picks and shovels we scooped out a deep hole in the centre of the island, which, to the delight of all, soon became filled with the wished-for fluid.

Our joy was of short continuance. We tasted the water. It was briny as the billows of the ocean. It was the sea-water itself—that went and came with the tides.

Next morning, the captain and six men were despatched in the pinnace—in the hope of then finding some ship to take us off, or reaching some inhabited island—where they might obtain the means of assisting us.

They took with them nearly all the water that remained—leaving over seventy people to depend on the milk of cocoa-nuts as a substitute.

To go out to sea in an open boat, with but a short allowance of water, and some salt beef, was not a very pleasant undertaking; but the captain and his crew seemed highly elated at even this opportunity of getting away from the island. They preferred their chances to ours.

Although the island was small, there was a sufficient quantity of fruit growing upon it to have supported us for many weeks. The chief trouble to be apprehended, was from the lawless wretches who comprised a large minority of the passengers.

After the shipwreck, these men became possessed with the idea: that they were no longer to be under any restraint. The only law they appeared disposed to regard was, that of might; and there was a sufficient number of them to give trouble should they combine in any evil design.

The old convicts, of course, felt sympathy for, and aided one another, while those of the passengers that were honestly inclined, gave themselves too little concern, on the score of combination.

The consequences were, that matters soon proceeded to a state of dangerous insubordination; and each hour it was becoming more evident, that those who wished to live without molesting others, or being molested themselves, must enter into a league against the scoundrels, who would otherwise devote the whole community to destruction.

Volume Two—Chapter Twelve.

Government Agreed Upon.

The more respectable of the castaways were now convinced that some form of government was necessary; and that it should be a strong one. Some who had been willing to acknowledge the authority of the officers of the brig while aboard their craft, would now no longer concede it to them; and yet authority of some kind was essential to our salvation.

We had much to do. The boat had gone away in search of assistance. It might be lost; and the captain and crew along with it. Even if they should succeed in reaching some inhabited land, they might never return to us? There was no wisdom in trusting to that source for relief. We must do something for ourselves.

A new vessel might be built from the materials of the wreck; but to accomplish this we should have to adopt some form of government, and submit to its authority.

There was another and still stronger reason why some ruling power should be established. The cocoa-nuts grew at a height rather inconvenient for a hungry or thirsty man to reach them; and a readier and simpler way of obtaining them was by felling the trees. As we were well supplied with axes brought from the wreck, those so inclined were able to effect this object; and, before we had been three days ashore, many of the trees were thus ruthlessly levelled to the ground.

Considering, that we might have to reside on the island for weeks, or even months, and that our only substitute for water was the milk to be obtained from these cocoa-nuts, it was evident that the trees should not be destroyed.

A meeting of all hands was at length got together; and a committee of five appointed, to form some regulations by which we should all agree to be governed.

Next day, something in the shape of order was inaugurated. We were divided into three parties—to each of which special duties were assigned. One party was entrusted with the business of carpentering. They were to take the wreck to pieces, and construct out of the fragments a new vessel. This party comprised half of the able-bodied men on the island; and was placed under the control of the first officer of the brig—with the carpenter to instruct them in their new duties.

Another party was appointed to act as fishermen—which calling also included the gathering of such shell-fish as could be found along the shore.

The third party—principally composed of the invalids—were to act as cooks, and fill other light offices, while a few young men who were expert in climbing the cocoa-nut trees, were specially appointed for procuring the nuts.

A chief statute of our improvised code was: that any one who should cut down, or in any way injure, a cocoa-nut tree, so as to cause its destruction, was, on conviction of the offence, to be shot!

The punishment may appear out of proportion to the offence; but when it is considered that our very existence might depend on the preservation of these precious trees, it will be seen at once, that the crime was of no light character.

A majority of those who voted for this resolution were in earnest; and I am positive that, any one acting in opposition to it, would have suffered the punishment of death.

Some of the old convicts were much opposed to the arrangements thus made; but they were compelled to submit, and act in accordance with them.

These men were masters of the island when we first landed; and seemed to think, they had the right to help themselves to whatever they wished, without regard to the general good.

Two of these "Sydney birds," who chanced to be a shade worse than their fellows—were specially informed, that if they should be caught violating the rules we had established, no mercy would be shown them.

A man of some influence amongst the more respectable of the passengers, had detected one of these worthies in possession of some articles that had been taken out of his chest on board the brig. He not only compelled a quick surrender of the misappropriated chattel, but promised for the future to watch for an opportunity of sending the thief where he would be in no danger of repeating the theft. Several others threw out hints to the two men to behave themselves—telling them that their only chance of life would be to act honestly, otherwise they would certainly meet with immediate chastisement. Such hints were effectual; and for a time the peace of the community remained undisturbed.

Three weeks passed—during which the work of ship-building progressed, as well as could be expected. The wreck had been taken to pieces, and floated ashore; and from the materials a tolerable commencement had been made in the construction of a new craft.

At this time serious fears began to be entertained, that many of us must die for the want of water. The cocoa-nuts were each day becoming scarcer; the trees did not grow them as fast as they were consumed; and a close watch was kept on the actions of every one in the community—in order that no one should have more than his share.

This duty was very harassing: as it had to be performed by the honest and respectable men, who were far from being the majority among us.

To our great relief, we were one night favoured by a fall of rain.

It rained but very little—a mere shower—and we had a good deal of trouble in collecting it. All the shirts on the island, clean or dirty, as they chanced to be, were spread out upon the grass; and, when saturated with the rain, were wrung into vessels.

Every exertion was made to save as much water as possible; and not without some success: for a sufficient quantity was collected to place us beyond the fear of want for several days longer.

Some of the men began to suffer severely from the want of tobacco. Only those, who had originally acted in the salvage of the wreck, were in possession of this precious commodity—having freely helped themselves while in the performance of that duty. Some of them did not refuse to sell a portion of their stock; and small plugs of tobacco, weighing about a quarter of a pound, readily found purchasers at ten dollars the plug!

One man, on paying his "eagle" for a pair of these plugs, was heard to remark: "Well! this is the second time I've bought this tobacco, though the price has been awfully raised since my first purchase. I know these plugs well. They've been taken out of my own chest!"

The person from whom the tobacco was purchased seemed highly amused, and not a little flattered. He was proud to think the purchaser did not take him for a fool!

It gradually became the conviction of all: that we should have to depend on our own vessel for getting away from the island. It was not a very agreeable prospect: since we knew that we should have to put to sea, with but little food and less water. Even from the first, it had seemed exceedingly doubtful that the captain would ever return.

Some were of the opinion that he could not, even if inclined; that he knew not the position of the island, on which we had been cast away; and, consequently, could give no instructions about finding it—even should he be so fortunate as to fall in with a ship.

There were many probabilities in favour of this belief; and those who entertained it did not fail to bring them forward.

"If he knew where the island lay," argued they, "why was the brig run ashore upon it on a calm, clear night?"

Certainly this question suggested a very discouraging answer.

At the end of the fifth week, our new vessel was nearly completed; and we set industriously to the collecting of shell-fish, cocoa-nuts, and other articles of food, to serve as stores for our intended voyage.

The craft we had constructed was not a very beautiful creature to look at; but I have no doubt it would have answered the purpose for which we had designed it.

By good fortune, we were never called upon to make trial of its sailing qualities. Just as we were about to launch it, a ship was seen bearing down for the island!

Before her anchor was dropped, a boat was seen shoving off for the shore; and, soon after, we had the pleasure of looking once more on the cheerful, honest countenance of the old Dutch skipper.

He had not deserted us in our distress, as some had conjectured: and he *did* know the situation of the island, as was proved by his bringing the ship back to it.

At the time of his departure, he had not a friend amongst the passengers of the "Ceres." There was not one on that occasion to speak a word in his favour. But now, as soon as he set foot on the island, he was hailed with three hearty cheers, and there was a struggle among the crowd who surrounded him: as to who should be the first to show their gratitude by a grasp of the hand!

Volume Two—Chapter Thirteen.

A Hungry Passage.

The ship thus brought to our rescue was a New England whaler, that had been cruising about in pursuit of the sperm whale. The captain asked six hundred dollars for taking our whole community to New Zealand.

The demand was by no means extortionate. Indeed, it was a moderate sum—considering the trouble and expense he would have to incur: since he had already lost a good deal of time on his way to the island.

The voyage to New Zealand might occupy several weeks—during which time we would be consuming no small quantity of his stores.

But although this price was not too much for the Yankee skipper to ask, it was more than the Dutch skipper was able to pay: since the latter had not got the money.

The passengers were called upon to subscribe the amount. Most of them objected. They had paid a passage once, they said, and would not pay it over again.

To this the captain of the whaler made a very reasonable rejoinder. If there were just grounds for believing that the money could not be obtained, he would have to take us without it: for he could never leave so many men on so small an island, where they might perish for want of food and water. But as we did not claim to be out of funds, the fault would be our own if he departed without us, which he would certainly do, unless the passage-money was paid. He also gave us warning, that we might expect to put up with many inconveniences upon his ship. She was not a passenger-vessel, nor was he supplied with provisions for so many people.

It was clear that the six hundred dollars must be raised some way or other; and a movement was immediately set on foot to collect it.

Many of the passengers declared that they had no money. Some of them spoke the truth; but the difficulty was to learn who did, and who did not.

Amongst others, who solemnly declared that they had no money, was a ruffian, who had been selling tobacco at the rate of forty dollars per pound. This fact was communicated by the individual, who had repurchased, and paid so dearly, for his own weed.

The fellow was now emphatically informed, that unless he paid his share of the passage-money, he would be left behind upon the island.

This threat had the desired effect. He succeeded in finding the required cash; and after much wrangling, the sum of six hundred dollars was at length made up.

Next day we were taken aboard the whaler; and sailed away from the island in a direct course for the port of Auckland.

I never made a more disagreeable voyage than on board that whaler. There were several reasons that rendered the passage unpleasant. One was, that all on board were in an ill-conditioned frame of mind; and, consequently, had no relish for being either civil or sociable. The diggers had been detained several weeks—on their way to a land they were anxious to reach in the shortest possible time—and they now were to be landed at Auckland instead of Sydney. Another voyage would have to be made, before they could arrive at the gold fields of Australia—of which they had been hearing such attractive tales.

We were not even favoured with a fair breeze. On the contrary, the wind blew most of the way against us; and the ship had to make about three hundred miles, while carrying us only fifty in the right direction.

The whaler, moreover, was an old tub—good enough for her proper purpose, but ill adapted for carrying impatient passengers on their way to a new gold field.

She was kept as much into the wind as possible; but withal made so much lee-way, that her course was side-ways—in the same manner as a pig would go into a battle.

There were no accommodations either for sleeping, or eating the little food we were allowed; and we were compelled to rough it in the most literal sense of the phrase.

By the time we should have reached Auckland, we were not half the distance; and both the provisions and water of the ship were well nigh consumed.

Between seventy and eighty hungry and thirsty men—added to the original crew of the whaler—had made a greater destruction of his ship's stores than the captain had calculated upon; and the third week, after leaving the island, we were put on an allowance of one quart of water per diem to each individual. Meat was no longer served out to us; and simple, though not very sweet, biscuits became our food. We were also allowed rice; but this, without garnishing, was still more insipid than the biscuits.

We thought it hard fare, and complained accordingly, although we had but little reason for doing so. We could only blame our fate, or our fortune; and so the captain of the whaler was accustomed to tell us.

"I warned you," he would say, "that you might expect to have a hard time of it. I'm sure I did not advertise for you to take passage in my vessel, and you have no reason to complain. I do the best for you I can. You are growling about having to eat rice. Millions of people live on it for years, while working hard. You have only to live on it for a few days, and do nothing. I hope, for both our sakes, it won't last long."

It was just, because they were *doing nothing* that the grumblers were so loud in their complaints.

In justice to many of the passengers, I should state, that those who complained the most were the very men who had paid nothing towards remunerating the captain for his services. They were some of the worst characters aboard; and, without making any allowance for the circumstances under which we were placed, found fault with everything on the whaler. I believe, they did so for the simple reason that she was an American ship.

Luckily we reached Auckland at last, though not a day too soon: for by the time we sighted land the patience of the passengers with each other, and their temper towards the captain, were well nigh exhausted. Had we remained at sea a few hours longer, some strange scenes would have taken place on the whaler, which all aboard of her would not have survived to describe.

No doubt the Yankee captain saw us go over the side of his ship with much heart-felt satisfaction, though certainly this feeling was not all to himself. His late passengers, one and all, equally participated in it.

I saw but very little of Auckland, or rather of the country around it; but, from that little, I formed a very favourable opinion of its natural resources and abilities; and I believe that colony to be a good home for English emigrants.

Being myself a Rolling Stone, I did not regard it with the eyes of a settler; and therefore I might be doing injustice either to the colony itself, or to intending emigrants, by saying much about it.

Guided by recent experiences, there is one thing I can allege in favour of New Zealand as a colony, which, in my opinion, makes it superior to any other; that is, that a home can be there had *farther away from London*, than in any other colonial settlement with which I am acquainted.

From Auckland to reach any part of Australia required a further outlay of six pounds sterling.

The gold-diggers thought this rather hard—alleging that they had already paid their passage twice; but they were forced to submit to circumstances.

For myself, after remaining in Auckland a few days, I obtained a passage in a small vessel sailing for Sydney, which port we reached, after a short and pleasant run of nine days' duration.

I had been exactly five months in getting from San Francisco to Sydney—a voyage that, under ordinary circumstances, might have been made in fifty days!

Volume Two—Chapter Fourteen.

The Guardians of the Orphan.

I had at length reached the place where, in all probability, I should find my long-lost mother.

A few days might find me happy, with my relatives restored to me, and all of us on our way to Liverpool—where I should see Lenore!

I felt a very singular sort of pleasure, in the anticipation of an interview with my mother and sister. They would not know me: for I was but a boy, when I parted from them in Dublin. They would scarce believe that the fair-skinned, curly-haired, little "Rolling Stone," could have become changed to a large bearded man—with a brow tanned by the South Sea gales, and the hot tropical beams of a Californian sun.

Before leaving San Francisco I had obtained the address of the grandparents of Mr Leary's child; and also of several other people in Sydney—who would be likely to have known something of Leary himself residing there.

From some of these persons I hoped to obtain information, that would guide me in the search after my relatives.

Mr Davis—the father of the unfortunate girl who had eloped with Leary—was a respectable shopkeeper in the grocery line.

As there could be no great difficulty in finding his shop, I resolved to make my first call upon the grocer.

Notwithstanding my hatred to Leary, I felt some interest in the child he had helped to make an orphan. I wished to ascertain, whether it had been safely delivered into the charge of its grandparents—as also the gold, which the Californian miners had so liberally contributed towards its support.

The next day after landing in Sydney, I made my call upon Mr Davis.

I found his shop without any difficulty; and in it himself—an honest-looking man, apparently about fifty years of age.

His business appeared to be in a flourishing condition: for the establishment was a large one, and to all appearance well-stocked with the articles required in a retail grocery.

There were two young men behind the counter, besides Mr Davis himself, who, as I entered, was in the act of serving a customer.

On the old gentleman being told, that if he was not too much engaged, I should like a few minutes' conversation with him, he handed the customer over to one of his assistants; and conducted me into a sitting-room that adjoined the shop.

After complying with his request to be seated, I told him, I had lately arrived from California, where I had heard of him, and that I had now called to see him, on a business to me of some importance. I added, that the communication I had to make might awaken some unpleasant thoughts; but that I deemed it better to make it, rather than run the risk of incurring his displeasure, by not communicating with him at all.

Mr Davis then civilly demanded to know the nature of my business, though from his tone I could tell, that he already half comprehended it.

"If I am not mistaken," said I, "you have a child here, that has been sent you from California?"

"Yes," answered he, "one was brought to me from there, about four months ago. I was told that it was my grandchild; and I received it as such."

"And have you also received a sum of money, that was to have been intrusted to your care, for its benefit?" I asked.

"I have; and that was some proof to me that the child was really my grandchild."

To this sage observation of the grocer, I replied, by making to him a full disclosure of my object in visiting Sydney; and that I had called on himself to learn, if possible, something concerning my own mother.

"You could not have come to a better place to obtain that information," said he; "a woman calling herself Mrs Leary, and claiming to be the wife of the man who had been known here by the name of Mathews, calls here almost every day. If she be your mother, you will have no difficulty in finding her: she is a dress-maker, and my wife can tell you where she resides."

My task had proved much easier than I had any reason to expect; and I was now only impatient to obtain the address; and hasten to embrace my long-lost mother.

"Do not be too fast," said the cautious Mr Davis. "Wait until you have learnt something more. Let me ask you two or three questions. Do you know how the man Mathews died?"

"Yes: I saw him die."

"Then you know for what reason he was put to death?"

"I do," was my answer. "And you—?"

"I too—alas! too certainly," rejoined Mr Davis in a sorrowful tone. "But stay!" he continued, "I have something more to say to you, before you see the woman who calls herself his wife, and whom you believe to be your mother. She does not know that Mathews is dead. I did not wish it to go abroad, that my daughter had been murdered, and that the man with whom she eloped had been hanged for the deed. Her running away with him was sorrow and shame enough, without our acquaintances knowing any more. They think that my daughter died in a natural way; and that the man Mathews, has merely sent the child back to us, that we might bring it up for him. The woman, you think is your mother, believes this also; and that Mathews is still alive, and will soon return. She seems to love him, more than she does her own life. I have informed you of this, so that you may know how to act. She comes here often to see the child—because her husband was its father. She is a strange woman: for she seems to love the little creature as though it was her own; and I have no doubt would willingly take sole charge of it on herself, were we to allow her."

All this was strange information, and such as gave me exceeding pain. It was evident that my unfortunate mother had profited nothing by the experience of the past. She was as much infatuated with Leary as ever—notwithstanding that he had again deserted her, after she had made a voyage of sixteen thousand miles to rejoin him!

I saw Mrs Davis and the young Leary. It was an interesting child—a boy, and bore no resemblance to the father, that I could perceive. Had it done so, I should have hated it; and so did I declare myself in the presence of its grandmother. In reply to this avowal, the old lady informed me that Mrs Leary and I held a different opinion upon the point of the child's resemblance: for she thought it a perfect image of its father, and that was the reason why she was so dotingly fond of it!

"Thank God!" said the grandmother, "that I myself think as you do. No. The child has no resemblance to its unworthy father. I am happy in thinking, that in every feature of its face it is like its mother—my own unfortunate child. I could not love it were it not for that; but now I don't know what I should do without it. God has surely sent us this little creature, as some compensation for the loss we sustained by being deprived of our dear daughter!"

The grief of the bereaved mother could not be witnessed without pain; and leaving her with the child in her arms, I withdrew.

Volume Two—Chapter Fifteen.

A Meeting with a Long-Lost Mother.

From Mrs Davis I had obtained my mother's address; and I went at once in search of the place.

Passing along the street, to which I had been directed, I saw a small, but neat-looking shop, with the words "*Mrs Leary, Milliner and Dress-Maker*" painted over the door. I had journeyed far in search of my mother; I had just arrived from a long voyage—which it had taken three ships to enable me to complete. The weariness of spirit, and impatience caused by the delay, had been a source of much misery to me; but now that the object of my search was found—and there was nothing further to do than enter the house and greet my long-lost relatives—strange enough, I felt as if there was no more need for haste! Instead of at once stepping into the house, I passed nearly an hour in the street—pacing up and down it, altogether undetermined how to act.

During that hour my thoughts were busy, both with the past and future: for I knew that in the interview I was about to hold with my mother, topics must come into our conversation of a peculiar kind, and such as required the most serious reflection on my part, before making myself known to her.

Should I make her acquainted with the ignominious termination of Mr Leary's career; and by that means endeavour to put an end to her strange infatuation for him? If what Mrs Davis had told me regarding her should turn out to be true, I almost felt as if I could no longer regard her as a mother. Indeed, when I reflected on her affection for such a wretch as Leary, I could not help some risings of regret, that I should have lost so much time, and endured so many hardships, in search of a relative who could be guilty of such incurable folly.

Notwithstanding the time spent in pacing through the street, I could determine on no definite course of action; and, at length, resolving to be guided by circumstances, I stepped up to the house, and knocked at the door.

It was opened by a young woman, about nineteen years of age.

I should not have known who she was, had I not expected to meet relatives; but the girl was beautiful, and just such as I should have expected to find my sister Martha. My thoughts had so often dwelt upon my little sister; that I had drawn in my mind an imaginary portrait of her. Her blue eyes and bright hair, as well as the cast of her countenance, and form of her features, had ever remained fresh and perfect in my memory. I had only to gaze on the young girl before me, refer to my mental picture of little Martha, remember that eleven years had passed since last I saw her, and be certain that I had found my sister.

I knew it was she; but I said nothing to make the recognition mutual. I simply asked for Mrs Leary.

I was invited in; and requested to take a seat.

The apartment, into which I was conducted, seemed to be used as a sitting-room as well as a shop; and from its general appearance I could tell that my mother and sister were not doing a very flourishing business. There was enough, however, to satisfy me, that they were earning their living in a respectable manner.

To prevent being misunderstood, I will state, that, by a respectable manner, I mean that they, to all appearance, were supporting themselves by honest industry; and in my opinion there can be no greater evidence, that they were living a life that should command respect.

The young girl, without a suspicion of the character of her visitor, left me to summon the person for whom I had made inquiry; and in a few minutes time, Mrs Leary herself entered from an adjoining room. I saw at a glance that she was the woman I remembered as *mother*!

The face appeared older and more careworn; but the features were the same, that had lived so long in my memory.

It would be impossible to describe the strange emotions that crowded into my soul on once more beholding my long-lost, unfortunate mother. I know not why I should have been so strongly affected. Some may argue that a weak intellect is easily excited by trifles. They may be correct; but there is another phenomenon. A great passion can never have existence in a little soul; and I know that at that moment, a storm of strong passions was raging within mine.

I tried to speak, but could not. Language was not made for the thoughts that at that moment stirred within me.

It was not until I had been twice asked by my mother, what was my business, that I perceived the necessity of saying something.

But what was I to say? Tell her that I was her son?

This was what common sense would have dictated; but, just at that crisis, I did not happen to have any sense of this quality about me. My thoughts were wandering from the days of childhood up to that hour; they were in as much confusion, as though my brains had been stirred about with a wooden spoon.

I contrived to stammer out something at last; and I believe the words were, "I have come to see you."

"If that is your only business," said my mother, "now that you have seen me, you may go again."

How familiar was the sound of her voice! It seemed to have been echoing, for years, from wall to wall in the mansion of my memory.

I made no effort to avail myself of the permission she had so curtly granted; but continued gazing at the two—my eyes alternately turning from mother to daughter—in a manner that must have appeared rude enough.

"Do you hear me?" said the old lady. "If you have no business here, why don't you go away?"

There was an energy in her tone that touched another chord of memory. "It is certainly my mother," thought I, "and I am at home once more."

My soul was overwhelmed with a thousand emotions—more strong than had ever stirred it before. I know not whether they were of pleasure or of pain: for I could not analyse them then, and have never felt them before or since.

My actions were involuntary: for my thoughts were too much occupied to guide them.

A sofa stood near; and, throwing myself upon it, I tried to realise the fact that eleven years had passed, since parting with my relatives a boy, and that I had met them again, and was a boy no longer!

"Martha!" cried my mother, "go and bring a policeman!"

The young girl had been gazing at me, long and earnestly. She continued her gaze, without heeding the command thus addressed to her.

"Mother," rejoined she, after an interval, "we have seen this man before; I'm sure I have."

"Did you not once live in Dublin, sir?" she asked, turning to me.

"Yes, I once lived there—when a boy," I answered.

"Then I must be mistaken," said she; "but I really thought I had seen you there."

There was something so very absurd in this remark, that I could not help noticing it—even in my abstracted state of mind; and this very absurdity had the effect of awakening me from my reverie.

It then suddenly occurred to the young girl, that she had not been in Dublin since she was a child herself; and, at the time she left that city, a young man of my appearance could not have been much more than a boy.

"Perhaps, I am right after all?" said she. "I do believe that I've seen you in Dublin. Mother!" she added, turning to the old lady; "He knows who we are."

Martha's first remark—about having seen me in Dublin—brought upon me the earnest gaze of my mother. She had often told me that when a man I would look like my father; and perhaps my features awakened within her some recollections of the past.

She came up to me; and, speaking in a low, earnest voice, said: "Tell me who you are!"

I arose to my feet, trembling in every limb.

"Tell me who you are! What is your name?" she exclaimed—becoming nearly as much excited as myself.

I could no longer refrain from declaring myself; and I made answer:—

"I am the Rolling Stone."

Had I been a small and weak man, I should have been crushed and suffocated by the embraces of my mother and sister—so demonstrative were they in their expressions of surprise and joy!

As soon as our excitement had, to some extent, subsided; and we were able to converse a rational manner, I inquired after my brother William.

"I left him apprenticed to a harness-maker in Liverpool," answered my mother.

"But where is he now?" I asked; "that was long ago."

My mother began to weep; and Martha made answer for her.

"William ran away from his master; and we have never heard of him since."

I requested to be informed what efforts had been made to find him. I was then told that my mother had written two or three times to the harness-maker; and from him had learnt that he had used every exertion, to discover the whereabouts of his runaway apprentice, but without success.

It appeared that my mother never liked to hear any one speak of William: for she had some unpleasant regrets at having left him behind her in Liverpool.

I consoled her, by saying that I had plenty of money, that William should be advertised for, and found; and that we should all again live happily together—as we had in years long gone by.

In all my life I was never more happy than on that evening. The future was full of hope.

It was true that much had yet to be done before my purposes could be fully accomplished. But a man with nothing to do, cannot be contented. We must ever have something to attain, or life is not worth the having.

I had yet something to live for. I had still a task to perform that might require much time and toil. I had yet to win Lenore!

Volume Two—Chapter Sixteen.

Mystified by Martha.

The next day I had a long conversation with my mother—as to what we should do in the future.

It resulted in my proposing, that we should return immediately to Liverpool.

"No! no!" protested she, with an eagerness that astonished me; "I cannot think of that. I must wait for the return of my husband."

"Your husband!"

"Yes! yes! Mr Leary. He has gone to California; but I have reason to believe that he will soon be back."

"Now that you have spoken of *him*," said I, "please to tell me all about him; and how he has used you since I left home."

"He has always been very kind to me," she answered, "very kind indeed. He has gone to the diggings in California, where I have no doubt but what he will do well, and come back with plenty of money."

"But I was told in Dublin that he deserted you there," said I. "Was that very kind indeed?"

"It is true; he did leave me there; but the business was doing badly, and he couldn't help going. I have no doubt but what he was sorry for it afterwards."

"Then you followed him here, and lived with him again?"

"Yes; and we were very happy."

"But I have been told by Mr Davis—whom you know—that he again deserted you here, and ran away to California with another woman. Is that true?"

"He did go to California," answered my foolish mother, "and I suppose that Miss Davis went with him; but I blame her more than him: for I'm sure she led him astray, or he would not have gone with her. However, I'll not say much against her: for I hear she is dead now, poor thing!"

"Knowing that she has deserted you twice, what leads you to think that he will again return to you?"

"Because *I know that he loves me*! He was always so kind and affectionate. The woman, who led him astray, is no longer alive to misguide him; and I know he will comeback to me."

"My poor deceived, trusting, foolish mother!"

I only muttered the words—she did not hear them.

"Besides," continued she, "gold is now being found here in Australia. Many of the miners are coming home again. I'm sure he will be among them. It is true, he is a little wild for his years; but he will not always be so. He will return to his wife; and we shall be once more happy."

"Mother! Am I to understand that you refuse to accompany me to England?"

"Rowland, my son," said she, in a reproachful tone, "how can you ask me to go away from here, when I tell you that I am every day expecting my husband to return? Wait awhile, till he comes; and then we will all go together."

Certainly to have said anything more to her on the subject would have been folly. It would be no use in trying to reason with her, after that proposal. The idea of my going aboard of a ship, on a long voyage, accompanied by Mr Leary—even supposing the man to have been in the land of the living—was too incongruous to be entertained and at the same time preserve tranquillity of spirit.

I was tempted to tell her, that Mr Leary had met the reward of his long career of crime—or, at least, a part of it—but, when I reflected on her extreme delusions concerning the man, I feared that such a communication might be dangerous to her mind.

From Martha I learnt what was indeed already known to me: that our mother had been all along willing and ready to sacrifice not only her own happiness, but that of her children, for the sake of this vile caitiff. My sister told me, that when they reached Liverpool, and found that Mr Leary had gone to Sydney, my mother determined to follow him immediately; and that William had been left behind in Liverpool, because she thought that coming without him she would be better received by the wretch whom she called her husband.

On reaching Sydney, they had found Mr Leary passing under the name of Mathews. He was at first disposed to have nothing to do with his Dublin wife; but having come to the knowledge that she was in possession of about fifteen pounds of the money received for her lease, he changed his mind; and lived with her, until he had spent every penny of it in drink and dissipation.

"Until he sailed for California," said Martha, "he used to come every day, and stay awhile with mother—whenever he thought that he could obtain a shilling by doing so; and then we saw him no more. Ah, Rowland! I have had much suffering since we were together. Many days have I gone without eating a morsel—in order that money might be saved for Mr Leary. Oh! I hope we shall never see him again!"

"You never will see him again," said I; "he is gone, where our poor mother will be troubled with him no more: he is dead."

Martha was an impulsive creature; and in her excitement at hearing the news, exclaimed—

"Thank God for it! No! no!" she continued, as if repenting what she had said, "I don't mean that; but if he is dead, it will be well for mother; he will never trouble her again."

I made known to my sister all the particulars of Leary's death. She agreed with me in the idea I had already entertained: that the intelligence could not with safety be communicated to our mother.

"I don't believe," said Martha, "that any woman in this world ever loved a man so much as mother does Mr Leary. I am sure, Rowland, it would kill her, to hear what you have just told me."

"But we must bring her to know it in some way," said I; "She must be told of his death: for I can see that she will not consent to leave Sydney, so long as she believes him to be alive. We cannot return to England, and leave her here; and it is evident she won't go with us, while she thinks there is the slightest chance of his coming back. We must tell her that he is dead, and take chance of the consequences."

My sister made no rejoinder to my proposal; and, while speaking, I fancied that my words, instead of being welcome, were having an unpleasant effect upon her!

Judging by the expression upon her features, I did not think it was fear for the result of any communication I might make to our mother, though what caused it, I could not guess.

Whenever I had spoken about returning to Europe, I observed that my sister did not appear at all gratified with my proposal, but the contrary!

I could not comprehend, why she should object to an arrangement, that was intended for the happiness of all. There was some mystery about her behaviour, that was soon to receive an elucidation—to me as unexpected, as it was painful.

Volume Two—Chapter Seventeen.

My Mother Mad!

I was anxious at once to set sail for Liverpool—taking my mother and sister along with me. Of the money I had brought from San Francisco, there was still left a sufficient sum to accomplish this purpose; but should I remain much longer in Sydney, it would not be enough. I had determined not to leave my relatives in the colony; and the next day a long consultation took place, between myself and Martha, as to how we should induce our mother to return to England. My idea was, to let her know that Leary was dead—then tell her plainly of the crime he had committed, as also the manner of his death. Surely, on knowing these things, she would no longer remain blind to his wickedness; but would see the folly of her own conduct, and try to forget the past, in a future, to be happily spent in the society of her children?

So fancied I. To my surprise, Martha seemed opposed to this plan of action, though without assigning any very definite reasons for opposing it.

"Why not be contented, and live here, Rowland?" said she; "Australia is a fine country; and thousands are every year coming to it from England. If we were there, we would probably wish to be back here. Then why not remain where we are?"

My sister may have thought this argument very rational, and likely to affect me. It did; but in a different way from that intended. Perhaps my desire to return to Lenore hindered me from appreciating the truth it contained.

I left Martha, undetermined how to act, and a good deal dissatisfied with the result of our interview. It had produced within me a vague sense of pain. I could not imagine why my sister was so unwilling to leave the colony, which she evidently was.

I was desirous to do everything in my power, to make my new-found relatives happy. I could not think of leaving them, once more unprotected and in poverty; and yet I could not, even for them, resign the only hope I had of again seeing Lenore.

I returned to the hotel, where I was staying. My thoughts were far from being pleasant companions; and I took up a newspaper, in hopes of finding some relief from the reflections that harassed my spirit. Almost the first paragraph that came under my eye was the following:—

Another Atrocity in California.—Murder of an English Subject.—We have just received reliable information of another outrage having been committed in California, on one of those who have been so unfortunate as to leave these shores for that land of bloodshed and crime. It appears, from the intelligence we have received, that a woman was, or was supposed to have been, murdered, at the diggings near Sonora. The American population of the place, inspired by their prejudices against English colonists from Australia, and by their love for what, to them, seems a favourite amusement—Lynch Law—seized the first man from the colonies they could find; and hung him upon the nearest tree!

We understand the unfortunate victim of this outrage is Mr Mathews—a highly respectable person from this city. We call upon the Government of the Mother Country to protect Her Majesty's subjects from these constantly recurring outrages of lawless American mobs. Let it demand of the United States Government, that the perpetrators of this crime shall be brought to punishment. That so many of Her Majesty's loyal subjects have been murdered, by blind infuriated mobs of Yankees, is enough to make any true Englishman blush with shame for the Government that permits it.

There is one circumstance connected with the above outrage, which illustrates American character; and which every Englishman will read with disgust. When the rope was placed around the neck of the unfortunate victim, a young man stepped forward, and claimed him as his father! This same ruffian gave the word to the mob, to pull the rope that hoisted their unfortunate victim into eternity! So characteristic a piece of American wit was, of course, received by a yell of laughter from the senseless mob. Comment on this case is unnecessary.

Regarding this article as a literary curiosity, I purchased a copy of the paper containing it, by preserving which, I have been enabled here to reproduce it *in extenso*.

On reading the precious statement, one thing became very plain, that my mother could not remain much longer ignorant of Mr Leary's death; and, therefore, the sooner it should be communicated to her, in some delicate manner, the better it might be. It must be done, either by Martha or myself and at once.

I returned forthwith to the house—in time to witness a scene of great excitement. My mother had just read in the Sydney paper, the article above quoted; and the only description I can give, of the condition into which it had thrown her, would be to say, that she was mad—a raving lunatic!

Some women, on the receipt of similar news, would have fainted. A little cold water, or hartshorn, would have restored them to consciousness; and their sorrows would in time have become subdued. My mother's grief was not of this evanescent kind. Affection for Mathew Leary absorbed her whole soul, which had received a mortal wound, on learning the fate that had unexpectedly, but justly, befallen the wretch.

"Rowland!" she screamed out, as I entered the house! "He is dead! He is murdered. He has been hung innocently, by a mob of wretches in California."

I resolved to do what is sometimes called "taking the bull by the horns."

"Yes, you are right, mother," said I. "If you mean Mr Leary, he *was hung innocently*; for the men who did the deed were guilty of no wrong. Mathew Leary deserved the fate that has befallen him."

My mother's intellect appeared to have been sharpened by her affliction, for she seemed to remember every word of the article she had read.

"Rowland!" she screamed, "you have come from California. You aided in murdering him. Ha! It was you who insulted him in the hour of death, by calling him father. O God! it was you."

The idea of my insulting Mathew Leary, by calling him father, seemed to me the most wonderful and original conception, that ever emanated from the human mind.

"Ha!" continued my mother, hissing out the words. "It was you that gave the word to the others—the word that brought him to death? You are a murderer! You are not my son! I curse you! Take my curse and begone! No, don't go yet! Wait 'till I've done with you!"

As she said this, she made a rush at me; and, before I could get beyond her reach, a handful of hair was plucked from my head!

When finally hindered from farther assailing me, she commenced dragging out her own hair, all the while raving like a maniac!

She became so violent at length, that it was found necessary to tie her down; and, acting under the orders of a physician, who had been suddenly summoned to the house, I took my departure—leaving poor Martha, weeping by the side of a frantic woman, whom we had the misfortune to call mother.

How long to me appeared the hours of that dreary night. I passed them in an agony of thought, that would have been sufficient punishment, even for Mr Leary—supposing him to have been possessed of a soul capable of feeling it.

I actually made such reflection while tossing upon my sleepless couch!

It had one good effect; it summoned reason to my aid; and I asked myself: Why was I not like him, with a soul incapable of sorrow? What was there to cause me the agony I was enduring? I was young, and in good health: why was I not happy? Because my mother had gone mad with grief for the death of a wicked man? Surely that could be no cause for the misery I myself suffered, or should not have been to a person of proper sense? My mother had been guilty of folly, and was reaping its reward. Why should I allow myself to be punished also? It could not aid her: why should I give way to it?

"But your sister is also in sorrow," whispered some demon into the ear of my spirit, "and how can you be happy?"

"So are thousands of others in sorrow, and ever will be," answered reason. "Let those be happy who can. The fool who makes himself wretched because others are, will ever meet misery, and ever deserve it."

Selfish reason counselled in vain: for care had mounted my soul, and could not be cast off.

Volume Two—Chapter Eighteen.

A Melancholy End.

The next morning, I was forbidden by the physician to come into my mother's presence.

He said, that her life depended on her being kept tranquil; and he had learnt enough to know, that nothing would be more certain to injure her than the sight of myself. He feared that she would have an attack of brain fever, which would probably have a fatal termination.

I saw Martha; and conversed with her for a few minutes. My poor sister had also passed a sleepless night; and, like myself, was in great distress of mind.

Her affliction was even greater than mine: for she had never, like me, been separated from her mother.

The physician's fears were too soon realised. Before the day passed, he pronounced his patient to be under a dangerous attack of brain fever—a disease that, in New South Wales, does not trifle long with its victims.

That night the sufferings of my unhappy mother ceased—I hope, for ever.

For all that had passed, I felt sincere sorrow at her loss. For years had I been anticipating an exquisite pleasure—in sometime finding my relatives and providing them with a good home. I had found my mother at last, only to give me a fresh sorrow—and then behold her a corpse!

If this narrative had been a work of fiction, I should perhaps have shaped it in a different fashion. I should have told how all my long-cherished anticipations had been happily realised. In dealing with fiction, we can command, even fate, to fulfil our desires; but in a narrative of real adventures, we must deal with fate as it has presented itself, however much it may be opposed to our ideas of dramatic justice.

There are moments, generally met in affliction, when the most incredulous man may become the slave of superstition. Such was the case with myself, at that crisis, when sorrow for the loss of my mother, was strong upon me. I began to fancy that my presence boded death to every acquaintance or friend, with whom I chanced to come in contact.

Memory brought before me, the fate of Hiram, on our "prospecting" expedition in California, as also the melancholy end of the unfortunate Richard Guinane.

My truest friend, Stormy Jack, had met a violent death, soon after coming to reside with me; and now, immediately after finding my mother, I had to follow her remains to the grave!

Soon after we had buried our mother, I consulted Martha, as to what we should do. I was still desirous of returning to Liverpool; and, of course, taking my sister along with me. I proposed that we should start, without further loss of time.

"I am sorry you are not pleased with the colony," said she. "I know you would be, if you were to stay here a little longer. Then you would never wish to return."

"Do not think me so foolish," I answered, "as to believe that I have come to this place with the intention of remaining; and wish to leave it, without giving it a fair trial. I came here on business, that is now accomplished; and why should I stay longer, when business calls me elsewhere?"

"Rowland, my brother!" cried Martha, commencing to weep. "Why will you *go* and forsake me?"

"I do not wish to forsake you, Martha," said I. "On the contrary, I wish you to go along with me. I am not a penniless adventurer now; and would not ask you to accompany me to Liverpool, if I were not able to provide you with a home there, I offer you that, sister. Will you accept of it?"

"Rowland! Rowland!!" she exclaimed; "do not leave me! You are, perhaps, the only relative I have in the world. Oh! you will not desert me."

"Silence, Martha," said I. "Do not answer me again in that manner; or we part immediately, and perhaps for ever. Did you not understand me? I asked you to go with me to Liverpool; and you answer, by intreating me not to desert you. Say you are willing to go with me; or let me know the reason why you are not!"

"I do not wish to go to Liverpool," replied she; "I do not wish to leave Sydney. I have lived here several years. It is my home: and I don't like to leave it—I *cannot* leave it, Rowland!"

Though far from a satisfactory answer, I saw it was all I was likely to get, and that I should have to be contented with it. I asked no further questions—the subject was too painful.

I suspected that my sister's reasons for not wishing to leave Sydney, were akin to those that had hindered my mother from consenting to go with me. In all likelihood, my poor sister had some Mr Leary for whom she was waiting; and for whom she was suffering a similar infatuation?

It was an unpleasant reflection; and aroused all the selfishness of my nature. I asked myself: why I should not seek my own happiness in preference to looking after that of others, and meeting with worse than disappointment?

Perhaps it was selfishness that had caused me to cross the Pacific in search of my relations? I am inclined to think it was: for I certainly did fancy, that, the way to secure my own happiness was to find them and endeavour to make them happy. As my efforts had resulted in disappointment, why should I follow the pursuit any longer—at least, in the same fashion?

My sister was of age. She was entitled to be left to herself—in whatever way she wished to seek her own welfare. She had a right to remain in the colony, if she chose to do so.

I could see the absurdity of her trying to keep me from Lenore: and could therefore concede to her the right of remaining in the colony. Her motive for remaining in Sydney, might be as strong as mine was for returning to Liverpool?

I had the full affection of a brother for Martha; and yet I could be persuaded to leave her behind. Should I succeed in overcoming her objections—or in any manner force her to accompany me—perhaps misfortune might be the result: and then the fault would be mine.

At this time, there were many inducements for my remaining in the colonies. Astounding discoveries of gold were being daily made in Victoria; and the diggings of New South Wales were richly rewarding all those who toiled in them.

Moreover, I had been somewhat fascinated by the free, romantic life of the gold-hunter; and was strongly tempted once more to try my fortune upon the gold fields.

Still there was a greater attraction in Liverpool. I had been too long absent from Lenore; and must return to her. The desire of making money, or of aiding my relatives, could no longer detain me. I must learn, whether the future was worth warring for—whether my reward was to be, Lenore.

I told my sister that I should not any more urge her to accompany me—that I should go alone, and leave her, with my best wishes for her future welfare. I did not even require her to tell me the true reasons why she was not willing to leave Sydney: for I was determined we should part in friendship. I merely remarked that, we must no more be lost to each other's knowledge; but that we should correspond regularly. I impressed upon her at parting—ever to remember that she had a brother to whom she could apply, in case her unexplained conduct should ever bring regret.

My sister seemed much affected by my parting words; and I could tell that her motive for remaining behind was one of no ordinary strength. I resolved, before leaving her, to place her beyond the danger of immediate want.

A woman, apparently respectable, wished some one with a little money to join her in the same business, in which my mother and Martha had been engaged.

I was able to give my sister what money the woman required; and, before leaving, I had the satisfaction to see her established in the business, and settled in a comfortable home.

There was nothing farther to detain me in Sydney—nothing, as I fondly fancied, but the sea between myself and Lenore!

Volume Two—Chapter Nineteen.

News from Lenore.

A large clipper ship was about to sail for Liverpool; and I paid it a visit—in order to inspect the accommodations it might afford for a passenger.

I made up my mind to go by this vessel; and selected a berth in the second cabin. Before leaving the clipper, I came in contact with her steward; and was surprised at finding in him an old acquaintance.

I was agreeably surprised: for it was Mason—the man who had been steward of the ship Lenore—already known to the reader, as one of the men, who had assisted in setting me right with Mrs Hyland and her daughter. Mason was pleased to meet me again; and we had a talk over old times.

He told me, that since leaving Liverpool he had heard of Adkins; that he was the first officer of an American ship; and had won the reputation of being a great bully.

I told the steward in return that I had heard of Adkins myself at a later date—that I had in fact, seen him, in California, where I had been a witness to his death, and that he had been killed for indulging in the very propensity spoken of.

Mason and Adkins had never been friends, when sailing together; and I knew that this bit of information would not be received by the old steward in any very unpleasant manner. Nor was I mistaken.

"You remember Mrs Hyland, and her daughter?" said Mason, as we continued to talk. "What am I thinking of? Of course you do: since in Liverpool the captain's house was almost your home."

"Certainly," I answered; "I can never forget *them*."

On saying this, I spoke the words of truth.

"Mrs Hyland is now living in London," the steward continued. "She is residing with her daughter, who is married."

"What!" I exclaimed, "Lenore Hyland—married?"

"Yes. Have you not heard of it? She married the captain of a ship in the Australia trade, who, after the marriage, took her and her mother to London."

"Are you sure—that—that—you cannot be mistaken?" I asked, gasping for breath.

"Yes, quite sure," replied Mason. "What's the matter? you don't appear to be pleased at it?"

"Oh nothing—nothing. But what reason have you for thinking she is married?" I asked, trying to appear indifferent.

"Only that I heard so. Besides, I saw her at the Captain's house in London where I called on business. I had some notion of going a voyage with him."

"But are you sure the person you saw was Lenore—the daughter of Captain Hyland?"

"Certainly. How could I be mistaken? You know I was at Captain Hyland's house several times, and saw her there—to say nothing of that scene we had with Adkins, when we were all in Liverpool together. I could not be mistaken: for I spoke to her the time I was at her house in London. She was married about two years before to the captain of the Australian ship—a man old enough to be her father."

What reason had I to doubt Mason's word? None.

I went ashore with a soul-sickening sensation, that caused me to wish myself as free from the cares of this life, as the mother I had lately lowered into her grave.

How dark seemed the world!

The sun seemed no longer shining, to give light; but only to warm my woe.

The beacon that had been guiding my actions so brightly and well, had become suddenly extinguished; and I was left in a night of sorrow, as dark, as I should have deserved, had my great love been for crime instead of Lenore!

What had I done to be cursed with this, the greatest, misfortune Fate can bestow?

Where was my reward for the wear of body and soul, through long years of toil, and with that conscientious and steadfast spirit, the wise tell us, must surely win? What had *I* won? Only an immortal woe!

Thenceforth was I to be in truth, a "Rolling Stone," for the only attraction that could have bound me to one place, or to anything—even to life itself—had for ever departed from my soul.

The world before me seemed not the one through which I had been hitherto straying. I seemed to have fallen from some bright field of manly strife, down, far down, into a dark and dreary land—there to wander friendless, unheeded and unloved, vainly seeking for something, I knew not what, and without the hope, or even the desire of finding it!

I could not blame Lenore. She had broken no faith with me: none had been plighted between us. I had not even talked to her of love.

Had she promised to await my return—had she ever confessed any affection for me—some indignation, or contempt for her perfidy, might have arisen to rescue me from my fearful reflections.

But I was denied even this slight source of consolation. There was nothing for which I could blame her—nothing to aid me in conquering the hopeless passion, that still burned within my soul.

I had been a fool to build such a vast superstructure of hope on a foundation so flimsy and fanciful.

It had fallen; and every faculty of my mind seemed crushed amid the ruins.

In one way only was I fortunate. I was in a land where gold fields of extraordinary richness, had been discovered; and I knew, that there is no occupation followed by man—calculated to so much concentrate his thoughts upon the present, and abstract them from the past—as that of gold hunting.

Join a new rush to the gold fields, all ye who are weary in soul, and sorrow-laden, and the past will soon sink unheeded under the excitement of the present.

I knew that this was the very thing I now required; and, from the moment of receiving the unwelcome tidings communicated by Mason, I relinquished all thought of returning to Liverpool.

I did not tell my sister Martha of this sudden change in my designs; but, requesting her not to write, until she should first hear from me, I bade her farewell—leaving her in great grief, at my departure.

Twenty-four hours after, I was passing out of the harbour of Sydney—in a steamer bound for the city of Melbourne.

Volume Two—Chapter Twenty.

The Victoria Diggings.

My passage from Sydney to Melbourne, was made in the steamer "Shamrock," and, after landing on the shore of Port Philip, I tried to believe myself free from all that could attract my thoughts to other lands.

I endeavoured to fancy myself once more a youth—with everything to win, and nothing to lose.

The scenes I encountered in the young colony, favoured my efforts; and after a time, I began to take an interest in much that was transpiring around me.

I could not very well do otherwise: since, to a great deal I saw in Melbourne, my attention was called, in a most disagreeable manner.

Never had I been amongst so large a population, where society was in so uncivilised a condition. The number of men and women encountered in the streets in a state of beastly intoxication—the number of both sexes, to be seen with black eyes, and other evidences, that told of many a mutual "misunderstanding,"—the horridly profane language issuing out of the public-houses, as you passed them—in short, everything that met either the eye or ear of the stranger, proclaimed to him, in a sense not to be mistaken, that Melbourne must be the abode of a depraved people. There, for the first time in my life, I saw men allowed to take their seats at the breakfast tables of an hotel, while in a state of staggering intoxication!

With much that was disgusting to witness, there were some spectacles that were rather amusing. A majority of the men seen walking the streets—or encountered in the bar-rooms of public-houses—carried grand riding whips; and a great many wore glittering spurs—who had never been upon the back of horse!

The hotel keepers of Melbourne did not care for the custom of respectable people, just landed in the colony; but preferred the patronage of men from the mines—diggers who would deposit with them, the proceeds of their labour, in bags of gold dust; and remain drunk, until told there was but five pounds of the deposit left—just enough to carry them back to the diggings!

I am not speaking of Melbourne at the present time; but the Melbourne of ten years ago. It is now a fine city, where a part of all the world's produce may be obtained for a reasonable price. Most of the inhabitants of the Melbourne of 1853—owing to the facility of acquiring the means—have long since killed themselves off by drink and dissipation; and a population of more respectable citizens, from the mother country, now supply their places.

I made but a short stay in this colonial Gomorrah. Disgusted with the city, and everything in it, a few days after my arrival, I started off for the McIvor diggings.

I travelled in company with several others, who were going to the same place—to which we had "chartered" a horse and dray for carrying our "swags."

One of my travelling companions was drunk, the night before leaving Melbourne; and, in consequence, could eat no breakfast on the morning when we were about to start. He had neglected to provide himself with food for the journey; and depended on getting his meals at eating-houses along the road.

Before the day was over, he had become very hungry; but would not accept of any food offered him by the others.

"No thank'ee," he would say, when asked to have something. "I'll wait. We shall stop at a coffee-house before night; and I'll make it a caution to the man as keeps it. I'll eat all before me. My word! but I'll make it a warning to him, whoever he be. He'll not want to keep a coffee-house any longer."

This curious threat was repeated several times during the day; and we all expected, when evening should arrive, to see something wonderful in the way of consuming provisions.

We at length reached the coffee-house, where we intended to stay for the night; and called for our dinners. When told to sit down, we did so; and there was placed before us a shoulder of mutton, from which, as was evident by the havoc made upon it, several hungry men had already dined.

A loaf, baked in the ashes—known in the colonies as a "damper"—some tea, in which had been boiled a little sugar, some salt, and a pickle bottle with some dirty vinegar in it, were the concomitants of the shoulder, or "knuckle" of mutton. I had sate down to many such meals before; and was therefore in no way disappointed. But the man who had been all day without eating seemed to be very differently affected. According to custom, he had to prepay his four shillings, before taking his seat at the table; and on seeing what he was to get for his money, he seemed rather chagrined.

"My word!" cried he; "I did say that I'd make it a warning to the landlord; but my word!—he's made it a warning to me. I sate down hungry, but I shall get up starving."

None of us could reasonably doubt the truth, thus naïvely enunciated by our travelling companion.

After reaching the diggings at McIvor, I entered into partnership with one of the men, who had travelled with me from Melbourne. We purchased a tent and tools; and at once set to work to gather gold.

Judge Lynch was very much wanted on the diggings of McIvor—as well as throughout all Victoria, during the first three years after gold had been discovered there.

Those, who claimed to be the most respectable of the colonists, did not want an English colony disgraced by "Lynch Law"—a wonderful bugbear to the English ear—so they allowed it to be disgraced by ten times the number of thefts and robberies than ever took place in California—which they were pleased to style "the land of bloodshed and crime."

In California miners never required to take their tools home with them at night. They could leave them on their claims; and be confident of finding them there next morning. It was not so in Victoria, where the greatest care could not always prevent the digger from having such property stolen. I have seen—in a copy of the "Melbourne Argus," of November 5th, 1852—two hundred and sixty-six advertisements offering rewards for stolen property! Yet "The London Times," November 6th, 1852, speaks of these same colonies in the following terms:—"It is gratifying to learn that English love of law and common sense there predominate."

As most of the thefts there committed were of articles, too insignificant to pay for advertising their loss, the reader may imagine what was the state of society in Victoria at that time; and how far "English love of law and common sense predominated!"

It was only one of the thousand falsehoods propagated by the truculent scribblers of this unprincipled journal; and for which they may some day be called to account.

But few of those, who committed crimes in the diggings, were ever brought to trial; or in any way made answerable for their misdeeds. Prisoners were sometimes sent down to Melbourne to be tried; but as no one wished to be at an expense of thirty or forty pounds, travel a hundred miles, and lose three or four weeks of valuable time to prosecute them, the result was usually an acquittal; and crime was committed with impunity.

While at McIvor, a thief entered my tent during my absence from it; and stole therefrom a spyglass that had been given me by Captain Hyland—with some other little articles that I had carried long and far, and valued in proportion.

I afterwards got back the glass by the aid of the police; and very likely might have had the thief convicted and punished—had I felt inclined to forsake a good claim, take a long journey to Melbourne, and spend about forty pounds in appearing against him!

As I did not wish to undertake all this trouble *pro bono publico*, the criminal remained unpunished.

Becoming tired of McIvor, I went on to Fryer's Creek. I there met with a fellow-passenger from California—named Edmund Lee—with whom I joined partnership; but after toiling awhile without much success, we proceeded to a large rush at Jones' Creek—a distance of thirty-five miles from Fryer's.

We started in the afternoon; and stopped the first night at a place called Castlemain.

That evening I saw more drunken men than I had met during a whole year spent in the diggings of California—where the sale of intoxicating liquor was unrestricted, while on the gold fields of Victoria it was strictly prohibited by law! Indeed, about four hundred mounted troopers and policemen were in Castlemain at the time, for the purpose of maintaining "English law and order;" and those selling intoxicating drinks were liable to a fine of fifty pounds or imprisonment, or both! One vice, so prevalent in California, was not to be observed on the gold fields of Victoria. In the latter there were no gambling-houses.

After leaving Castlemain, we walked about twenty-five miles; and stopped all night at "Simpson's Station."

On this pasture I was told there were sixteen thousand head of sheep.

Before reaching Simpson's, we passed a station, on which the sheep were infested with a disease, resembling the "shab." Carcasses of the dead were everywhere to be seen; and those, that were still alive, were hardly able to drag along the few locks of wool clinging to their sky-coloured skins!

On Sunday, the 14th day of August, 1853, we reached the diggings on Jones' Creek, where we found about ten thousand people, but no place where we could procure a meal of victuals, or a night's lodging!

That the reader may have some idea of the hardships to which diggers were then often exposed, I shall make known of the manner of our life, while residing at Jones' Creek.

We first purchased some blankets; and with these, some poles and pieces of string, we constructed a sort of tent. At none of the stores could we find a utensil for cooking meat; and we were compelled to broil it over the fire on the end of a stick. Sometimes we could buy bread that had come from Bendigo, for which we had to pay six shillings the loaf of three and a half pounds weight! When unable to get this, we had to purchase flour at a proportionate price, knead it into dough, and roast it in the ashes.

There was no place of amusement at Jones' Creek; and a strong police force was stationed there, to suppress the sale of liquors; or, rather, to arrest those who sold it; and also to hunt diggers for what was called the "Gold Licence."

The precious metal at this place was found very unevenly distributed through the gullies; and while some were making fortunes by collecting it, others were getting next to nothing.

The gold was found in "nuggets"—lying in "pockets" of the slate rock; and not a fragment could be obtained till these pockets had been explored.

The day after our arrival, my partner and I marked off two claims. Being unable to hold them both, we took our choice of the two; and gave the other one away to some men, with whom we had become slightly acquainted.

The top earth from both claims was removed—disclosing not a speck of gold in that we had retained, while twenty-four pounds weight were picked out—without washing—from the claim we had given away!

Lee and I remained at Jones' Creek three weeks, worked hard, made nothing, and then started back for Fryer's, where our late partners were still toiling.

On our way back we halted for dinner—where some men with a dray load of stores,—on their way to one of the diggings, had also stopped for their mid-day meal.

We had neglected to bring any sugar with us; and wished to buy some for our coffee. The men with the dray did not wish to sell any; but we insisted on having it at any price.

"We'll let you have a pannikin full of sugar," said one, "but shall charge you ten shillings for it."

"All right," said my companion, Edmund Lee. "It's cheap enough—considering."

The man gave us the sugar; and then refused to take the money! He was not so avaricious, as we had supposed. He had thought, by asking ten times the usual price, to send us away, without being obliged to part with what he might himself soon stand in need of!

On the evening of the second day of our journey, about nine o'clock, we reached the banks of Campbell's Creek—within four miles of the place we were making for.

Rain had been falling all the day; and the stream was so swollen, that we could not safely cross it in the darkness.

The rain continued falling, and we spread our wet blankets on the ground. We prayed in vain for sleep, since we got none throughout that long, dreary night.

Next morning we arose early—more weary than when we had lain down; and, after fording the stream, we kept on to Fryer's Creek—which we reached in a couple of hours.

We had been without food, since the noon of the day before; and from the way we swallowed our breakfast, our former mates might have imagined we had eaten nothing during the whole time of our absence!

Volume Two—Chapter Twenty One.

The Stolen Nugget.

I worked a claim in German Gully, Fryer's Creek, in partnership with two men, of whom I knew very little; and with whom—except during our hours of labour—I held scarce any intercourse.

One of them was a married man; and dwelt in a large tent with his wife and family. The other lived by himself in a very small tent—that stood near that of his mate. Though both were strangers to me, these men knew each other well; or, at all events, had been associates for several months. I had been taken into their partnership, to enable them to work a claim, which had proved too extensive for two. The three of us, thus temporarily acting together, were not what is called on the diggings "regular mates," though my two partners stood to one another in this relationship.

The claim proved much better than they had expected; and I could tell, by their behaviour, that they felt some regret, at having admitted me into the partnership.

We were about three weeks engaged in completing our task, when the gold we had obtained was divided into three equal portions—each taking his share. The expenses incurred in the work were then settled; and the partnership was considered at an end—each being free to go where he pleased.

On the morning after, I was up at an early hour; but, early as it was, I noticed that the little tent, belonging to the single man, was no longer in its place. I thought its owner might have pitched it in a fresh spot; but, on looking all around, I could not see it.

My reflection was, that the single man must have gone away from the ground.

I did not care a straw, whether he had or not. If I had a wish one way or the other, it was to know that he *had* gone: for he was an individual whose *room* would by most people have been preferred to his *company*. For all that, I was somewhat surprised at his disappearance, first, because he had not said anything of his intention to take leave of us in that unceremonious manner; and, secondly, because, I did not expect him to part from his mate, until some quarrel should separate them. As I had heard no dispute—and one could not have occurred, without my hearing it—the man's absence was a mystery to me.

It was soon after explained by his comrade, who came over to my tent, as I suppose, for that very purpose.

"Have you noticed," said he, "that Tom's gone away?"

"Yes," I answered; "I see that his tent has been removed; and I supposed that he had gone."

"When I woke up this morning," continued the married man, "and saw that he had left between two days, I was never more surprised in my life."

"Indeed!"

I had a good deal of respect for Tom, and fancied he had the same for me. I thought we should work together, as long as we stayed on the diggings; and for him to leave, without saying a word about his going, quite stunned me. My wife, however, was not at all surprised at it—when I told her that he had gone away. She said she expected it; and only wondered he had had the cheek to stay so long.

"I asked her what she meant. By way of reply she brought me this nugget."

As the man finished speaking, he produced from his pocket a lump of gold—weighing about eighteen ounces—and held it up before my eyes.

"But what has this to do with your partner's leaving you?" I asked.

"That's just the question I put to my wife," said the man.

"And what answer did she make?"

"She said, that, after we had been about a week working in the claim, she was one day making some bread; and when she had used up the last dust of flour in the tent, she found that she wanted a handful to sprinkle over the outside of the damper—to keep it from sticking to the pan. With her hands in the dough, she didn't care to go to the store for any; but stepped across to Tom's tent to get a little out of his bag. There was no harm in this: for we were so well acquainted with him, that we knew he would not consider it much of a liberty. My wife had often before been into his hut, to borrow different articles; and Tom knew of it, and of course had said, all right. Well, on the day I am speaking of, she went in after the flour; and, on putting her hand into the bag to take some out, she laid her fingers on this here lump of yellow metal. Don't you see it all now? It's plain as a pike-staff. Tom had found the nugget, while working alone in the claim; and intended to keep it for himself, without letting either of us know anything about it. He was going to rob us of our share of the gold. He has turned out a damned thief."

"Certainly it looks like it," said I.

"I know it," emphatically asserted Tom's old associate. "I know it: for he has worked with me all the time he has been on the diggings; and he had no chance to get this nugget anywhere else. Besides, his having it hid in the flour-bag is proof that he didn't come honestly by it. He never intended to let us know anything about it. My wife is a sharp woman; and could see all this, the moment she laid her hands upon the nugget. She didn't let it go neyther; but brought it away with her. When Tom missed it—which he must have done that very day—he never said a word about his loss. He was afraid to say anything about it, because he knew I would ask him how he came by it, and why he had not mentioned it before. That of itself is proof of his having stolen it out of our claim."

There was no doubt but that the married man and his "sharp" wife were correct in their conjecture, which was a satisfactory explanation of Tom's strange conduct, in taking midnight leave of us. He had kept silent, about losing the nugget, because he was not certain how or where it had gone; and he had not left immediately after discovering his loss, because the claim was too good to be given up for such a trifle. By this attempt to rob us, he had lost the share of the nugget—which he would have been entitled to—while his fears, doubts, and other unpleasant reflections, arising out of the transaction, must have punished him far more effectually than the loss of the lump of gold. He could not have been in a very pleasant humour with himself, while silently taking down his little tent, and sneaking off in the middle of the night to some other diggings, where he might chance to be unknown. I have often witnessed ludicrous illustrations of the old adage, that "honesty is the best policy;" but never one plainer, or better, than Tom's unsuccessful attempt at abstracting the nugget.

There is, perhaps, no occupation, in which men have finer opportunities of robbing their partners, than that of gold-digging. And yet I believe that instances of the kind—that is, of one mate robbing another—are very rare upon the gold fields. During my long experience in the diggings—both of California and Australia—I knew of but two such cases.

The man who brought me the nugget, taken from Tom's tent, was, like the majority of gold-diggers, an honest person. His disclosing the secret was proof of this: since it involved the sharing of the gold with me, which he at once offered to do.

I did not accept of his generous offer; but allowed him to keep the whole of it; or, rather, presented it to his "very clever wife,"—who had certainly done something towards earning a share in it.

Volume Two—Chapter Twenty Two.

A Fearful Fright.

After finishing my explorations on Fryer's Creek, I went, in company with my "regular mates," to Ballarat, which was the place where "jeweller's shops" were then being discovered.

The gold on this field was found in "leads"—that lay about one hundred and sixty feet below the surface of the ground.

The leads were generally but one claim in width; and no party could obtain a claim on either of them, without first having a fight to get, and several others to keep, possession of it.

My mates and I succeeded in entering a claim on Sinclair's Hill; and, during the time we were working it, we had five distinct encounters with would-be intruders—in each of which my friend Edmund Lee had an opportunity of distinguishing himself; and, by his fistic prowess, gained great applause from a crowd of admiring spectators.

I have often been in places where my life was in danger, and where the passion of fear had been intensely excited within me; but never was I more frightened than on one occasion—while engaged in this claim upon Sinclair's Hill.

We were sinking the shaft; and I was down in it—at a depth of one hundred and twenty feet from the surface of the earth. One of my mates—as the readiest place to get clear of it—had thrown his oil-cloth coat over the windlass. The coat, thus carelessly placed, slipped off; and came down the shaft—in its descent causing a rustling, roaring noise, that, to me below, sounded somewhat like thunder!

I looked up. All was dark above; and the idea occurred to me, that the shaft had given way at the "drift"—a place about sixty feet above my head, where we had gone through a strata of wet sand. The noisy coat at length reached the bottom, and I found myself unhurt; but, so frightened had I been, that I was unable to go on with my work—until after I had gone up to the surface, swallowed a glass of brandy, and taken a few draws of the pipe!

The business of mining, in the Victoria diggings, is attended with considerable danger; and those who conduct it should be men of temperate habits—as well as possessed of some judgment. Every one on the gold fields, being his own master—and guided only by his own will—of course there are many who work in a reckless manner, and often under the influence of drink. As a consequence, accidents are, or were at that time, of daily occurrence.

When an accident resulted from intoxication, it was generally not the drunken man himself—but his mate—who was the sufferer—the latter having a bucket, or some heavy implement, dropped upon his head, from a height of a hundred feet.

Gold miners, as a class, are exceedingly indifferent to danger; and careless about the means of avoiding it. They will often continue to work in a shaft, that they know must soon "cave" in; but they do so under the hope, that the accident will occur during the night, or while they are at dinner. So long as there is a possibility of their escaping, hope tells them they are "all right"—too often a deceitful tale.

While engaged in gold-digging, I had frequent opportunities of testing a doctrine often put forward by tobacco-smokers: that the "weed" is a powerful antidote to fear. Several times have I been under ground, where I believed myself in danger; and have been haunted by fear that kept me in continued agony, until my pipe was lit—when my apprehensions seemed at once to vanish literally in a cloud of smoke!

There is something in the use of tobacco, that is unexplained, or untaught, in any work of philosophy, natural or unnatural, that I have yet read. The practice of smoking is generally condemned, by those who do not smoke. But certainly, there are times, when a man is the better for burning a little tobacco, although the immoderate use of it, like all other earthly blessings, may be converted into a curse.

My readers may think, that a disquisition on tobacco can have but little to do with the Adventures of a Rolling Stone. But why should they object to knowing my opinions on things in general, since the adventures themselves have been often either caused or controlled by these very opinions? I have entered into a minute detail of my experience in mining affairs, under the belief, that no sensible reader will think it uninteresting; and, still continuing in this belief, I purpose going a *little* farther into the subject.

While engaged in gold-digging, I have often been led to notice the influence of the mind over the physical system.

In washing dirt that contains but little gold, the body soon becomes weary—so much so, that the work is indeed toil. On the other hand, when the "dirt" is "rich," the digger can exert himself energetically from sunrise to sunset, without feeling fatigue at the termination of such a long spell of labour.

In the business of mining—as in most other occupations—there are certain schemes and tricks, by which men may deceive each other, and sometimes themselves. Gold is often very ingeniously inserted into fragments of quartz rock—in order to facilitate the sale of shares in a "reef."

I made the acquaintance of several diggers who had been deceived in this way; and whose eyes became opened to the trick, only after the tricksters had got out of their reach. On the other hand, I once saw a digger refuse to purchase a share in a reef, from which "splendid specimens" had been procured—fearing that some trickery was about to be practised upon him. One month afterwards, I saw him give, for the same share, just twenty times the amount that he had been first asked for it!

I remember a party of "Tasmanians," who had turned up a large extent of ground, in a claim on Bendigo. The richest of the earth they washed as it was got out; and of the rest they had made a large heap, of what is called "wash dirt, Number 2."

This, they knew, would not much more than pay for the washing; and, as a new "rush" had just been heard of, at a place some miles off, they resolved to sell their "wash dirt, Number 2."

Living near by the diggings was a sort of doctor, who used to speculate, in various ways, in the business of gold-mining. To this individual the Tasmanian diggers betook themselves; and told him, that they had received private intelligence, from the new rush; and that they must start for it immediately, or lose the chance of making their fortunes. For that reason, they wished to sell their "wash dirt," which they knew to be worth at least two ounces to the "load;" but, as they must be off to the "new rush," they were not going to haggle about price; and would take twelve ounces for the pile—they thought, in all, about thirty loads.

The doctor promised to go down the next morning, and have a look at it. In the evening the "Tasmanians" repaired to an acquaintance, who was unknown to the doctor; and requested him to be sauntering about their dirt-heap in the morning, and to have with him a washing-dish. They further instructed him—in the event of his being asked to wash a dish of the dirt—that he was to take a handful from that part of the heap, where he might observe a few specks of white quartz.

Next morning the doctor came, as he had promised; but declined to negotiate, without first having some of the dirt washed, and ascertaining the "prospect."

"We have no objection to that," said one of the proprietors of the dirt-heap, speaking in a confident tone.

"Oh! not the slightest, doctor," added a second of the party.

"Yonder's a man with a washing-dish," remarked a third. "Suppose you get him to prove some of it?"

The man, apparently unconnected with any of the party, was at once called up; and was told, that the dirt was to be sold; and that the intending purchaser wished to see a "prospect" washed, by some person not interested in the sale. He was then asked, if he had any objections to wash a dish or two from the heap.

Of course he had not—not the slightest—anything to oblige them.

"Take a little from everywhere," said one of the owners, "and that will show what the average will yield."

The confederate did as requested; and obtained a "prospect" that proclaimed the dirt probably to contain about four ounces to the load.

The doctor was in a great hurry to give the diggers their price—and in less than ten minutes became the owner of the heap.

The dirt had been, what the diggers call, "salted," and, as was afterwards proved, the speculating doctor did not get from it enough gold to pay the expenses of washing!

At Ballarat my partners and I were successful in our attempts at gold hunting; and yet we were not satisfied with the place. Very few diggers are ever contented with the spot upon which they happen to be. Rumours of richer fields elsewhere are always floating about on the air; and these are too easily credited.

In the latter part of the year 1853, a report reached the diggings of Victoria: that very rich "placers" had been discovered in Peru.

There is now good reason for believing, that these stories were originated in Melbourne; that they were set afoot, and propagated by ship agents and skippers, who wished to send their ships to Callao, and wanted passengers to take in them—or, rather, wanted the money which these passengers would have to pay.

Private letters were shown—purporting to have come from Peru—that gave glowing descriptions of the abundance of gold glittering among the "barrancas" of the Andes.

The Colonial papers did what they could to restrain the rising excitement; and, although they were partly successful, their counter-statements did not prevent many hundreds from becoming victims, to the trickery of the dishonest persons, at that time engaged in the shipping business of Melbourne.

A majority of those, who were deluded into going to Peru, were Americans, Canadians, and Frenchmen—probably for the reason that they were more dissatisfied with Australia, than the colonists themselves.

Amongst the victims of the "Callao fever" I have to record myself—along with two of my partners—Edmund Lea and another. All three of us being too simple-minded to suspect the trick, or too ready to yield to temptation, we set off for Melbourne; and thence set sail across the far-stretching Pacific.

Volume Two—Chapter Twenty Three.

The Callao Gold Fever.

There could not well have been a more uninteresting voyage, than the one we made to Callao. There was about one hundred and fifty passengers on board—most of them young and wild adventurers.

The master of the vessel had the good sense *not* to attempt the game of starving us. Had he done so, it would have obtained for him an unpleasant popularity. We had no ground for complaint on the score of food.

The principal amusement on board the ship was that of gambling; but it was carried on in a quiet manner; and we had no rows leading to any serious disaster. We had no particular excitement of any kind; and for this reason I have pronounced the voyage uninteresting. For all that, it was not an unpleasant one. I have no hesitation in asserting, that, with the same number of diggers of the pure Australian type, that long voyage, before its termination, would have resembled a "hell aboard ship."

When we at length reached Callao, it was simply to find ourselves laughed at for leaving Victoria! We had left behind us a land of gold; and made a long sea voyage to discover that we had been "gulled."

No one appeared to be at all disappointed. Every one was heard to say, "It's just as I expected!" I may have said so myself—I don't remember whether I did or not—but I admit now, that I thought myself "some" deceived; and I believe that each of my fellow-passengers felt something like myself: and that was, strongly inclined to kill either himself—or some one else—for having been so damnably duped.

To have heard most of them talk, you could scarce have believed, that there had been any disappointment! Many alleged that they had been dissatisfied with the colonies; and had only come to Peru to see that celebrated country—which they had long desired to do!

Some of them claimed, that they had only left the gold fields of Victoria on a sea voyage—in order to recruit their strength; and that they intended to return, and pursue the avocation of gold-digging with greater energy than ever!

Most of the Americans declared, that, they were on their way home across the Isthmus of Panama!

No one would acknowledge, that he had been made a fool of. Each, according to his own showing, had come to Callao for some wise purpose, which he was anxious to explain to the rest—notwithstanding the obvious difficulty of obtaining credence for his story.

About half of those, who were the victims of this gold-digging delusion, became also victims to the fevers of Peru. Some proceeded up the coast to California; others *did* go home by the Isthmus of Panama; while a few, and only a few, returned to Australia.

In Callao I parted with my friend Edmund Lea, who was one of those who took the Panama route, on his way back to the United States.

He was returning to a happy home, where he would meet those—and there were many of them—who would rejoice at his return.

There was no such home for me. I was alone in the world—a Rolling Stone—with no one to love—no one who cared for me—and no place, except the spot under my feet, that I could call home.

Lea was a young man who won the esteem of all with whom he came in contact—at least, all whose respect was of any value.

I parted from him with much regret. Before bidding adieu, we made arrangements to correspond with each other; and I have heard from him several times since. He is now, or ought to be, living in Lowell, in the State of Massachusets.

In the first ship "up" for Melbourne, I engaged a passage—resolved upon returning to the gold fields of Victoria.

The vessel had arrived from Melbourne only three weeks before—freighted with a full cargo of deluded diggers; and the captain was now about to extract from them some more of their money, by taking them back!

On board there was one young man, who had come to Peru as a passenger. He had not the money to take him back; and, being a seaman, he had joined the ship as one of her crew. We sailed late in the afternoon, and were some time getting out of the harbour. About ten o'clock at night this young man was at the wheel, where he was spoken to by the captain in a very harsh, unpleasant tone. It was said that the skipper was intoxicated; and that he not only spoke in the manner described, but struck the young sailor without the slightest cause or provocation. The exact truth will perhaps never be told. The night was very dark; and all that was certainly known is: that the sailor drew his knife, plunged it into the captain's body; and then jumped overboard into the sea!

As the captain had evidently received a mortal wound, the ship was put about; and brought back to her anchorage within the harbour. The captain was carried below; and for three or four hours he did nothing but swear, and threaten to kill the sailor who had stabbed him. His senses had forsaken him; and it was impossible to make him understand, that the young man had leaped overboard, and was in all probability at that moment fifty fathoms under the sea.

The captain had a wife and two children aboard; and what with the noise made by them, and his own wild ravings, not a soul, either among crew or passengers, slept during that night. By six o'clock in the morning, the wounded man had ceased to live.

Three days after, another captain was sent aboard by the agents; and we again set sail for Melbourne.

Nothing was heard of the sailor previous to our leaving the port or ever afterwards. At the time he jumped overboard lights were to be seen, shining on many vessels in the harbour; and some believed that he might have reached either a ship, or the shore. There was not much probability of his having been saved. Both ships and shore were too distant for him to have swum to either. In all likelihood he preceded the captain, into that unknown world from which there is no return.

Very few, either of the passengers or crew, blamed the young sailor for what he had done. The captain had the reputation of being a "bully;" and his having commenced practising his tyranny so early on the voyage—and especially on the man at the wheel, who, while there, should have remained unmolested—gave evidence that had he continued to command the ship, our passage across the Pacific might have proved of a character anything but "peaceful."

The skipper, who succeeded him, was a man of a different disposition. He soon became a favourite with all on board; and we had both a quick and pleasant passage to Melbourne—where we arrived without any further accident or obstruction.

When setting foot for the second time on Australian soil, I found the city of Melbourne greatly changed—I am happy to say—for the better.

An attempt was being made at keeping the streets clean. Old buildings had been taken down; and new ones erected in their stead. The citizens, too, were better dressed; and looked, as well as acted, more like human beings.

At the public-houses customers were served with food fitting to eat; and were also treated with some show of civility. The number of people who formerly seemed to think, that a public-house keeper held a higher social position than the governor himself, had become greatly diminished. They were now in a decided minority.

Men were no longer afraid, during night hours, to trust themselves alone in the streets; and they did not, as formerly, issue in armed bands from the public-houses to protect themselves from being robbed, while going to their homes, or repairing to places of amusement.

Men found lying drunk in the gutters were now in some danger of being placed upon a stretcher, and taken away by the police.

The convict element was greatly upon the decrease; and the profane language, imported from the slums of London, was not so disgustingly universal.

I have hurried through the narrative of my voyages from Melbourne to Callao, and back, for two reasons. First, because nothing very interesting occurred to me during either; and secondly, because I feel somewhat ashamed at having been so ridiculously deluded; and have therefore no desire to dwell upon the details of that ill-starred expedition.

Volume Two—Chapter Twenty Four.

The Yarra-Yarra.

Soon after my return from Callao, I accompanied two acquaintances, upon a hunting expedition up the Yarra-Yarra.

There is some beautiful scenery along the banks of this river—beautiful, as curves of shining water, bordered by noble forms of vegetable life, can make it.

There is some pleasure to be found in a hunting excursion in Australia—although it does not exactly consist in the successful pursuit of game.

In the morning and afternoon, when your shadow is far prolonged over the greensward—and you breathe the free genial atmosphere of that sunny clime—an exhilarating effect is produced upon your spirits, a sort of joyous consciousness of the possession of youth, health, and happiness. To breathe the evening atmosphere of Australia is to become inspired with hope. If despair should visit the soul of one, to whom fate has been unkind, it will come in the mid-day hours; but even then, the philosopher may find a tranquil contentment by lying under the shade of a "she oak," and imbibing the smoke of the Nicotian weed.

One of my companions in the chase chanced to have—living about twenty miles up the river—an acquaintance, who had often invited him to make a visit to his "station."

Our comrade had decided to accept the invitation—taking the two of us along with him, though we were in no haste to reach our destination—so long as we could find amusement by the way.

The squatters, living on their "stations"—at a distance from large towns, or assemblages of the digging population—are noted for their hospitality. They lead, in general, a lonely life; and, for this reason, visitors with whom they can converse, and who can bring them the latest news from the world of society, are ever welcome.

Both the climate and customs of Australia make visitors less troublesome to their hosts, than in almost any other part of the world.

The traveller is usually provided with his own blankets, carried in a roll; and these, wrapped around him in the open air, he prefers to the best bed his host could provide for him.

All that we should require from our comrade's acquaintance would be his company, with plenty of substantial food; and with this last article the squatters of Australia are abundantly supplied.

Not wishing to make a toil, of an excursion intended for amusement, we had purchased an old horse, on which we had packed our blankets, with a few articles of food to sustain us, till we should reach the station of the squatter.

We might have accomplished the journey in a single day; but walking twenty miles within twelve hours, was too much like work; and, on the first night, after leaving Melbourne, we had only made about half the distance!

We had sauntered leisurely along, and spent at least three or four hours under the shade of the trees growing by the side of the road.

This style of travelling appeared to suit the old horse, as much as his masters. It was an animal that had seen its best days; and seemed averse to any movement that called for a high degree of speed. Like most of his kind, in the colonies, he was as much at home in one place as another; and, wherever we stopped for repose, he appeared to think that the halt was made for his especial accommodation.

We did not make much effort to undeceive him. He had seen hard times; and we were, probably, the best masters that had ever owned him.

On the second morning, shortly after resuming our journey, we observed some hills, thickly covered with timber—at some distance to the right of our road. We diverged from the direct path—to see whether we could not find a kangaroo, or some other harmless creature, possessing a happy existence, that might be put an end to.

This undertaking was a success—so far as the kangaroos were concerned—since we were not able to do injury to any of these creatures.

We caught a glimpse of two or three of them, at a distance; but, after roaming about the timbered ranges for several hours, we did not succeed to get within killing distance of any of them.

We returned to the bank of the river—just in time to form our bivouac, before the night fell upon us—having accomplished during the day, about four miles in the direction in which we intended going!

"I am a little disgusted with hunting," said one of my companions, whose name was Vane. "I move that in the morning we keep on to the station; and see what amusement is to be found there."

This proposition was carried, by a majority of three. The horse, being indifferent on the subject, was permitted to remain neutral.

"What amusement shall we find at your friend's house?" asked Vane of my other companion—who was the one acquainted with the squatter we were on the way to visit.

"Well, I suppose we can have some hunting there," replied the individual thus interrogated; and who always answered, in a polite manner, to the name of "Cannon."

"No, thank you!" said Vane. "We've had enough of that sort of thing to-day. I don't want any more of it."

"But at the station we shall be provided with horses," suggested Cannon; "and, when we get sight of a kangaroo, we can run the animal down."

"That makes a difference," said Vane; "and I don't mind trying it for a day. But is there no other amusement, to be had at your friend's house?"

"Not that I know of—unless you make love to my friend's pretty daughter."

"Ah! that *would* be amusement," exclaimed Vane, evidently a little stirred by the communication.

"Is she good-looking?" he asked.

"Yes, extremely good-looking. But, remember, comrades," continued Cannon, "I will allow no serious love-making."

"Give yourself no uneasiness about that," rejoined Vane. "In love affairs, I am never serious. Are you?" he asked, turning to me.

"Yes, very serious," I answered, thinking of Lenore.

"Then you will never be successful," said Vane.

I passed half-an-hour in a fruitless endeavour to comprehend the philosophy of this remark, after which I fell asleep.

Next morning, we resumed our route for the squatters' station; and had got about three miles along the road, when we came to a plain, entirely destitute of timber. Upon this plain was a drove of about a hundred horses. They remained motionless, with heads erect, and nostrils spread, until we had approached within fifty yards of them. They then turned, and galloped off at the top of their speed.

At this moment, a change suddenly showed itself in the demeanour of our old roadster. We had been driving him before us, for the last mile or two, with great difficulty; but, on seeing his congeners take to flight, he suddenly threw up his head; and, either calling out to the drove that he was coming, or to us that he was going, he started towards them. Before we could get hold of his bridle, he was beyond reach—going at a rate that promised soon to place him among the foremost of the herd.

We had supposed that our hack belonged to some "serious family" of horses; and that the natural sedateness of his disposition had been augmented by years of toil and starvation. We were never more disappointed, than on seeing him forsake us in the fashion he did. A two-year old could not have gone more gaily.

Cannon and Vane started off in pursuit of him; but, as I had a little more experience in colonial horses, than either of my companions, I bade good-bye both to our roadster and my roll of blankets; and, stretching myself under the shade of a tree, I resolved to await their return.

I did wait. One hour passed, then another, and a third; and still my companions did not come back.

"I am a fool for remaining here," reflected I. "The squatters station cannot be more than five miles distant; and they have probably gone there? The herd of horses undoubtedly belongs to it; and my companions have followed them home?"

Influenced by these conjectures, I once more rose to my feet; and continued the journey, that had been so unexpectedly interrupted.

Volume Two—Chapter Twenty Five.

Jessie.

The path led me along the bank of a river. It was the Yarra-Yarra.

As I moved onward, I began to perceive, that I had not been such a fool, after all, in having waited awhile for my companions. My long quiet reverie, in the shade of the tree, had refreshed me. I had escaped the hot sunshine; and I should now be able to reach my destination, during the cool hours of evening.

I did not wish to arrive at the station before Cannon: as I should require him to introduce me.

My solitary journey was altogether an agreeable one. The bright waters of the Yarra-Yarra flowed by my side, while the gentle breeze, as it came softly sighing through the peppermint-trees, fanned my brow.

After advancing, as I supposed, a distance of about four miles—hearing only the cries of the screaming cockatoo, and the horribly human voice of the laughing jackass—I was suddenly and agreeably surprised by the barking of a dog. The animal could not be far off; and it was also in the direction I was going—up the river.

"The station cannot be distant?" thought I; and eager to catch a glimpse of it, I hastened forward. I had scarce made a step further, when I was startled by a piercing scream. It was a human voice—the voice of a woman. She who gave utterance to it must be near the spot—concealed by some wattle-bushes on the bank of the river?

I rushed forward; and glided through the bushes into the open ground beyond. I perceived a young woman just on the point of leaping into the river!

My abrupt appearance seemed to cause a change in her design. Suddenly turning towards me, she pointed to the water, at the same time exclaiming, "Save her! O, save her!"

Looking in the direction thus indicated, I saw something like a child—a little girl—struggling on the surface of the water. Partly supported by the drapery of her dress, she was drifting down with the current. The next instant I was in the water, with the child in my arms.

The bank of the river, for some distance below, was too high and steep for me to climb out again. After making two or three ineffectual attempts, I gave it up; and, supporting myself and the child by a swimming stroke, I permitted the current to carry us down, until I had reached a place where it was possible to scramble ashore.

The young girl upon the bank had done all she could to assist me, while I was endeavouring to climb out; but, fearing, from the state of excitement in which she appeared to be, that she would herself tumble in, I had commanded her to desist.

On my relinquishing the attempt to ascend the steep bank, she appeared to think that I had done so in despair; and that both the child and I were irrecoverably lost.

Her screams recommenced, while her movements betokened something like a determination to join company with us in the water. This, I believe, she would have done, had I not at that instant reached a place, where the bank shelved down to the surface, and where I at length succeeded in getting my feet upon dry land. In another moment I had placed the child in her arms.

For some time after my getting out of the water, the attention of the young girl was wholly engrossed by the little creature I had rescued; and, without fear of my scrutiny being noticed, I had a good opportunity of observing her.

As she stood before me, affectionately caressing her little companion, I thought that there could be on this earth but one other so lovely—one Lenore.

She appeared to be about sixteen years of age. I had often heard of "golden hair," and always had regarded the expression as a very foolish figure of speech. I could do so no longer on looking at the hair of that Australian maiden. Its hue was even less peculiar than its quantity. There seemed more than a delicate form could carry.

I could not tell the colour of her eyes; but I saw that they emitted a soft brilliant light, resembling the outburst of an autumn sun.

When she became satisfied that the child was unharmed, she proceeded to thank me for the service I had done, in "preserving the life of her sister."

I interrupted her expressions of gratitude, by offering to accompany her to her home. The child, after the fright it had sustained, seemed hardly able to stand; and I proposed to carry it in my arms. My proposal was accepted; and we proceeded on up the river.

An animal called in the colonies a "Kangaroo dog," led the way; and to this quadruped the young girl directed my attention.

"Rosa was running in advance of me," said she, "and was playing with the dog. It was he that pushed her into the river. I fear, our mother will not allow us to come out again, though I am very fond of straying along the Yarra-Yarra. We have not far to go," she added; "the house is just behind that hill, you see before us. It is not quite a mile to it."

I was pleased to hear this: for Rosa was about five years of age, and of a weight that I did not desire to walk under for any great distance.

I had forgotten all about my gun. I had dropped it, when jumping into the river; and only remembered it now, long after we had left the spot. On turning towards my companion, I saw that she had it in her hands.

During our progress towards her home, I was constantly making comparisons between my companion and Lenore. They were mental, and involuntary. She and Lenore were the two most lovely objects I had ever seen; and yet they were altogether unlike. Lenore was dark, reserved, and dignified, though the expression of her features and the silent glance of her eye denoted, that her soul contained volumes of warm poetic fancy that might never be expressed in words.

The young girl by my side was fair and free-spoken; she talked almost continuously; and I could plainly perceive, that every thought of her mind must find expression in speech.

Before we had reached the house, I had learnt the simple history of her life. She was the daughter of Mr H—, the friend of Cannon—for whose station we were bound.

She was the one about whom Cannon had bantered Vane—telling him that he might amuse himself by making love to her. Cannon had never spoken a truer word in his life, than when he said that she was "extremely good-looking." If the description was at all incorrect, it was because it was too tame. She was more than good-looking—she was beautiful.

I learnt from her that her name was Jessie, that her life was very lonely on the station—where the appearance of a stranger, whatever he might be, was an unusual event; and that she was much pleased that an acquaintance of her father had sent word, that he was about to visit them with two of his friends.

"That acquaintance is Mr Cannon?" said I, interrogatively.

"Yes; and you are one of the friends who was to come with him," rejoined she, with a woman's instinct, jumping to the correct conclusion. "Oh! we shall be so happy to have you with us!"

We had still that mile further to go; but although Rosa was no light weight to carry, the distance appeared as nothing.

Before we had reached her home, Jessie H— seemed to be an old acquaintance. I felt assured that my visit to her father's station would prove a pleasant one.

On arriving at the house there ensued a scene of excitement, of which little Rosa's mishap was the cause.

Jessie seemed determined to make me the hero of the hour; and I had to listen to profuse expressions of gratitude from her father and mother—all for bringing a child out of the water—an act that a Newfoundland dog would have performed, quite as cleverly as I.

Little Rosa was the favourite of the family; and their thanks for what I had done were in proportion to the affection entertained for her.

When they had succeeded in making me feel very uncomfortable, and appear very much like a fool, I had to listen to some nonsense from my travelling companions Vane and Cannon—who had arrived at the station nearly an hour before. Their badinage was to the effect, that I had got the start of them, in the amusement of love-making to the beautiful Jessie.

My companions had been unsuccessful in the pursuit of our packhorse. He had gone quite off into the "bush"—carrying his cargo along with him.

We never saw either again!

Volume Two—Chapter Twenty Six.

Australian Amusements.

The owner of the station, Mr H—, followed the kindred occupations of grazier and wool-grower; and, to judge by the appearance of his home, he had carried on this combined business to some advantage. He was a simple, kind-hearted man, about fifty years of age; and, having been a colonist for more than twenty years, he understood how to make our visit to his home as pleasant, as circumstances would admit.

The day after our arrival, we were inducted into the mysteries of a "kangaroo hunt." In chase of an "old-man kangaroo" we had a fine run, of about three miles, through the bush; and the affair was pronounced by Vane, who claimed the character of a sportsman, to be a more exciting chase than any fox-hunt he had ever witnessed in the old country. To be "in at the death" of a fox is to be present at a scene of considerable excitement; but it is tame, when compared with the termination of a kangaroo chase. When an "old-man kangaroo" is brought to bay—after having come to the conclusion that he has jumped far enough—then comes the true tug of war.

The venerable gentleman places his back against a tree; and resists further molestation in a most determined manner. He shows fight in his own way—by lifting up one of his hind legs, and bringing it down again with a sudden "slap"—all the time supporting himself in an upright attitude on the other. The blow does not cause a sudden jar, like the kick of a horse; but by means of his long, sharp claws, the kangaroo will tear the skin from the body of a dog, or any other assailant, that may imprudently come within reach.

Vane and Cannon knew that I had been a sailor. They expected, therefore, some amusement in seeing me "navigate" a horse across the rough country—among the standing and prostrated trees of an Australian "bush."

They did not know, that I had been more than two years in the saddle—as a United States dragoon; and that I had ridden over heaps of dead and wounded men—over crippled horses and broken carriages—as well as thousands of miles across the desert plains and through the dense forests of America.

They were taken somewhat by surprise, on beholding my horsemanship; and Vane flattered me with the hope, that a few years' practice would make me as good a hunter as himself!

We returned home with a game-bag—containing two dead kangaroos; and next day, at dinner, indulged in the luxury of "kangaroo-tail" soup.

Our amusement, for the following day, was a fishing excursion along the Yarra-Yarra.

We caught an abundance of fish; but they were so small, that angling for them appeared to be an amusement more fit for children than men; and we soon became weary of the rod and line.

Each day, on returning home to the station, we enjoyed the society of the beautiful Jessie.

As already stated, this young lady was an accomplished conversationist—though her teaching had been only that of Nature. She could carry on a conversation with all three of us at once; and on a different subject with each.

I believe that Vane fell in love with her at first sight; and his whole behaviour betokened, that he intended paying no attention to the command or request which had been made by the man who introduced him.

I knew very little about love affairs; but something whispered me that, if Vane should form a serious attachment for Jessie H— it would end in his disappointment and chagrin. Something told me, she would not reciprocate his affection—however fond it might be.

At the same time, I could perceive in the young lady a partiality for myself. I did not attempt to discover the reason for this. It might have been because my introduction to her had been made, under circumstances such as often win a woman's love. She might have admired my personal appearance. Why not? I was young; and had been often told that I possessed good looks. Why should Jessie H— not fall in love with me, as well as another?

As I reflected thus, conscience whispered to me, that I should take leave of Mr H—'s family; and return to Melbourne.

I did not do so; and I give the reason. Jessie H— was so enchantingly lovely, and her conversation so interesting, that I could not make up my mind to separate from her.

Several times I had mentally resolved to bid adieu to my new acquaintances; but my resolutions remained unfulfilled. I stayed at the station, under the fascinations of the charmer.

Our diversions were of different kinds. One day we would visit a tribe of native blacks living up the river, where we would be treated to astonishing spectacles of their manners, and customs, especially their exploits with the boomerang and spear.

Our mornings would be spent in kangaroo hunting; and our evenings in the society of the beautiful Jessie.

One day we made an excursion—all going well mounted—to a grazing station about fifteen miles from that of Mr H—. Our object was to assist the proprietor in running a large drove of his young cattle into a pen—for the purpose of having them branded.

The animals were almost wild; and we had an exciting day's sport, in getting them inside the inclosure. Several feats of horsemanship were exhibited by the different graziers, who assisted at the ceremony. The affair reminded me of what I had seen in California, upon the large grazing estates—"ganaderias" of that country. We were home again before dinner time; and in the evening I was again thrown into the company of Jessie.

I could not help reading her thoughts. They were easily interpreted: for she made no attempt to conceal what others might have desired to keep secret. Before I had been a week in her company, I was flattered with full evidence, that the warmest love of a warm-hearted girl was, or might be, mine.

There are few that do not sometimes stray from the path of rectitude—even knowingly and willingly. By staying longer at the station of Mr H— when convinced that the happiness of another depended on my leaving it—I was, perhaps, acting as most others would have done; but I knew I was doing wrong. It brought its own punishment, as wickedness will.

Jessie loved me. I was now sure of it. Several circumstances had combined to bring this misfortune upon her. Grateful for the service I had done in saving their child, her father and mother acted, as if they could not treat me with sufficient consideration. Little Rosa herself thought me the most remarkable man in the world; and was always talking of me to her sister.

It was natural for a girl like Jessie to love some one; and she had met but few, from whom she could make a choice. There was nothing strange in her young affections becoming centred on me; and they had done so. Conscience told me that I should at once take myself from her presence; but the fascination of that presence proved stronger than my sense of duty; and I remained—each day, becoming more enthralled by the spell of her beauty.

Why was it wrong in me to stay by the side of Jessie H—? Lenore Hyland had forsaken me; and why should I not love another? Where could I hope to find a woman more beautiful, more truthful, more worthy of being loved, or more capable of loving than Jessie. The task of learning to love her seemed every day to grow less difficult; and why should I bring the process to an abrupt termination?

These considerations required my most profound reflection. They obtained it—at least I thought so;—but the reflections of a man, under the fascinating influence of female beauty, are seldom guided by wisdom. Certainly mine were not, else I would not have allowed the hopes and happiness of my life to have been wrested from me by the loss of Lenore.

Volume Two—Chapter Twenty Seven.

"Love but One!"

"What should I do?" This was the question that presented itself to my mind, almost every hour of the day. It called energetically for an answer.

I loved Lenore Hyland—I felt that I ever should, as long as life was left me. Such being the case, was it right for me to endeavour to gain the affections of an unsophisticated girl like Jessie H—? Would it be honourable of me to take advantage of that incident—which had no doubt favoured her first inclination towards me? To win her heart, and then forsake her, would be to inflict upon her the same sorrow I was myself suffering for the loss of Lenore.

Lenore was still more dear to me than life; and I had only lived since losing her, because I believed it a crime to die, until some Supreme Power should call me to come. And yet should I ever return to Liverpool, and find Lenore a widow—even though she should wish it—I could never marry her!

"She can never be mine," thought I. "She never loved me; or she would have waited for my return. Why, then, should I not love Jessie, and make her my wife?"

There are many who would have adopted this alternative; and without thinking there was any wrong in it.

I did, however. I knew that I could never love Jessie, as I had loved Lenore—to whose memory I could not help proving true, notwithstanding that she had abandoned me for another. This feeling on my part may have been folly—to a degree scarce surpassed by my mother's infatuation for Mr Leary; but to know that a certain course of action is foolish, does not always prevent one from pursuing it.

"Shall I marry Jessie, and become contented—perhaps happy? Or shall I remain single—true to the memory of the lost Lenore—and continue the aimless, wandering, wretched existence I have lately experienced?"

Long and violent was the struggle within my soul, before I could determine upon the answers to these self-asked questions. I knew that I could love Jessie; but never as I should. "Would it be right, then, for me to marry her?" I answered the last question by putting another. "Should I myself wish to have a wife, who loved another man, and yet pretended for me an affection she did not feel?"

I need scarcely say, that this interrogatory received an instantaneous response in the negative. It determined me to separate from Jessie H—, and at once. To remain any longer in her society—to stay even another day under the roof of her father's house, would be a crime for which I could never forgive myself. To-morrow I should start for Melbourne.

I had been walking on the bank of the river, when these reflections, and the final resolve, passed through my mind. I was turning to go back to the house, when I saw Jessie straying near. She approached me, as if by accident.

"Miss H—," said I, "I am going to take leave of you."

"Going to leave me!" she exclaimed, her voice quivering as she spoke.

"Yes; I must start for Melbourne to-morrow morning."

She remained silent for some seconds; and I could see that the colour had forsaken her checks.

"I am very sorry," she said at length, "very sorry to hear it."

"Sorry!" I repeated, hardly knowing what I said, "why should that grieve you?"

I should not have asked such a question; and, as soon as I had done so, I perceived the mistake I had made.

She offered no reply to it; but sate down upon the bank; and rested her head upon her hands. An expression had come over her countenance, unmistakeably of a painful character; and I could see that her eyes were fast filling with tears.

"Surely this girl loves me? And surely I could love her?"

I know not how these two mental interrogatories were answered. I only know that, instead of rejoicing in the knowledge that I had gained her love, I was made miserable by the thought.

I raised her to her feet; and allowed her head to rest upon my shoulder.

"Miss H—," said I, "can it be that you show so much emotion, merely at parting with a friend?"

"Ah!" she replied, "I have thought of you as a friend; but such a one as I never knew before. My life has been lonely. We are here, as you know, shut out from all intercourse with the world. We can form but few friendships. Yours has been to me like some unknown joy of life. You have been my only thought, since I first saw you."

"You must try to forget me—to forget that we have ever met; and I will try to forget you. *I should* only think of you as a friend!"

For a second she stood gazing upon me in silence. Then tremblingly put the question:

"You love another?"

"I do, although I love without hope. It is one who can never be mine—one I may, perhaps, never see again. She and I were playmates when young. I fancied she loved me; but she did not: she has married another."

"How very strange! To me it seems impossible!"

The artless innocence of these observations, proved the purity of the mind from which they could emanate.

"And yet," continued she, "for one who has acted in that manner, you can still feel love?"

"Alas! such is my unfortunate fate."

"Oh! sir, if you but knew the heart you are casting away from you!—its truth—its devotion and constancy—you would never leave me; but stay here and be happy. You would learn to love me. You could not hate one, who loves you as I can; and will to the end of my life!"

I could make no reply to this speech. Sweet as it might have been to the ears of some, I listened to it only with pain. I scarce knew either what to say, or do; and I was only relieved, from my painful embarrassment, when our steps brought us back to the house.

I loved Lenore for what she had been; and regarded her now as lost—as dead; yet I determined to remain true to her. My affections were not wandering fancies—finding a home wherever circumstances might offer it. I could "love but one."

Jessie H— was beautiful, innocent, and affectionate; but all these qualities could not conquer my love for Lenore; and honour commanded me to depart speedily from her presence.

Shortly after entering the house, she retired to her own room; and I saw no more of her for the night.

Before doing so myself, I took leave of Mr and Mrs H—, telling them that I must be off by daybreak in the morning.

My companions, Vane and Cannon, declared their unwillingness to accompany me; and used every argument to dissuade me from such an abrupt departure; but their arguments were only thrown away upon me. I had formed the determination; and nothing could have influenced me to abandon it. On becoming assured of this, they at length consented to go along with me.

Mr and Mrs H— did not urge me very strenuously to remain; and I believe that their silent eloquence could have been explained: by the supposition that it arose, from a regard for the happiness of their daughter.

We took our departure from the station at an early hour of the morning—before any of the household—except some of the domestics—were astir.

This manner of leaving may appear unceremonious; and would be so, in many parts of the world. But it is nothing unusual in Australia—where early setting out upon a journey is almost the universal fashion.

I did not care for the company of Vane and Cannon, on the way back to Melbourne. I would much rather have dispensed with it: as I wished to be alone. I wanted an opportunity for reflection—such as that journey would have afforded me. The society of Jessie H— had revived many memories within me. It had rekindled my passion for Lenore—strengthened my regrets for the past, and my despair for the future.

As I walked at a rapid pace, my companions fell behind—until, at length, I lost of them altogether.

Before the hour of noon, I had reached the city of Melbourne—sorry to think I had ever left it, to go upon an excursion, that had ended only in adding to the discontent already too firmly established within my bosom.

Volume Two—Chapter Twenty Eight.

Unsuitable Associates.

Once more I found myself without a home, without an occupation, and without any plans for the future—with a spirit undecided—depending on some slight circumstance as to what course I should next take.

Such a position is ever unpleasant. I knew this, from the fact of having been too often placed in it; and being well accustomed to the disagreeable reflections attending it.

I was anxious to decide, upon something to do. What should it be? What part of the world should I next visit? Why had I come back to Melbourne at all? Was it to make more money; or spend what I had already made? These, and a thousand other interrogatories succeeded each other in my mind; but to none of them could I give an intelligent answer.

While in this state of indecision, I came near losing a portion of my self-respect. There was a good deal to seduce me into habits of dissipation; and not much to restrain me from them. I had no longer the motives, to guard me against evil courses, that had once guided me. What could I gain, by always keeping on my best behaviour? Ever since first leaving home, I had endeavoured to conduct myself, as well as my limited knowledge would allow. What had I gained by it? Nothing, except, perhaps, a little vanity. Was this worth all the exertion I had made by resisting temptation?

Having little else to do, I spent some time in considering the question. The result was: satisfaction at the course I had pursued, and a determination to continue it.

A little vanity is, perhaps, after all, not such a bad thing. If a man cannot win the good opinion of others, he should endeavour to keep on proper terms with himself; and this he cannot do, without conducting himself in a proper manner. Because Fortune had not dealt with me, as I had wished, that was no reason why I should take her for an example, and imitate her unkindness. A man in adversity is too often deserted by his acquaintances; but this is no argument for turning against himself and becoming his own enemy. I determined not to act in a manner so stupid. I had too much self-respect, or pride, or vanity, to do so. Call it by what name you please, it served me at that time in good stead: for it was this, and nothing else, that restrained me from entering upon a course of dissipation.

My companions Vane and Cannon were good examples of men, who act without any fixed principles or firm resolve. They had both been, in the old country, what is called a "little wild," and had come to the colonies not from any inclination on their own part, but rather at the instance of their relatives and friends. They had been *sent* out, in fact—in the hope of their getting *tamed* by the hardships of colonial life.

I have known thousands of genteel young men similarly expatriated; and who, armed with letters of introduction and recommendation, had landed in the colonies, under the belief that they were very much wanted there. Never was there a greater delusion—as most of them had afterwards reason to know. The only people required in Australia are those of good habits—combined with some brains, or else a willingness to work. The "fast youths" packed off to get them out of the way, are generally deficient in these essential requisites—otherwise they might have found employment at home.

Unwilling to work, they arrive in the colonies with too good an opinion of themselves and too low an opinion of the people there. Although leaving England under the belief that there may be greater people left behind, they feel confident that they will stand foremost in Australia.

Some of these young gentlemen have the sense soon to discover their mistake; and many of them turn to hard work, with a will that does them credit. My companions Cannon and Vane were not of this kidney. Neither would consent to do anything, that savoured of "toil;" and with all their letters of introduction—backed by the influence of the friends to whom they had come introduced—they were unable to procure what they had been led to expect—easy situations under "government."

According to their showing, there was something wrong in the system; and the fault was with the colonial government and people. They could not understand that those who are called upon to govern a young colony—and put together the machinery of its social state—require to know something: and that they who, in their native land, have proved incapable of performing any useful duty, will be found still more useless, in a land where the highest capability is required.

Both had been unfortunate in having friends, who, while apparently behaving too well to them, had in reality been treating them in a cruel manner. They had been brought up in idleness—with the idea that labour is vulgar, and disgraceful to a gentleman. With these views they had been thrust forth upon a wide world—to war with life's battles, as it were, undisciplined and unarmed. Neither had the spirit successfully to contend against the adverse circumstances, in which they now found themselves; and they appeared to think that the best way for combating their misfortune was to betake themselves to a course of dissipation.

I endeavoured to persuade them, to go up to the diggings with me, and try to make their fortune by honest and honourable labour; but both rejected my counsel—Vane even receiving it with scorn. They would not soil their soft hands by bringing them in contact with the dirty earth! They had as little inclination for such menial labour, as I for many habits in which they indulged, and which to my way of thinking were far more menial than gold-digging.

They had been educated as gentlemen—I had not. Their ways were not my ways; and, seeing this, I resolved to cut their acquaintance. They were naturally not bad fellows; but they had faults, arising from a defective education, that rendered their company undesirable—especially in a place like Melbourne.

They were both pleasant companions; and in many respects I could have liked them; but as they were trying to live in Melbourne on nothing a year, I saw they would not be the right sort of associates for me.

To do them justice, they seemed to be aware of this themselves, more especially Cannon. One day he had the honesty to confess to me, that he was afraid he could not lead the life of a respectable gentleman any longer.

"Why?" I asked; "can you not get work?"

"No," he answered with a sneer; "I'm not going to drive bullocks, or dry-nurse a flock of sheep, for any man. I must live in some other manner—whether it be considered respectable or not."

"What can you do?" I inquired.

"Haven't an idea. I only know, Stone, that I shall be 'spongeing' on you, if you don't cut my acquaintance."

"And, when you can live on your acquaintance no longer, what then?"

"Then I must turn billiard-marker. My friends have sent me here, as they said, to make my fortune, but, as I believe, only to get rid of any further trouble with me at home. They have succeeded in their purpose: for I don't believe that I shall ever rise the 'tin' to return to England, although I should deucedly like to do so."

"Why should you wish to go where you are not wanted? Why not set to work; and become independent, by your own exertions?"

"Ah! my friend, you forget that we have not been brought up alike. You have had sensible parents, or guardians, who have done something to prepare you for that sort of thing, while I have been brought up foolishly by those who have tried hard to make me believe myself wiser than other people. What seems easy to you, is altogether impossible to me. You have been educated in a world that has taught you some wisdom, while I have been trained by a family that has only made a fool of me. I have been taught to believe that a man should owe everything to his ancestors; and you, that he should be indebted only to himself. Therefore, it's idle to talk about the matter—we can never agree."

I saw that there was no use in urging Cannon to attempt doing any thing in the colonies, as long as he could perceive no object to be gained by exerting himself.

Just then, I was myself slightly inclined to take a similar view of things. I had hoped and toiled to make myself as perfect, as was possible for a human being, placed in my circumstances. What had I gained by it? Nothing. What could I expect to gain? Nothing. Influenced by these thoughts, I remained for some time in doubt, whether I should return to the diggings or not. Life there, was, after all, only an excitement. It was not happiness.

Several times the temptation came strong upon me, to go back to Jessie; and see if I could find happiness with her. In striving to overcome this temptation, I was, perhaps, acting not so unlike my companions—Vane and Cannon: I was refusing to accept of fortune's favours, when they could so easily have been won.

They were in a growing colony, where, with labour, they might easily have obtained a high position—yet they would not exert themselves. I was playing a very similar part; for I saw how I might become happy—at all events, how I might live without unhappiness—yet I rejected the opportunity fortune had thus set before me. I would only consent to accept happiness on my own terms; and my obstinacy was not so very different from that which was the besetting sin of my companions.

I never felt more like a Rolling Stone, than when in Melbourne upon that occasion; but the sensation was not peculiar to myself: for the city contained thousands of people who had been everywhere; and were ready, at an hour's notice, to go there again!

Volume Two—Chapter Twenty Nine.

Farrell's Story Continued.

I at length succeeded in making up my mind to leave Melbourne; and, having parted with Vane and Cannon, I proceeded alone to Geelong—on my way to the gold fields of Ballarat. It was my first visit to Geelong; and I made it a short one; but, short as it was, I came to the conclusion, that if the people of Geelong had, within the two previous years, advanced in civilisation as rapidly as those of Melbourne, they must have been in a dreadfully degraded state before: since I found the social, moral, and intellectual condition of the place, if possible, still lower than that which had disgusted me on my first visit to Melbourne—and this is saying a deal.

The principal business of the Geelongers appeared to be that of drinking; and at this they were, to a high degree, industrious. Almost every one, with whom I came in contact, used obscene language, and were, or appeared to be, in every way more depraved, ignorant, and brutish, than any people to be found out of England itself.

From Geelong I went on to Ballarat—a distance of forty-eight miles—in a conveyance drawn by four horses; and paid for my accommodation the smart sum of six sovereigns.

On my arrival, I once more pitched my tent on the richest gold field known to the world.

Gold-diggers had been called "lucky vagabonds" by the then Attorney-General of Victoria. Perhaps he was right; but, whatever name had been given them, I was well pleased at finding myself once more in their company; and ready to share their toils, chances, and disappointments.

There is something in gold hunting that unsettles a man's mind, and makes him unfit for the ordinary occupations of life; and yet the calling itself is exactly suited to the state of mind it thus produces.

In this respect it is perhaps, unfortunately—too like the profession of the gamester.

No other occupation could have been so well adapted to my state of mind. I had no hopes to realise—no object to accomplish, but that of forgetting the past, and guarding my thoughts from straying into the future.

Such being the case, it was with much satisfaction that I again found myself a "lucky vagabond"—amidst the ever-varying scenes of excitement, to be witnessed on the gold fields of Ballarat.

The first acquaintance I encountered, after my arrival at the place, was Farrell—the Californian gold-digger—whom I had last seen in San Francisco.

As a matter of course, we stepped into the nearest hotel, to have a glass together.

"I suppose," said Farrell, as soon as we were seated—"you have no objection to listen to the conclusion of that little romance—the second chapter of which I made you acquainted with in San Francisco?"

"Not the slightest," I answered. "Although I felt sorry for what had happened to you, I confess I was very much amused at what you told me. But the most interesting part of the romance—as you call it—had not transpired. I shall be very glad to hear more of it."

"Well," proceeded Farrell, "you shall. As I told you they would, Foster and my wife came out to California; and, as I expected, to San Francisco. However, they had come ashore so very secretly and quietly, that I did not succeed in finding them, until they had been about ten days in the city.

"Foster took a house in Sacramento Street, furnished it with the money I had sent home to maintain my faithless wife; and laid in a stock of liquors. He intended to commence business in the grog-selling line; and was about opening the establishment, when I found them out.

"As soon as I did so, I went straight to the house—prepared for some sport.

"Foster and my wife were out shopping, and, no doubt, spending what remained of my money. The new tavern was in charge of a young man, whom they had engaged as a barkeeper.

"I immediately took possession of the whole concern—the house, and everything in it.

"I then discharged the barkeeper from their employment; and, the instant after, engaged him in my own service.

"I remained in that house for nine weeks—managing the business which Foster had intended to profit by; and then sold out for five thousand dollars.

"Neither Foster nor my wife, to my knowledge, ever came near the place—at all events, they never showed their faces in the house. They had found out, by some means, that I was in possession; and that had proved sufficient to make them surrender their claim without a contest.

"After selling out, I found leisure to look about me; and make further enquiries concerning the precious pair. I learnt that they had gone up to Sacramento city—where they had both taken situations in a public-house, managed by some other man. They had no longer any money, to go into business for themselves.

"I was still determined to see them; and started off for Sacramento.

"They must have had some one on the watch; for, on reaching the place, I found they had left only two hours before! As my anger had been for some time evaporating, I had no desire to pursue them any farther. The fact is, I felt a degree of freedom—after the loss of my wife—that went far towards reconciling me to the man who had relieved me of her. Besides, there was something in the idea of having turned Foster out of his finely furnished house in San Francisco, that made me think myself nearly square with him; and I did not care to take any more trouble, simply for the sake of troubling them.

"I returned to San Francisco; and from that place took passage in a ship just sailing for Melbourne.

"My anger has now entirely passed away; and yet I know I am still having some revenge—in addition to that I have already got. Wherever they may be, they are not living happily. They know that they have done wrong; and I'd lay a wager, there's not an hour of the day that they're not thinking of me, and dreading that I will make my appearance.

"I can return to my native land, and be happy. They cannot. I never wish to see either of them again: for I have become philosophical, and am willing that their crime should bring about its own punishment."

I congratulated Farrell on the philosophy that had enabled him so successfully to regain his tranquillity of spirit; and, after giving each other mutual directions for meeting again, we parted company.

Volume Two—Chapter Thirty.

Odd Fashions in the Gold Fields.

Farrell's philosophical resolve—to trouble the delinquents no more—formed the subject of my reflections, as I walked towards my tent. It was an illustration of the power which circumstances may have, in allaying even the strongest passion: for I knew that, when first made acquainted with his dishonour, the man had felt both deeply and resentfully.

I could not help applying the lesson to myself. "Is it possible," thought I, "that any circumstances can ever arise to allay my longings for Lenore? Is there in time a power that will yet appease them?"

My sentimental reflections were interrupted, by a scene that was of a different character—altogether comical. Not far from the place where I had parted with Farrell, I saw a crowd collected around a tent. Two miners, who had been "regular mates," were quarrelling; and their neighbours had gathered upon the ground, to be edified by an abundance of vituperative eloquence.

After the two men had, for a considerable time, amused the bystanders with their dispute, there appeared to be but one point upon which they could agree. That was that they should remain "mates" no longer.

The tent, some provisions in it, along with their mining tools and cooking utensils, they owned in common: having shared between them the expense attending their purchase.

As these things could not be divided to the satisfaction of both parties, it was proposed that each should remove from the tent, whatever was fairly entitled to be called his "private property," and that everything held in common—including the tent itself—should be burnt! This proposal was at once agreed to.

Each then brought forth from the tent his roll of blankets, and along with some other purely "personal effects." The ropes, picks, shovels, and buckets—that chanced to be lying outside the tent—were then "chucked" inside; after which, a match was applied to the dry canvass, and the diggers' dwelling was instantly in flames. The two disputants then walked coolly away from the place—each carrying his bag upon his back; one going to the east, the other to the west, amidst the cheers of the spectators—all of whom seemed greatly to admire this original mode of dissolving a partnership.

Law is so expensive and uncertain in all newly-established communities, that even sensible people do not like to resort to it, in the settlement of their disputes. Perhaps in this respect, the citizens of older communities might imitate the gold-diggers to advantage.

While in California, I was witness to another incident illustrative of the unwillingness to resort to the judgments of a legal tribunal. It was a case of two gold-diggers, who had been working together, and were about to dissolve partnership. Among the property they had owned in common was a fine mule. Each was desirous of becoming sole possessor of the animal; but neither would consent to give the other the price demanded for parting with his share. The difficulty might have been arranged by arbitration; but, neither desiring to be under any obligation to a third party, they adopted a more independent plan for settling the dispute.

"I'll give you fifty dollars for your share of the mule," proposed one, "or I'll take a hundred for mine? I want the animal."

"And I'll give you fifty for your share, or take a hundred for mine?" said the other, "I want it too."

"I'll make you another offer," said the first. "We'll play a game of 'Euker,' and whoever wins shall have the mule?"

The third challenge was accepted. The game was played; and the difficulty settled in five minutes, without any expense or ill-feeling arising out of it!

A disposition to settle doubts and difficulties by chance—that "unspiritual god"—is very common, among those who have long followed the occupation of gold hunting—for the reason, no doubt, that there is so much chance or uncertainty in the calling itself. Gold-diggers become familiarised to a sort of fatalism; and, in consequence, allow many questions to be decided by chance, that should be submitted to the test of reason.

I have seen a miner after working out a rich claim, toss up a dollar, to decide whether he should return home or not! The piece of money fell wrong side down; and the man remained at the diggings; and for aught I know, may be there still, working for a "pennyweight per diem."

And yet I do not always condemn this mode of relieving the intellect from the agony of doubt.

I once met two miners in San Francisco—to which place they had come from different diggings, for the purpose of having a few days' rest after months of toil. They had been shipmates to California; and now meeting again, each told the other of the way fortune had served him, since they had parted.

"I have got together two thousand three hundred dollars," said one. "I came out here to make up a pile of four thousand. If I had that, I'd go home."

"I have done nearly as well," said the other; "I have about two thousand; and if I had what we have both got, I'd go home; and never touch pick or shovel again."

"Ah! so would I," sighed the first.

"Well, then," challenged his old shipmate, "I'll tell you what we can do. We both want to go back home, with not less than four thousand dollars. We need not *both* be disappointed. One of us can go; and let the other stay. I'll cut a pack of cards with you; and the one who cuts highest, shall take four thousand dollars, and go home. The odd two or three hundred will be enough, to carry the loser back to the diggings. What say you, old hoss?"

This proposal was instantly accepted. The man, who had made it, lost his two thousand dollars; and next morning he handed the money over to his more fortunate friend, shook hands with him, and started back for the diggings!

This story may seem improbable, to those who have never been in California in its best days; but I can vouch for its truth.

After parting with Farrell, I seemed destined to witness a variety of incidents on that same evening; and of both characters—comic and tragical.

Shortly after passing the crowd, who had assisted at the dispute of the two miners, I came in sight of another concourse of people—in the middle of which appeared two or three policemen. They were gathered around the shaft of an abandoned claim. I went up to see what the excitement was about; and learnt, that a Chinaman had been found suspended in the shaft.

The Celestial had committed suicide, by hanging himself; and the plan he had adopted for terminating his existence, seemed, from its ingenuity, to have met with as much admiration from this crowd, as had been bestowed by the other one on the mode of settling their dispute, which had been adopted by the two diggers.

The Chinaman, knowing that the shaft was a deep one, had placed a large log of wood across the top of it. To the middle of this he had tied the end of a rope about fifteen feet long. The other end he had fastened, loop fashion, around his neck; and then jumped down the shaft. No Jack Ketch could have performed the operation for him, in a more effectual manner.

I afterwards learnt that the Chinaman had been an opium eater; and that he had secretly squandered some gold, in which his mates owned shares. The crime preying on his conscience—perhaps, when he had no opium to fortify it—was supposed to be the cause of his committing the act of self-destruction.

Volume Two—Chapter Thirty One.

A Disagreeable Partnership.

For two or three days I strolled about the diggings, looking for some opportunity of setting myself to work. On the Eureka lead I found five men holding a claim, that stood a good chance of being "on the line." It was within four claims of a place where gold was being taken out; and the "lead" would have to take a sharp turn to escape this place. A shaft had already been sunk to the depth of twenty feet, that would have to go down about ninety feet further. It would require eight hands to work the claim; and the five who owned it wished to sell some shares—for the purpose of making up the number.

The price asked was fifty pounds each; and, not seeing any better prospect of getting into a partnership, I purchased a share; and paid over the money.

I did not much like the appearance of my new partners. None of them looked like men accustomed to do hard work, or earn their livelihood in any respectable way. They seemed better suited for standing behind a counter, to sell gloves and ribbons, than for the occupation of gold-digging. But that the claim was likely to prove rich, I should not have chosen them as working associates.

One of the number was named John Darby. He was one of those individuals, who can never avail themselves of the fine opportunities afforded, for saying nothing. Darby's tongue was constantly on the go, and would often give utterance to a thousand words that did not contain a single idea. His eloquence was of the voluble kind, and very painful to the ear—being nothing but sound, without one grain of sense. His voice often reminded me of the clattering of the flour-mills I had heard in Callao. Whenever he would mount a hobby, and get his tongue freely going, the air seemed to vibrate with the movement of ten thousand demons, each hurling a fire-ball into the brain of the listener!

According to his own account, Darby had been ten times shipwrecked on the voyage of life. Several times, by not being able to marry as he wished; and once, when he was too successful in this design. The latter misfortune he regarded as being more serious than all the others.

Physically, as well as morally and intellectually, my gold-digging companion, John Darby was a singular creature. He did not weigh more than ten stone—though he was six feet one inch high standing in his shoes.

He had a small round head, from which hung long bay-coloured tresses of hair; and these he every day submitted to a careful dressing *à la Nazarene*.

Another member of our interesting "firm," who went by the name of "George," was simply an educated idiot.

In the opinion of many persons the man who has received a book education—whatever his natural abilities—must be a highly intelligent person. For my part, I think different; and I have adopted my belief, from an extensive experience of mankind.

It has been my misfortune to meet with many men of the class called "educated," who knew absolutely nothing that was worth the knowing; and George was one of these. He had received college instruction, yet no one could spend five minutes in his company without thinking of the phrase "ignorant idiot."

Like most people of his class, his folly was made amusingly conspicuous, by his assumption of an intellectual superiority over the rest of his companions.

Like most people, too, he had his vexations, the greatest being that his superiority was not always acknowledged. On the contrary, he was often chagrined by the discovery: that the light of his genius—like that of the lamp that burned in Tullia's grave—could not be seen of men. His eccentricities were at times amusing. Perhaps he had not been created in vain, though it was difficult to determine what had been the design of bestowing existence upon such a man—unless to warn others against the absurdities, by which he daily distinguished himself. He was a living lesson in the sixth volume of the great work of Nature; and none could study him, without subjecting themselves to a severe self-examination. Useless as I may have supposed the existence of this man to be, I must acknowledge myself indebted to him for many valuable lessons. My observation of his follies had the effect of awakening within me certain trains of thought, that removed from my own mind many strong prejudices hitherto possessing it. In this sense, I might say, that, he had not been created in vain, though his intended mission could not have been that of delving for gold on the fields of Ballarat.

Another of our firm had been an apothecary's assistant in London; and had but recently made his *début* on the diggings. He could not think of anything else, nor talk on any other subject, than the "shop," and what it contained; and I could not help fancying myself close to a chemical laboratory, whenever this individual came near me.

The other two partners of the concern used to make their appearance on the claim, about ten o'clock in the morning; and generally in a state of semi-intoxication.

These two men kept my mind in a constant state of trepidation—that is, when they were at work with me. I could never feel safe, in the shaft below, when I knew that either of the two was at the windlass.

Any man, in the least degree affected by drink, is a dangerous associate in the working of a gold mine—especially when entrusted with the charge of the windlass. He may not see when a bucket wants landing; or, when trying to lower it, he may hang the handle over the wrong hook—an almost certain consequence of which will be the crushing in of the skull of whoever may have the misfortune to be below!

No wonder that I felt some apprehension, while toiling in the companionship of my intoxicated partners.

Volume Two—Chapter Thirty Two.

A Sudden Dissolution of Partnership.

So much did my apprehensions prey upon me, that I had some idea of selling out my share and forsaking the partnership; but I had not been very long in the concern, before becoming convinced that we were sinking a shaft into one of the richest claims upon the line.

It was alike evident to me, that a great deal of hard labour would have to be performed, before the gold could be got out of it; and that my associates were the wrong men for this sort of thing.

Fortunately at this crisis a man of a different character purchased one of the two shares, that had remained unsold. Fearing that the other share might fall into the hands of some trifler like the rest of my original partners, I purchased it myself; and then underlet it to a young fellow, with whom I had formed an acquaintance. This young man had been hitherto unsuccessful at gold-digging. His name was John Oakes; and I had learnt from him that, he was by profession a sailor, yet—unlike the majority of sailors met with on the gold fields—he was a man of temperate habits; and seemed determined to save money, if he could only get hold of it.

Up to this time he had not found an opportunity of acting upon his good resolves: for every claim, in which he had taken a share, had turned out a failure.

Before telling Oakes of my intentions towards him, I simply informed him, that I had purchased the eighth share in our claim, and offered to underlet it to him.

"There's nothing I'd have liked better," said he, "than to get into a claim along with you. You are always lucky; and I should have been sure of getting something at last; but unfortunately I haven't the money to pay what you have advanced."

"Never mind that," rejoined I. "The claim is pretty safe to be on the lead; and you can pay me, when you have obtained your gold out of it."

"Then I accept your offer," said Oakes, apparently much gratified. "I need not tell you, how kind I think it of you to make it. I feel sure it will bring me a change of luck. I've never had but one decent claim, since I've been on the diggings; and the gold I got out of that was stolen from me. Rather, should I say, I was robbed of it. Did I ever tell you how that happened?"

"No—not that I remember."

"Well, then, let me tell you now. There were three of us in partnership, in a good claim on Eagle-Hawk Gully, Bendigo. We got out of it about forty-eight pounds of pure gold. During the time we were at work, we used to take the gold—as quick as we cleaned it out—to the Escort Office; and leave it there on deposit, until we should finish the job.

"When we had worked out the claim, we all went together to the office, and drew out the deposit.

"My two mates lived in a tent by themselves; and they proposed that we should go there—for the purpose of dividing our 'spoil.'

"On the way, we stopped at a tavern—with the owner of which they were acquainted, where they borrowed some gold weights and scales. They also purchased a bottle of brandy—to assist us, as they said, in the pleasant task that we had to perform.

"We then continued on to their tent. After going inside, we closed the door—so that no one should interrupt us, or see what we were about.

"Before proceeding to business, each of my mates drank a 'taut' of the brandy; and, although I did not care for it, to keep from quarrelling with them, I took a thimbleful myself. Immediately after swallowing that brandy—although, as I have said, there was only a thimbleful of it, I became insensible; and knew nothing of what passed afterwards. I did not recover my senses, until the next morning, when I found my two mates gone, and nothing in the tent except myself! They had taken the whole of the gold—including my share— along with them; and I have never set eyes upon either of them since.

"That lesson has cured me for ever of any propensity for strong drink, besides making me very particular as to the men I work with. What sort of fellows are they in the claim with you?"

"That is a subject on which I was just going to speak to you," said I. "They are not of the right sort for the work we have to do: one of them is an old woman, another a young one, and a third is worse than either. Two others are drunkards. There is only one—and he lately entered with us—who can be depended on for doing any work."

"It's unfortunate," said Oakes; "but I mustn't lose the chance of a good claim, for all that. I've no other prospect of getting one. I'll come over in the morning; and go to work with you. Perhaps, when the shaft is sunk, and we get a sight of the gold, there may be a reformation amongst your mates."

Next morning, at seven o'clock, Oakes made his appearance upon the claim. George and the apothecary came up a little later; and were soon followed by Mr John Darby.

When Oakes and Darby met, they recognised each other as old acquaintances.

"Is it possible, Darby, that I find *you* still in the colony?" asked Oakes. "I thought that you had long ago started for England."

"No; I did not intend going home," replied Darby, evidently not too well pleased at encountering his old acquaintance. "I only went to Melbourne for a few days—to recruit my health, which was never very good at Bendigo. After getting all right again, I came out here."

Darby continued talking as if against time; and, as we were looking out with some impatience for the two drunkards, we allowed him to go on without interruption.

I had requested all the members of the "firm" to be early upon the ground on that particular morning. A full company had now been made up; and I wanted to come to some understanding with my partners—about a more energetic "exploration" of the claim.

The two "swipers," as they were called, soon after made their appearance; and, as they drew near, I could perceive that another recognition had taken place.

On seeing the new partner, both turned sharp round; and then started off, at a brisk pace, in the opposite direction!

For a moment Oakes appeared surprised—as if uncertain what to make of it. All at once, however, his comprehension became clearer; and, calling to me to follow him, he set off in pursuit of the fugitives.

The two had diverged from each other in their flight; and, as they had already got a good start of us, both were successful in making their escape. When Oakes and I came together again, he informed me, that the men were his old mates, who had robbed him on the Bendigo diggings!

We repaired to the police encampment; and, after procuring a force, proceeded to the tent of the runaways.

As a matter of course, we found that the birds had flown; and could not be discovered anywhere upon the diggings.

We were no more troubled with them, as "sleeping partners" in the claim.

Volume Two—Chapter Thirty Three.

A Frightful Nugget.

When Oakes and I got back from our search after the thieves, we discovered that still another defection had taken place in the firm. During the interval of our absence, Mr John Darby had sold his share, to a person, who had the appearance of having work in him, after which that talkative gentleman had quietly slipped away from the spot.

I had noticed that he had not seemed highly delighted with the idea of my friend Oakes coming into the company; and I presumed that this was the cause of his sudden desertion of us.

On making my conjecture known to Oakes, I received from him the following explanation:

"I knew Darby," said Oakes, "when he first arrived in the colonies. He had come over here, as many others do, under the belief that hard work was degrading to a gentleman, such as he loudly proclaimed himself to be. Suffering under this affliction, he would not condescend to become a miner, but obtained a situation in the government camp at Bendigo.

"One day I had the misfortune to pass an hour in his company—during which he seemed struck with a fit of temporary sensibility, and declared his intention to take to gold-digging.

"Toiling to get gold," said he, "is manual labour, I admit; still it is not degrading to a man of fine sensibilities. I'm told that there are men of all the learned professions engaged in mining; and that a celebrated author is now a gold-digger at the Ovens. Gold-diggers have no masters; and I have even heard, that they affect to despise us government people at the camp."

I afterwards ascertained that Mr Darby had been dismissed from the government employment, just before making these remarks; and to this cause, no doubt, might be assigned the change, that had taken place in his views regarding "labour."

Not long after that interview with him, he made his appearance near where I was working, in the Bendigo diggings. He had some mining tools with him—such as gold-diggers sometimes buy for the amusement of their children. He appeared as if he intended to pick up a fortune, without soiling his hands with the dirt, since both of them were gloved!

Paying no heed to some derisive cries that greeted him as he came upon the ground, he strutted on, looking out for a claim.

The place, he at length selected for his début in gold-digging, was chosen with some apparent judgment.

Seeing two old shafts, about ten yards apart, that had the appearance of having been well worked, he supposed the ground between them must also be worth working; and just half-way between the two he commenced sinking another.

The soil of the place was shallow—not over eight feet in depth—and Darby, inspired by high hopes, toiled industriously for the greater part of a day. At the end of each hour it could be seen that his head had descended nearer to the level of the earth; and, before leaving off in the evening, he had got waist deep into the dirt.

Next morning he was again at work, at a very early hour.

"I sha'n't be surprised," said he to one of his neighbours who was passing, "if I should find a jeweller's shop here. If it turns out well, I shall be on my way home to-morrow. As good luck would have it, the Great Britain sails for England next week."

"I shall not be surprised at your good luck," replied the miner, with a significant smile; "at least, not any more than you'll be astonished at finding no gold in that hole."

"I won't be at all astonished," retorted Darby; "astonishment is a vulgar feeling, that I'm not in the habit of indulging in. So far as that goes, it would make little difference to me, whether I found no gold at all—a nugget the size of myself—or the devil."

Darby continued toiling for nearly an hour longer. At the end of this time, he was seen suddenly to spring up out of the hole; and run with all the speed, his tottering limbs could command, in the direction of his tent—falling down, once or twice, on the way!

Some of the diggers had the curiosity to go, and look down the hole he had made—in the hope of discovering the cause of his so suddenly forsaking it. To their surprise they saw a human corpse! It was partly uncovered. The face, with its half decayed features, had been exposed to view by the spade of Mr Darby, who had been all the time engaged in re-opening an old tunnel excavated by their former owners between the two worked-out claims.

Some man had been murdered; and his body concealed in the tunnel. Of course the miner who had "chaffed" Darby in passing knew nothing of this. He only knew that a tunnel was there; and that Darby would get no gold out of the shaft he was sinking; but the man was as much astonished as any of us, on seeing the horrible "nugget" that had rewarded the labours of the "gentleman gold-digger."

We heard that afternoon that Darby—immediately after receiving payment for his share in our claim—had started off to Melbourne, with the intention of returning to England. He had still retained enough pride of character, or vanity, or whatever it might be called, to dread the ridicule, that he knew must await him, should Oakes tell us the story of that Bendigo nugget.

His defection was a fortunate circumstance for us: as it led to our procuring, in his place, a partner capable of performing a full share of the toil we had before us.

On that day Fortune appeared determined to favour us. Before night we had disposed of the two shares, abandoned by the "swipers," to a couple of first-class miners.

Next morning we all went to work with a will. Even George and the apothecary—stimulated by the example of the others—did their best to imitate it.

This, however, was on their part only a spasmodic effort. Before many days had elapsed, the toil proved too great for their powers of endurance; and each entered into an agreement with a "working partner," who was to have one-half of their gold in return for the labour of getting it out for them.

After this arrangement had been made, we could count on a proper working company; and our progress in the *exploitation* of the mine was, thenceforth, both regular and rapid.

We had not been long engaged upon the claim, when we discovered that it *was* "on the line," and our toil was lightened by the golden prospects thus predicated.

I was struck with the interest which Oakes appeared to feel in the result. He would scarce take time, either for eating or sleeping, and, I believe, he would have continued to toil twenty-two hours, out of the twenty-four, had we allowed him!

When the claim was at length worked out, and the gold divided, Oakes came to me, and paid back the fifty pounds I had advanced towards the purchase of his share.

"You have made my fortune," said he, "and I am going home with it to-morrow. It is not a large one; but it is all I require. I must now tell you what I intend to do with the money—as I believe that will be some reward to you, for your generosity in taking me into the claim. I have a father, who has been in prison for seven years for debt; and all for the paltry sum of a hundred and sixty pounds! Six years ago, I left home, and turned sailor, only that I might get my passage to some foreign land—where I might make the money to pay this debt, and take my father out of prison. I knew I could never raise it in England—where some of our governing people tell us we are so prosperous, and contented! One hundred and sixty pounds was a large sum, for a young fellow like me to get together. I knew I could never make it up, by following the sea; and I had begun to despair of ever doing so, until I got aboard of a ship in Cape Town bound for Melbourne. Of course I joined the ship, with the intention of escaping from her, when we should reach Melbourne. I need hardly tell you, that I succeeded. One night, as we were lying anchored in Hobson's Bay, off Williamston, I slipped into the water; and, by swimming more than a mile, I reached the shore. Soon after, I found my way to the Bendigo diggings.

"While working out that claim on Eagle-Hawk Gully—of which I have told you—I was the happiest man on earth: but, when I discovered that my mates had absconded with my gold, I was driven nearly distracted. It was a cruel disappointment to a man, anxious to liberate an honest father from prison, as well as extricate a mother and two sisters from a situation of extreme misery.

"Since then I have had no good luck—until you got me into this claim we have just completed. Thank God, I've got the money at last; and may He only grant that I shall live to reach old England with it, in time to relieve my suffering relatives. That is all I care for in this world; and if I can accomplish it, I shall be willing to die."

At my request Oakes promised to write to me from Melbourne; and let me know in what ship he would sail.

This promise was kept, for, the week after, I received a letter from him, informing me—that he had embarked in the ship "Kent," bound for London.

I could not help offering up a silent prayer, that favouring winds would safely waft him to his native shore; and that his long-cherished hopes might meet with a happy realisation.

End of Volume Two.

Volume Three—Chapter One.

An Adventure with a "Black fellow."

Shortly after the departure of Oakes, I went to a little rush, on Slaty Creek, on the Creswick's Creek Gold-fields, about thirteen miles from Ballarat.

I was accompanied by two others, with whom I had lately been working. Soon after arriving at the rush, we took possession of a claim; and proceeded to "prospect" it.

After sinking a small hole on the claim, and washing some of the earth from the bottom of it, we found a little gold—not what we thought "payable," and yet the "prospect" was so good that we did not like to forsake the claim. In hopes that it might contain richer "dirt" than what we had found, we determined to stay by it a while longer.

To sink our shaft to any advantage, we needed a crowbar. There were some very large stones in the ground that could not be moved without one. A crowbar was an article we did not possess; and as we could not find one at the two or three stores established on Slaty Creek, I walked over, one evening, to Creswick Creek—a distance of some three or four miles—intending to purchase one there.

By the time I reached the township, made my purchase, and started towards home, it had got to be ten o'clock. About half a mile from Creswick, on the road homeward, I had to pass a camp of native blacks.

These people, in morality and social habits, are upon a scale, perhaps, as low, as humanity can reach. The sole object of their existence is, to obtain strong drink. For that, they will sometimes work at gathering bark and poles; or they will look about for stray specks of gold—in places where the miners have been working, and which have been abandoned.

Any one, who understands the strength of their aversion to labour, may form some idea of the desire these blacks have for drink: when it is known that they will sometimes do the one for the sake of getting the other!

An Australian native black, after becoming degraded by intercourse with the whites, will sell his mother, sister, or wife, for brandy!

The party, whose camp I was compelled to pass, had evidently met with some success, in their various ways of obtaining brandy during that day, for from the noise they were making, I judged that all, or nearly all of them, must be in a state of intoxication.

Not wishing to be annoyed, by their begging for tobacco—which I knew they would be certain to do, should they see me—I resolved to keep out of their way. Instead of following the direct path—which led on through the place where they had erected their "*mia-mias*" or huts—I made a détour of their encampment. After passing well round it, I turned once more towards the road to Slaty Creek, which, after a time, I succeeded in regaining.

I had scarce got well upon the track, when I was confronted by a big "black fellow," apparently beside himself with drink.

As a general rule, the native blacks, seen roaming about the *gold-fields* of Victoria, are seldom guilty of malignant violence towards the whites; but the man, whom it was now my misfortune to meet, proved an exception to this rule: for the reason, no doubt, that he was maddened with alcohol.

As he approached me, I saw that he was brandishing a "waddy waddy," or club. I strove to avoid him; but found, that although mad with drink, he was active upon his limbs, and able to hinder me from making a retreat. Had I attempted to run away, I should have been brought to a stop—by a blow from his "waddy waddy."

I saw that my best chance of safety would be in standing firm, and defending myself.

The fellow made two desperate lounges at me with his club, which, with some difficulty, I managed to dodge—and all the while that he was delivering his murderous assault, he kept shouting to me, in his native gibberish—apparently making some important communication, but the nature of which I had not the slightest idea.

Just as I was beginning to consider the affair serious, and was preparing to act on the offensive, the black made a third blow with his waddy waddy. This I was unable, altogether, to avoid; and the club struck heavily against one of my legs.

Irritated by the pain produced, I could no longer control my temper; and, grasping the crowbar with both hands, I aimed a blow at the black fellow's head.

93

I did not strike with the intention of killing the man. I only knew that my life was in danger; and that I was suffering great pain from the wound I had received. This, however, had irritated me beyond the power of controlling myself; and, no doubt, my whole strength was given to the stroke.

The crowbar descended upon the black fellow's naked crown; and never shall I forget the horrible sound made by the crashing in of his skull. It was not only horrible, but sickening; and for a moment, completely unmanned me. It was not the mere thought, that I had broken a man's head, that unmanned me, for I had both witnessed, and taken part, in many a sanguinary scene before that—without feeling any such remorseful emotion. It was the horrid sound—caused by the crashing in of his skull—that not only overcame me, but, for a time, rendered me faint, sick, and disgusted with the world, and all it contained.

That sound echoed in my ears for hours afterwards; and, ever since that time, I have carefully avoided being near any place where a "free fight" was about to take place—lest it might be my misfortune to hear a similar sound.

The day after, it was reported, that the blacks were entertaining themselves with a funeral. I did not learn the particulars of the ceremony; but, presume it was similar to a funeral I had witnessed among a tribe of the same people on Fryer's Creek, in July, 1853. One of their number had been killed, by another of the tribe; and, on the next day, I was present at the performance of their funeral rites, over the remains of the murdered man.

A grave was dug, about five feet deep—into which the body was lowered, and a sheet of bark laid over it. The earth was then filled in; and while this was being done, by one man, two others stood inside the grave, stamping upon the dirt, and treading it down, as firm as they could make it!

What could have been their object in thus *packing* the dead body, I never understood, unless it was done, under the impression, that the corpse might come to life again, without this precaution being taken to keep it under ground!

Volume Three—Chapter Two.

Farrell and His Wife, Once More.

Three weeks "prospecting," at Slaty Creek, convinced me that it was not the place for a gold-digger to make his fortune, without the severest labour; and for this reason, I left it—returning to Ballarat.

On arriving at the latter place, I went to see my old Californian acquaintance, Farrell. The instant I set eyes on him, and he on me, his features plainly proclaimed that he had something to tell me, which he deemed very amusing.

"Farrell," said I, "you are working a rich claim; I see fortune written on your face."

"Nothing of the kind," he answered; "I have just finished a tolerable spell of digging, it is true; and shall start for home to-morrow. But it ain't that; I have better news still."

"Better news? What can it be!"

"I've seen Foster, and my wife. Ha! ha! they've been living in sight of my tent for the last four months; and I never knew they were there until two days ago!"

"Then you have seen Foster?"

"Certainly, I have!"

"What did you do to him?"

"Nothing. Fate is giving me all the revenge I want; and I would not interfere with her designs—not for the world. In saying that Foster is the most miserable object I've seen for many years. I speak only the truth. He has a rheumatic fever, and hasn't been able to stir out of his tent for six weeks. He will probably never go out of it again—that is, alive. Now, I call that fun; isn't it?"

"Not much for Foster, I should think. But how came you to find them?"

"I was in my tent, one morning, when I heard a woman talking to my partner, who happened to be outside just by the door. The woman was wanting to get some washing to do. She said, that her husband had been a long time ill; and that they hadn't a shilling to live upon. I thought her voice sounded familiar to me; and, taking a peep out of the tent, I saw at once it was my runaway wife! I waited till she walked away; and then, slipping out, I followed her to her own tent. She went inside, without seeing me; and then I stepped in after her, and stood quietly surveying the guilty pair.

"My wife went off into a fit of 'highstrikes,' while Foster lay trembling, like a craven, expecting every moment to be killed. 'Don't be frightened,' said I, 'I haven't the slightest intention to put you out of your misery. I like revenge too well for that. You have some more trouble to see yet, I hope; and I'm not going to do anything that might hinder you from seeing it.

"I waited till my wife became sufficiently composed to comprehend what was going on; and then, after thanking her for the kindness she had done me—by relieving me of all further trouble with her—I bid them 'good day,' and walked off, leaving them to reflect upon the interview.

"To-day, I have just been to visit them again; and the want and misery, they appear to be suffering, gave me no little pleasure. They looked as though they had not had a morsel to eat for a week; and I could not see a scrap—of either bread or meat—in their tent.

"I told them, not to give themselves any further uneasiness, on my account, for I wasn't going to molest them any more. 'I've made a little fortune here,' said I, 'and intend starting for New York State to-morrow. Have you any message to send to your friends?' I asked of Foster. The poor devil could not, or would not, make me a reply. 'Have *you*, Mary,' said I, turning to my wife. She could only answer with sobs. 'It is a miserable, wretched life, at the best, on these diggings,' I remarked. I am going to leave it, and once more seek happiness in my native land. Excuse me, Mr Foster, and you, Mrs F., for not helping you in your distress. I know that there is an All-wise Creator, who will reward both of you, as your conduct deserves; and it would be presumptuous in me to take any of the work out of his hands. I leave you here, with full confidence in the belief, that divine justice will be impartially administered to all.

"Now that was what I call good talking,—what do you say?"

"Very good, indeed," I answered. "But are you really going to leave them in that manner?"

"Certainly, I am. I never intend to see either of them again. When I was coming away from their tent, my wife followed me out, went down on her knees, and piteously entreated me to aid her, in returning to her parents. She declared, that she never knew my worth, until she had foolishly lost me; and that she now loved me more than ever she had done—my little finger, more than Foster's whole body—which it would not have been difficult to make me believe. She said, she would not ask me to let her live with me again; but, that if I would give her money to return home, she would pass the remainder of her days in praying for me.

"No, Mary," said I, "do not think so unjustly of me, as to suppose I could do that. I love you too well, to stand in the way of your receiving the reward you have deserved; and, besides, you should not desert Forter, whom you have followed so far—now that the poor fellow is in affliction. My affection for you is too sincere, to think of allowing you to commit so great a wrong?

"Having delivered this exordium, I turned and left her. Now that is what I call revenge. What's your opinion?"

"What is revenge to one man, may not be to another," was my answer. "If it pleases you to act so, of course, I have nothing to say against it."

"And what would *you* do?"

"I should give the woman some money, enough to enable her to return to her parents. As for the man, I should leave him to his fate."

"Then you would act very foolishly,—as I would, if I followed your advice. The woman having got home, would be there to annoy me. I wish to go back to my native place; and be happy there for the rest of my days. How could that be—living along side a wife who had so disgraced me?"

I could say nothing more to dissuade Farrell from his purpose; and we parted company—he shortly after starting for Melbourne, to take passage for New York.

The after-fate of his faithless wife, and her wretched paramour, some other must record: for, from that hour, I never heard of either of them again.

Volume Three—Chapter Three.

The Rush to Avoca.

After passing four or five days in looking about the Canadian, Eureka, and Gravel-pits, "leads" on the Ballarat Gold-fields, and finding no favourable opportunity of getting into a good claim, I determined to proceed to Avoca river, for which place a big "rush" was just starting—that, by all accounts, would turn out a success.

The day after I had formed this resolution, I saw a man with a horse and dray, just departing for Avoca.

The man was willing to take a light load of diggers' "swags;" and, rolling up my tent and blankets, I put them upon his dray.

The drayman did not succeed in getting all the freight he required: for there was but one other digger besides myself, who furnished him with anything to carry. As he, and a partner he had, were anxious to reach the new gold-field as soon as possible, they determined to start, without waiting to make up a load.

All being ready, we set out at once for the "sweet vale of Avoca."

The drayman's partner was a man known in the diggings, by the name of "Bat." I had often seen "Bat," and was acquainted with two or three other diggers, who knew him well. He was famed at Ballarat, for having the largest mind of any man in the place; but it was also generally known, that in his mind, the proportion of selfishness, to all other feelings and faculties, was ninety-nine to one.

The reason why Bat's soul was thought to be so large was, that, otherwise it could not have contained the amount of disgusting selfishness, which it daily exhibited.

He was only miserly about spending money, that might result to the benefit, or injury, of any one but himself. In the gratification of his own desires, he was a thorough spendthrift.

I had heard one of the miners tell a story, illustrative of Bat's disposition. For amusement, the miner had made an experiment, to see, to what extent, selfishness would, as he expressed it, "carry Bat on the way to hell."

He enticed this large-souled individual, to go with him on a "spree;" upon which, he treated him five times in succession.

Bat had by this time imbibed a strong desire for more drink; and after waiting for some time for his companion to treat him again, he slipped to one side, and took a drink alone—without asking the other to join him.

After this, the miner treated him twice more; and not long after, Bat again drank alone, at his own expense!

By this time both of them had become pretty well intoxicated; and the spree came to a termination, by Bat's receiving a terrible thrashing from the *convive*, who had been vainly tempting him to spend his money.

Bat's mate, the drayman, knew but little about him—only having joined him as a partner the evening before we started for the Avoca.

On the first day of our journey, late in the afternoon, we arrived at a roadside grog-shop; and all went in for something to drink. Inside the house, were three ill-looking men, who had the appearance of having once *lived in Van Dieman's Land*. The shop was a very colonial affair; and, after drinking some poison, called rum, we all came out—leaving Bat weighing some gold, which he had taken out of a leather bag, in presence of all the company. It was to pay for a bottle of brandy, which, as we were going to camp out for the night, he had purchased—for the purpose of making himself comfortable.

Darkness overtook us about a mile or so beyond the grog-shop; and water being near the place, we resolved to stay by it for the night.

Bat came up, just after we had kindled our fire; and drank some tea along with us. He had brought with him two bottles of brandy, instead of one, the second being for his mate, the drayman, who had commissioned him to buy it for him. Seeing these two bottles of brandy in the camp, I did not care about staying on the spot. I believed that the drayman, Bat, and the other digger who accompanied them, would get drunk; and I did not fancy to remain in their company.

I took up my blankets; and, going about two hundred yards off from the camp—to a grove of bushes—I rolled myself in my cover, and slept soundly till the morning.

At sunrise I awoke; and went back to rejoin my travelling companions.

On drawing near the encampment, I saw that something was wrong; and I hastened forward. Bat was not there, but the drayman was, and also the digger. Both were tied with their hands behind their backs, and, furthermore, fastened to the wheels of the dray. I saw that both of them were gagged!

I lost no time in releasing them from their unpleasant imprisonment; and as soon as I had ungagged them, they told me what had happened. About the middle of the night, four men had come up, armed with revolvers, which they had held to the heads of the drayman and digger, while they tied and gagged them. The two were then robbed of all their money, after which, the bush-rangers went their way— taking along with them the drayman's horse.

"But where is Bat?" I asked.

"We don't know," was the reply. "He went away soon after you did."

Circumstances looked suspicious against Bat; but only to me: for the others understood all that had happened. Bat had determined to keep his bottle of brandy to himself. By remaining with the others, he could not well drink it all without asking them to have a share, as he had already been treated by his partner. To avoid doing so he had stolen away to the bush, where he could drink his liquor alone.

"The men who robbed us," said the disconsolate drayman, "could be no others than them we saw in the grog-shop; and it was my mate Bat who drew them on to us: for they seemed greatly disappointed, and swore fearfully at not finding him. He flashed his gold-dust before them yesterday; and, of course they came after us to get it. I wish they had got every ounce of it. He deserved to be robbed for tempting them."

"Have you lost much?" I asked, of the drayman.

"No," answered he. "Luckily, I had not much to lose—only seventeen pounds. But I care more about my old horse, for I've owned him over three years."

The digger had lost twelve pounds in cash, and a gold nugget of seven ounces weight.

While both were lamenting their mishap, Bat made his appearance from the bush; and began finding fault with his mate, for not having breakfast ready, and the horse harnessed for a start. The effects of the bottle of brandy had only increased the disagreeable peculiarities of Bat's character; and given him a good appetite.

He was now told what had happened, which made him a little more amiable. But his amiableness could be traced to the fact of his being conceited of the swinish selfishness of which he had been guilty. He seemed highly delighted to think he had had the good fortune to escape the mischance that had befallen his companions; and, instead of sympathising with them, he actually boasted of his luck, putting it forward as a proof of his possessing more than ordinary sagacity.

"Will you have a little brandy?" asked his mate, in a tone of voice that told me the offer was not made in a friendly spirit. "There's a drop left in my bottle, which, luckily, the bush-rangers did not get hold of."

"Of course I will," answered Bat. "Brandy is a thing I never refuse, especially when on the road, and after camping out all night. Let's have it."

The drayman produced his bottle, along with his tin pannikin. The former was about half full, and its contents were poured into the cup.

When Bat reached forth his hand to take hold of the vessel, the brandy was thrown into his face; and the next instant he himself fell heavily to the earth—from the effects of a blow administered by the clenched fist of the drayman!

Bat rose to his feet, and tried to show fight; but no efforts he could make, either offensive or defensive, hindered him from getting his deserts. It was the first time I had ever been pleased at the sight of one man punishing another.

After getting a thorough thrashing from his irate partner, Bat took up his blankets, and then started back along the road towards Ballarat—having, for some reason or other, changed his mind about going to Avoca.

I paid the drayman what I had agreed to give him for taking my "swag;" and, accompanied by the digger, who had been robbed along with him, I continued my journey afoot—each of us carrying his own blankets and tent. We left the poor drayman alone with his dray, in what the Yankees call a "fix," for he dare not leave the vehicle, and the goods it contained, to go in search of a horse, and without one it would be impossible for him to transport his property from the place.

I would have stopped along with him for a day or two, and lent him some assistance, had it not been, that he was one of those unfortunate creatures so often met in the Australian colonies, who seldom speak without using some of the filthy language imported there from the slums of London. For this reason I left him to get out of his difficulty the best way he could; and, for all I know to the contrary, he is still keeping guard over his dray, and the miscellaneous lading it contained.

Volume Three—Chapter Four.

The "Sweet Vale of Avoca."

We arrived near the Avoca diggings late in the afternoon. Seeing a good spot for pitching a tent, my companion stopped, and proposed that we should go no further: as that place was exactly suited to his mind.

"All right," said I. "If it suits you—you had better stay there."

While the digger was disencumbering himself of his load, I walked on. I did so, because my travelling companion was a man whose acquaintance I did not care to cultivate any further. I did not take the trouble to satisfy myself of any reason for leaving him in this unceremonious manner. I only knew that I did not like his society; and, therefore, did not desire to pitch my tent near him—lest I might have more of it.

My principle objection to remaining with the man was this. I had formed an idea, that nothing was to be gained from him—neither knowledge, amusement, friendship, money, nor anything else—unless, perhaps, it might have been, a worse opinion of mankind; and this of itself, was just ground for my giving him the good-bye.

After going a little farther on, I pitched my tent in a place I made choice for myself.

Next morning I walked forth, to have a look at the new gold-field.

There are not many spectacles more interesting to the miner, than that termed a "rush" to a gold-field newly discovered, and reported to be "rich."

The scene is one of the greatest excitement. On the ground to which the "rush" is directed, all the vices and amusements to be met with in large cities, soon make their appearance. Where, perhaps, a month before, not a human being could have been seen, taverns, with magnificent interior decorations, billiard-rooms, bowling-alleys, rifle-galleries, theatres, and dancing-saloons, will be erected; in short, a city, where, but a few weeks ago, there was nothing but the "howling" wilderness!

On my arrival at the Avoca diggings, I marked out a "claim," and for several days my occupation was that of "shepherding" it.

To "shepherd a claim," is to keep possession of, and merely retain it—until, by the working of other claims near, a tolerably correct opinion may be formed: as to whether yours will be worth digging or not.

The system of shepherding claims, is only practised where the gold lies some distance below the surface; and where the claim can only be prospected at the expense of some money and trouble.

The claim I had marked out, was a large one—larger in extent than one person was entitled to hold. For this reason, on the third day, after I had taken possession of it, another man bespoke a share in it along with me.

I did not like the look of this man; and would have objected to working with him; but he would not consent to divide the ground; and the only way I could get clear of him was, to yield up the claim altogether. This I did not wish to do: for it stood, or rather "lay," in a good position for being "on the lead."

I have said that I did not like the look of the intruder. This dislike to him arose, from the circumstance of his having a strong "Vandemonian expression" of countenance; and I had a great prejudice against those who, in the colonies, are called "old lags."

We "shepherded" the claim together for a few days, when the prospect of its being on the lead, became so fair, that we at length commenced sinking a shaft.

The more I saw of my companion, while we were toiling together, the weaker grew my aversion to him; until, at length, I began to entertain for him a certain feeling of respect. This increased, as we became better acquainted.

I learnt that he was not from Tasmania, but from New South Wales; and my prejudice against the "Sydneyites" was even stronger (having been formed in California,) than against the "old hands" from Van Dieman's Land.

The "Vandemonians," generally speaking, have some good traits about them, that are seldom met amongst those from the "Sydney side." The convicts from the former place, have more generosity in their wickedness, less disposition to turn approvers on their companions in crime, while at the same time, they display more manliness and daring in their misdeeds, than do the "Sydney birds."

One would think, there could not be much difference between the criminals of the two colonies: since both originally come from the same school; but the characteristics distinguishing classes of *transportees*, change with the circumstances into which they may be thrown.

My new partner proved to be like few of the "downey coves" I had encountered in the diggings: for I found in him, a man possessing many good principles, from which he could not be easily tempted to depart.

He did not deny having been a convict, though, on the other hand—unlike most of his class—he never boasted of it.

"Drinks all round," can usually be won from an old convict in the following manner:—

Offer to lay a wager, that you can tell for what crime he had been transported; and as his own word is generally the only evidence to be obtained for deciding the wager, ten to one it will be accepted. Tell him then: that he was "lagged for poaching," and he will immediately acknowledge that he has lost, and cheerfully pay for the "drinks all round."

This game could not have been played with the subject of my sketch: since he freely acknowledged the crime for which he had been transported: it was for killing a policeman.

One evening, as we sate in our tent, he related to me the story of his life; but, before giving it to my readers, I must treat them to a little explanation.

This narrative is entitled the "Adventures of a Rolling Stone," and such being its title, there may be a complaint of its inappropriateness: because it also details the adventures of others. But part of the occupation of the hero, has been to observe what was going on around him; and, therefore, a faithful account, not only of what he did, but what he saw and heard—or in any way learnt—should be included in a true narrative of his adventures. Hearing a man relate the particulars of his past life, was to the "Rolling Stone," an event in his own history; and, therefore, has he recorded it.

The reality of what is here written may be doubted; and the question will be asked:—how it was, that nearly every man who came in contact with the "Rolling Stone," had a history to relate, and also related it?

The answer may be found in the following explanation:—

A majority of the men met with on the gold-fields of California and Australia, are universally, or at least generally, unlike those they have left behind them in the lands of their birth. Most gold-diggers are men of character, of some kind or other; and have, through their follies or misfortunes, made for themselves a history. There will almost always be found some passage of interest in the story of their lives—often in the event itself, which has forced them into exile, and caused them to wander thousands of miles away from their homes and their friends.

When it is further remembered: that the principle amusement of the most respectable of the gold-diggers, is that of holding social converse in their tents, or around their evening camp-fires, it will appear less strange, that amongst so many "men of character" one should become acquainted with not a few "romances of real life"—such as that of the "Vandemonian" who became my associate in the "sweet vale of Avoca," and which is here recorded, as one of many a "convict's story," of which I have been the confidant.

Volume Three—Chapter Five.

A Convict's Story.

"You have expressed a desire to hear the story of my life," said my mining partner. "I make you welcome to it. There is not much of my history that I should be ashamed to tell you of; but with that little I shall not trouble you. I have never done anything very bad,—that is, I have never robbed anybody, nor stolen anything that I did not really want.

"I am a native of Birmingham, in which town I resided until I was about twenty years of age.

"My father was a confirmed drunkard; and the little money he used to earn by working as a journeyman cutler, was pretty certain to be spent in gin.

"The support of himself, and four young children fell upon my mother, myself, and a brother—who was one year younger than I. In all Birmingham, there were not two boys more dutiful to their parents, more kind to their younger brothers and sisters, more industrious, and less selfish, than my brother and myself—at the time I am speaking of.

"Our hours were wholly occupied in doing all we could, to supply the wants of my father's family.

"We sometimes attended an evening school. There we learnt to read and write; but even the time devoted to this, we would have considered as squandered, if we could have been doing anything else—to benefit the unfortunate family to which we belonged.

"One evening, after we had got to be grown up to manhood, my younger brother and I were returning from our work, when we saw our father at some distance off, in the middle of the street. We saw that he was intoxicated. Three policemen were around him—two of them with hands upon him.

"As usual with my father on such occasions, he was refractory; and the policemen were handling him in a very rough manner. One of them had struck him on the head with his baton, and my father's face was covered with blood.

"My brother and I ran up, and offered to take him quietly home—if the policemen would allow us to do so; but as he had assaulted them, and torn their clothes, they refused to let us have him, and insisted in locking him up. My brother and I, then offered to take him to the lock-up ourselves; and, taking him by the hand, I entreated him to go quietly along with us.

"The policeman rudely pushed me aside, again collared my father, and commenced dragging him onward. Once more we interfered—though this time, only to entice our father to go with the policemen, without making any resistance.

"At that moment, one of the constables shouted 'a rescue;' and the three, without further provocation, commenced an assault upon my brother and myself.

"One of them seized me by the throat; and struck me several times on the head with his baton. We struggled awhile, and then both fell to the ground. I turned my head, while trying to get up again, and saw my brother lying on the pavement, with his face covered all over with blood. The policeman, who had fallen with me, still retained his clutch upon my throat; and again commenced beating me as soon as we had both recovered our feet. A loose stone, weighing about ten pounds, was lying upon the pavement. I seized hold of it, and struck my antagonist on the forehead. He fell like a bullock. When I looked around, I saw that my father—who was a very powerful man—had conquered the other two policemen. He seemed suddenly to have recovered from his intoxication; and now helped me to carry the constable I had felled, to the nearest public-house—where the man died a few hours after the affray.

"I was tried for manslaughter; and sentenced to ten years transportation.

"Not until then, did evil thoughts ever make their home in my mind.

"Up till the time I was torn from my relatives—for whom I had a great affection—and from the girl whom I fondly loved, I am willing to be responsible to God and man, for every thought I had, or every act I did. Ever since, having been deprived of liberty—dragged from all near and dear—with every social tie broken—and robbed of everything for which I cared to live—I do not think myself to blame for anything I may have done. I have been only a link in a chain of circumstances—a victim of the transportation system of England, that transforms incipient crime into hardened villainy.

"On arriving in New South Wales, I was placed in a gang with other convicts; and put to the business of pushing a wheel-barrow. We were employed in removing a hill, from the place where nature had set it: for no other reason, I believe, than for the purpose of keeping us from being idle! The labour was not severe; but the life was a very weary one. It was not the work that made it so to me. I was used to work, and did not dislike it, if there had been any sense in the task we had to perform. But I had no more idea of what my labour was for, than the wheel-barrow with which I performed it; and therefore I could feel no more interest in the work, than did the barrow itself.

"My toil was not sweetened with the reflection that it was in behalf of those I loved. On the contrary, I knew that the best years of my life were being uselessly squandered, while my mother and her children were perhaps suffering for food!

"I often asked myself the question: why I had been sent from home? It could not have been to reform me, and make me lead a better life, after the expiration of the term for which I had been sentenced. It could not have been for that: for no youth could have been more innocent of all evil intentions than I was, up to the time of my unfortunate affair with the policeman. All the philosophers of earth could not devise a scheme better adapted to corrupt the morals of a young man—make him forget all the good he had ever learnt—harden his soul against all the better feelings of human nature—and transform him from a weak frail mortal, with good intentions, into a very demon—than the transportation system of England.

"From the age of twenty years, until that of thirty, I consider the most valuable part of a man's existence; and as this whole period was taken from me, I naturally regarded the future of my life, as scarce worth possessing. I became recklessly indifferent as to what my actions might be; and from that time they were wholly guided by the circumstances of the hour.

"Each month, I either heard, or saw, something calculated to conduct me still further along the path of crime. I do not say that all my companions were bad men; but most of them were: since my daily associates were thieves, and men guilty of crimes even worse than theft I am willing to acknowledge—which is more than some of them would do—that the fact of their being convicts was strong evidence of their being wicked men.

"After having spent nearly a year, between the trams of the wheel-barrow in the neighbourhood of Sydney, I was despatched with a gang to do some labourer's work up the country.

"Most of the men in this gang, were wickeder than those, with whom I had previously been associated. This was perhaps owing to the fact that my new companions had been longer abroad, and were of course better trained to the transportation system.

"Some of them were suffering great agony through the want of tobacco and strong drink, in both of which—being many of them 'ticket-of-leave' holders—they had lately had a chance of freely indulging. That you may know something of the character of these men, and of the craving they had for tobacco, I shall tell you what I saw some of them do.

"Many of the wardens—as is usually the case—were greatly disliked by the convicts; and the latter, of course, took every opportunity of showing their hatred towards them.

"One morning, the gang refused to go to work—owing to a part of the usual allowance of food having been stopped from one of them, as they said, for no good reason. The overseer, in place of sending for the superintendent, attempted to force them to their tasks; and the result was a 'row.'

"In the skrimmage that followed, one of the wardens—a man especially disliked by the convicts—was killed, while the overseer himself was carried senseless from the ground.

"The dead warden had been a sailor, and liked his 'quid.' He was generally to be seen with his mouth full of tobacco, and this was the case at the time he was killed. I saw the quid taken from his mouth, scarce ten minutes after he had become a corpse, by one of the convicts, who the instant after transferred it to his own!

"The overseer, at the time he got knocked down, was smoking a pipe. Scarce three minutes after, I saw the same pipe in the mouth of one of the men; and from its head was rolling a thick cloud of smoke!

"The fire in the pipe had not been allowed to expire; and the man who was smoking it was one of those afterwards hung for the murder of the warden!"

Volume Three—Chapter Six.

Squatters' Justice.

The old convict, as if reminded by the queer incidents he had related: that he himself stood in need of a smoke, here took out his pipe. After filling and lighting it, he resumed his narrative.

"Owing to refractory conduct on my part, and a dislike to crawling for the purpose of currying favour with overseers, I did not get a 'ticket-of-leave' until five years after landing in the colony.

"I then received one—with permission to go as shepherd to a 'squatter's station' up the country. For acting in this capacity, I was to receive ten pounds a year of wages.

"I found the shepherd's life a very weary one. The labour was not sufficient to keep me from thinking. During the whole day I had but little to do—except to indulge in regrets for the past, and despair of the future. Each day was so much like the one preceding it, that the time was not only monotonous, but terribly tiresome.

"Had I deserted my employment, I knew that I should be re-captured; and a new sentence passed upon me. My only hope of obtaining full freedom—at the end of my ten years' term—was by doing my duty as well as I could.

"One morning, after I had been about ten months in my shepherd's berth, as I was letting the sheep out of the enclosure, the squatter who owned the station, his overseer, and another man, came riding up.

"The sun was more than half an hour above the horizon; and as I ought to have had the sheep out upon the grass by sunrise, I was afraid the squatter would blame me for neglecting my duty. I was agreeably surprised at his not doing so.

"He bade me 'good morning,' lit his pipe, took a look at the sheep; and then rode away along with the others.

"This treatment, instead of making me more neglectful, only rendered me more attentive to my duty; and every morning for three weeks after, the sheep were out of the yard by the first appearance of day-break.

"It was summer time, and the nights being very short, I could not always wake myself at such an early hour. The consequence was, that about three weeks before the expiration of the year, for which I was bound, my employer again caught me napping—nearly an hour after sun-up—with the sheep still in the penn.

"The squatter would listen to no excuse. I was taken direct before a magistrate—who was also a 'squatter'—and charged with neglect of duty.

"The charge was of course proved; and I was dismissed from my employment.

"You may think that this was no punishment; but you will have a different opinion when you hear more. My year of apprenticeship not being quite up, my wages were forfeited; and I was told, that I ought to be thankful for the mercy shown me: in my not getting severely flogged, and sent back to the authorities, with a black mark against my name!

"I probably did my duty, as well as any man the squatter expected to get; and I had good reason to know, that I had been dismissed only to give my rascally employer the opportunity of withholding the balance of my wages, that would soon have been due to me!

"The only magistrates in the grazing country, were the squatters themselves; and they used to play into each other's hands in that fashion. There was no justice for convicts, who were treated but little better than slaves.

"Three months after leaving my situation, I came across an 'old hand,' who had been cheated out of his wages, by the very same squatter who had robbed me, and in precisely the same manner.

"This man proposed to me that we should take revenge—by burning down the squatter's wool-sheds.

"I refused to have anything to do with the undertaking; and from what the man then said, I supposed that he had relinquished the idea. That night, however, altogether unknown to me, he set fire to the sheds—causing the squatter a loss of about three thousand pounds worth of property. The next day I was arrested and committed for trial—along with the old hand, who had urged me to aid him in obtaining his revenge.

"On the trial, circumstantial evidence was so strong against the incendiary, that he was found guilty. But as he continued to assert his innocence, of course he could say nothing that would clear me; and I was also found guilty—though the only evidence against me was, that I had been seen in his company eight hours before the crime was committed, and that I had been dismissed from service by the proprietor of the sheds!

"This was thought sufficient evidence upon which to sentence me to five years hard labour on the roads—the first two years of the term to be passed in irons!

"I now despaired of ever seeing home again; and became, like many other convicts, so reckless as to have no thought for the future, and not to care whether my deeds were right or wrong.

"Had I acted as many of the very worst convicts are in the habit of doing—that is, fawning upon the overseers—I might have regained my liberty in two years and a half; but I never could crawl, or play the hypocrite; and all the less so, that I knew my sentence was unjust. Neither could I allow the ill-usage of others to pass without complaint; and frequently did I complain. For doing this, I had to serve the full term of my sentence, while others, much worse than myself, by using a little deception, obtained their liberty on 'tickets-of-leave.'

"After the term of my transportation had expired, I was no better than most of the 'old hands.' If I have not committed all the crimes of which many of them are guilty, the reason is, that I had not the temptation: for, I acknowledge, that I have now completely lost the moral power to restrain me from crime.

"I happened to be free when gold was discovered in New South Wales; and, of course. I hastened to the place. After the discovery of the richer diggings here, I came overland to try them.

"In my gold seeking, I cannot complain of want of success; and I have not spent all that I have made.

"I am thinking of going back to England—although my visit to my native country cannot be a very pleasant one. I have, probably, some brothers and sisters still living; but, notwithstanding the strong affection I once had for them, they are nothing to me now. All human feeling has been flogged, starved, and tortured out of me.

"Sometimes, when I reflect on the degradations I have endured, I am ashamed to think of myself as a human being.

"When I look back to the innocent and happy days of my boyhood—of what I aspired to be—only an honest, respectable, hard-working man, when I contrast those days, and those humble hopes, with the scenes I have since passed through, and my present condition—my back scarred with repeated floggings, and my limbs marked by the wear of iron fetters—I am not unwilling to die.

"I am glad to learn that a change has been made in the mode of punishing crime in the mother country. It has not been done too soon: for, bad as many of the convicts are—who are transported from the large cities of the United Kingdom—they cannot be otherwise than made worse, by the system followed here. A convict coming to this country meets with no associations, precepts, or examples, that tend to reform him; but, on the contrary, every evil passion and propensity is strengthened, if it has existed before; and imbibed, if it has not.

"Having told you a good deal of my past, I should like to be able to add something of my future; but cannot. Some men are very ingenious in inventing food for hope: I am not. I don't know for what I am living: for every good and earnest motive seems to have been stifled within me. Hope, love, despair, revenge, and all the other mental powers that move man to action, are dead within my heart. I having nothing more to tell you of myself; and probably never shall have."

So ended the sad story of the convict.

Volume Three—Chapter Seven.

Raffling Away a Wife.

Our claim on the Avoca "lead" turned out to be worth working; and we had five or six weeks of hard toil before us. My mate continued temperate and industrious; and we got along together without any misunderstanding.

One day we were informed by a man passing our tent, that a very interesting affair was to come off that evening—at a certain grog-shop not far from where we lived.

My partner was strongly advised to be there: as there would be a spectacle worth witnessing.

"Shall you go?" I asked, after the man had gone.

"No—not alone," replied he, "the place has a bad name; and I know that one of the parties concerned in what is to take place is a bad bird. You go along with me, and you'll see some amusement."

"Have you any idea what it's to be?" I inquired.

"Yes. I think they are going to have a raffle."

"A raffle! There's nothing very interesting about that!"

"That depends," significantly rejoined my partner. "Supposing it is a woman that's to be raffled for?"

"A woman to be raffled for!"

"So I believe. There is a Hobart Town man here, who has a young wife, with whom he has been quarrelling for the last month. He has found out that it is impossible to live with her any longer; and is going to put her up to be raffled for."

I had seen a negro slave disposed of in this fashion in the city of New Orleans; but had never heard of a man raffling away his wife; and the oddness of the thing determined me to go. Having signified my intention to my mate, he promised to take me to the place, and also take care of me while there.

The reader may think his promised protection unnecessary—after my having managed for so many years to take care of myself. But I knew that amongst "old hands," the protection or friendship, of one of their own "kidney" was worth having; and I certainly would not have gone, without some one to introduce, and look after me—one such as my mining partner, who knew their ways, and would give them to understand, that I was not to be molested.

At that time on the gold-field of Avoca, there were probably about ten men to one woman; and a man, who was so fortunate as to possess a wife, was thought to be a very lucky individual indeed. Any woman, however ugly she might have appeared in other lands, would there have passed for a Venus. Knowing this to be the state of things, I was not surprised, when, on reaching the grog-shop with my companion, we found a large crowd of between thirty and forty men assembled around it. In one way only was I astonished; and that was, that the majority of those present were not "old hands," but rather the contrary.

This observation was also made by my companion, who shook his head significantly, but said nothing.

I did not understand what meaning he intended to convey by this gesture—at least not at the time.

From the appearance of the crowd collected round the grog-shop, I had no doubt but that I should be well rewarded for my trouble in walking to the place. I could see that some pains had been taken in selecting the company: for it appeared to be composed of that class of young miners—known as "fast," and "flush"—that is with money to spend, and the disposition to spend it.

The woman who was to be disposed of was in the room, seated on the edge of a table, and swinging her legs about with perfect nonchalance. One of her eyes bore, in distinct characters of a purplish hue, some evidence of a very late disagreement with her husband, or some one else. She seemed much pleased at the commotion she was causing; and quite indifferent as to its results. She was about twenty-three years of age; and rather good-looking.

The husband was about forty years old; and was a vulgar looking wretch—even for a "Vandemonian." His features were twisted into a disgusting leer, from which I could well fancy they were but seldom relieved.

I was not surprised at the woman seeming pleased at the idea of parting with him. My wonder was, how he had ever been allowed to obtain the power of disposing of her.

There was not a man in the room, or perhaps on the diggings, that any creature entitled to the name of woman, should not have preferred, to the ugly animal who claimed to be her husband.

I could perceive from the woman's behaviour, that she possessed a violent temper, which to an ignorant brute of a man, would no doubt render her difficult of being managed. But there appeared to be nothing more against her—at least, nothing to prevent a man of common sense from living with her, and having no more serious misunderstandings, than such as are usually required to vary the monotony of connubial life.

The business of getting up the raffle, and carrying it through, was managed by a young man, who played the part of mutual friend—the proprietor of the article at stake, being to all appearance too drunk, or too ignorant, to act as master of the ceremonies.

After a sufficient number of persons was thought to have arrived upon the ground, it was decided to go on with the business of discovering: to whom fate should decree the future ownership of the woman.

"Gentlemen!" said the mutual friend, rising up, and placing himself upon a chair, "I suppose you all know the game that's up here to-night? I believe that most of you be aware, that my friend 'Brumming' here, can't agree with his old woman, nor she with him; and he have come to the resolution of getting rid of her. He thinks he'd be better off without a woman, than with one, 'specially with one as he can't agree with. And she thinks any other man be better than Ned 'Brumming.' Such being the case, they think they had better part. Now, 'Brumming' wants a little money to take him over to the other side; and to rise it for him, his friends have been called together, and his woman is going to be put up at a raffle for fifty pounds—twenty-five chances at two pounds a chance. Mrs Brumming is willing to live with any man, as will support her, and use her kindly. Who is going to help poor Ned Brumming? What name shall I first put down on this 'ere paper?"

"Dirty Dick," "Jack Rag," "Hell Fryer," "Shiny Bright," and several other names were called out—to the number of twenty.

It was then announced that five names were still wanted to complete the list.

"I'll take a chance," said a man stepping forward to the table, where the names were being written out.

The individual thus presenting himself, bore every evidence of having obtained a passage to the colonies at the expense of his native country—about twenty-five years before.

"What name shall I put down?" asked the youthful master of the ceremonies.

"Jimmy from Town."

"Jimmy from hell!" screamed the woman. "You had better save your money Jimmy from Town. I wouldn't live with an old beast like you, if you were to win me ten times over."

The prospect of losing his two pounds, and gaining nothing, caused the old convict to retire, which he did, apparently with no very good grace.

"We must pay something for this entertainment," whispered my mate; "I will go halves with you in a chance."

As he said this, he slipped a sovereign into my hand.

I did not fully understand what my partner meant. He surely could not be thinking of our winning the woman, and owning her in partnership, as we did our mining claim?

But as he had said something about our paying for the entertainment—and having trusted myself to him before I came away from my tent—I gave the name of "Rolly," to the manager of the raffle, and put down the two pounds.

Two others then came forward, took a chance each, and paid their stakes. There were now only two more "tickets" to dispose of.

Amongst the first who had entered their name upon the list, was a young miner, who to all appearance, took a greater interest in the proceedings than any person present.

I saw the woman give him a glance, that might be interpreted into the words, "I wish *you* would win me." He appeared to notice it, and take the hint: for he immediately entered himself for another chance.

The remaining share was then taken by somebody else; and the ceremony of throwing the dice was commenced.

Each was to have three throws, taking three dice at each throw; and the man who should score the highest number, was to win the woman.

A name would be called out, as it stood on the list; the owner of it would then come forward, and throw the dice—when the number he should score would be recorded against his name.

All the numbers made, chanced to be very low, none of them reaching over thirty-eight—until I had finished "tossing the bones," when I was told that the aggregate recorded in my favour was *forty-seven*.

I felt as good as certain that the woman was mine: for the chances were more than a hundred to one against any of the five others who were to throw after me.

The young fellow who had paid for two shares, looked very blank: his remaining chance was now scarce worth a shilling.

"I will give you fifteen pounds for your throw," said he, addressing himself to me.

I glanced at my mate, and saw him give his head a slight inclination: as a sign for me to accept the offer—which I did.

The money was paid down; and after all had finished tossing, number forty-seven was declared the winner. This had been my score. The woman, therefore, belonged to the young man, who had bought it from me. She was at once handed over to him; and inaugurated the "nuptials" by flinging her arms around his neck, and giving him a sonorous "buss" upon the cheek!

After we came away from the place, I learnt from my mate, that the affair was what he called "a sell."

"Then why did you propose that we should take a chance?" I asked.

"Why," he replied, with a significant shrug, "well, I'll tell you. I was told to come to the raffle, because I was working with you—who they thought would be likely to take a share. Had you not taken one, they would have supposed that I had cautioned you not to do so; and I should have made enemies amongst some of the old hands—who look upon me as, being in all things, one of themselves."

"And you think that the woman will not live with the young man who won her?"

"I'm sure of it. She'll go along with him for awhile; but she won't stay with him. She'll run away from him—join, Brumming, again—and the two will repeat the same dodge at some other diggings."

I divided the fifteen pounds with my partner; and retired to my tent—well pleased that I had so disposed of my chance, and no little amused at the grotesque chapter of "life on the Avoca," it had been my fortune to be witness to.

A few weeks after the occurrence, I read in a newspaper: that the police on the Bendigo diggings had arrested a man for trying to dispose of his wife by a raffle; and I have no doubt that the man was "poor old Ned Brumming!"

Volume Three—Chapter Eight.

Caught in his Own Trap.

A "claim," adjoining the one in which my partner and I were working, was much richer than ours. The primitive rock lay farther below the surface—showing that there had been a basin in the creek, or river, that hundreds of years before had flowed over the "vale of Avoca."

In this basin had been deposited a great quantity of earth containing gold: for the soil was thickly impregnated with the precious metal.

This claim was owned by three men. Two of them appeared to be respectable young fellows; and I incidentally learnt from them, that they had been playmates in boyhood, shipmates on their voyage to the colony, and had worked together ever since their arrival at the diggings. An old convict was the third partner of these two young men. He had first marked out the claim, and for a while kept sole possession of it; but, seeing that he would be unable to manage it by himself, he had allowed the other two to take shares in it.

They had joined the convict only for that one job; and had done so, because they could not find any other favourable opportunity for "getting on the line."

One day, when I was standing by at the windlass of our own shaft, I saw the old convict come towards his claim—apparently after having been to his dinner.

I had observed one of the young men let himself down the shaft, but a few minutes before. Soon after, I heard his voice from below calling to the convict—who had placed himself by the windlass, after his arrival. I then saw the latter lower the rope, and hoist the young man to the surface. The old convict was then lowered down; and, as soon as he had detached himself from the rope below, I noticed that the young man hastily drew it up and in a manner that betrayed some extraordinary excitement.

"Hoist up your mate, and bring him here," he called to me. "Quick! I've something terrible to tell you of."

I called to my partner to get on the tackle; and, as soon as he had done so, I drew him up out of the shaft.

While I was doing this, the young man who had called to me, summoned some others in the same manner; and five or six men who chanced to be near, hastened up to the spot.

As soon as we were assembled around him, the young fellow began:

"I have a strange story to tell you all," said he. "My friend has been murdered; and the man who has committed the crime is below. We have him sure. Will some one go to the 'camp' for the police? I shall not leave this spot, till I see the murderer in their custody, or see him dead."

The commotion, caused by this startling announcement, brought several others to the place; and a crowd was soon collected around the claim. Two or three started off for the police encampment.

While waiting for their return, the young man, who had called us around him, gave an explanation of his conduct in having summoned us thus strangely.

"I came up out of the shaft," said he, "about half-past eleven o'clock; and went home to cook dinner for myself and my friend. I left him along with our other mate—the murderer—who is now below, at work, stowing away some of the pipe-clay that we had finished working with. I expected him to follow me to his dinner in about half-an-hour after. I waited for him till nearly one; and as he did not come, I ate my dinner alone, and then returned here to go on with the work.

"When I came back, I could see no one. I called down the shaft, thinking both were below.

"As there was no answer, I let myself down by the rope, intending to go to work by myself. I supposed that my mates had strayed off to some grog-shop—where they might spend a good part of the afternoon. They had done this once before; and I thought they might do it again.

"After getting below, I lit the candle; and looked about to see what they had been doing, since I left them at eleven o'clock.

"The first thing that met my eyes, was the toe of a boot sticking out of the pipe-clay—where we had been stowing it away, in the worked-out part of the shaft. What, thought I, is their object in burying the boot there?

"I took hold of it—there was just enough of it protruding out of the pipe-clay to enable me to get a grasp of it. I felt that there was a foot in it. It was a boot belonging to my friend. I knew it—notwithstanding its being plastered over with the clay. I drew out the boot; and along with it the body of the man to whom it belonged. He was dead! I think it is probable he was not quite dead, when covered up; and that in his death-spasm he had somehow moved his foot, causing it to protrude a little out of the clay.

"I have no doubt," continued the young miner, "that my seeing that boot has saved my own life: for the man who has murdered my friend, would have served me in the same way, had we both been down below, and I ignorant of what he had already done.

"Just as I was about climbing up the rope to get out, I saw the man who is now below here, preparing to let himself down. I called to him, in my natural tone of voice; and told him that I wanted to go above for a minute—to get a drink. This, no doubt, put him off his guard; and he helped me up.

"I then asked him what had become of Bill—that was my friend's name.

"'He did not come home to dinner,' said I, 'and he is not below.'

"'When we came up to go to dinner,' said he, 'and were about starting away from here, I saw Bill meet a stranger, and shake hands with him. They went off together.'

"I suggested that he might probably have strayed off upon a spree; and that we were not likely to get any more work out of him that day. I added, that, after I had had my drink, we could both go below, and work without him. This seemed to please my other partner—who at once desired to be let down into the shaft.

"I lowered him at his request—telling him I should follow soon after.

"He and his victim are now in the shaft. Had he succeeded in killing both of us, he would not only have got all the gold we had obtained in the claim, but some more besides." This story excited in the minds of all present, a feeling of horror, joined to a keen desire for retribution. Several shouted out to the old convict—commanding him to come up; that his crime was known, and escape would be impossible.

The murderer must have heard every word; but no answer was returned either to the threats or commands of those above. There was no occasion for the latter, either to be in haste, or in any way uneasy about the man making his escape. He could not possibly get clear from the trap, into which his partner had so adroitly cajoled him. He must either come out of the shaft, or starve at the bottom of it.

The policemen, soon after, arrived upon the ground; and were made acquainted with all the circumstances.

One of them hailed the convict—commanding him "in the Queen's name" to come up.

"You are our prisoner," said the policeman, "you cannot escape; and you may as well surrender at once."

There was no answer.

One of the policemen then placed himself in a bowline knot at the end of the rope; and was gently lowered down into the shaft—several men standing by at the windlass.

"Hold there!" cried the convict from below. "The instant you reach the bottom, I'll drive my pick-axe through you."

The men at the windlass ceased turning—leaving the policeman suspended half way down the shaft.

He was a man of superior courage; and, cocking his revolver, he called to the convict: that he was going down anyhow—adding, that the first move made to molest him in the execution of his duty, would be a signal for him to blow out the brains of the man who should make it.

He then called to the miners at the windlass to "lower away."

"Drop your pick!" shouted the policeman, as he came near the bottom of the shaft—at the same time covering the convict with his revolver.

The murderer saw the folly of resisting. It was impossible for him to escape—even could he have killed the officer, and a dozen more besides.

Some of the "Queen's Jewellery" was soon adjusted upon his wrists; and the rope, having been fastened around his body, he was hoisted up into the light of heaven.

The policemen were going to stop, until they could examine the body of the murdered man; but they perceived that the indignation of the crowd was fast rising to such a pitch, that it was necessary for the prisoner to be carried to some place of security—else he might be taken out of their hands.

None of the spectators seemed anxious either to rescue, or kill the man. Each one appeared to be satisfied by getting a kick or blow at him. The mind of every honest miner on the ground had been shocked by the cruel crime that had been committed; and each appeared to think he had himself a score of revenge to wipe off against the perpetrator.

Each wished to calm his outraged feelings, by inflicting some chastisement upon the criminal; and still leave to the justice of God and the law, the task of punishing him for the murder.

The police did their best to protect their prisoner; but on their way to their station, they were followed by an indignant crowd of miners, who kicked and scratched the old convict, till he was nearly lifeless in their hands.

When the body of the murdered man had been brought out of the shaft, it was found that the sharp point of a pick-axe had been driven through his skull. The wound was in the back part of the head—proving that the victim had received the blow from behind, and most probably without any warning. A similar fate would undoubtedly have befallen his friend, had he not made the discovery which enabled him to avert it.

The murderer was sent down to Melbourne to be locked up, till the sitting of the Criminal Court.

The day after the funeral of the murdered man, the only one of the three partners left to work out the claim, made his appearance upon the spot.

Before commencing work, he came over to me; and we had a long conversation together.

"If I had only myself to think of," said he, "I would have nothing farther to do with this claim. It cannot be very pleasant to me to work in it, after what has occurred. The young man who has been killed, was my playmate in boyhood, and my constant companion ever since we left home together. I shall have to carry back to his father, mother, and sisters, the news of his sad fate. His relatives are very poor people; and it took every penny they could scrape together to furnish him with the means for coming out here. My duty to them, and to his memory, is the sole cause of my continuing any longer to work the claim. However painful the task may be, I must perform it. I shall obtain all the gold it may yield; and every speck to which my murdered friend should have been entitled, shall be paid over to his relatives. I know that they had rather see himself return penniless to them, than to have all the gold of Australia; but for all that he shall not be robbed, as well as murdered.

"I have often heard him speak of the pleasure it would give him to return to his relations with his gold. I can only show my respect for his wishes, by taking them the money to which he would have been entitled, had he lived, to work out his claim. It shall be done without his aid; but his relations shall have the yield of it, all the same as if he had lived."

Whenever the windlass was to be used in bringing up the "wash dirt" from below—or the surviving partner wanted assistance in any way—it was cheerfully rendered by the miners at work in the adjoining claims.

By the time he had completed his task, he was summoned to Melbourne, as a witness on the trial of the murderer; and, after his leaving the Avoca diggings, I saw him no more.

I afterwards learnt from the Melbourne Argus: that the old convict was found guilty of the murder, and ended his earthly existence on the gallows.

Volume Three—Chapter Nine.

A Lark with the "Licence-Hunters."

After we had completed the working of our claim in the Avoca lead, my partner—who had told me that his name was Brown—signified his intention of returning home to England.

"I have saved between three and four hundred pounds," said he, "and shouldn't know what to do with it here. I've been thinking of going home for several years past; and now's the time to do it."

Instead of attempting to dissuade him, I rather encouraged him in his design, telling him that, if dissatisfied with his visit to his native country, he could return to the diggings—before they should get worked-out—and try his fortune once more.

He had heard me speak of going myself back to England some time or other; and he urged me to make the voyage along with him.

I should probably have acceded to his request,—had he not pressed me so strongly; but I have a great aversion to doing anything, that I am vehemently solicited to do.

If there is anything which will make me do the very thing I know to be wrong, it is when some one counsels me too pressingly *against* doing it. I have a great *penchant* for being guided by my own judgment; and I believe that very little good is done by giving advice, to those who are old enough to think and act for themselves.

In answer to my partner's request, I told him that I should probably return to England in about a year; but was not then ready to go.

Though a little disappointed at my not accompanying him, Brown and I parted on good terms. He left full directions with me for finding him in Birmingham—should I ever go to that city; and warmly urged upon me to call and see him. I gave him a promise to do so.

"I believe you are a respectable, right-thinking man," said he, as we shook hands at parting; "you have treated me, as though I was the same; and that's more than I have been accustomed to for the last score of years."

On leaving me, Brown proceeded direct to Melbourne, where he took ship for England.

For two or three days after he had left me, I looked about the diggings—undecided what I should next do.

One afternoon, while sauntering at a little distance, from my tent, I saw some policemen, with a squad of mounted troopers, out on the patrol. A "licensing commissioner" at their head, proved that they were looking for "unlicenced" miners.

I never went abroad without a miner's licence in my pocket; but I felt a strong dislike to showing it—solely on account of the manner, in which the demand to do so was usually made.

I shall have something to say about "licence-hunting" in another chapter—where the subject will be introduced, and more fully discussed. My present purpose is to relate a little adventure which occurred to me at Avoca—of which the licence-hunters were the heroes. It was this episode, that first awakened within my mind some thoughts about the infamous system of drawing a revenue, from the most honest and industrious portion of the population.

It is usual for diggers—who are not provided with a licence—on seeing the police out upon their scouting excursions, either to take to the bush, or hide themselves in the shaft, or tunnel, of some mining claim. This is done to avoid being searched; and, as a matter of course, carried before a magistrate, and fined five pounds for—*trespassing on the Crown lands*!

On the occasion in question, when I saw the licence-hunters out on their usual errand, it came into my head to have a little amusement with them. I had been going idle for two or three days, and wanted something to amuse me—as well as give exercise to my limbs.

When the policemen had got within about a hundred yards of where I was standing, I pretended to see them for the first time; and started off at a run. They saw me, as I intended they should; and two or three of them gave chase—under the full belief that I was an unlicenced digger. They that first followed me were afoot; and they soon learnt that the farther they pursued, the greater became the distance between them and me. Two of the mounted troopers now left the side of the Commissioner; and joined in the chase—spurring their horses into a gallop.

I was running in the direction of my own tent; and contrived to reach it, before the troopers overtook me.

By the time they had got up to the tent, I was standing in the opening of the canvass; and received them by demanding their business.

"We wish to see your licence," said one.

I took from my pocket the piece of paper, legally authorising me to "search for, dig, and remove gold from the crown lands of the colony." I handed it to the trooper.

He appeared much disappointed, at finding it was "all right."

"What made you run away from us?" he demanded angrily.

"What made you think I was running away from you?" I inquired in turn.

"What made you run at all?" put in the second trooper.

"Because I was in haste to reach home," I answered.

The two then talked together in a low voice, after which one of them told me that I must go along with them.

"For what reason?" I asked; but received no answer. They were either unwilling, or unable, to give me a reason.

The two policemen, who had pursued me on foot, now came up; and all four insisted on my being taken along with them, a prisoner, to the police camp!

I refused to come out of the tent; and cautioned them not to enter it—without showing me their warrant, or some authority for the intrusion.

They paid no attention to what I said; but stepping inside the tent, rudely conducted me out of it.

I accompanied them without making resistance—thinking that when brought before a magistrate, I should get them reprimanded for what they had done.

In the afternoon, I was arraigned before, the "bench," and charged with molesting and interfering with the police in the execution of their duty! My accusers told their story; and I was called upon for my defence.

I informed the magistrate, that I had never been an unlicenced miner for a single day, since I had been on the diggings; and I entered upon a long speech—to prove, that in moving about the gold-fields, I had the right to travel at any rate of speed I might choose; and that I had unlawfully been dragged out of my tent—which being my "castle," should not have been invaded in the manner it had been.

This was what I intended to have said; but I did not get the opportunity of making my forensic display: for the magistrate cut me short, by stating, that I had been playing what the diggers call a "lark," and by doing so, had drawn the police from their duty. They had been seeking for those who really had *not* licences; and who, through my misbehaviour, might have been able to make their escape!

In conclusion, this sapient justice fined me forty shillings!

There was an *injustice* about this decision—as well as the manner in which I had been treated—that aroused my indignation. I had broken no law, I had done nothing but what any free subject had a right to do, yet I had been treated as a criminal, and mulcted of my money—in fact, robbed of two pounds sterling!

After this affair, I was disgusted with Avoca; and, in less than an hour after, I rolled up my blankets, and took the road for Ballarat—this being the place to which I always turned, when not knowing where else to go.

Everyone must have some place that they look upon as a home—a point from which to start or take departure. Mine was Ballarat: for the reason that I liked that place better than any other in the colony.

I had made more money on the Ballarat diggings than elsewhere in Australia; and I had never left the place to go to any other, without having cause to regret the change. This time, I determined, on my return to Ballarat, to stay there—until I should be ready to bid a final adieu to Australia.

Volume Three—Chapter Ten.

Digger-Hunting.

Soon after my arrival at Ballarat, the mining population of the place was roused to a state of great excitement—by being constantly worried about their gold licences.

All engaged in the occupation of mining, were required to take out a monthly licence, for which one pound ten shillings had to be paid. Each miner was required to carry this licence upon his person; and produce it whenever desired to do so, by the commissioner, or any official acting under his authority.

It was not to the tax of eighteen pounds per annum that the miners objected; but to the manner in which it was levied and enforced.

The diggers did not like to be so often accosted by a body of armed men, and compelled to show a piece of paper—in the event of them not having it about them, to be dragged off to the court, and fined five pounds.

After some show of opposition to this tax—or rather to the way of enforcing it—had begun to exhibit itself, the government officials became more industrious than ever at their occupation of "digger-hunting." A commissioner, with a band of mounted troopers, might have been seen out every day—scouring the country far and near, and commanding every man they met to produce his licence. Not unfrequently an honest miner would be required to exhibit the disagreeable document as often as four or five times a day!

The diggers soon got tired of this sort of thing, which was enough to have exasperated men of a more tranquil tone of mind, than gold-diggers usually are.

Meetings were called and attended by many hundreds of miners, at which strong resolutions were passed; to resist the arrest of any man, who should be taken up for not having a gold licence.

These resolutions could not be effectually carried into effect, without some organisation amongst those who had passed them.

This was to a certain extent accomplished; by about four hundred diggers forming themselves into an organised band, and commencing to drill and discipline in a sort of military fashion.

Thinking the wrongs of the diggers a sufficient justification for this action on their part, I joined one of the companies thus formed—with the full determination to assist, as far as lay in my power, in the removal of the injustice complained of.

I did not think there was anything in English law—properly understood and administered—that would allow thousands of men to be constantly hunted, harassed and insulted by bands of armed police, demanding to see a piece of paper; but perhaps my experience of the way "justice" was administered at Avoca, had something to do in guiding my resolution to resist it at Ballarat.

At our meetings, the diggers indignantly declared their determination to overthrow the system that made them game for the minions of the Government; and to prove that they were in earnest in what they said, many of them were seen to tear up their licences upon the spot, and light their pipes with the torn fragments of the paper!

From that time, whenever an attempt was made by the police to arrest a man without a licence, it was resisted by large mobs of diggers; and on two or three occasions both police and troopers were compelled to retreat to their encampment.

The police force on Ballarat was soon increased in number; and a large body of regular troops was sent up from Melbourne.

The diggers saw that they could no longer oppose this force, without maintaining a body of their own men in arms; and for this purpose a select number was chosen, who, having been regularly organised into companies, formed a camp on the Eureka lead.

Some of the lying officials of the government have represented this camp to have been strongly fortified—the lie being propagated to secure them greater credit, for their bravery in capturing it!

The statement was altogether untrue. The Eureka stockade was nothing more than an inclosure formed with slabs of timber—such as were used to wall in the shafts sunk on wet leads—and could no more be called a fortification, than the hurdles used by farmers for penning up a flock of sheep.

The importance attached to the movement, on the part of the government officials, was ludicrous in the extreme.

Martial law was proclaimed in Ballarat; and several hundred pounds were expended in filling bags of sand, and fortifying the Treasury at Melbourne—about one hundred miles from the scene of the *emeute*!

The idea of the diggers marching to Melbourne, and molesting the Government property there, was simply ridiculous. The authorities must have held an opinion of the men they governed, not very complimentary to the liege subjects of Her Majesty.

Because the miners objected to being hunted and worried for a piece of paper—proving that they had paid eighteen pounds per annum of tax, more than any other class of the population—the Government officials seemed to think that a causeless rebellion had broken out, which threatened to overthrow the whole British Empire; and which nothing but low scheming and barbarous action could quell.

Thousands of ounces of gold were lying on deposit in the Escort Office at Ballarat; yet had the mutineers taken the place, I am confident this treasure would have been protected, and restored to its rightful owners.

But there was no intention on the part of the diggers, either to touch Ballarat, or its gold. They only maintained an armed body at the Eureka Stockade, because they could in no other way resist the raids of the troopers who were sent out licence-hunting. They were as innocent of all intention to overthrow the Government; "loot" the Escort Office at Ballarat; or march upon Melbourne, as babes unborn.

Their only object was to have English law properly administered to them; or rather, to resist the violation of it by the minions who had been appointed to its execution.

This the Government might have learnt—and probably did learn—from the policemen disguised as diggers, who took part in the proceedings at the Eureka Stockade, for these communicated all they learnt, and no doubt a good deal more, to the officials in the Government camp.

Volume Three—Chapter Eleven.

A Genius in the Diggings.

When I went to join the insurgents at the Stockade, I was accompanied by a man, who had been living in a tent near my own—a German, whom I only knew by the name of "Karl." He was as singular a man, as was to be met amongst the many incomprehensible characters found on a gold-field. He was only twenty-five years of age, though he had already travelled over much of the world, and spoke several languages fluently. He knew something of the literature, science, arts, and customs of almost every nation, ancient or modern; and having a wonderful memory, as well as a great command of language, he could be very entertaining in conversation. My attention was first called to the extraordinary power of his memory, by hearing him once talking on the relative merits of the poets.

He appeared to know all the poetical writings of the English, German, and Italian authors by heart: as he could repeat long passages from any of them, when called upon.

I remember, amongst many severe criticisms which he gave us on the poetry of Byron, his quoting the phrases of "sad knee," "melodious tears," "cloudy groan," "poetic marble," "loud hill," "foolish flower," "learned fingers," and "silly sword," all of which he mentioned were absurd expressions.

The reader may think my sketch of this individual overdrawn, when I add, that in addition to his other accomplishments, he was not only a musician of great skill, but, in my opinion, a musical prodigy; and excited more astonishment and admiration by his musical talents, than by any other of the many accomplishments he possessed.

Often would he wander alone, where nature was most lovely; and from her surrounding beauties, add inspiration to the melody that filled his soul.

The notes of birds, the whispering of the winds, and the murmuring of the streams, were all caught and combined, or harmoniously arranged in enchanting melodies, which he would reproduce on his violin, after returning to his tent, in strains that seemed enraptured.

Never did I listen to the music made by him, without thinking myself a better man: for all the gentler sentiments of my soul would be awakened, and expanded into action under its influence. For hours would the sounds echo in my memory—making me forget the sorrows of the past, as well as the cares of the future; and turning my thoughts to an ideal world, where material ugliness is unknown.

I defy any man with a soul superior to that of a monkey, to have been guilty of a mean or dishonest action, after listening to a tune composed and played by Karl the German.

I do not call myself a judge of music, or of the relative merits of different musicians, and only form this opinion from the effect produced on my mind by his performance.

I am not easily excited by musical, or dramatic representations; but Mario's magnificent rendering of the death scene in "Lucrezia Borgia," or the astounding recklessness Alboni is accustomed to throw into the "Brindisi," could never awaken within my soul such deep thoughts, as those often stirred by the simple strains of Karl's violin.

Though possessing all these great natural abilities—strengthened by travel, and experience in both men and books—Karl was a slave to one habit, that rendered all his talents unavailing, and hindered him from ever rising to the station, he might otherwise have held among men.

He was a confirmed drunkard; and could never be kept sober, so long as there was a shilling in his pocket!

Pride had hitherto restrained him from seeking professional engagement, and exhibiting his musical talents to the world, although, according to his own story, he had been brought up to the profession of a musician. He was even becoming celebrated in it, when the demon of intemperance made his acquaintance, and dragged him down to the lowest depths of poverty and despair.

Once, when in Melbourne, starvation drove him to seek an interview with the manager of a theatre, who listened with wonder and admiration to the soul-entrancing melody he produced.

A sum far beyond his expectations was offered; and money advanced to enable him to make a respectable appearance; but on the night in which his *début* was to have been made, he was not forthcoming! He had been found in the street, drunk and disorderly, and was carried to the lock-up—where he passed the evening among policemen, instead of exhibiting himself before a delighted audience on the stage of a theatre!

I know that he used every effort to subdue this passion for strong drink. But all proved unavailing. Notwithstanding the strength of his mind in other respects, he could not resist the fatal fascination.

Small minds may be subdued and controlled by worldly interests; but the power to curb the action of a large and active intellect may not always lie within itself.

Karl wished to join the insurgents—as they were called—at the Eureka Stockade; and although myself anxious that their number should be augmented as much as possible, I endeavoured to persuade him against having anything to do with the disturbance.

The truth was, that I thought foreigners had at that time too much to say about the manner in which the colony was governed.

Although I could not deny that the faults of which they complained, in reality existed, yet I believed that they were not the persons who had the right to correct them. Many of the foreign diggers had a deal more to say, about the misgovernment of the colony, than any of Her Majesty's subjects; and I did not like to hear them talk treason. They had come to the colony for the purpose of making money—because Australia offered superior advantages for that purpose—and I thought that they should have been satisfied with the government found there, without taking upon themselves to reform its abuses.

I explained all this to Karl; but, while admitting the truth of what I said, he still adhered to his determination to take a part in the revolution of Eureka.

"Several times," said he, "have I had armed men command me to show a licence, and I have also been imprisoned, because I did not have that piece of paper in my pocket. I have several times been insulted in the colony, because I am not an Englishman. I care but little which gets the worst of this struggle—the minions of the government or its subjects. Where the blood of either, or both, is to flow, there I wish to be."

I said nothing more to dissuade Karl from following this singular wish; but permitted him to accompany me to the stockade—where he was enrolled in one of the companies.

Volume Three—Chapter Twelve.

The Eureka Rout.

I have stated that about four hundred men were kept under arms at Ballarat, to oppose the amusement of digger-hunting, so much indulged in by the government officials. The former had now made their rendezvous at the stockade on the Eureka.

They were accustomed to meet in the day, and get drilled by officers, whom they had appointed for this duty. During the night, most of them, who were residents of Ballarat, returned thither, and slept in their tents, while others, who had come from Creswick's Creek and the more distant gold-fields—to take part in the affair—remained at the boarding houses of the township.

On the night of the 2nd of December, 1854, there were about one hundred and seventy men in the stockade.

Having entered into the cause, I determined to devote my whole time to it; and on that night I was there among the rest.

The diggers, who were present, supposed they had as much right to stay in the stockade as elsewhere.

They certainly were not interfering with the officials in the execution of their duty; nor, in any way, making a disturbance.

There was no just cause why they should have been attacked on that particular night. It is true, that during the previous week, the troopers had been opposed by the diggers they were hunting; and had in some cases been prevented from making arrests. But the authorities need not have supposed, that the men in the Eureka Stockade were the same who had offered this resistance. They could only have thought so, and acted on the belief, by a singular stretch of imagination.

About half-past eleven o'clock, an alarm was given, that the soldiers were approaching the stockade. All turned out, and were prepared to defend themselves; but the alarm proved a false one.

At one o'clock in the morning there was another alarm, which also proved to be without any just cause.

At half-past two, there was still another false report, to which only a very few paid any attention: as the men had got tired of being so often roused from their slumbers without any cause. Only about half of their number turned out at this time; and these were laughed at by the others—for allowing themselves to be unnecessarily frightened.

About half-past four in the morning—just as the first faint light of day was seen on the eastern horizon—the camp was again set in commotion by the fourth alarm.

This time there was a real cause: since soldiers and troopers could be seen through the twilight, riding towards the stockade.

On the 3rd day of December, 1854, at half-past four o'clock on that holy Sabbath morning, the people in the Eureka Stockade were attacked by English soldiers, and troopers in the pay of the Victorian Government. As the attack was altogether unexpected, they were of course unprepared to repel or resist it.

It would have been little less than folly to have attempted resistance: for the assailants numbered three hundred and ninety men, all well armed and mounted, while the diggers, were less than half that number, and most of us only provided with fowling pieces.

When the signal of attack was given, it was done in a manner that started the sleeping diggers to their legs; and these soon proved to be the most useful members of their bodies. The majority refused to obey the orders of their officers—which was to reserve their fire, until our assailants should come near.

Most discharged their guns at the enemy, while still only dimly seen through the mist of the morning. After firing once, they fled. In an instant, the troopers were upon us.

A few of the diggers upon this occasion proved themselves men of heroic courage. I saw young Ross, who commanded a company, shot dead at the head of his men—while vainly trying to induce them to stand firm.

It seemed but a minute after the signal had been sounded, before the troopers broke down the palisades; and began shooting and hacking at us with their swords.

"I'm a Rolling Stone," thought I, "and do not like staying too long in one spot. The Eureka Stockade is not the place for me."

After making this reflection, I sprang over the palisades; and went off at a speed, that enabled me soon to distance many of my comrades who had started in advance of me.

Amongst others passed in my flight, was Karl, the German, who still persevered in his determination not to desert his digger associates: since he was accompanying them in their retreat.

He had not fled, however, until assured that our defeat was certain: for I saw him inside the stockade, firing his revolver, shortly before I came away myself.

I did not stay to speak to him: for the troopers were closely pursuing us; and cutting down with their swords any man they could overtake.

A majority of the routed diggers fled towards a tract of ground, that had been what the miners call, "worked-out."

This ground was so perforated with holes, that the troopers were unable to gallop their horses over it. Fortunate for the fugitives that these abandoned diggings lay so near the stockade—otherwise the slaughter would have been much greater than it was—in all probability amounting to half the number of the men who had been gathered there.

The pursuit was not continued very far. The troopers soon lost all traces of those they were galloping after. Some of the diggers succeeded in reaching the bush, while others concealed themselves in the shafts of the worked-out claims; and, after a time, the soldiers were recalled to exult over their easy victory.

The regular soldiers of Her Majesty's army took some prisoners in the stockade; but so far as I saw, or could afterwards ascertain, the mounted policemen of the Colonial Government, made no attempt to capture a single digger. They showed no quarter; but cut down, and in some instances horribly mutilated, all with whom they came in contact.

Many of the routed diggers remained concealed in the bush, and other places of refuge, all that day; but, perceiving no necessity for this, as soon as the pursuit was over, I returned to my tent. In the afternoon, when quiet had to a certain extent been restored, I walked over to view the scene of strife, and take a look at the unclaimed corpses. Twenty-eight miners had been shot dead upon the spot; but many more were missing—of whose fate nothing was ever afterwards known. A few probably fell, or were thrown, into some of the deep holes, through which the pursuit had been carried.

Some of the dead had acquaintances and friends about Ballarat, who afterwards removed their bodies, for the purpose of burial.

I saw several corpses that had been collected in one place, and were waiting for recognition. Amongst them was that of a young Austrian, whom I had known. His body had been pierced with five gun shot wounds—any one of which would have proved fatal.

There was one corpse so mutilated and disfigured with sabre cuts, that the features could not be recognised by any with whom, when alive, the man had been acquainted. It was that of a miner who had a family in Ballarat. His body was afterwards identified by his wife, but only through some articles that were found in the pockets of his coat.

I never saw, or heard of Karl after that fatal morning. Several days elapsed; and his tent, that stood near my own, remained unclaimed by its owner. It was still guarded by his dog, which I fed on its chain—as some of my neighbours jocularly remarked—to keep it alive, for the pleasure of hearing it howl. Karl had probably fallen down one of the deep holes, on the abandoned diggings, over which we had been pursued.

At length, becoming weary of listening to the piteous howling of the dog, I set the animal at liberty, and on doing so, gave it a kick—this being the only means I could think of, to let it know that I wished to cut its further acquaintance. It was an ugly, mangy creature; and all the respect I felt for the memory of its lost master, could not induce me to be troubled with it any longer.

Four men were arrested, and tried as ringleaders in the "Ballarat rebellion." They were charged with treason—with an intent to overthrow her Majesty's Government, and take from Queen Victoria the Crown of England! The Governor and his ministers wished the world to be informed, that they had succeeded in quelling a revolution, that threatened destruction to the whole British empire!

They thirsted for more blood; but they did not get it. The jury, before whom the prisoners were tried, acquitted them; and they were once more set at liberty.

Not long after, the licensing system was abolished; and in its stead an export duty of two shillings and sixpence per ounce, was levied upon the gold. This was certainly a more natural method of collecting the revenue; and in every way more satisfactory. By it, the unsuccessful miner was not called upon to pay as much as one who had been fortunate; and the diggers were no longer annoyed and insulted by the minions of the Licensing Commission.

Volume Three—Chapter Thirteen.

Buried Alive.

From Ballarat, I went to the great rush at Mount Blackwood; and pitched my tent on a part of that gold-field, known as the "Red Hill."

Mount Blackwood was more heavily and thickly timbered, than any other of the Victorian gold-fields. The surface of the ground was very uneven; and the soil on the rocks of but little depth. It was difficult to find a horizontal space, of sufficient size, for the pitching of an ordinary miner's tent; and to see such stupendous trees growing on the steep hill-sides, with scarce soil enough to cover their roots, was matter of surprise to everybody who came to Mount Blackwood.

About three weeks after the rush had commenced—and after several thousand people had gathered there—we were visited one night by a terrific gale, or more properly speaking, a "hurricane."

Hundreds of large trees—which owing to the shallow soil, could not take deep root in the rock underneath—were blown down.

The night was very dark; and no one could see from what side a tree might at any moment come crashing. A space of ground, out of reach of the fallen trunks, was not to be found on the gold-field. The consequence was, that thirteen people were killed for certain; and many more severely injured, all through the falling of the trees.

But the number of fatal accidents, caused by the hurricane of that night, was probably never known.

The night was one of horror and fear to more than eight thousand people—each of whom knew not the minute that death might be his portion. A miner and his wife, while endeavouring to escape to a place of safety, were crushed under the same tree. Had they remained in their tent, they would have escaped uninjured! But what was still more singular in this unfortunate incident; the woman, when struck by the tree, was carrying a child, which received not the slightest injury, while both the parents were killed on the spot!

The day after the storm, Mount Blackwood presented a very forlorn appearance. Hundreds of trees had been prostrated by the wind; and nearly every tent had been thrown down.

Ever since that night, I can understand the fear, that some sailors entertain, of *a storm upon land*.

I had very little success in gold digging at Mount Blackwood; but while there, an incident occurred that was interesting to me; so much so, as to be deserving of a place among these my adventures.

I expect to die some time; but fervently hope and pray, that my existence may not be terminated by *suffocation*—either by means of a rope, or otherwise. I profess to have a horror of that mode of death: for the simple reason that I have made trial of it, and found the sensation anything but pleasant.

While at Mount Blackwood, I worked a claim in company with three others.

I was taken into this partnership, by a man I had known at Ballarat. He went by the name of "Yorkey"—from his being a Yorkshireman—and was the only one of the "firm" with whom I formed much acquaintance.

I was at work in a tunnel of the claim, where we had not used sufficient caution in supporting the top of the tunnel with timber.

Although the shaft was not a wide one, the earth being a little damp, and composed of loose shingle, required propping up. As I had neglected this, about a cart load of the shingle fell down, burying me completely under it.

The weight upon my limbs was so great, that I could not move them; and I lay as if I had been chained to the spot.

At the time, two of my mining partners were also below, working in another part of the tunnel. Of course they heard the little earthquake, and came to my assistance.

The task of digging me out, proved more difficult than they expected: for there was not room for both my mates to work at the same time—besides, they could not handle either pick or shovel to any great effect, lest they might injure my limbs.

We had been called up for dinner; and I was on the point of climbing out of the tunnel, just at the moment the earth fell in.

Our mates above, had grown impatient at our delay; and commenced shouting for us to come up. I heard one of those below responding to them. I could not understand what he said; but afterwards learnt, that he was merely telling them what had happened.

Never shall I forget the strange sound of that man's voice. I suppose, for the reason that I was buried in the earth, it seemed unearthly. I could form no idea of the distance the speaker was from me. His voice seemed to come from some place thousands of miles away—in fact from another world. I was sensible that some mischance had occurred—that I was buried alive, and in great agony; but the voice I heard seemed to proceed from the remotest part of an immense cavern in some planet, far down in the depths of space. It commanded me to come thither: and I thought I was preparing to obey that command, by ceasing to live; but the necessary preparation for another existence appeared to require a long time in being completed.

In my struggles for respiration, I fancied that stones and earth were passing through my lungs; and hours, days and weeks seemed to be spent in this sort of agony. It was real agony—so real as not to beget insensibility. On the contrary, my consciousness of existence remained both clear and active.

I wondered why I did not die of starvation; and tried to discover if there was any principle in nature that would enable a person, when buried alive, to resist the demands of hunger and live for ever without food. It seemed impossible for me to die. One vast world appeared to be compressing me against another; but they could not both crush out the agony of my existence.

At length the thought occurred to me that I was dead; and that in another world I was undergoing punishment for crimes committed in that I had left.

"What have I ever done," thought I, "that this horrible torture should be inflicted on me?"

Every link in memory's chain was presented to my mental examination, and minutely examined.

They were all perfect to my view; but none of them seemed connected with any act in the past, that should have consigned me to the torture I was suffering.

My agony at last produced its effect; and I was released from it. I gradually became unconscious, or nearly so. There was still a sensation of pain—of something indescribably wrong; but the keen sensibility of it, both mental and bodily, had now passed away. This semi-unconscious state did not seem the result of the accident that had befallen me. I thought it had arisen from long years of mental care and bodily suffering; and was the involuntary repose of a spirit exhausted by sheer contention, with all the ills that men may endure upon earth. Then I felt myself transferred from this state to another quite different—one of true physical pain, intense and excruciating, though it no longer resembled the indescribable horror I had experienced, while trying to inhale the rocks that were crushing the life out of me.

My head was now uncovered; and I was breathing fast and freely.

Though in great pain, I was now conscious of all that was transpiring.

I could hear the voice of 'Yorkey,' speaking in his native Yorkshire dialect, and encouraging me with the statement that I would soon be out of danger.

Notwithstanding the pain I still suffered, I was happy—I believe never more so in my life. The horrible agony I had been enduring for the want of breath had passed away; and, as I recognised the voice of the kind-hearted Yorkshireman, I knew that everything would be done for me that man could do.

I was not mistaken: for 'Yorkey' soon after succeeded in getting my arms and legs extracted from the shingle; and I was hoisted up to the surface of the earth.

Previous to this accident, I had but a faint idea of how much I valued life, or rather how much I had hitherto undervalued the endurance of death.

My sufferings, whilst buried in the tunnel, were almost as great as those I had felt on first learning the loss of Lenore!

This accident had the effect of sadly disgusting me with the romantic occupation of gold digging—at all events it made me weary of a digger's life on Mount Blackwood—where the best claim I could discover, paid but very little more than the expenses incurred in working it.

I thought Mount Blackwood, for several reasons, the most disagreeable part of Victoria I had ever visited, excepting Geelong. I had a bad impression of the place on first reaching it; and working hard for several weeks, without making anything, did not do much towards removing that impression. I determined, therefore, to go back to Ballarat—not a little dissatisfied with myself for having left it. After my experience of the Avoca diggings, I had resolved to remain permanently at Ballarat—believing it to be the best gold-field in the Colony—but I had allowed false reports of the richness of Mount Blackwood to affect this resolution; and I was not without the consolation of knowing, that the misfortunes that befel me at the latter place were attributable to my own folly; in lending a too ready ear to idle exaggerations.

Volume Three—Chapter Fourteen.

The "Elephant" and His Mate.

For several days after my "exhumation," I was compelled to remain in my tent, an invalid.

When at length I became able to take the road, I started back for Ballarat, where I arrived after an arduous journey on foot, that lasted nearly three days.

On again becoming fairly settled on this far-famed gold-field, I purchased a share in a claim on the "Gravel-pits" lead.

This speculation proved fortunate: for the prospect turned out a good one. The gold I expected to obtain from my claim—added to what I had previously accumulated—promised to amount to a considerable sum. With this, I should have been willing to relinquish the hardships of a miner's life, and follow some less laborious occupation.

When I thought of doing so, however, certain difficulties always presented themselves.

What should I do? What other profession could I follow? These were interrogatories, not easily answered.

Where I should go, after leaving the diggings, was a subject for profound consideration. For what reason should I go anywhere? What purpose had I to accomplish by going anywhere, or doing anything? While asking myself these questions, I thought of Jessie, though not with pleasure, for then within my mind would arise a temptation hard to resist.

Unable to shape out any plan, I left it to circumstances; and toiled on from day to day, with no more interest in the future than the shovel I held in my hands!

How very different it appeared to be with the two young men, who were part owners of the claim, in which I had purchased a share!

Our "firm" was a large concern, owned by ten of us in all; and out of the number, there were but two who appeared to be toiling for an object. The majority of mankind think they are living and working for some purpose; but many of them are mistaken. They have some wishes, with a faint desire to see them fulfilled. But few there are who labour with that determined resolve that cannot be shaken, or set aside by the circumstances of the hour. Men do not often struggle with the determined spirit, that is ever certain to insure success.

The most superficial observer could not have failed to perceive, that the two young men I have mentioned were acting under the influence of some motive stronger than common.

The energy they displayed in their toil, the firmness they exhibited in resisting the many temptations set before them, their disregard of the past, their anxiety for the present, and confidence in the future—all told me that they were toiling for a purpose. They acted, as if they had never met with any serious disappointment in life; and as if they fully believed that Fortune's smiles might be won by those who deserve them.

I knew they must be happy in this belief: for I once indulged in it myself. I could envy them, while hoping that, unlike me, the object for which they were exerting themselves might be accomplished. I had seen many young men—both in California and Australia—yielding to the temptations that beset them; and squandering the most valuable part of their lives in dissipation—scattering the very gold, in the accumulation of which they had already sacrificed both health and strength. It was a pleasure, therefore, to witness the behaviour of these two young miners, actuated by principles too pure and strong to be conquered by the follies that had ruined so many. For this reason, I could not help wishing them success; and I sincerely hoped that virtue, in their case, might meet with its reward.

Nearly everyone has some cause for self-gratification—some little revenue of happiness that makes him resigned to all ordinary conditions of life.

My two companions wished to acquire a certain sum of money, for a certain purpose. They had every reason to believe their wishes would be fulfilled; and were contented in their toil. Such was once the case with myself; but my circumstances had sadly changed. I had nothing to accomplish, nothing to hope for.

And yet this unfortunate state of existence was not without some reflections, that partially reconciled me to my fate. Others were toiling with hopes that might end in disappointment; and I was not. Apprehensions for the future that might trouble them, were no longer a source of anxiety to me!

One of the young men, whom I have thus ceremoniously introduced, was named Alexander Olliphant. He was better known amongst us as "the Elephant"—a distinction partly suggested by his name, and partly owing to his herculean strength. He was a native of the colonies—New South Wales—though he differed very much in personal appearance from the majority of the native-born inhabitants of that colony, who are generally of a slender make. "The Elephant" was about six feet in height, but of a stout build, and possessing great physical strength. Although born and brought up in New South Wales, his conversation proclaimed him familiar with most of the sights to be witnessed in London, Paris, and many others of the large cities of Europe. He appeared to have been well educated; and altogether there was a mystery about the man, that I could not comprehend. I did not try to fathom it. Men working together on the gold-fields are seldom inquisitive; and two mates will often associate, throughout the whole period of their partnership without either becoming acquainted with a single circumstance of the past life of the other—often, indeed, without even learning each other's family names!

I was along with Edmund Lee—already mentioned in my narrative—for many months; and yet he never heard my name, until the hour of our parting in Callao—when we were entering into an arrangement to correspond with each other!

The second of the young men I have spoken about, was known to us simply as, "Sailor Bill." He seldom had anything to say to anyone. We only knew, that he had been a sailor; and that he was to all appearance everything an honest fellow should be. He had worked with Olliphant for more than a year; and, although the two appeared to be on intimate terms of acquaintance—and actually were warm friends—neither knew anything of the private history of the other!

As soon as we should have completed our claim on the Gravel-pits lead, Olliphant and Bill had declared their intention of proceeding to Melbourne—to return to the diggings no more. They had been both fortunate, they said—having obtained the full amount for which they had been toiling, and something more.

They were going to realise those hopes and wishes, that had cheered and inspired them through the weary hours of their gold digging life.

They were both quite young. Perhaps they had parents in poverty, whom they were intending to relieve? Perhaps others might be waiting for their return, and would be made happy by it? The joy of anticipating such a happiness was once mine; and I could imagine the agreeable emotions that must have occupied the thoughts of my two companions—once my own—to be mine no more.

They were going to give up gold digging—with spirits light, and hopes bright, perhaps to enter upon some new and pleasanter sphere of action, while I could bethink me of nothing that would ever more restore my lost happiness. For me there was nothing but to continue the monotonous existence my comrades were so soon to forsake.

Volume Three—Chapter Fifteen.

A Dinner-Party of Diggers.

Our claim was at length completed, and we—the shareholders—with some of our friends determined to hold a little jollification. We engaged a private room in the hotel, where we had divided our gold; and, after settling all accounts, we sat down to as good a dinner, as the landlord could place upon his table.

After dinner, our pipes were lit; and the only business before us, was to find some amusement for the rest of the evening.

"Rule Britannia," "The Red, White, and Blue," and "The Flag that braved a Thousand Years," were sung, and duly applauded. The poet of the company then gave us a song of his own composing, which, whatever may have been its merits, met with the approval of the company.

As it was understood that "the Elephant" and "Bill" were going to give up gold digging for good, and were to start for Melbourne the next day, one of the party came out with a proposal, warmly seconded by the rest.

"Elephant," said the person thus proposing, "now that you and Bill have made your fortunes, and are going to give up the business, suppose you tell us all what you intend doing with your money—so that, when we have made our fortune, we shall have your example to guide us in spending it?"

The individual who made this request, had once been a convict in Tasmania. He was rather a good-looking man, about forty-five years of age, and went by the name of Norton. The little bird called "rumour," had chirupped about the diggings many tales of his former achievements in crime—all of which, however, seemed to have been forgotten.

The reader may ask, why those of our company, who professed to be respectable men, should associate with one who had manifestly been a transported felon?

The answer is, that we were in circumstances very different from those who might think of putting such a question. Ten or twelve men were required for working a mine on the Gravel-pits; and where nearly all the people of the place were strangers to each other, a man could not very well make choice of his companions, at least not all of them. Norton had bought a share in the claim from one of the first holders of it; and all that the rest of us could require of him, was, that he should perform his share of the work.

On such an occasion as that of dividing the gold, he had as much right to be one of the company, as any other shareholder.

"I will agree to what you propose, on one condition," responded the Elephant, to the proposal of Norton; "and I have no doubt but that my friend, Bill, will do the same. But in order that you should understand what I intend doing in the future, it will be necessary that you should be told something of my past. This I am willing to make known, if you, Norton, will give us a true account of the principal events of your life; and Bill will probably gratify your curiosity on the same terms?"

"Oh certainly," said Bill; "if Norton will give us his history, I'll give mine."

The idea of an old convict giving us a true account of his misfortunes and crimes, was thought to be a very happy one; and the whole company were amused at the way the "Elephant" had defeated Norton's attempt to gratify his curiosity: for they had no idea that the convict would make a "confession." But to the surprise of all, he accepted the terms; and declared himself ready and willing to tell "the truth, the whole truth, and nothing but the truth."

Olliphant and Bill could not retreat from the position they had taken, and Norton was called upon to commence. The glasses were again filled, and the short black pipes relit.

The company kept profound silence—showing the deep interest they felt in hearing the life narrative of a man, with whose crimes rumour had already made them partially acquainted.

"I am," began Norton, "the son of a poor man—a day labourer, and was born in the north of Scotland. Inspired by the hopes common to youth, I married early. In consequence, I had to endure the misery every man must meet, who is cursed with poverty, and blessed with a family he is unable to support.

"The mutual affection my wife and I entertained for each other, only increased our wretchedness. It was agony to see one who loved me, having to endure the privations and hardships to which our poverty subjected us.

"By almost superhuman exertions, and by living half-starved, I managed at last to scrape together a sufficient sum to take me to America—where I hoped to be able to provide a home for my wife and child.

"I had not the means to take them along with me, though I left enough to secure, what I thought, would be a permanent home for them until I should return.

"My wife had a brother—an only relative—who lived in a lonely house among the hills. He and his wife kindly agreed to give my old woman a home, until I should either return, or send for her.

"I will not weary you with the particulars of what I did in America—more than to state that I went to the copper mines near Lake Superior; and that I was not there a year, before I was so fortunate as to find a rich vein of ore, which I sold to a mining company for 6,000 dollars.

"I sent my wife a part of this money, along with the intelligence, that I would soon return for her. With the rest, I purchased a small farm in the southern part of the State of Ohio; and leaving a man in charge of it, I returned to Scotland for my family.

"I got back in the middle of winter—in December. It was a very cold morning, when I arrived in sight of the hovel, that contained all I loved most dear on earth. It was Christmas Day; and, in order to have the pleasure of spending it along with my wife, I had walked all the night before. When I drew near the house, I noticed that the snow—that had been falling for two days—lay untrodden around the door!

"I hurried up inside, when I saw, lying on the floor, and partly covered with rags, my wife and child. They were what men call—*dead*!

"The appearance of the hut, and of the dead bodies, told me all. They had died of cold and hunger.

"I afterwards learnt, that my brother-in-law had died some time before; and that his wife immediately afterwards had gone away from the hovel to join some of her own relatives, who lived near the border.

"My poor wife had disposed of every thing that would sell for a penny; and had in vain endeavoured to find employment. The distance of the hut from any neighbour, had prevented her from receiving assistance in the last hours of her existence: for no one had been aware of the state of destitution to which she had been reduced.

"During the severe storm preceding her decease, she had probably lingered too long in the hut to be able to escape from it; and had miserably perished, as in a prison.

"Neither she, nor the child, could have been dead for any length of time. Their corpses were scarcely cold; and it was horrible for me to think, that I had been walking in the greatest haste throughout all that stormy night, and yet had arrived too late to rescue them!

"When sitting by their lifeless forms, in an agony of mind that words cannot describe, I was disturbed by the arrival of a stranger. It turned out to be the post carrier, who stepping inside the hut, handed me a letter. At a glance, I saw it was the letter I had sent from America—enclosing a draft for twenty-five pounds.

"Why has this letter not been delivered before?" I inquired of the man, speaking as calmly as I could.

"He apologised, by saying that the letter had only been in his possession *four days*; and that no one could expect him to come that distance in a snow storm, when he had no other letter to deliver on the way!

"I took up an old chair—the only article of furniture in the house—and knocked the man senseless to the floor.

"His skull was broken by the blow; and he soon after died.

"I was tried, and convicted of manslaughter, for which I received a sentence of ten years transportation.

"At the end of three years, I obtained a ticket-of-leave for good conduct. And now, gentlemen, I have nothing more to tell you, that would be worth your listening to."

At the conclusion of Norton's narrative, several of the company, who seemed to be restraining themselves with great difficulty, broke into loud shouts of laughter. Norton did not appear to be at all displeased at this, as I thought, unseemly exhibition!

I afterwards learnt why he had taken it in such good part. It was generally known, that he had been transported for robbing a postman; and the cause of their mirth was the contrast between the general belief, and his own special account of the crime.

For my part, I could not join in their mirth. His story had been told with such an air of truth, that I could not bring myself to disbelieve it. If not true, the man deserved some consideration for the talent he had exhibited in the construction of his story: for never was truth better counterfeited, or fiction more cunningly concealed, under an air of ingenuous sincerity.

Volume Three—Chapter Sixteen.

The "Elephant's" Autobiography.

When tranquillity had been again restored, the "Elephant" was called on for his autobiography—which was given nearly as follows:—

"My father is a 'squatter' in New South Wales—where I was myself born.

"At the age of seventeen, I was sent to England to be educated; and, being well supplied with money, the design of those who sent me was not defeated: for I did learn a good deal—although the knowledge I obtained, was not exactly of the kind my parents had meant me to acquire.

"I possessed the strength, and soon acquired the skill, to defeat all my fellow students in rowing or sculling a boat. I was also the best hand amongst them with a bat. I became perfect in many other branches of knowledge, of like utility. During my sojourn in Europe, I made several trips to Paris—where I obtained an insight into the manners and customs of that gay capital.

"My father had a sister living in London—a rich widow, who had an only daughter. I called on them two or three times, as I could not well avoid doing so. I was not infatuated with my cousin, nor did my visits beget in my mind any great affection for my aunt.

"Her husband had been dead several years before that time. He had been related to a family of title, and on his death had left a fortune to his widow of about fifty thousand pounds.

"My father considered his sister a person of great consequence in the kingdom; and used to keep up a regular correspondence with her.

"When I was about twenty-two, I received a letter from him, commanding me forthwith to marry my cousin!

"He had made the match with my aunt, without consulting my wishes.

"The deluded man thought the plan he had formed for me, would make me a very great personage. But I could not regard the affair in the same light.

"Soon after receiving my father's orders, my aunt sent me a note—containing a request for me to call upon her.

"I complied; and found that she considered the thing as quite settled, that I was forthwith to marry my cousin. In fact, my aunt at this interview had a good deal to say about preparations for the ceremony!

"My cousin was neither personally good-looking, nor interesting in any way. On the contrary, she had a disposition exceedingly disagreeable; and, to crown all, she was a full half-dozen years older than myself.

"Soon after that interview with my English relatives, I embarked for Sydney. I had been for some time anxious to return home. As I have told you, New South Wales is my native country; and I prefer it to any other. I had seen enough of Europe; and longed to gallop a horse over the broad plains of my native land.

"On my return home, and reporting that I had *not* married my rich cousin, my father flew into a great passion, and refused to have anything farther to do with me.

"I tried to reason with him; but it was of no use. It ended by his turning me out of his house; and telling me to go and earn my own living. This I did for some time, by driving a hackney coach through the streets of Sydney.

"My father, on finding that I was man enough to take care of myself, without requiring any assistance from him, began to take a little interest in my affairs. In doing so, he discovered something else—that caused him quite as much displeasure as my refusal to marry my English cousin.

"He learnt that I was making serious love to a poor, but honest girl, who, with her mother, scarce earned a subsistence, by toiling fourteen hours a day with her needle.

"To think I should let slip a woman with fifty thousand pounds—and who could claim relationship with a family of title—and then marry a poor sewing girl, was proof to my father that I was a downright idiot; and, from that hour, he refused to acknowledge me as his son.

"When gold was discovered in these diggings, I gave up my hackney business, took an affectionate leave of my girl; and came out here.

"I've been lucky; and I shall start to-morrow for Sydney. I shall find the one I love waiting for me—I hope, with some impatience; and, if I don't miscalculate time, we shall be married, before I've been a week in Sydney.

"I am young, and have health and strength. With these advantages, I should not consider myself a man, if, in a new world like this, I allowed my warmest inclinations to be subdued by the selfish worldly influences, that control the thoughts and actions of European people."

I believe the company were a little disappointed in the "Elephant's" story. From the remarkable character of the man, and the evidence of superior polish and education—exhibited both in his bearing and conversation—all had expected a more interesting narrative—something more than the tale he had told us, and which was altogether too simple to excite their admiration. Some of them could not help expressing their surprise—at what they pronounced the silliness of the "Elephant," in "sacking" a fine lady with *fifty thousand pounds*, and an aristocratic connection, for a poor Sydney sempstress. To many of them, this part of the story seemed scarce credible, though, for my part, I believed every word of it.

Reasoning from what I knew of the character of the narrator, I felt convinced that he was incapable of telling an untruth—even to amuse his audience; and I doubted not that he had refused his rich English cousin; and was really going to marry the poor sewing girl of Sydney.

In judging of the Elephant—to use his own words—I did not allow my "inclinations to be subdued by the selfish worldly influences, that control the thoughts and actions of European people."

Volume Three—Chapter Seventeen.

Sailor Bill's Life Yarn.

As the autobiography of the "Elephant," had been of too common-place a character to create any excitement, there was but little interruption in the proceedings; and Sailor Bill, according to the conditions, was next called upon to spin the yarn of his life.

Without any formality, he at once responded to the call.

"When a very small boy," began he, "I was what is called a gutter urchin, or 'mud lark,' about the streets and docks of Liverpool. It was not exactly the business for which I had been intended. When very young, I had been bound apprentice to a trade I did not much like, and to a master I liked still less. In fact, I hated the master so much, as to run away both from him and his trade; and became a ragged wanderer in the streets.

"The profits of this profession were not so great, as to allow me to contract habits of idleness, though, somehow or other, I managed to live by it for nearly a year.

"I was one day overhauling some rubbish, that had been thrown into a gutter, when a man ran against me; and his feet becoming entangled in the rags that composed my costume, he was tripped up, and fell into the mud.

"He immediately got to his feet again; and shook me, until he was so exhausted and agitated, that he could do so no longer.

"While he was doing so, I was not idle. With my nails, teeth, and feet, I scratched, bit, and kicked him—with all the energy passion could produce.

"My desperate resistance, instead of further provoking, seemed to make a favourable impression on the mind of the man: for, as soon as he had ceased shaking me, he declared that I was 'a noble little wretch,' a 'courageous little vagrant,' and many other pet expressions equally conflicting.

"Then taking me by the hand, he led me along by his side, at the same time questioning me about my home and parents.

"Having satisfied himself, that he had as good a right to me as anybody—and perhaps a better by my being in his possession—he continued to drag me onward, all the while muttering to himself, 'Dirty little vagabond! give him in charge to the police. Spirited boy! give him in charge of my steward.'

"Favourably impressed with the general expression of his features, I offered no resistance to his taking me where he liked. The fact is, I did not care what became of me, for I was independent of either fortune or circumstances.

"I was finally carried on board of a ship; and handed over to the care of her steward, where, for the first time in three years, I had my body covered with a complete suit of clothes.

"The man who had thus taken possession of me, was a good-natured, eccentric old bachelor, about fifty years of age; and was master and owner of the ship, that traded between Liverpool and Kingston, Jamaica.

"I remained with this man seven years; and under his tuition, I obtained something of an education. Had I been his own son, he could not have shown more zeal, or taken greater pains to teach me.

"During all that time, his ship was my only home; and I had nothing to tempt me away from it. It was all the world to me; and of that world I was not long in acquiring a knowledge.

"I was about twenty-one years of age, when I was made first officer of the ship. My father—for as such I had got to esteem the man who raised me from rags, and out of mud, to something like a human existence—was going to make one more voyage with me, and then lie by for the rest of his life—leaving me master of the ship.

"We were on our return from Kingston, very deeply laden, when we encountered a severe gale. For some time, we allowed the ship to run with the wind—in order that we might keep on our course; but the storm increased; and this could not be done with safety. We were preparing to lay her head to sea, when a wave rolled over the stern, and swept the decks fore and aft. The captain—my generous protector—and two of the sailors, were washed overboard; and we could do nothing to save them. All three were lost.

"I took the ship to Liverpool, where a wealthy merchant succeeded to the captain's property. To make way for some friend of the new owner, I was discharged from the service—after receiving the few pounds due to me as wages.

"The commotion caused by the discovery of the Australian gold-fields, had then reached Liverpool; and seamen were shipping to Melbourne, asking only the nominal wages of one shilling a month! I was able to get a situation as second officer of a brig bound for that port.

"We had one hundred and twelve passengers; and amongst them was a bankrupt London merchant, emigrating with a large stock of pride, and a small stock of merchandise, to the golden land. He was accompanied by his wife, and a beautiful daughter. To me, this young lady appeared lovely, modest, intelligent; in short, everything that a young man—who for the first time had felt the tender passion, could wish its object to be.

"I had frequent opportunities of conversing with her—when she would be seated outside on the poop; and many of my happiest moments were passed in her society, in those delightful evenings one experiences while crossing the Line.

"I was at length made perfectly happy, by the knowledge that there was one being in the world who felt an interest in my welfare.

"I soon saw that my attentions to his daughter, were displeasing to the proud merchant; and I was told by the girl herself: that she had been commanded to discourage my addresses.

"I sought an interview with the father; and demanded from him his reasons for thus rejecting me. I was simply told: that the girl was his daughter, and that I was only a sailor!

"That same evening, when on duty, I was spoken to by the captain in a harsh and ungentlemanly manner. I was in no pleasant humour at the time: and to be thus addressed, in hearing of so many people—but more especially in the presence of her I loved—was a degradation I could not endure. I could not restrain myself, from making a sharp and angry reply.

"The captain was a man of very quick temper; and, enraged at my insolence, he struck me in the face with his open hand. For this insult, I instantly knocked him down upon the deck.

"The remainder of the voyage I passed in irons. On arriving at Williamston, I was sentenced to two months' imprisonment—during which time I was confined on board a hulk anchored in Hobson's Bay.

"I made an attempt to escape; and, being unsuccessful, I received a further sentence of two months' hard labour on the hulk.

"When at length I received my liberty, I hastened to Melbourne. There I made inquiries for the merchant, in hopes of being able to obtain an interview with his daughter, who was then the only being on earth, for whom I entertained the slightest feeling of friendship.

"I succeeded in finding the young lady; and was conducted into the presence of her mother—who, somewhat to my surprise, received me in the most cordial manner!

"The old merchant was dead. He had died within a month after landing; and the goods he had brought with him to the colony—not being suited to the market—had been sold for little more than the freight out from England had cost. His widow and her daughter were living by their own industry—which, I need hardly tell you, was something they had never done before."

Here Sailor Bill paused—as if he had got to the end of his story.

But his listeners were not contented with such a termination. They believed there must be something more to come—perhaps more interesting than anything yet revealed; and they clamoured for him to go on, and give them the finale.

"There's nothing more," said Bill, in response to the calls of the company; "at least nothing that would interest any of you."

"Let us be the judges of that," cried one. "Come, Bill, your story is not complete—finish it—finish it!"

"I'm sorry myself it's not finished," rejoined he. "It won't be, I suppose, until I get back to Melbourne."

"What then?" inquired several voices.

"Well then," said Bill, forced into a reluctant confession, "I suppose it will end by my getting spliced."

"And to the young lady, with whom you spent those pleasant evenings on the poop?"

"Exactly so. I've written to her, to say I'm coming to Melbourne. I intend to take her and her mother back to England—where they've long wished to go. Of course it would never do to make such a voyage, without first splicing the main brace, and securing the craft against all the dangers of the sea. For that reason, I've proposed to the young lady, that she and I make the voyage as man and wife; and I'm happy to tell you that my proposal has been accepted. Now you've got the whole of my *yarn*."

And with this characteristic ending, Sailor Bill brought his story to a termination.

Volume Three—Chapter Eighteen.

My Brother William.

The next morning, I arose early, and went to Olliphant's tent—to take leave of him, and his companion Bill.

I accompanied them to the public-house, from which the stage coach to Geelong was to start. We stepped inside the house, to have a glass together.

"There's a question," said Bill, "that I've often thought of putting to you. I've heard you called Rowland. Excuse my appearing to be inquisitive; but I have a strong reason for it. You have some other name. Will you tell me what it is?"

There is something extraordinary in the power and quickness of thought. Suddenly a conviction came over my mind: that I had found my brother! I felt sure of it. Memory did not assist me much, in making the discovery. It seemed to come upon me, as if by inspiration!

It is true, I had something to guide me, in coming to this conclusion. Sailor Bill had evidently, at some time or other, known a person by the name of Rowland. It at once entered my mind, that I must be the individual of whom he had this distant recollection.

"My name," said I, in answer to his question, "is your own. Is not yours Stone?"

"It is," rejoined he, "William Stone."

"Then we are brothers!"

"You are the Rolling Stone!" exclaimed Bill, grasping my hand. "How strange that I did not ask the question, when I first heard you called Rowland!"

The excitement caused by our mutual recognition, was of the most pleasurable character; and, for some moments after the first words, we both remained speechless.

'The Elephant' was nearly as much astonished as ourselves, at the discovery thus made. "What a fool I've been," said he, "not to have seen long ago that you were brothers. If ever there were two brothers, I could swear that you two were the pair. I have been blind not to have told you before—what you have at last found out for yourselves."

We had no time to do more than exchange mutual congratulations: for the stage coach was about to start. I immediately paid for a seat; and set off along with them for Geelong. At the moment, I had along with me all the gold I had gathered. I had brought it out, for the purpose of taking it to the Escort Office—as soon as I should bid adieu to my friends. There was nothing else of much importance to detain me in Ballarat; and I parted from the place at less than a moment's notice.

My brother and I found plenty of employment for our tongues, while making the journey to Melbourne.

I asked him, if he had been aware of our mother's having followed Mr Leary to Australia.

"Yes," said he, "I knew, when she left me in Liverpool, that she was going to follow the brute out there; and I concluded she had done so."

"And have you never thought of trying to find her, while you were in Sydney?"

"No," said my brother, in a tone of solemnity, "when she deserted me in Liverpool, to go after that wretch, I felt that I had lost a mother; and it is my belief, that a mother once lost is never found again."

"But did it not occur to you that you should have tried to find Martha? Do you intend leaving the colonies without making some effort to discover our sister?"

"Poor little Martha!" exclaimed William, "she was a dear little child. I would, indeed, like to see her again. Suppose we both try to find her? I do not believe that if we discover her, we need have any fear of being ashamed of her. She was once a little angel; and I am sure she will be a good girl, wherever she is—Oh! I should like to see Martha once more; but to tell the truth Rowland, I do not care for ever seeing mother again!"

I then informed my brother, that his wishes might yet be gratified; and, as we continued our journey, I gave him a detailed history of the affairs of the family—so far as I was myself acquainted with them.

It was by no means an agreeable mode of transit, travelling by stage coach in the state the roads of Victoria were at the time, yet that was the happiest day I had ever passed in the colony. William and I kept up our conversation all day long. We had hardly a word for our companion, Olliphant; and we were under the necessity of apologising to him.

"Don't mention it," said the good-hearted Elephant. "I am as happy as either of you. You are two fellows of the right sort; and I'm glad you have found each other."

On our arrival in Melbourne, we all went together to the Union Hotel. After engaging rooms, we proceeded to the purchase of some clothes—in order that we might make a respectable appearance in the streets of the city. My brother was in breathless haste to get himself rigged out; and we knew his reason. He intended to spend the evening in the society of his future wife and her mother.

At an early hour in the afternoon, he took leave of us.

Olliphant and I were compelled to kill the time the best way we could; but the trouble of doing so was not great: since there are but few cities of equal size with Melbourne, where so much time and money are devoted to the purpose of amusement.

Next day, I accepted an invitation from my brother, to accompany him on a visit to his sweetheart. She and her mother were living in a small house in Collingwood. When we arrived at the door, it was opened by a rather delicate ladylike woman, about forty years of age. She received my brother with a pleasant smile; and I was introduced to Mrs Morell.

The young lady soon made her appearance, from an adjoining room; and, after greeting my brother in a manner that gave me gratification to witness, I was introduced to her.

Sarah Morell was, what might have been called by any one, a pretty girl. She had not the beauty of my lost Lenore, nor was she perhaps even as beautiful as my sister Martha; but there was a sweet expression in her features, a charm in her smile, and a music in her gentle voice, that were all equally attractive; and I could not help thinking, that my brother had made choice of a woman worthy of his honest and confiding love.

She talked but little, during the interview—allowing most of the conversation to be carried on by her mother; but, from the little she did say; and the glance of her eyes—as she fixed them on the manly form of my brother—I could tell that he was beloved.

By that glance, I could read pride and reverence for the man upon whom she had bestowed her heart; and that she felt for him that affection I once hoped to win from Lenore.

How superior was my brother's fate to mine! He was beloved by the one he loved. He was in her presence; and they were soon to be man and wife. He was happy—happy as youth can be, when blessed with hope, love, wealth, and health. I was happy also; but it consisted only in seeing others blessed with the happiness, which I was myself denied.

After passing some hours in the cheerful companionship, of Mrs and Miss Morell, my brother and I returned to our hotel—where we found 'The Elephant' in a very unamiable mood. He had just ascertained, that he would have to stay three days longer in Melbourne: as there was no steamer to start for Sydney before the third day from that time.

117

After a council held between my brother and myself, it was resolved that I should go on to Sydney with the Elephant; and try to induce our sister Martha to accompany me back to Melbourne. The pleasure of meeting a long-lost brother, and of being present at his wedding, we hoped, would be sufficient inducement to cause her to change her resolution, and consent to live with relatives, who were only too anxious to support and protect her.

Since William had been told of our mother's death, he appeared to take much more interest in Martha's welfare; and urged upon me, not to come back to Melbourne, without bringing her along with me. We could not, he said, feel happy, returning to England, and leaving our sister alone in the colonies.

I promised to use every effort in the accomplishment of his wishes—which, of course, were but the echoes of my own.

Miss Morell, on hearing that her lover had a sister in Sydney, insisted on the marriage being postponed, until Martha should arrive.

"I am willing to be married the very day your sister comes," said she, adding in her artless manner, "I shall wait with great impatience until I have seen her."

It is hardly necessary to say, that these conditions redoubled William's anxiety for the speedy arrival of our sister; and, before taking leave of him, I was compelled to make a most emphatic promise of a speedy return. Olliphant, without knowing the object of my visit to Sydney, was gratified to hear that we were to continue our travelling companionship still further; and in joyous spirits we stepped aboard the steamer bound to that place.

Volume Three—Chapter Nineteen.

A Milliner's Yarn.

The Melbourne steamer made the port of Sydney, at a late hour of the night. On landing, we proceeded direct to a hotel, where, after some difficulty, we obtained accommodation for the night.

In the morning, after eating our breakfast—which in Sydney is the most important meal of the day—my companion and I walked out into the streets. We soon parted company—each taking a different direction, since each had his own affairs to attend to.

I proceeded direct to the house where I had left my sister, two years before. I was both surprised, and disappointed, at not finding her there; and perceiving that the house was no longer a milliner's shop.

I inquired for the people who formerly occupied the premises; but could learn nothing of them.

"I am justly served," thought I, "I should have corresponded with my sister; and this disappointment could not have happened."

My relatives had been lost to me once. That should have been a warning. I should have taken precautions against a recurrence of this misfortune. Instead of doing so, I had led Martha to believe, that I had gone back to England; and during my absence had never written to her. I now perceived how foolishly I had acted; and felt as if I deserved never to see my sister again.

I should have been more deeply aggrieved by my conduct, but that I still entertained the hope of being able to find her.

Sydney was not a large city; and if my sister was still within its limits, there was no reason why I should not discover her whereabouts—especially with the energy and perseverance I determined to make use of in the search.

This search I lost no time in instituting. I turned into the next street—though rather mechanically than otherwise: for I was still undecided as to how I should act.

All at once I remembered, that the woman, with whom Martha had gone into partnership, was a Mrs Green. I remembered, too, hearing Mrs Green say, that she had resided in Sydney for several years. Some one, therefore, should know her; and, if she could be found, it was natural to infer, that I should learn something of Martha.

While sauntering along the street, into which I had entered, my eye fell upon a little shop, which bore the sign of a milliner over the window. That should be the place for me to commence my inquiries. I entered the shop, where I saw standing behind a counter the worst-looking woman I had ever beheld. She was not ugly, from having a positively hideous face, or ill-formed features; but rather from the spirit that gave expression to both. It was a combination of wicked passions—comprising self-esteem, insolence, avarice, and everything that makes human nature despicable. The woman was dressed in a style that seemed to say: "vanity for sale."

I asked her, if she could give me any intelligence of a Mrs Green, who formerly kept a milliner's shop in the next street.

A disgusting grin suddenly spread over the features of the woman, as she promptly replied, "Yes; Mrs Green was chased out of Sydney over a year ago. She thought to smash my business; but she got smashed herself."

"Can you tell me where she is to be found?" I inquired.

"Yes. She saw it wasn't no use to try to carry on business against me; and she's hooked it to Melbourne."

"There was a young woman with her, named Martha Stone," I continued, "can you tell me where *she* is?"

"Yes. She's another beauty. I am not at all astonished at young men inquirin' for *her*. Don't think I am, mister. I've kept that lady from starving for the last six months; and I'm about tired of it, I can tell you. This is a nice world we live in, sure enough. What might you be wantin' with Miss Stone?"

"I wish to know where she is to be found—nothing more," I answered.

"Certainly. You wish to know where she is! Of course you do. Why not?" said the disgusting creature, in a tone, and with a significant leer, that I have ever since been vainly endeavouring to forget. "What right have you to think, that I should know where any such a person lives?" continued the woman. "I wish you to understand, sir, that *I am a lady*."

I should certainly never have thought it, without being told; but, not the least grateful for the information, I answered:

"You say, that you know where Miss Stone is to be found. I am her brother, and wish to find her."

"Oh! that's it, is it?" retorted the woman with a look of evident disappointment. Then, turning round, and forcing her neck someway up a narrow staircase, she screamed out, "Susan! Susan!"

Soon after, a very young girl—apparently half-starved—made her appearance at the bottom of the stairs.

"Susan," said the only woman I ever hated at first sight, "tell this man, where Miss Stone lives."

There was something not so bad in the creature after all; and I began to fancy, I had been wronging her.

"Please, sir," said Susan, pointing with outstretched arm towards one of the sides of the shop, "go up this street, till you come to the baker's shop; then turn round this way, and go on till you pass the public-house with the picture of the horse on it; then turn that way, and go on till you come to where the house was burnt down; cross the street there, and go on to the house where they sell lollies; go by that, and at the turning beyond go this way until you come to the house with the green window blinds—"

"That will do," I exclaimed. "I don't want to lose my senses, as well as my sister. Can you tell me, Susan, the name of the street, and the number of the house, in which Miss Stone resides?"

"No, sir, thank you," answered Susan.

"Can you go there—if this lady will give you leave?"

"Yes, sir, if you please," said the girl, glancing timidly at her mistress.

I thought the mistress would refuse; and even hoped she would. Anxious as I was to find my sister, I did not like to receive even so slight a favour from one whom I had hated with so very little exertion.

The woman, contrary to my expectations, consented to the child's going out to show me the way; and I am so uncharitable as to believe, that her consent was given with the hope that, in finding my sister, I should meet with some chagrin!

I followed Susan through the streets, until we came to a dirty, wretched suburb of the city, where the girl pointed out a house, and told me to knock at the door.

Giving the poor little slavey half-a-crown, I sent her away; and, the next minute, my sister was sobbing in my arms.

Everything in the room proclaimed her to be in the greatest poverty. Strange that I did not regret it; but, on the contrary, was gratified by the appearance of her destitution! It was proof that she was still virtuous and honest. Moreover, I fancied she would now be the more willing to accept the protection, I had come to offer her. She was under the impression, that I had just returned from England. When I undeceived her on this point, she seemed much grieved, that I had been so long in the colonies, without letting her know it.

I soon learnt from her the simple story of her life, since our last parting. At the time she had joined Mrs Green in business, the latter was deeply in debt; and, in about three months after, all the stock in the little shop was sold off to meet Mrs Green's liabilities. Their business was broken up; and Mrs Green had gone to Melbourne—as her rival had stated. Martha had obtained employment in two or three milliner's establishments in the city; and, as she blushingly told me, had good reasons for leaving them all.

She was now making a sort of livelihood, by working for anyone who chanced to have sewing to give her; and was obtaining occasional, but ill paid employment, from the lady who had assisted me in finding her.

"Oh, Rowland!" said Martha, "that woman is the worst that ever lived. She never lets me have a piece of sewing, at a price that will allow me more than bread and water, and yet I have been obliged to take it from her, because I cannot get enough sewing elsewhere. I often work from six o'clock in the morning till ten at night—when I can get anything to do; and yet I've often been very, very hungry. I'm sure it is as bad here, as the stories I've heard about poor sempstresses in London. Ah, brother! Good girls are not wanted in this place. People seem only to care for those who are bad; and while they have everything they wish, girls like me must live as you see I've been doing. Oh, Rowland! is it not a cruel world?"

I was much gratified at hearing my sister talk in this manner: for each word was evidence, that she had been leading an honourable life; and, moreover, her despondency led me to believe: that she would no longer oppose my projects, as she had previously done.

It was all for the best, that she had not done as I wished her two years before. Had she then consented to returning with me to England, I should have gone thither—notwithstanding my disappointment about Lenore. By doing so, I should have missed meeting my brother—besides I should have lost the opportunity of making above fifteen hundred pounds—which I had gathered on the gold-fields of Victoria.

Volume Three—Chapter Twenty.

My Sister still Obstinate.

I had been some little time in my sister's company, before telling her of my intentions regarding her. I had allowed her to indulge in such conjectures about my designs, as the circumstances might suggest.

"I am very glad, Rowland," said she, "that you have made up your mind to stay in the colonies. I hope you will live in Sydney. Oh! we would be so happy! You have come to stay here, have you not? Say yes, brother; and make me happy! Say you will not leave me any more?"

"I do not wish to leave you, dear sister," said I; "and I hope that you have now learnt a lesson, that will make you willing to accept the offer I am going to make you. I have come, Martha, to take you with me to Melbourne."

"What reason can you have, for wishing me to go to Melbourne? It cannot be a better place than Sydney?"

"Are you still unwilling to leave Sydney?" I asked, with a painful presentiment, that I was once more to be baulked in my design of making my poor sister happy.

"Brother," she replied, "I am not willing to go to Melbourne. I don't wish to leave Sydney—at least, not yet."

"Would you not like to see your brother William?" I asked.

"What! William! dear little Willie! Have you heard of him, Rowland? Do you know where he is?"

"Yes. He is in Melbourne; and very anxious to see you. I have come to take you to him. Will you go?"

"I must see William—my long-lost brother William! I must see him. How came you to find him, Rowland? Tell me all about it. Why did he not come here along with you?"

"We met by mere chance—on the diggings of Victoria; and, hearing me called Rowland, he asked my other name. We then recognised one another. Little Willie—as you call him—is now a tall, fine-looking young man. Next week he is going to be married to a beautiful girl. I have come to take you to the wedding. Will you go, Martha?"

"I don't know. I must see brother William. What shall I do? What shall I do? I cannot leave Sydney."

"Martha," said I, "I am your brother; and am willing to assist you in any manner possible. I am older than you; and we have no parents. I have the right to some authority over you; and now demand the reason, why you are not willing to go with me to Melbourne?"

My sister remained silent.

"Give me a straightforward answer," I cried in a tone that partook of command. "Tell me why you will not go?"

"Oh, brother!—because—because I am waiting here for some one—one who has promised—to return to me."

"A man, of course?"

"Yes, yes—a man—a true man, Rowland."

"Where has he gone; and how long is it, since you have seen him?" I asked, unable to conceal my indignant sorrow.

"He went to the diggings in Victoria, a little more than two years ago. Before going, he told me to wait, until he should come back; and then he would marry me."

"Martha! is it possible that this is your only reason for not going with me?"

"It is—my only one—I cannot go. *I must wait for him!*"

"Then you are as foolish, as our poor mother was in waiting for Mr Leary. The man who promised to return and marry you, has probably forgotten both his promise and you, long before this. Very likely he has married some other. I thought you had more sense, than to believe every idle word spoken by idle tongues. The man for whom you are making yourself miserable, would laugh at your simplicity, if he only knew of it. He has probably forgotten your name. Cease to think of him, dear sister; and make both yourself, and your brothers, happy!"

"Do not call me a fool, Rowland—do not think me one! I know I should be, if I was waiting for any common man; but the one I love is not a common man. He promised to return; and unless he dies, I am sure he will keep his word. I know it would be folly to have trusted most men as I've done him; but he's not like others. I shall yet be happy. To wait for him is but my duty; do not urge me to neglect it."

"Oh, Martha! our poor mother thought about Mr Leary, just as you do about this man. She thought him true to her—the best husband in the world! You may be as much mistaken as she was. I advise you to think no more of him, but go with me. Look around you! See the wretched state in which you are living! Leave it for a happy home, with those who will truly love you."

"Do not talk to me so, Rowland, or you will drive me mad. I wish to go with you, and wish to see William; but I cannot, and must not leave Sydney!"

It was evident to me, that my sister was afflicted with the same delusion, that had enslaved our mother even unto death; and, with much regret, I became conscious of the folly of trying to induce her to act in a rational manner. I saw that common sense, reason, persuasion, or threats, would all be alike unavailing to obtain compliance with my wishes. The little I had seen of her sex, had impressed me with the belief that no woman ever exhibited such blind faith and full confidence in a man worthy of the least regard; and I was willing to stake my existence, that my sister's lover was a fellow of no principle—some low blackguard of a similar stamp to the late Mr Leary. I could not suppose him to be quite so bad as Leary: for that to me would have appeared impossible.

I was greatly chagrined to think my kind intentions towards Martha should be thwarted by her folly. I was even angry. Perhaps it was unmanly in me to be so. My sister was unfortunate. No doubt she had been deluded; and could not help her misfortune. She was more an object for pity than anger; but I was angry, and could not restrain myself from showing it. Conscious of my upright and disinterested regard for her, I could not help thinking it ungrateful of her, thus to oppose my designs for her welfare.

"Martha," said I, "I ask you once more to go with me. By doing so, you will fulfil a sister's duty as well as seek your own welfare. Reject my offer now, and it will never be made again: for we shall part for ever, I will leave you to the misery, you seem not only to desire, but deserve."

"Rowland! Rowland!" exclaimed she, throwing her arms around my neck, "I cannot part from you thus. Do not leave me. You must not—you must not!"

"Will you go with me?" I asked, too much excited to listen patiently to her entreaties.

"Rowland, do not ask me! May heaven help me; I cannot go!"

"Then, farewell!" I cried, "farewell for ever!" and as I uttered the parting speech, I tore myself from her embrace, and hurried half frantic out of the room.

Volume Three—Chapter Twenty One.

My Sister's Sweetheart.

On leaving the house, my soul was stirred by conflicting emotions. I was wild with disappointment, sorrow and indignation.

It was wrong to part with my poor sister in such fashion; and my conscience told me so, before I had proceeded two hundred yards along the street. I should at least have given her some money, to relieve her from the extreme necessity which she was evidently in.

A moment's reflection, as I stopped in the street, told me it was my duty to do this, if nothing more.

I thought of sending her a few pounds after getting back to the hotel. Then succeeded the reflection, that to do so would be more trouble, than to turn back, and give it to her myself. This thought decided me to return to the house, and see her once more. I retraced my steps; and again knocked at the door.

For some moments there was no answer; and I knocked again. I waited for nearly two minutes; and still there was no sign of my summons being answered.

I was on the point of bursting in the door, when it was opened by a man, whose huge frame almost filled the entrance from jamb to jamb. It was the Elephant! The truth instantly flashed upon my mind. It was for *him* my sister had been waiting! She—was the sempstress for whom he had been toiling—the young girl spoken of in his story—she, whom he had said, he was going to return and marry!

Martha had flung herself into a chair; and appeared insensible.

I cannot remember that either Olliphant or I spoke on seeing one another. Each was too much surprised at meeting the other. And yet neither of us thought, there was anything strange in the circumstance. Let those, who can, explain the singularity of our sentiments at that encounter. I cannot, and therefore shall not make the attempt. The attention of both of us was soon called to Martha, who had recovered consciousness.

"I thank God!" she cried out addressing me, "I thank God, Rowland, you have returned. You see, he has come back!" she continued, placing her hand on the broad shoulder of 'the Elephant.' "I knew he would. I told you he was certain to come; and that it was not possible for him to deceive me. This is my brother, Alex," she added, turning to Olliphant. "He wanted me to leave you; but don't blame him: for he did not know you, as I did. I've seen hard times, Alex; but the joy of this moment more than repays me for all."

It was some time before Olliphant and I had an opportunity of communicating with each other: for Martha seemed determined that no one should have anything to say but herself.

"What fools we have been!" exclaimed Olliphant, as soon as his sweetheart gave him a chance of speaking. "Had you told me that your name was Stone, and that you had a sister in Sydney, how much more pleasure we should have had in one another's society! You have nearly missed finding your brother; and either you or I have nearly lost your sister by keeping your name a secret. I know that for a man to talk to others of his family affairs is not strict etiquette; but the rules of that are often made by those who are only respected because they are unknown; or rather, because nothing concerning them can be told to their credit."

"You and I have been friends," continued the Elephant, still addressing his discourse to me. "Why should we have cared for etiquette? We ought to have acted independently of its requirements. Depend upon it, that open-hearted candour is ever preferable to secrecy."

I assured Olliphant, that I was convinced of the truth of this doctrine by late events; and that it was also my belief, an honest man has very little on his mind that need be concealed from his acquaintances.

The scene that followed was one of unalloyed happiness. It ended in the determination—that we should all three at once proceed to Melbourne; and that Olliphant and Martha should be married at the same time that my brother was to be united to Miss Morell.

It was ludicrous to witness the change, that had suddenly taken place in the sentiments of Martha. She no longer offered the slightest objection to leaving Sydney; but on the contrary, declared herself delighted at the prospect of going to Melbourne—a place, she said, she had been long desirous of seeing!

During the evening, the little slavey, Sarah, came over from the milliner's shop, with a bundle of sewing materials—which Martha was required to make up immediately.

"Tell your mistress," said Martha, "that I cannot afford to do any more work for her: for she does not pay me enough for it. Tell her, that I hope she will not be much disappointed; but that I really cannot sew any more for her. Will you tell her that?"

"Yes, thank you!" said Sarah, "but I don't think she'll be much disappointed: for she said she did not think you would do any more work now; and she only sent it to see."

We had enough to talk about that evening. Olliphant had been acquainted with our poor mother; and expressed much regret that she had died so unhappily.

We all had explanations to make; and Olliphant and I listened with equal interest to a long recital of my sister's struggle to maintain herself, and to an explanation of her sorrow at being unable to comply with my request, when I had entreated her to leave Sydney.

This confession was as pleasant to me as to the Elephant; but perhaps still pleasanter was it for him to hear that, during his long absence, she had never felt a doubt about his returning, and that such a suspicion had never remained for an instant in her mind.

As events had turned out, I could not regret that my sister had been, what I had too rashly termed foolish; and that her faith in Olliphant's promise had remained unshaken under such strong temptations, as those to which she had been subjected.

She had proved herself worthy of a good husband; and there was no one, whom I should have preferred seeing her united to, before the man, for whom she had so long and patiently waited.

Volume Three—Chapter Twenty Two.

At Sea.

On the third day after my arrival in Sydney, I started back for Melbourne, in the steamer "Warratah," accompanied by Olliphant and Martha.

On arriving at Melbourne, my sister was taken to the residence of Mrs Morell, where she had the pleasure of meeting her brother William; and making the acquaintance of her future sister-in-law.

Sarah Morell and Martha became warm friends upon sight; and on the evening of our return, a more happy party, than the one assembled in Mrs Morell's cottage, could not have been found in the colony.

At intervals, a thought of my own life-long disappointment would flash across my mind; but the sight of so many happy faces around me, would soon restore me to a feeling of tranquil contentment.

Next day, preparations were made for the double marriage, which took place shortly after.

The occasion was not marked by any grand ceremonial display—such as I have often witnessed at the "weddings" of lucky gold-diggers. All the arrangements were conducted with the same sense of propriety and taste, that appeared to have guided the previous conduct of the principal parties concerned.

My brother's honeymoon tour, was to be a voyage in the first ship that should sail for England. As I did not much like the idea of separating from him so soon; and, having no great desire to return to the diggings, I resolved to accompany him.

Olliphant and Martha only remained in Melbourne, until they should see us off, when they intended returning to Sydney to reside permanently in that city. The Elephant had gathered gold enough to set him up in some respectable business; and it was but natural he should prefer New South Wales—his native country—to any other. I knew that to my sister, all places were now alike; so long as she should be with her husband.

I do not much like travelling in a ship, where there is a large number of passengers. It is something like going out for a walk, along a street crowded with people. When there are many passengers in a vessel, there are likely to be some of a very disagreeable disposition, that will be sure to make itself manifest during the voyage. Moreover, in a crowded ship, the regulations require to be more rigidly enforced—thus rendering the passage more irksome to all. There is much greater freedom of action, and generally more amusement, on board a ship carrying only a limited number of passengers. For this reason, we took passage in the first cabin of a small vessel—where we knew there would be only about twenty others besides ourselves.

The ship was bound direct for the port of London; the captain, whose name was Nowell, was to all appearance a gentleman; the accommodation, as regarded room and other necessary requirements, was satisfactory; and we set sail, with every prospect of a pleasant voyage.

As Captain Nowell was a man of sociable inclinings, he soon became a favourite with all his passengers. Between him and myself an intimacy arose; and I passed much of my time in his company—either at chess, or in talking about subjects connected with his calling, which I had not altogether forgotten. He appeared to take an interest in my future welfare; so much so, as frequently to converse with me on the subject of my getting married.

"Lucky gold-diggers," said he, "often go home in my ship in search of a wife; and not unfrequently get cheated in the quality of the article. As I have some experience in matrimonial matters, you can't do better than let me choose a wife for you. Besides," he continued, "I have a young lady in view, that I think would just suit you. I have long been in search of a good husband for her; but have not yet met with a man, to whom I should think of confiding her happiness. From what I have seen of you, Mr Stone, I fancy I could trust her to your keeping."

Though perfectly indifferent about the captain's protégée, I could not help acknowledging the compliment.

"I only ask of you," he continued, "to make no rash engagements, after you arrive in England. Do nothing in that line till you have seen the girl; and then if you don't like her, there's no harm done."

I thanked the captain for his offer; and sighed, as I thought of the cruel fate, that had placed an impassible barrier between me and Lenore.

There is one thing in my narrative, that may appear remarkable to the reader—perhaps scarce truthful; and that is, the facility with which I made so many friends. An explanation of this may not be out of place.

I was always in earnest in what little I had to say. No one could converse long with me, without discovering that I was sincere in what I said. I do not claim this as a trait of character peculiar to myself; but I do affirm—as far as my experience has instructed me—that it is not so with the majority of mankind. Language is too often used, as the means for concealing thoughts—instead of expressing them.

Thousands of people say what they do not mean; and sometimes gain friends by it. But it is a friendship false as it is fleeting; and often confers on him who obtains it, more disappointment and trouble, than he would be likely to have with avowed enemies.

Nothing transpired during our home voyage, worthy of particular notice. After passing some small islands, that lie near the coast of Port Philip, we never sighted land again for three months!

On the ninety-second day of our voyage, the cheering cry of "Land ho!" resounded through the ship; and, hastening on deck, we looked upon the white cliffs of Dover.

Great was the joy of Mrs Morell and her daughter, at once more beholding their native shores; and I could envy my brother, who had contributed so much to the happiness of others, and at the same time so successfully established his own.

We landed at Portsmouth; and proceeded to London by rail. Before parting with Captain Nowell—who had to remain a few days with his ship—I promised to visit him in his London house—the address of which he had already made known to me.

A few hours after, I entered, for the first time, within the limits of the world's metropolis.

Volume Three—Chapter Twenty Three.

Life in London.

After staying one night at a hotel, we went into private lodgings at Brompton.

For several days after our arrival, my brother was employed in the pleasant duty of escorting his wife and mother-in-law—on a round of visits to their numerous old acquaintances, while I was left to wander alone through the streets of the stupendous city. I had anticipated some little pleasure in visiting the far-famed metropolis; but in this I was disappointed; and soon began to feel regret for having left behind me the free life I had been pursuing on the gold-fields.

I had some business, however, to transact, even in London. The gold I had obtained in California—along with that bequeathed to me by poor old Stormy Jack—had been forwarded to the Bank of England; and about a week after my arrival, I went down to the city, to draw out the money deposit that was due to me. On presenting myself to the cashier, I was told that it would be necessary for me to bring some responsible person, to say that my name was Rowland Stone. This individual must be known to the authorities of the Bank.

This requirement placed me in a little dilemma. Where was I to find a sponsor? I was a perfect stranger in London. So were my travelling companions. I knew not a soul belonging to the great city—much less one who should be known to the magnates of the Bank.

To whom should I apply?

When I had mentally repeated this question, for the twentieth time, I bethought me of Captain Nowell. He should be the very man.

I at once hailed a cab; and drove to the address he had given me. Fortunately he had arrived from Portsmouth; and was at home.

Without a moment's hesitation, he accompanied me to the Bank, where everything was satisfactorily arranged. Instead of drawing out the deposit, I added to it, by paying in an additional sum—consisting of the gold I had gathered in Australia. My only object in troubling myself about it at the time, was to make sure that the gold I had forwarded from California had arrived safely, and was otherwise "all right."

Before parting with Captain Nowell, he requested to know why I had not gone to his house to see him sooner.

"Your coming to-day," he said, "was not a visit; and I shan't take it as such. You only came to trouble me on business for which you needed me, or probably I should not have seen you at all. You must pay me a regular visit. Come to-morrow; or any time that best suits your convenience. You know my style at sea? You'll find me just the same ashore. Don't forget that I've something to show you—something you had better have a look at, before you choose elsewhere."

I gave the kind-hearted Captain my promise to call upon him—though not from any inclination to be assisted by him in the way he seemed to wish. The finding a wife was a thing that was far—very far from my thoughts.

Several days had elapsed after my interview with Captain Nowell; and each day I was becoming more discontented, with the life I was leading in London. My brother, his wife, and Mrs Morell, were very kind to me; and strove to make me as happy as possible. But much of their time was taken up in paying visits, or spent in amusements, in which I could feel no interest. I soon found that to be contented, it would be necessary for me, either to take an active part in the busy scenes of life, or be in possession of great domestic happiness. The latter I could never expect to attain; and London appeared to present no employment so well suited to my disposition and habits, as that I had followed upon the gold-fields.

I might have passed some of my time very pleasantly in the company of Captain Nowell; but I was prevented from availing myself of that pleasure—even of paying my promised visit to him—by the very thing that might otherwise have attracted me. I had no desire to form the acquaintance of the young lady, he had spoken of; and for me to call at his house might give occasion for him, as well as others, to think differently.

I admit that I may have been over-scrupulous in this matter: since Captain Nowell and I had become fast, and intimate friends. But from what he had already said, I could not visit the young lady, and remain indifferent to her, without the conclusion being come to, that I thought her unworthy of my regard, and that, after seeing, I had formed an unfavourable opinion of her. It may have been silliness on my part; allowing such a thought to prevent my visiting a friend; but, as I had not come to London wife-hunting, I did not desire others to think that I had. To me, matrimony was no more a pleasant subject for contemplation—especially when it referred to myself—and the few words, spoken to me by the captain on that theme, had been sufficient to defeat the only object he probably had any particular wish to attain: that I should call upon him and partake of his hospitality.

About a month after our arrival in London, I inquired at the General Post Office for letters from Australia; and had the pleasure of receiving two. One was from Olliphant, the other from my sister. Martha's was a true woman's letter: that could be read once by the recipient, and then easily forgotten. It was full of kind words for all of us in London; but the only information to be obtained from it was, that she thought well of everybody, and was herself exceedingly happy.

Perhaps I was more gratified with the contents of Olliphant's letter, from which I select the following extract:—

"On our return to Sydney, I learnt that my father had just got back from a visit to England—which he had long before determined on making. I was very anxious to see him, in the hope that we might become friends again; but, knowing that the first advances towards a reconciliation must come from himself, I would not go to him. I could not think of acknowledging myself sorry, for having done that which I knew to be right. The only step I could make, towards the accomplishment of my wishes, was to put myself in communication with a mutual friend; and let him know that I had returned to Sydney. I did not omit to add, that I had returned from the diggings with a full purse: for I knew that this would also be communicated to my father, and might have some effect upon him of a favourable character.

"It appeared as if I had not been mistaken. Three days after, the governor called at the hotel where I was staying; and met me as a father should meet a son, whom he has not seen for more than three years. I was no little surprised at the turn things had taken: for, knowing the old gentleman's obstinate disposition, I did not expect a settlement either so prompt, or satisfactory. I presumed it would take some time and trouble, to get on good terms with him again.

"He seemed greatly pleased with Martha's appearance; and they became fast friends all at once.

"'I like the look of you,' said he to her, 'and am willing to believe that you are worthy of Alex; and that is saying a good deal for you. Ah, my son,' continued he, addressing himself to me, 'had you brought home your London cousin for a wife—as I commanded you to do—should certainly have horsewhipped you on your return. When I came to see her in London, I soon changed my mind about her. She is nothing but an ugly silly fool; and too conceited to know it. I admire your spirit for disobeying orders, and marrying a girl, whom I am not ashamed to acknowledge as my daughter.'

"We shall leave town to-morrow for my father's station; and the only thing we require now to make us perfectly happy, is the company of yourself, William and his wife, I hope that after you have tried the 'Old Country' for a few weeks, you will believe, as I do, that it is only a place for flunkeys and snobs; and that every young man of enterprise and energy should come out here, where life can be spent to some purpose—worthy of the toil that all ought to endure. I shall expect to see you in Sydney within the next year."

There was a strong suspicion in my mind, that "The Elephant" was right, in believing I would soon return to the colonies. Why should I remain in London? I could be nothing there. It was different with my brother. He might now be happy anywhere. He only wanted a spot, where he might tranquilly await his final departure from the world, while I was a Rolling Stone that must roll on—or be miserable.

The more consideration I gave to the circumstance, the more determined did I become to part from London: and go to some land, where youth and health were worth possessing. I could feel that the blessings, Nature had bestowed on me were not worth much in London, where men are enslaved by customs and laws that subject the million to the dominion of the few. I determined, therefore, on going, where I should be regarded as the equal of those around me, where there was room for me to move, without the danger of being crushed by a crowd of self-sufficient creatures—most of whom were in reality more insignificant than myself. I should join "The Elephant" in New South Wales; and perhaps become a man of some influence in a land where the sun is to be seen every day.

I at this time regretted, that I had ever been a Rolling Stone. I believed that a man may be happier who has never wandered from home to learn lessons of discontent, and become the slave of desires, that in one place can never be gratified. Each spot of earth has its peculiar advantages, and is in some respects superior to all others. By wandering in many lands, and partaking of their respective pleasures, we become imbued with many desires to which we look back with regret when they can no longer be gratified. After residing in a tropical climate, who can encounter the chilling blasts of a northern winter, without longing:

"For green verandahs hung with flowers,
For marble founts, and orange bowers?"

And when nearly cooked by the scorching sun—when tortured at every turn by reptiles, and maddened by the worry of winged insects—we sigh for the bracing breezes of a northern clime, and the social joys of the homes which are there found—a happiness such as my brother might now be permitted to enjoy, but which was for ever denied to me.

With such reflections constantly passing through my mind, I felt that London, large as it was, could not contain me much longer; and I only waited, until some slight turning of Fortune's wheel would bestir me to make a fresh start for the Antipodes.

Volume Three—Chapter Twenty Four.

Old Acquaintances.

One day, while riding inside a "bus" along the Strand, and gazing out through the slides, I amused myself by looking at the "fares" seated upon the "knife-board," or rather their images, reflected in the plate-glass windows of the shops in front of which we were passing.

While thus engaged, my attention became more especially fixed upon one of my fellow passengers so reflected; and, on continuing my second-hand scrutiny, I became convinced that an old acquaintance was directly over my head. I requested the conductor to stop the "bus," and, upon his doing so, I got out, and climbed to the top of it. On raising my eyes to a level with the roof, I saw that I had not been mistaken. Cannon, whom I had last seen in Melbourne, was one of the row of individuals that occupied the knife-board.

We got off the "bus" at Charing Cross, stepped into Morley's Hotel, and ordered "dinner for two."

"Cannon," said I, "how came you to be here? I left you in Melbourne, without any money. How did you get a passage home?"

"Well," replied Cannon, with a peculiar grin, "it's easily explained. My well-wishing friends here sent me a little money, which came to hand, shortly after I saw you. I knew why they did it. They were afraid, that I might get hard up out there, and, someway or other find my way home. They weren't so cunning as they thought themselves. On receiving their cheque, I did with it, just what they didn't intend I should do. I paid my passage home with the money, for fear I mightn't have the chance again; and I'll take precious good care, they don't send me out of England a second time—not if I can help it."

"What has become of Vane?" I asked.

"Vane! the damned insidious viper! I don't like to say anything about him. He had some money left him here; and got back to England, before I did. He's here now."

"And how are our friends up the Yarra Yarra. Have you heard anything of them, since we were there together?"

"Yes; and seen them, too—several times. They were well the last time I saw them. I mean well in bodily health; but I think a little wrong in the mind. They became great friends with that fellow Vane."

I noticed that Cannon, although he had said that he did not like to say anything about Vane, kept continually alluding to him during the two or three hours that we were together; and always spoke of him with some show of animosity.

I could see that the two men were friends no longer. I was not inquisitive as to the cause of their misunderstanding—probably for the reason, that I took very little interest in the affairs of either.

"Are you in any business here?" asked Cannon, when we were about to separate.

"No," I replied, "I don't desire to go into business in London; and, as I can find but little to amuse me, I am thinking of returning to Australia."

"Ah! that's strange," rejoined Cannon. "Perhaps the reason why you are not amused, is because you are a stranger here, and have but little society. Come along with me, and I will introduce you to some of my friends, who can show you some London life. Will you promise to meet me here to-morrow, at half-past ten o'clock?"

I did not like giving the promise; but Cannon would take no denial; and, having nothing else to do, I agreed to meet him, at the time and place he had mentioned. After that we shook hands, and parted.

Though not particularly caring about either of them, I liked Vane less than I did Cannon. I was not at all surprised to find that a disagreement had sprung up between them. In fact, I would rather have felt surprised, to hear that they had remained so long in each other's society without having had a quarrel. Cannon, with all his faults, had some good qualities about him, enough to have rendered him unsuitable as a "chum" for the other; and I had anticipated a speedy termination of their friendship. I knew that Vane must have done something very displeasing to Cannon, else the other would scarce have made use of such strong expressions, while speaking of his old associate. Cannon, when not excited by passion, was rather guarded in his language; and rarely expressed his opinions in a rash or inconsiderate manner.

Next morning, I met him according to appointment; and we drove to a cottage in Saint John's Wood—where he proposed introducing me to some of his English acquaintances. We were conducted into a parlour; and the servant was requested to announce, "Mr Cannon and friend."

The door was soon after opened; and Jessie H— stood before me!

On seeing me, she did not speak; but dropped down into a sofa; and for some time seemed unconscious, that there was anyone in the room.

It was cruel of Cannon thus to bring us again together; and yet he did not appear to be the least punished, although present at a scene that was painful to both of us. On the contrary, he seemed rather pleased at the emotion called forth upon the occasion.

Jessie soon recovered command of herself, but I could easily perceive, that her tranquil demeanour was artificial and assumed—altogether unlike her natural bearing, when I knew her on the banks of the Yarra Yarra.

Cannon strove hard to keep alive a conversation; but the task of doing so was left altogether to himself. I could give him but little help; and from Jessie he received no assistance whatever. The painful interview was interrupted by the entrance of Mr H—, whose deportment towards us, seemed even more altered than that of his daughter.

I could easily perceive, that he did not regard either Cannon, or myself, with any feeling of cordiality.

We were soon after joined by Mrs H—, who met us in a more friendly manner than her husband; and yet she, too, seemed acting under some restraint.

While Cannon engaged the attention of Mr and Mrs H—, I had a few words with Jessie.

She requested me to call, and see them again; but, not liking the manner in which her father had received me, I declined making a promise. To my surprise—and a little to my regret—she insisted upon it; and appointed the next morning, at eleven o'clock—when she and her mother would be alone.

"I am very unhappy, Rowland," muttered she, in an undertone. "I seldom see anyone whom I care for. Do come, and see us to-morrow. Will you promise?"

I could not be so rude—might I say cruel—as to refuse.

Our stay was not prolonged. Before we came away, Mrs H— also invited us to call again; but I noticed that this invitation, when given, was not intended to be heard by her husband.

"Little Rose is at school," said she, "and you must come to see her. She is always talking of you. When she hears that you are in London, she will be wild to see you."

After our departure, my companion, who already knew my address, gave me his; and we separated, under a mutual agreement to meet soon again.

There was much, in what had just transpired, that I could not comprehend.

Why had Cannon not told me that Mr H— and his family were in London, before taking me to see them? Why had he pretended that he was going to introduce me to some of his London friends? I could answer these questions only by supposing, that he believed I would not have accompanied him, had I known on whom we were about to call.

He might well have believed this—remembering the unceremonious manner in which I had parted from his friends, at the time we visited them on the Yarra Yarra. But why should he wish me to visit them again—if he thought that I had no desire to do so?

This was a question for which I could find no reasonable answer. I felt certain he must have acted from some motive, but what it was, I could not surmise. Perhaps I should learn something about it next day, during the visit I had promised to make to Jessie. She was artless and confiding; so much so, that I felt certain she would tell me all that had taken place, since that painful parting on the banks of the Yarra Yarra.

Long after leaving the house in Saint John's Wood, I found occupation for my thoughts. I was the victim of reflections, both varied and vexatious.

By causing us to come together again, Fate seemed to intend the infliction of a curse, and not the bestowal of a blessing!

I asked myself many questions. Would a further acquaintance with Jessie subdue within my soul the memories of Lenore? Did I wish that such should be the case?

Over these questions I pondered long, and painfully—only to find them unanswered.

Jessie H— was beautiful beyond a doubt. There was a charm in her beauty that might have won many a heart; and mine had not been in different to it. There was music in her voice—as it gave utterance to the thoughts of her pure, artless mind to which I liked to listen. And yet there was something in my remembrance of Lenore—who had never loved me, and who could never be mine—sweeter and more enchanting than the music of Jessie's voice, or the beauty of her person!

Volume Three—Chapter Twenty Five.

Jessie's Suitor.

Next morning I repeated my visit to Saint John's Wood. I again saw Jessie. She expressed herself much pleased to see me; but upon her features was an expression that pained me to behold. That face, once bright and joyous, and still beautiful, gave evidence that some secret sorrow was weighing upon her heart.

"I know not whether I ought to be glad, or grieved, Rowland," said she. "I am certainly pleased to see you. Nothing could give me greater joy; and yet I know that our meeting again must bring me much sorrow."

"How can this be?" I asked, pretending not to understand her.

"Ever since you left us on the Yarra Yarra, I have been trying to forget you. I had resolved not to see you again. And now, alas! my resolves have all been in vain. I know it is a misfortune for me to have met you; and yet I seem to welcome it. It was wrong of you to come here yesterday; and yet I could bless you for coming."

"My calling here yesterday," said I, "may have been an unfortunate circumstance, though not any fault of mine. I knew not, until I entered this house, but that you were still in Australia. Mr Cannon deceived me; he proposed introducing me to some of his London friends who lived here. Had I known on whom we were going to call, for my own happiness, I should not have accompanied him."

"Rowland, you are cruel!"

"How can you say so, when you've told me it was wrong for me to come? Jessie! there is something in this I do not understand. Tell me, why it is wrong for me to have seen you, while, at the same time, you say you are pleased at it?"

"Rowland, spare me! Speak no more of this. Let us talk of other things."

I did my best to obey her; and we conversed nearly an hour, upon such topics as suggested themselves, until our *tête-à-tête* was interrupted by the entrance of Mrs H—.

I could not well bid adieu to them, without promising to call again: for I had not yet seen little Rosa.

After my return home, I sate down to reflect upon the conversation I had had with Jessie—as also to seek some explanation of what had appeared mysterious in the conduct, not only of Cannon, but of Jessie's father and mother.

I had learnt that Mr H—, like many of the Australian wool growers, after having made his fortune in the colonies, had returned to his native land—intending to end his days in London.

I had also learnt that Vane—after that occasion on which he accompanied Cannon and myself, had often revisited the family on the Yarra Yarra; and had become a professed candidate for the hand of Jessie.

In the colony he had received but little encouragement to continue his advances, either from her father or mother. Since their arrival in London, however, Vane had come into possession of some property; and Mr H— had not only listened with favour to his proposals, but was strongly urging his daughter to do the same.

A matrimonial alliance with Vane would have been considered advantageous by most people in the social position of the H— family; and Jessie, like many other young ladies, was likely to be married to a man, who held but a second place in her affections.

Thousands do this, without surrendering themselves to a life of misery; and Jessie H— could scarce be expected to differ from others of her age and sex. In fact, as I soon afterwards learnt, she had yielded to her father's solicitations, rather than to the suit of the wooer; and had given a reluctant consent to the marriage. It was to take place in about ten days from that time.

I also learnt that Vane and Cannon had quarrelled, before leaving Melbourne. I did not ascertain the exact cause. It was no business of mine; and I did not care to be made acquainted with it. With the conduct of the latter I had some reason to be dissatisfied. He had endeavoured to make use of me, as a means of obtaining revenge against his enemy—Vane.

I could not think of any other object he might have, in bringing me once more into the presence of Jessie.

To a certain extent he had succeeded in his design. Without vanity I could not shut my eyes to the fact of Jessie's aversion to her marriage with Vane; and I was convinced that, after seeing me, it became stronger.

I was by no means pleased at the idea of being made a cat's paw for the gratification of Cannon's revenge; and, next day, when his name was announced at my lodgings, I resolved that that meeting should be our last.

"Mr Cannon," said I, before he had even seated himself, "will you tell me why you took me to see Jessie H—, when you had reason to believe that neither of us desired to meet the other again?"

"I had no reason for thinking anything of the kind," replied he. "On the contrary, there was much to make me believe differently. I have a great respect for Mr H— and his family; and I don't mean to flatter, when I tell you, I have the same for yourself. What harm was there in bringing together those whom I respect? and desire to see friends? But you want some explanation. You shall have it. It is this:—you have seen Vane, and know something about him. I know more of him, than you. He is a conceited, trifling fellow, without the slightest truth or principle in him. True, his society was amusing. I overlooked his faults; and bore with him for a long time. When I saw that he was trying to take advantage of the introduction I had given him to the daughter of my friend—a young lady of whom he is in no sense worthy—I then became his enemy. I acknowledge having taken you to see her in a somewhat surreptitious fashion; and, moreover, that I did it with a design: that of thwarting the intentions of Vane. But I deny having done it as you suppose, because he is my enemy. It was not that; but my friendship to Mr H—, and his family, that induced me to act as I did. While we were on the Yarra Yarra, I could not fail to notice that you were not wholly indifferent to the beauty of Miss H—; and also, that she had the discernment to see, that you were worthy of her esteem. Where was the harm, then, in my bringing you once more together? You are mistaken in thinking, that I was using you to give annoyance to an enemy. On the contrary, I claim to have been only guilty of studying the happiness of my friends."

To Cannon's explanation I could make no answer. He was better in an argument than I; and what he had said, left me without any reason to believe, that he knew either of Jessie's being engaged to Vane, or that their marriage was shortly to take place. From his point of view, I could not much blame him for what he had done.

I had received Cannon with the resolve to have nothing more to do with him, after our interview should end; but he had given me a fair explanation of his conduct, and we parted without any ill-will.

I had promised to call again upon Jessie. It was after my last visit to her, that I had learnt of her approaching marriage with Vane; and, on receiving this intelligence, I regretted having made the promise. I had two reasons for regretting it. To see her again could only add to her unhappiness; and perhaps to me might be a cause of self-reproach.

Nothing but sorrow could spring from our again seeing one another—a sorrow that might be mutual—and, in spite of the promise I had given, I determined we should meet no more.

Volume Three—Chapter Twenty Six.

Mrs Nagger.

My brother William had rented a house in Brompton, engaged two female servants, and commenced house-keeping after the manner of most Londoners.

In his house I was permitted to occupy two apartments—a parlour, and bed-room.

The servant, who attended to these rooms, possessed a character, marked by some peculiarities that were rather amusing. She was over fifty years of age; and carried about the house a face that most people would have considered unpleasant.

I did not. I only believed that Mrs Nagger—such was her name—might have experienced several disappointments in her life; and that the expression, caused by the latest and last of them, had become so indelibly stamped upon her features, as not to be removed by any hope of future happiness.

Like a good many of her sex, Mrs Nagger's tongue was seldom at rest, though the words she uttered were but few, and generally limited to the exclamatory phrase, "More's the pity!" followed by the confession, "That's all I can say."

I had, sometimes, cause to complain of the coffee, which the old housekeeper used to set before me—fancying it inferior to any, I had met elsewhere.

"Mrs Nagger," I would say—laying an emphasis on the Mrs, of which she seemed no little vain—"I do not think this is coffee at all. What do you suppose it to be?"

"Indeed I don't know, sir; and more's the pity!"

"And this milk," I would continue, "I fancy it must have been taken from an iron-tailed cow."

"Yes, sir; and more's the pity! That's all I can say."

I soon learnt that the old creature was quite right in her simple confession. "More's the pity" was about all she could say; and I was not sorry that it was so.

One day I was honoured by a visit from Cannon, who, being some years older than myself, and having rather an elevated opinion of his own wisdom, volunteered to offer me a little advice.

"Stone," said he, "why don't you settle down, and live happily like your brother? If I had your opportunity of doing so, I wouldn't put up with the miserable life I am leading, a week longer."

"What opportunity do you speak of?"

"Why that of marrying Jessie H—. Do not think me meddlesome, or impertinent. I take it for granted that you and I are sufficiently acquainted for me to take the liberty I am doing. The girl likes you; I know it, and it is a deuced shame to see a fine girl like her thrown away on such a puppy as Vane. Why don't you save her? She is everything a man could wish for—although she is a little different from most of the young ladies of London. In my opinion, she's all the better for that."

In thus addressing me, Cannon acted in a more ungentlemanly manner than I had ever known him to do, for he was not a man to intrude advice upon his friends—especially on matters of so serious a nature, as the one he had introduced.

Believing him to have some friendship for myself, more for the H— family, and a great antipathy to Vane, I listened to him without feeling offended.

"I am not insensible to the attractions of Miss H—," said I, "but the happiness, you speak of, can never be mine."

"Oh! I understand you," rejoined he. "You have been disappointed in love by some one else? So was I, once on a time—madly in love with a girl who married another, whom I suppose she liked better than me. At first I thought of committing suicide; but was prevented—I suppose, by fear. I was afflicted with very unpleasant thoughts, springing from this disappointment. They stuck to me for nearly three years. I got over them last, and I'll tell you how. I accidentally met the object of my affections. She was the mother of two rosy, apple-cheeked children; and presented a personal appearance that immediately disenchanted me. She was nearly as broad as she was long. I wondered how the deuce I could ever have been such a fool as to love the woman—more especially to have made myself so miserable about her. If you have been disappointed in the same manner, take my advice, and seek the remedy that restored me."

Absurd as Cannon's proposition might appear, I could not help thinking that there was some philosophy in it; and, without telling him of my intention, I determined on giving it further consideration.

To change the conversation, I rang the bell. I knew that Cannon was fond of a glass of Scotch whiskey; and, when Mrs Nagger made her appearance, I requested her to bring a bottle of Glenlivet into the room—along with some hot water and sugar. The "materials" were produced; and we proceeded to mixing the "toddy."

"This is the right brand," said Cannon, taking up the bottle, and scrutinising its label, "the very sort to my taste."

I could see the lips of Mrs Nagger slightly moving; and I knew that she was muttering the words, "more's the pity!" I have no doubt that she suffered a little at being deprived of the opportunity of giving her one idea a more audible manifestation.

Cannon did not suffer from any disappointment as to the quality of the liquor. At all events, he appeared to find it to his liking: for he became so exhilarated over it, that he did not leave until sunset; and not then, till he had prevailed upon me to accompany him—with the understanding, that we should spend the evening together.

"What's the use of your living in London," he asked, "if you stay all the time within doors? You appear even less inclined to see a little life, than when I met you in Melbourne. Why is it, Stone?"

"Because I came here to rest myself. A life spent in labour, has given me but few opportunities of acquiring that knowledge, that may be obtained from books; and now that I have a little leisure given me, I wish to make a good use of it."

"That's a very sensible design, no doubt," said Cannon, "but you must not follow it to-night. Come along with me; and I'll show you something of London."

I consented to accompany Cannon—on the condition of his taking me to some place where I could be amused in a quiet, simple manner—any spectacle suitable to a sailor, or gold-digger, and at which there might be no disgrace in being present.

"Take me to some place," said I, "that is neither too high nor too low. Let me see, or hear something I can understand—something that is popular with the majority of Londoners; so that I may be able to form an idea of their tastes and habits."

"All right," answered Cannon, "I'll take you to several places of the sort; and you can judge for yourself. You wish to witness the amusements most popular among, what might be called, the middle classes? Well, we shall first visit a concert hall, or music room. The Londoners profess to be a musical people; and it must be admitted that much, both of their time and money, is expended in listening to vocal and instrumental performances. It is in the theatres and music halls, that one may best meet the people of London—not the very lowest class of them; but those who profess, and fancy themselves up to a high standard of civilisation. Come on!"

Yielding myself to the guidance of my sage companion, I followed him into the street.

Volume Three—Chapter Twenty Seven.

London Concert Singers.

It was about nine o'clock in the evening, when we entered, what Cannon called, one of the most "respectable music halls" in London.

I discovered the "entertainment" to consist of one or more persons standing upon a stage, before a large assemblage of people, and screaming in such a manner, that not a word could be understood of the subject, about which they were supposed to be singing!

To make secure, against any chance of a sensible sound reaching the ears of the audience, several instruments of music were being played at the same time; and the combined effect of the screams, yells, moans, groans, and other agonising noises proceeding from both singers and musicians, nearly drove me distracted.

When an act of this "entertainment," was over; and the creatures producing it were on the point of retiring, the entire audience commenced clapping their hands, stamping their feet on the floor, and making other ridiculous demonstrations. In my simplicity, I fancied that this fracas arose from their satisfaction at getting rid of the hideous screaching that had come from the stage. I was told, however, that I was mistaken in this; and I afterwards learnt, that the clapping of hands and stamping of feet were intended to express the pleasure of the audience at what had been causing me positive pain!

I could see that these people had really been amused, or pretended that such had been the case; and I fervently prayed, that I should never be afflicted with the "refinement" that could cause me to take an interest in the exhibition which appeared to have amused them.

While the storm of applause was raging, a man would spring up, and announce the name of the next performer, or performers—though not a word of what he said could be heard. During this "intellectual" entertainment, the audience were urged to give orders for refreshments, which were served to them by men moving about in "hammer-claw coats" and white "chokers."

For the "refreshments" partaken of, an exorbitant price was charged; and then something had to be paid to the ghoul-like creatures who placed them before you.

So enlightened are the people of the world's metropolis, that a man is expected to fee the waiter who sets his dinner before him.

An unenlightened people, who live far away from London, are such fools, as to think that when a dinner is ordered, the proprietor of the place is under some obligation to have it set on the table; but Londoners have reached a pitch of refinement—in the art of extortion and begging—that has conducted them to a different belief.

After staying in the "music hall" about an hour—and becoming thoroughly disgusted both with actors and audience—I succeeded in persuading my friend to take me away.

Our next visit was to a "tavern," where we were shown into a large parlour, full of people, though it was some time before I became certain of this fact, by the tobacco smoke that filled the apartment.

In this place also, part of the entertainment consisted of singing, though none of the singers were engaged professionally. A majority of those present, seemed to be acquainted with one another; and those who could sing, either volunteered, or sung at the request of the "company." A man sitting at the head of a long table, officiated as "chairman," and by knocking on the table with a small ivory hammer, gave notice when a song was to commence, at the same time commanding silence.

In this place, we actually heard songs sung in good taste, and with much feeling, for it was possible to understand both the words and the music. On leaving this tavern we repaired to another; and gained admission into the "parlour." We found it filled with linen draper's assistants, and other "counter jumpers."

Their principal amusement appeared to be, that of trying which could use the greatest quantity of slang and obscene language. It had been raining, as we entered the house; and a young man—too elaborately dressed to be a gentleman—who came in after us, reported to the rest of the company, that it was "raining like old boots."

Another well-dressed young man entertained the company with the important intelligence, that as soon as it should cease raining, he intended to "be off like a shot."

The individuals assembled in this tavern parlour, had a truly snobbish appearance. Their conversation was too obscene to be repeated, yet every sentence of ribaldry was received by the company with shouts of laughter!

My companion and I stayed but a few minutes among them. On going out from this place, we resolved to separate for the night, as I was quite satisfied with what I had seen of metropolitan amusements.

There are many disagreeable peculiarities about London life. It is the only place visited by me in all my wanderings, in which I had seen women insulted in the streets, and where I had been almost every day disgusted by listening to low language.

London, for all this, offers many advantages as a home. The latest and earliest news, from all parts of the world, is there to be obtained, as well as almost everything else—even good bread and coffee—if one will only take the trouble to search for them.

My brother had made London his home. It was the wish of his wife—backed by that of her mother—that he should do so. This resolution on his part, produced in my mind some unmanly envy; and perhaps a little discontent.

Why could fortune not have been equally kind to me, and linked my fate with Lenore. I had wandered widely over the world, and wished to wander no more. Had fate been kind, I might have found a happy home, even in London. But it was not to be; and I might seek for such in vain—in London, as elsewhere.

Might I not be mistaken? Might I not follow the counsel of Cannon with profit? By once more looking upon Lenore, might I not see something to lessen my misery?

The experiment was worth the trial. It was necessary for me to do something to vary the monotony of existence. Why not pay a visit to Lenore?

Why not once more look upon her; and, perhaps as Cannon had said, "get disenchanted." By so doing, I might still save Jessie, and along with her myself.

Why was the presence of Jessie less attractive than the memory of Lenore? She was not less beautiful. She was, perhaps, even more gentle and truthful; and I believed no one could love me more. Why then should I not follow Cannon's advice? Ah! such struggles of thought availed me nothing. They could not affect my resolution of returning to Australia. The more I reasoned, the more did I become convinced, that I loved only one—only Lenore!

Volume Three—Chapter Twenty Eight.

A "Blessed Baby."

I am afflicted by a mental peculiarity, which seems to be hereditary in my family. It is my fate to form attachments, that will not yield to circumstances, and cannot be subdued by any act of volition; attachments, in short, that are terminated only by death. Among the individuals of our family, this peculiarity has sometimes proved a blessing—at other times a misfortune. Such an infatuation for Mr Leary existed in the mind of my mother. It had been cured only by her death. My sister and brother had experienced a similar regard for the respective objects of their affection. In the case of both it appeared to have led to a blessing. I had been less fortunate than they; and perhaps not more so than my departed mother: for the memories of a young girl, met in early life, had blighted all my hopes, and chilled the aspirations of my youthful manhood.

It may seem strange that a young man who had seen something of the world—and gathered gold enough to enable him to meet the demands of every day life—should find any difficulty in choosing a wife. Perhaps I may be understood, when I state that I was unable to act as most men would have done in a similar situation. The idea of my being united to any other than Lenore, seemed to me something like sacrilege—a crime, I could neither contemplate nor commit.

This condition of mind was, in all probability, mere foolishness on my part; but I could neither help, nor control it. A man may have something to do in the shaping of his thoughts; but in general they are free from any act of volition; and my inability to conquer the affection I had formed for Lenore Hyland—from whatever source it proceeded—had been proved by long years of unsuccessful trying. My will had been powerless to effect this object.

I had once been astonished at the conduct of my mother. Her long-felt affection for Mr Leary had appeared to me the climax of human folly. After all, was it any greater than my own? I was a young man, possessing many advantages for a life of happiness. Thousands might have envied my chances. Yet I was not happy; and never likely to be. I was afflicted with an attachment that produced only misery—as hopelessly afflicted, as ever my poor mother had been; and that, too, for one whom it was wrong in me to love, since she was now the wife of another.

In one thing, it might be supposed, that I had the advantage of my unfortunate mother. I had the satisfaction of knowing, that my love had been bestowed upon a worthy object. For all this, my happiness was as effectually ruined—as had been my mother's, by an affection for the most worthless of men!

I believed myself to have been very unfortunate in life. The reader may not think so; but I can assure him, that the person who imagines himself unhappy, really is so—whether there be a true cause for it, or not. Call it by what name you will, folly, or misfortune—neither or both—my greatest pleasure was in permitting my thoughts to stray back to the happy hours I once spent in the society of Lenore; and my greatest sorrow was to reflect, that she was lost to me for ever!

My determination to return to Australia became fixed at length; and there seemed nothing to prevent me from at once carrying it into effect. Something whispered me, however, that before going to the other side of the world, I should once again look upon Lenore.

I knew not what prompted me to this resolve, for it soon became such. Cannon's counsel might have had something to do with it; but it was not altogether that. I was influenced by a higher motive.

I had heard that after her marriage, her husband had taken her to reside in London. I presumed, therefore, that she was in London at that moment; but, for any chance that there would be of my finding her, she might as well have been in the centre of the Saharan desert. I had no clue to her address—not the slightest. I did not even know the name of the man she had married. The steward, who at Sydney had told me the news, did not give the name; and at the time I was too terribly affected to think of asking it. It is true that I might have found her by advertising in the papers; but the circumstances were such, as to forbid my resorting to such means as that. I only desired to see her—not to speak to her. Nothing could have tempted me to exchange a word with her. I wished but to gaze once more upon her incomparable beauty—before betaking myself to a place where the opportunity could never occur again.

I thought of Cannon's conversation—of his plan for becoming disenchanted; but I had not the slightest idea, that, in my case, it would prove successful.

While reflecting, on how I might find Lenore, a happy idea came to my aid. She had lived in Liverpool—she had been married there. I was acquainted with some of Mrs Hyland's friends, who must still be in Liverpool. Surely they would know the name and address of the young lady, who was once Lenore Hyland? It would only cost me a journey to Liverpool—with some disagreeable souvenirs, to spring up in my mind while there—but my reward would be to gaze once again upon the beauty of Lenore.

I had seen in the papers, that Captain Nowell's vessel was to sail for Melbourne in a few days. I was pleased at this information: for I intended to take passage with him; and might anticipate a more pleasant voyage, than if I went with a stranger.

Before setting out for Liverpool, I wrote a note to Captain Nowell—informing him of my intention to go out in his ship; and requesting him to keep for me one of the best berths of his cabin. This business settled, I took the train for the metropolis of Lancashire. I was not over satisfied with myself while starting on this journey. I was troubled with a suspicion, that I was doing a very foolish thing. My conscience, however, became quieted by the reflection that it was of very little consequence, either to myself, or any one else, whether I went to Liverpool, or stayed in London. I was alone in the world—a rolling stone—and why should I not follow the guidance of my destiny?

I became better satisfied with my proceedings when I reflected that they would lead to my finding Lenore, and once more looking upon her.

I knew that by so doing my unhappiness might only be increased; but I fancied that even this would be a change from the dull aching misery, I had been so long enduring.

My railroad journey by Liverpool was not without an incident that interested me. In the carriage in which I had taken my seat, was a man—accompanied by his wife, their child, and a servant girl who nursed the "baby." I had not been ten minutes in the company of this interesting group, before I became convinced that it was worthy of being studied, although like a Latin lesson, the study was not altogether agreeable.

The husband was a striking example, of how a sensible man may sometimes be governed by a silly woman. The child was about two years and a half old; and the fact, that it had already learnt to cry, seemed to its mother something to be surprised at!

The selfishness which causes that painful reserve, or want of sociability, observable amongst the travelling English of the middle class, was in the case of the woman in question, subdued by a silly conceit about her child—which she appeared to regard as a little lump of concentrated perfection. Before we had been in the carriage half-an-hour, she had told me its age, the number of its teeth, what it did, and did not like to eat, along with several remarkable things it had been heard to say.

"But is it not strange," asked she, after a long speech in manifestation of its many virtues, "that a child of its age cannot walk?"

"There is nothing strange about it," muttered the husband, "how can the child learn to walk, when it never has an opportunity of trying? It'll never have a chance to try, as long as there is a servant girl in the United Kingdom strong enough to carry it about. I'll answer for that."

"John, dear, how can you talk so?" exclaimed the mother of the blessed baby, "you have not the least consideration, or you would not expect an infant to be a man."

During the two hours I shared the carriage with this interesting family, I heard that mother use to her child about one-fourth of all the words in the English language—adding to each word the additional syllable "ee."

When the father ventured to open his mouth, and speak to the child in plain English, the mother would accuse him of scolding it; and then the little demon would set up a loud yelling, from which it would not desist, until mother and nurse had called it every pet name they could think of—adding to each the endearing syllable "ee."

Becoming perfectly satisfied at the observations I had made of the peculiarities of this pleasant family, I took the first opportunity of "changing carriages;" and left the fond mother to enjoy, undisturbed, the caresses of her spoilt pet. Perhaps, had Fortune been a little kinder to myself, I might have felt less afflicted in such society. But as I had no intention of ever becoming a family man, I thought the knowledge of "what to avoid," was hardly worth acquiring—at the expense of being submitted to the annoyance that accompanied the lesson.

Volume Three—Chapter Twenty Nine.

Brown of Birmingham.

On my way to Liverpool, I took the route by Birmingham—with the intention of breaking my journey in the latter city.

I had two reasons for this. I wanted to see the great city of iron foundries; and, still more, my old mate—Brown, the convict—who had worked along with me on the diggings of Avoca.

The morning after reaching Birmingham, I went in search of the place, where Brown had told me to enquire for him.

Just before his departure from the diggings, he had seen a man fresh from Birmingham; and had learnt from him, that a young fellow—with whom he had once been acquainted—was then keeping a public-house formerly much frequented by his father.

The old convict had said, that from this tavern keeper he should be able to learn all about his family; and had directed me, in case of my ever coming to Birmingham, to inquire for himself at the same address.

I found the tavern without much trouble. It was what might be called, either in Birmingham or Glasgow, a "third class" public-house; but would not have been licensed for such a purpose in any other city.

I saw the landlord; and requested him to give me the address of "Richard Brown." After some hesitation, my request was complied with.

On proceeding to the place, I had the good fortune to find my old mate at home.

I had no occasion to regret paying him this visit: for the happiness it seemed to cause him, was worth making a long journey to confer.

"You are the only one," said he, "to whom I told my story in the colonies. You remember with what little hope I returned home; and I know you are just the man to be pleased at what I have to tell you."

"I am certainly pleased," said I, "at what I already see. I find you living in a quiet, comfortable home; and, to all appearance, contented."

"Yes," joyfully answered Brown, "and I am all that I appear, even more happy than you can imagine. But I must tell you all about it. On my return, I found my mother still living, and in a workhouse. My brother was married; and had a large family—fighting, as he and I used to do, against death from starvation. I did not go to my mother in the workhouse. I did not wish to meet her there, in presence of people who could not have understood my feelings. After learning that she was there, I took this house; and furnished it on the same day. My brother then went to the workhouse, took our mother out of it, brought her here, and told her it was her own home, and that everything she saw belonged to her. He then explained the puzzle—by bringing us together. The poor old lady was nearly mad with joy; and I believe that I was at that moment the happiest man in England. I am not certain, but that I am so yet. The pleasure I have had in placing my mother beyond the reach of want, and in aiding my brother—who only required the use of a few pounds, to enable him to make a comfortable living—has far more than repaid me, for all the hardships and sorrows of the past."

Before I parted from him, Brown opened a door, and called to his mother, requesting her to come in.

When she entered the room, I was introduced to her, as a friend who had known her son in Australia. She was a respectable-looking woman, about sixty-eight years of age; and her features bore an expression of cheerfulness and contentment that was pleasant to behold.

"I am greatly pleased to see thee," said she, addressing herself to me, "for thy presence here tells me, that my son had friends amongst respectable people when far away."

I took this as a compliment; and was as polite to her, as I knew how to be.

Brown informed me, that he was then engaged in the hay and corn business; and was making a little money—enough, he said, to prevent the gold-dust he had brought home with him from getting scattered. Notwithstanding what he had done for his mother and brother, he expected to find himself at the end of the year worth as much money, and a little more, than when he landed in England.

I know not what others may think of the incident here described; but I felt upon parting from Brown, that it had been worth all the trouble I had taken to call upon him; and I will, at any time, again undergo the same trouble to be present at a similar spectacle.

Under the guidance of my old mining partner, I visited many of the great manufacturing establishments of Birmingham; and, after seeing much to cause me both wonder and admiration, I proceeded on my journey to Liverpool.

Volume Three—Chapter Thirty.

In Search of Lenore.

From having resided so long in Captain Hyland's family, I was familiar, as already stated, with the names of many of their acquaintances. Amongst others, I remembered a Mrs Lanson, who had been on very intimate terms with Mrs Hyland and Lenore.

I knew her address; and from her, would be sure to obtain the information I desired. After arriving in Liverpool, I proceeded almost direct to her residence. At Captain Hylands house, I had often met Mrs Lanson; and on presenting myself, had no trouble in getting recognised. I was received with courtesy—even cordiality.

"I am very anxious," said I, "too see my old friends—Mrs Hyland and her daughter. Having been so long abroad, I have lost all knowledge of them. I knew that you could inform me, where they are to be found; and it is for that purpose I have taken the liberty of calling upon you."

"No liberty at all, Mr Stone," said the lady; "on the contrary, I'm very glad to see you. Of course, you've heard of the change that has taken place in Mrs Hyland's family; and that they are now living in London?" I answered in the affirmative. "The address is Number —, Denbigh Street, Pimlico. That is Captain Nowell's residence. Please remember me to them!"

Not many more words passed between Mrs Lanson, and myself. I know not whether she noticed my confusion, as I stammered out some common-place, leave-taking speech. I was too much excited to know what I did; or whether my behaviour was remarked upon.

It was not necessary for me to make a memorandum of the address thus given me. I had one already in my possession—which I had been carrying in my pocket for weeks. More than that, I had called at the house itself—on that occasion, when Captain Nowell accompanied me to the Bank.

I know not why this discovery should have given my mind such a painful shock. Why should the thought, that Lenore had married a man with whom I was acquainted, cause me a more bitter pain than any I had yet experienced?

Captain Nowell was a person, for whom I felt a sincere respect—amounting almost to regard. Why then was I so disagreeably surprised, to discover that he was the man who had found the happiness, I had myself lost? I knew not; and I only sought an answer to this mental interrogatory—in the hope, that, by finding it, I might be able to correct some fault that existed in my own mind. I had accomplished the object of my journey; and yet I returned to London with a heart aching from disappointment. I had learnt where Lenore could be seen; and had gone all the way to Liverpool to obtain that information, which might have been mine at an earlier period—had I but hearkened to the request of Captain Nowell to visit him at his house.

My reasons for keeping away from Denbigh Street were now ten times stronger than ever. I no longer felt a desire to see Lenore; and never wished to see Captain Nowell again.

My desire to depart from London was greatly strengthened by the discovery I had made; and, much as I disliked Liverpool, I resolved to return to it—for the purpose of taking passage thence to Melbourne: as I had learnt that there were several Melbourne ships soon to sail from that port.

On conferring with my brother William, he expressed his determination to remain in London. He had bought shares in a brewery; and had every prospect of doing well. He endeavoured to persuade me against returning to the colonies—urging me to go into some business in London, get anchored to a wife, and live happily like himself! Little did William suspect how impossible it would have been for me to follow his counsels.

The arguments he used, only increased my desire to be gone; and I determined to start next day for Liverpool.

Common politeness would not allow me to leave, without writing Captain Nowell a note. It was necessary I should let him know, that I had changed my mind about returning to the colonies in his ship.

On the morning after this last duty had been fulfilled—before I had taken my departure for the train—Captain Nowell was announced; and I could not well avoid seeing him.

"I have come after you," said he, as soon as he entered the room. "I'm sent to take you prisoner; and bring you before two ladies, whom you should have called upon long ago. You cannot escape—so come along immediately!"

"It is impossible for me to go with you, Captain Nowell," protested I, "I start for Liverpool by the next train; and I shall have scant time to get to the station."

"I tell you," said the Captain, "that I can take no refusal. Why—do you know what I have just learnt? My wife, and her daughter, are old acquaintances of yours. Don't you remember Mrs Hyland, and little Lenore? I happened to mention the name of Rowland Stone this morning—on reading your note of last night—and there was a row in the house instantly. My wife sent me off to bring you, as fast as a cab can carry us. Unless you go with me, we shall have a fight. I daren't go back, without you."

"Stop a minute!" I cried, or rather stammered out the words. "Let me ask you one question! What did you say about your wife?"

"I said that my wife, and her daughter, were old acquaintances of yours. I married the widow of Captain Hyland."

"Great heaven!" I exclaimed, "did you not marry his daughter?"

"No. What the devil makes you ask that? Marry Lenore Hyland! Why, Stone, I'm old enough to be the young lady's father; and I am that: since I married her mother."

"Come on!" I exclaimed, rushing towards the door. "Come on! I must see her immediately."

I hurried bare-headed into the street—followed by Captain Nowell, who brought my hat in his hand, and placed it on my head.

We hailed a cab; and ordered the driver to take us to Number —, Denbigh Street, Pimlico.

I thought that a horse had never moved so slow. I said everything I could, to induce cabby to drive faster. I did more than talk to him: I bribed him. I threatened, and cursed him—though the man seemed to make every endeavour to satisfy my impatience. The horse appeared to crawl. I thought of jumping out of the cab—in the belief that I could go faster afoot; but my companion prevented me.

We did reach Denbigh Street at last; but after a drive that seemed to me as long as any voyage I had ever made across the Atlantic Ocean.

I could not wait for the Captain to ring his own bell; but rang it myself.

On the instant that a servant girl answered the summons, I put the question:

"Where is Lenore?"

The girl's face assumed an expression of surprise; but, seeing me in the company of her master, she opened the door of a drawing-room; and I walked in.

Lenore Hyland was before me—more beautiful, if possible, than ever!

I was, no doubt, taking a great liberty, in the ardent demonstrations I at that moment made towards her; but my consciousness of this could not restrain me from doing as I did—though I may have acted like a madman.

"Lenore," I exclaimed, clasping her in my arms, "are you free? Is it true, that I have not lived and toiled in vain?"

The young lady made no answer—at least not in words; but there was something in her silence, that led me to think, she was not offended at my rudeness.

Gradually I recovered composure, sufficient to conduct myself in a more becoming manner, when the Captain called my attention to Mrs Nowell—in whom I recognised Mrs Hyland, the mother of Lenore.

My long continued misapprehension—so near leading to a life-long misery—was soon fully explained. Mason, whom I had met in Sydney—and with whom the error originated—had been himself the victim of a mistake.

He had called to see Captain Nowell on business; and the latter, not being at home, the old steward had asked to see his wife. Mrs Nowell being engaged at the time, her daughter had come out to receive him; and, as Mason had been formerly acquainted with Captain Hyland and his family, of course he recognised Lenore. This circumstance—along with something that had occurred in the short conversation between her and the steward—had led to the misapprehension; and Mason had left the house under the belief that Lenore Hyland was Captain Nowell's wife!

I never passed a more happy evening, than that upon which I again met Lenore—though my happiness did not spring, from the "disenchantment" promised by Cannon. I did not think of poor Jessie; and also forgot all about my intention of returning to the colonies, until reminded of it by Captain Nowell—as I was about to take leave of him and his family for the night.

"Stone," he said, "now that you have found your old friends, you must give them as much of your time as possible: for you know, in a few days, we are to sail for Australia."

This speech was accompanied by a glance, that told me the Captain did not expect my company upon his next voyage.

I proudly fancied that Lenore interpreted it, in the same sense as I had done: for the blush that broke over her beautiful cheeks, while adding bloom, at the same time led me to believe that my remaining in London would be consonant with her wishes.

Volume Three—Chapter Thirty One.

A Child of Nature.

One morning as I sat in my room, impatiently waiting for the hour when I could call upon Lenore; and pondering over the events of my past life—especially that latest one that had given such a happy turn to it—I was informed by Mrs Nagger that a lady was downstairs, who wished to see me.

"What is the ladylike?" I inquired, still thinking of Lenore.

"Like an angel in some great trouble," replied Mrs Nagger; "and more's the pity! sir, for she's a very nice young lady, I'm sure."

"Did she give any name?"

"No, sir; and more's the pity, for I should like to know it, but she seems very anxious to see you, and more's the pity, that she should be kept so long waiting."

I descended the stairs, entered the parlour, and stood face to face with Jessie H—.

She appeared to be suffering from some acute mental agony; and when I took her hand I could feel her fingers trembling in my grasp. A hectic flush overspread her cheeks; and her eyes looked as though she had been weeping. Her whole appearance was that of a person struggling to restrain the violent expression of some overwhelming sorrow.

"Jessie! What has happened?" I asked. "There is something wrong? You look as if there was—you look ill, Jessie."

"Yes," she made answer. "Something *has* happened; something that has destroyed my happiness for ever."

"Tell me what it is, Jessie. Tell me all. You know that I will assist you, in any way that is in my power."

"I do not know that, Rowland. There was a time when you might have saved me; but now it is too late—too late to appease my aching heart. I have waited a long while in anxious doubt; and, perhaps, would have died with the secret in my breast, had I not met you again. It would have been better so. Oh! Rowland, after meeting you once more in this strange land, all the memories of the past came over me, only to fill my soul with sadness and despair. Then it was that my long pent-up grief gave way; and my heart felt shattered. Rowland! I have come to you in my misery, not to accuse you of being its cause; but to tell you that you alone could have prevented it. No mortal could live with more happiness than I, did I but know that you had the slightest love for me. Even should we never meet again, there would be joy in the thought that your love was, or had been mine."

"Jessie! Can you speak thus when—"

"Peace, Rowland! hear me out. I am nearly mad. I will tell you all—all that I have suffered for you. For that reason have I come here. They want me to marry a man I do not love. Give me your counsel, Rowland! Is it not wrong for me to marry him, when I cannot love him—when I love only you?"

"Jessie, I cannot hear you talk thus. I told you, when we parted in Australia that I loved another. I have met that other since; and I find that she is still true to me. I hope never to hear you speak so despondingly again. To all, life is sorrow; and we should pray for strength to bear it. Fulfil cheerfully the promises you have made. We can still be friends and you may yet be happy."

I could perceive, by the quick heaving of her bosom, that her soul was agitated by powerful emotions, that only became stronger as I continued.

At length this agitation seemed to reach a climax, her arms were thrown wildly outwards; and without a word escaping from her lips, she fell heavily upon the floor. She had fainted!

I rang the bell, and called loudly for assistance. Mrs Nagger came hurrying into the room. I raised the insensible form; and held it in my arms—while the old housekeeper rubbed her hands, and applied such restoratives as were near. It seemed as if Jessie H— was never again to be restored to life. She lay against my bosom like a piece of cold white marble with not a movement to betoken that she was breathing.

I gently placed her on a couch—resting her pale cheek upon the pillow. I then requested Mrs Nagger to summon a doctor.

"It's no use, sir," said the woman, her words causing me a painful apprehension: for I thought that she meant to say there was no hope of recovery.

"It's no use, sir," repeated Mrs Nagger, "she'll be over it before the doctor could get here. She's only fainting; and more's the pity, that such a dear pretty creetur should know the trouble that's causing it. More's the pity! that's all I can say."

Mrs Nagger's prognosis proved correct, for Jessie soon recovered, and as she did so, my composure became partially restored.

I began to breathe more freely: for not being used to scenes of this kind, I had felt not only excited, but very much alarmed.

"Jessie," said I, as I saw her fix her eyes upon me, "you are ill—you have been fainting?"

"No," she answered, "I have only been thinking—thinking of what you have said. It was something about—"

She interrupted herself at sight of Mrs Nagger—whom she now noticed for the first time. The presence of the housekeeper appeared to make her conscious of what had occurred; and for some moments she remained silent—pressing her hands against her forehead.

Mrs Nagger perceiving, that she was the cause of some embarrassment, silently retired from the room.

"Rowland," said Jessie, after the woman had gone, "I have but a few words more to say. To-morrow I am to be married to Mr Vane. It is my father's wish; and, as I have been told that his wishes should be my own, I have consented to obey him. I have tried to love this man but in vain: for I love another. I love you, Rowland. I cannot govern my feelings; and too well do I remember your own words, when you said, we could only love one. I will leave you now, Rowland: I have told you all."

"Jessie," said I, "I am truly sorry for you; but I trust that after your marriage you will think differently; and will not allow any memories of the past to affect your happiness."

"I thank you for your good wishes," she answered, "I will, try to bear my cruel fate with composure. Farewell, Rowland! I shall now leave you. I shall go as I have come—alone."

As I took her hand in mine—to speak that parting, which was to be our last—she fixed her eyes upon me in a glance I shall not forget till my dying hour.

In another instant she was gone.

To me there was something more than painful in this visit from Jessie. It surprised me—as did also her bearing and language. Had she been at all like any other girl, the singularity would have been still more apparent; but she was not. Her conduct was not to be judged by the same standard, as if she had been a young lady educated in the highly civilised society of Europe. She was a child of Nature; and believed that to conceal her thoughts and affections, was a sin against herself—as well as against all whom they might regard. In all likelihood she fondly loved me; and regretted the promise she had given to become the wife of Vane. Such being the case, she may have deemed it her duty to make known to me the state of her mind, before she became irrevocably united to another; and this she had done regardless of consequences. In acting thus, Jessie H— might have been conscious of no wrong, nor could I see any, although had another behaved in a similar manner, my opinion would have been different.

A young lady, brought up in English society, that teaches her rigidly to conceal every warm affection and impulse of the heart, would have been acting wrong in doing as Jessie H— had done. In her betrothal to Vane, she had undoubtedly yielded to the wishes of her father, instead of following the dictates of her own mind; but such was not the case in her making that visit to me.

Her marriage was to take place the next day; and it may be supposed that she ought to have been engaged in making preparations for that important event. Such would the world decide to have been her duty. But her artless, pure, and confiding nature, rendered her independent of the opinions of the world; and she had made one last reckless effort to possess herself of the man she loved.

The effort had failed. Fate was against her.

I went to make my daily visit to Lenore; and Jessie, along with her grief, was for awhile forgotten.

Volume Three—Chapter Thirty Two.

Mrs Nagger.

Since meeting with Lenore, I had faithfully responded to the invitation of Captain Nowell. Most of my time had been devoted to his ladies; or rather, spent in the society of Lenore. Every day had witnessed the return of happy hours; and, strange to say, the happiest were experienced on the day of that sad parting with Jessie!

On that morning, Lenore had promised to be mine; and an early day had been appointed for our marriage.

In procuring her consent to our speedy union, I was aided by Captain Nowell, who wished to be present at the ceremony, and could not postpone the departure of his ship.

When Lenore and I came to compare notes, and make mutual confession, she expressed surprise that I should ever have thought her capable of marrying another!

"Did you not tell me, Rowland," said she, "to wait for your return, and you would then talk to me of love? I knew your motive for going away; and admired you for it. I firmly confided in what you told me. All the time of your absence, I believed you would come back to me; and I should have waited for many years longer. Ah! Rowland, I could never have loved another."

My journey to Liverpool—to ascertain the name and address of the man Lenore had *not* married—I had hitherto kept a secret, but a letter had arrived the evening before, which frustrated my designs. Mrs Lanson had written to her old friend, Mrs Nowell—giving a full account of my visit that had ended so abruptly. I was compelled to listen to a little pleasant raillery from Captain Nowell, who did not fail to banter me about the trouble I had taken, to learn what I might have discovered much sooner and easier—by simply keeping faith with him, in the promise I had made to call upon him.

"I told you aboard the ship," said he, "that I had something to show you worth looking at; and that you couldn't do better than visit me, before throwing yourself away elsewhere. See what it has cost you, neglecting to listen to my request. Now, is it not wonderful, that the plan I had arranged for your happiness, when we were seven thousand miles from this place, should be the very one that fate herself had in store for you?"

I agreed with Captain Nowell, that there was something very strange in the whole thing; and something more agreeable than strange.

I returned home highly elated with the prospect of my future happiness. I informed my brother and his wife of a change in my intentions—merely telling them that I had given up the design of returning to Australia. They were much gratified at this bit of news, for they had both used every argument to dissuade me from going back to the colonies.

"What has caused this sudden, and I must say sensible, abandonment of your former plans?" asked my brother.

"I have at last found one," I answered, "that I intend making my wife."

"Ah!" exclaimed William, "the one that you had lost?"

"Yes, the one that I had lost; but what makes you think there was such an one?"

"Oh! that was easily seen. Ever since meeting you on the Victoria diggings, I noticed about you the appearance of a man who had lost something—the mother of his children, for instance. I have never asked many particulars of your past life; but, until within the last few days, you looked very like a man who had no other hope, than that of being able to die sometime. Why, Rowland, you look at this minute, ten years younger, than you did three days ago!"

I could believe this: for the change that had taken place in my soul was like passing from night to day.

I was, indeed, happy, supremely happy: since Lenore had promised to be mine.

That day I did not think of poor Jessie, until after my return home, when Mrs Nagger, while setting my tea before me, put the question:

"Please, sir, how is the poor young lady who was here this morning? She was such a nice creetur, I'm anxious to hear if she be well again."

This was the most reasonable remark I had heard the old housekeeper make, during all my acquaintance with her. She had given utterance to a long speech, without once using her favourite expression. The fact was something wonderful; and that is probably the reason why I have recorded it.

In answer to her interrogatory, I told her, that I had neither seen nor heard of the young lady since the morning.

"Then more's the pity!" rejoined Mrs Nagger. "If men have no regard for such a lovely creetur as her, it's no wonder *I* have never found a husband. More's the pity, sir! That's all *I* can say."

Mrs Nagger was a good servant; but my sister-in-law and her mother were often displeased with her; on account of a disposition she often displayed for meddling too much with what did not, or should not have concerned her. She seemed to consider herself one of the family; and entitled to know the affairs of every member of it, although I believe she was prompted to this, by a feeling of friendship and good will.

"Nagger," I once heard my brother's wife say to her, "I think you give yourself much more trouble, than is required from you."

"More's the pity, ma'am!" answered Nagger.

"You must not interfere with what does not concern you," continued Mrs Stone. "If you do, I shall have to dispense with your services."

"If you do, ma'am, more's the pity! That's all I can say."

"I wish it *was* all you could say. Then, perhaps, we should agree very well."

"The more I don't trouble about your business," rejoined Mrs Nagger, "the more's the pity for us all!"

I believe that my sister-in-law knew this; or if not, she probably thought that a better servant would be difficult to obtain; and Nagger continued to keep her place.

I had promised to call again at Captain Nowell's, that same evening, and take my brother, his wife, and her mother, along with me.

The Captain wished to see them before setting sail; and had urged me to bring them to his house—a request with which I was but too ready to comply: as I was desirous to show Lenore to my relations. I communicated my intention to them; and asked if they had made any engagement for the evening.

"No, I think not. Have you, William?" asked Mrs Stone.

"Not that I know of," answered my brother, "unless it be to make ourselves happy at our own fireside."

"I am to be married in six days," said I, "and there is no time to lose in getting you acquainted with my intended. I have promised to take you all to see her this evening—if I can induce you to go. What say you? Will you accompany me?"

They looked at each other.

"I cannot tell," said Mrs Stone. "What do you say, mother? What do you think William. I am impatient to see Rowland's choice; but would it be etiquette for us to go to-night?"

"What do we care for etiquette?" said William. "I, for one, am above it. Let us go!"

An hour afterwards, we were all on the way to the residence of Captain Nowell.

On being ushered into the drawing-room, my relatives were surprised to meet an old acquaintance—the captain of the ship, on which they had voyaged some thousands of miles.

The Captain first introduced them to his wife; and then to his step-daughter. I had before mentioned her name to my brother—while giving him a brief history of the life I had led, after parting from him in Dublin.

On hearing the name, he gazed upon Lenore for a moment with evident admiration. Then turning to me, he inquired, "Is this the lost one, Rowland?"

I answered in the affirmative.

"I am reading a romance of real life," said William, as he grasped Lenore's hand, with a grasp no other but a true sailor could give.

Need I add that we passed that evening in the enjoyment of such happiness, as is only allowed to hearts that throb with innocence and honesty?

Volume Three—Chapter Thirty Three.

A Letter of Sad Significance.

Next morning, as I was on my way to Lenore, I thought of Jessie. I was reminded of her by the ringing of bells. It might not have been for her wedding; but no doubt at that same hour the bells of some church were tolling the announcement of the ceremony, that was to make her a wife.

Poor Jessie! I could not help feeling sorrow for her. That peal, that should have produced joy both to her and myself, fell upon my ear in tones of sadness! I fancied—nay, I knew it—that whatever might be her future fate, she was at that moment unhappy!

Engrossed as I was in my own happiness, it was not natural I should long dwell upon the misery of another; and I soon ceased to think of her.

"Jessie is not related to me, nor my family," thought I, by way of stifling my regrets, "she will soon forget her present griefs; and perhaps be as happy as myself."

I offered up a silent prayer, that such should be the event.

I saw Lenore; passed with her a pleasant hour or two; and then learnt that my company was on that day no longer required.

Great preparations were being made for the marriage. Every one in the house appeared to be busy—Lenore included—and as she could devote but little time to entertaining me, I took leave of her, and returned home.

On entering my room, I found a letter awaiting me. It lay upon the table; and, drawing near, I cast my eye over the superscription.

I saw that the writing was in a female hand, though not one familiar to me. From whom could the letter be? Something seemed to whisper in my ear the word "Jessie."

She could not have written to me—least of all at that hour—unless to communicate something of importance; and I hastily tore open the envelope.

I lay before my readers a copy of that ominous epistle:

"Rowland,

"The hour has arrived! The bells are ringing for the ceremony, yet I am sitting here in my chamber—alone—alone in my anguish! I hear hurried movements below, and the sounds of joyful voices—the voices of those who come to celebrate my wedding-day; and yet I move not!

"I know that my sorrows will soon be at an end! Before another hour has passed away, my soul will be wafted to another world! Yes, Rowland! start not—but when those eyes, which have long haunted me in my dreams shall be gazing on these lines, the poor, lone girl who loved you, and sought your love in return, will have ceased to exist. Her soul will be at rest from the agonies of this cruel world!

"Rowland! something tells me that I must not marry, that I must not enter yonder sacred edifice, and pledge myself to one when I love another. My conscience rebels against it. I will never do it! I will die!

"You told me you had found the long-lost one you love. May *she* know all the happiness that is denied to me! May every blessing from Heaven fall upon her head; and make her life one blissful dream—such as I once hoped might be mine!

"I know that when you read this, the first impulse of your manly heart will be to try to save me. But it will be too late! *Before you could reach me, I shall have closed my eyes in the sleep of death!* My last prayer shall be, that you may receive every earthly blessing; and that you may long live in happiness to love her you have chosen as your wife!

"Perhaps in your reveries, in solitude, or when your heart is sad—God grant that may never be! you may bestow a thought on her whose heart you won in a foreign land; and who, in her dying hour, breathed only prayers for your welfare. In such a time, and when such thoughts may wander through your mind, I would, that you may think my only sin in life was in loving you too truly!

"Farewell, Rowland! Farewell for ever!

"Jessie."

I rushed out into the street; and hailed a cab.

"Put your horse to his greatest speed," cried I to the driver, "Reach the house, as soon as ever you can!"

"What house?" asked the cabby.

I gave the address; and sprang into the vehicle.

The driver and horse both seemed to sympathise with my impatience: for each appeared to exert himself to the utmost.

I reached the street; but, before arriving at the house, I could see a crowd of people collected about the door.

Their movements betokened great agitation. Something very unusual had certainly happened. It was not like the excitement caused by a wedding: for—

"Then and there was hurrying to and fro,
And gathering tears, and tremblings of distress;
And cheeks all pale, which but an hour ago
Blushed at the praise of their own loveliness."

My arrival was not noticed by any member of the family. They were up-stairs, and I saw none of them; but from one of their guests, I obtained the details of the sad story. I was indeed, as Jessie had said in her letter, *too late!*

A few minutes before my arrival, she had been found dead in her dressing-room—with a bottle of prussic acid by her side!

I rushed back into the cab; and ordered the driver to take me home again. I was too much unmanned, to remain a minute longer in that house of woe.

I had suffered great mental agony on many previous occasions. When alone, with the body of my companion Hiram—whom I had neglected when on the "prospecting" expedition in California—my thoughts had been far from pleasant. They were not agreeable when I saw my friend, Richard Guinane, by his own act fall a corpse before my face. Great was the pain I felt, when standing by the side of poor Stormy Jack, and looking upon his last agonies. So was it, when my mother left me; but all these—even the grief I felt when told that Lenore was married, were nothing to the anguish I experienced, while riding home through the crowded streets of London, and trying to realise the awful reality that Jessie H— had committed suicide. A heart that but an hour ago had been throbbing with warm love—and that love for me—was now cold and still. A pure spirit, altogether devoted to me, had passed suddenly away—passed into eternity with a prayer upon her righteous lips; and that prayer for myself!

My anguish at her untimely end, was mingled with the fires of regret. I submitted my conscience to a strict self-examination. Had I ever deceived her, by pretending a love I did not feel? Was I, in any way, to blame for the sin she had committed? Did I, in any way, lead her to that act of self-destruction? Could her parents, in the agony of their grief, reproach me for anything?

These questions haunted me all that night; and I slept not. I even endeavoured to remember something in my conduct, which had been wrong. But I could not: for I had never talked to *her* of love. In all, that had passed between us, I had been true to Lenore.

In the voyage of her life, her hopes, as well as her existence, had been wrecked upon me; but I was no more to blame than the rock, unmarked on map or chart, against which some noble ship has been dashed to pieces.

In that sad letter, Jessie had expressed a hope that I would think of her, and believe her only guilty of the crime of having loved me too well.

That wish died with her; but obedience to it, still lives with me.

When I returned home, on the day of her death, I locked myself in my chamber; and read that letter over and over again. No thoughts—not even of Lenore—could keep the rain of sorrow from dimming my eyes, and drowning my cheeks.

My life may be long; faith, hope, and even love for Lenore, may become weak within me; but never shall be effaced from my heart, the deep feeling of sorrow for the sad fate of Jessie H—.

May her spirit be ever blessed of God!

Her last act was not that of self-murder. It was simply that of dying; and if in the manner she acted wrong, it was a wrong of which we may all be guilty. Let her not be condemned then, among those whose souls are tainted and distorted by the vanities and hypocrisies of so-called civilised society!

To her family and friends, there was a mystery about the cause of her death, that they could not unravel. Her letter to me would have explained all; but that letter I did not produce. It would only have added fuel to the fire of their grief—causing it to burn with greater fierceness, and perhaps to endure longer. I did not wish to add to their unhappiness. I had too much respect for her memory to exhibit that epistle to any one, and see it printed, with the usual vulgar commentary, in the papers of the day.

The unfortunate ending of her life is now an event of the past; and her parents have gone to rejoin her in another and happier world, else that letter would still have remained in the secret drawer—from which it has now been taken.

Volume Three—Chapter Thirty Four.

The Rolling Stone at Rest.

One bright May morning, from the turrets of two London churches pealed forth the sound of bells. Sadly discordant were they in tone, yet less so, than the causes for which they were being tolled. One was solemnly announcing the funeral of one, who had lived too long, or died too soon. Its mournful monotone proclaimed, that a spirit had departed from this world of woe, while the merry peals of the other betokened a ceremony of a far different character: that in which two souls were being united—to enjoy the supremest happiness upon earth.

It seemed a strange coincidence, that the very day chosen for my marriage with Lenore should be the one appointed for the funeral of Jessie H—. And yet such chanced to be the case.

I knew it; and the knowledge made me sad.

There was a time, when I would not have believed, that a cloud of sorrow could have cast its shadow over my soul, on the day I should be wedded to Lenore. But I did not then understand myself; or the circumstances in which Fate was capable of placing me.

Ten years have elapsed, since that day of mingled joy and sadness—ten years of, I may almost say, unalloyed happiness, in the companionship of a fond affectionate wife. During this time, I have made a few intimate friends; and there is not one of them would believe—from the quiet, contented manner in which I now pass my time that I had ever been a "Rolling Stone." Since becoming a "Benedict," I have not been altogether idle. Believing that no man can enjoy life, so well as he who takes a part in its affairs, I was not long settled in London, before entering into an occupation.

I am now in partnership with Captain Nowell, who has long since professionally forsaken the sea; and we are making a fair fortune, as ship agents and owners.

The only misunderstanding that has ever arisen between my brother William and myself, has been an occasional dispute: as to which of us is the happier.

We often hear from "the Elephant" and our sister Martha. The last letter received from them, informed us that we might soon expect to see them on a visit to the "old country."

After the melancholy event that deprived them of their daughter, Mr H— and his family could no longer endure a residence in England; but returned to their colonial home. They lived to see little Rosa married, and happy—some compensation, perhaps, for the sorrow caused by her sister's sad fate.

Cannon and Vane I only knew afterwards as occasional acquaintances. I have just heard of their meeting in Paris, where a quarrel occurred between them—resulting in a duel, in which the latter was killed. I have also heard, that, since the affair, Cannon has been seen at Baden-Baden—earning his livelihood as the croupier of a gaming table!

Mrs Nagger and my brother's wife did not continue many months under the same roof; and the old housekeeper is now a member of my household—a circumstance of which I am sometimes inclined to say in her own words, "More's the pity;" but this reflection is subdued, every time it arises, by respect for her many good qualities, and a regard for the welfare of my children.

Her days will probably be ended in my house; and, when that time comes, I shall perhaps feel inclined to erect over her grave a stone, bearing the inscription:

"Jane Nagger,
Died
And more's the pity!"

Yet, I hope that many years may pass, ere I shall be called upon to incur any such expense on her account.

There was a time when roaming through the world, and toiling for Lenore, I thought I was happy. When riding over the broad plateaux of Mexico, amidst the scenes of lonely grandeur that there surrounded me—as also when toiling amidst the scenes of busier life in California—I believed my existence to be one of perfect happiness. I was travelling, and toiling, for Lenore.

But now that years have passed, and Lenore is mine—I find that what I then deemed happiness was but a prophetic dream. It is while seated by my own tranquil hearth, with my children around me, and she by my side—that true happiness finds its home in my heart.

When I allow my thoughts to dwell solemnly on the gifts that God has bestowed upon me, I feel grateful to that Providence that has watched over my fortunes, and ruled my heart to love only one—*only* "Lost Lenore."

The End.

Manufactured by Amazon.ca
Acheson, AB

13840140R00077